Michael Marshall was born in England but spent his early years in the United States, South Africa and Australia. His critically-acclaimed novels have won a string of awards and his breakout blockbuster, *The Straw Men*, was a *Sunday Times* bestseller, consequently becoming an internationally bestselling sensation. Marshall has also worked extensively as a screenwriter, writing for clients in both LA and London. He lives in London, with his wife and son.

www.michaelmarshallsmith.com

KILLER MOVE

Bill Moore is a man with a plan. He's got a lucrative job selling condos in the Florida Keys, a great marriage, and a beautiful house . . . only, it's year six of his five-year-plan for world domination. So he decides it's time to get in tight with the people in power, the players who run the area like their personal kingdom. It all goes to plan, but then, at work, Bill finds a card left on his desk. The card, black on both sides, has one word printed in white: *Modified*. From that moment, his life gradually begins to change, in increasingly disturbing ways. Bill discovers, terrifyingly, that he's become the subject of a dark and deadly game . . . and that he has no choice but to fight back.

MICHAEL MARSHALL

KILLER
MOVE

Complete and Unabridged

CHARNWOOD
Leicester

First published in Great Britain in 2011 by
Orion Books, an imprint of
The Orion Publishing Group Ltd.
London

First Charnwood Edition
published 2012
by arrangement with
The Orion Publishing Group Ltd.
An Hachette UK Company
London

British Library CIP Data

Smith, Michael Marshall.
  Killer move.
  1. Real estate agents- -Florida- -Florida Keys- -
  Fiction. 2. Suspense fiction. 3. Large type books.
  I. Title
  823.9′2–dc23

  ISBN 978–1–4448–1087–5

Published by
F. A. Thorpe (Publishing)
Anstey, Leicestershire

Set by Words & Graphics Ltd.
Anstey, Leicestershire
Printed and bound in Great Britain by
T. J. International Ltd., Padstow, Cornwall

This book is printed on acid-free paper

For Jonny Geller

La vie contemplative est souvent misérable.
Il faut agir davantage, penser moins,
et ne pas se regarder vivre.

— Nicolas-Sébastien Chamfort,
Maximes et Pensées

Acknowledgments

Thanks to my editors, Jane Johnson and Jen Brehl, and also to Sarah Hodgson and Chris Smith; to my agent, Ralph Vicinanza; and to Paula and Nate.

Prologue

He stands in a corridor. He has been there for nearly an hour. For many this would feel like the final imposition, the last straw, the bitter end: something to ignite crimson threads of anger in the brain and provoke a tumble backward into the pit of clotted fury that consigned them here in the first place. It does not have this effect on John Hunter, however, and this is not just because he has always possessed certain reserves of calm, or even because this period is but the stubby tail of a far longer period of waiting. He has simply become aware, over the years, that all experience is more or less equal. So he waits.

The corridor is painted in rancid cream, a color that is presumably supposed to be calming. He will remember this place by it, along with the tang of rust and the orchestral complexity of a thousand mingled strains of male sweat. He has been offered a seat. He declines, deferentially, but without playing the fake submissive: a balanced performance he's had plenty of time to perfect. Waiting in a seated or standing position amounts to the same job, and so he stands.

His mind is a perfect blank.

★   ★   ★

Eventually a door opens, and a bluff, plump man wearing a crumpled blue suit steps out into the corridor.

'Sorry for the wait, John,' he says. He looks harassed, but in command.

Inside the office are bookshelves crammed with case files and texts on criminology and penal theory. There is a window that affords a view over the main prison yard. The man with his name on the door has occupied this space for seven years. During this time, it is said, he has made significant improvements to conditions within the facility and has published four highly regarded papers presenting carefully quantified analysis of the results. He has also lost much of his hair, revealing a pate sprinkled with sizable moles.

He sits himself behind the wide wooden desk. 'Minor crisis on D,' he mutters. 'Now averted, or at least postponed until the gods of chaos pay another visit. Which they will. Please — have a seat.'

Hunter does so, taking one of the two large plush chairs angled to face the warden's desk. He has been in this office before. The desk as usual holds a laptop, a half-used legal pad, two pens, a mobile phone in a leather belt-clip, and a photograph of a woman and three children so strikingly anonymous that it seems possible the official bought the picture preframed from a prop shop, as set dressing, in order to present himself exactly as he is expected to be. Perhaps, in reality, and outside these walls, he is roguishly single, spending the small hours of the night cruising S and M bars. It is equally possible that the warden is simply what he appears to be. Sometimes, remarkably, that is so.

He folds his hands together over his stomach and looks cheerfully across at the man sitting bolt upright in one of his chairs. 'So. Feeling good?'

'Very good, sir.'

'Not surprised. Been a long time.'

The man nods. He is privately of the opinion that only someone who has been incarcerated for sixteen years can have any understanding of how long a period that represents, but is aware this is not a fruitful direction for the discussion to take. During the course of preparing for three unsuccessful parole hearings, he has learned a good deal about fruitful discussion.

'Any questions? Any particular fears?'

'No sir. Not that I'm aware of. The counseling sessions have been real helpful.'

'I'm glad to hear it. Now, I know you do, but I've got to ask. You understand, and will fulfill, the conditions of your release and parole, blah blah blah?'

'Yes sir.'

'Don't want to see you back here, right?'

'With respect, sir, the feeling is mutual.'

The warden laughs. In a way, he is sorry to see this prisoner leave. He is not the only malleable man among a population dominated by feral recidivists and borderline psychopaths, but he is intelligent and reasonable and has — most important — responded well to the program of rehabilitation that the warden has accentuated

3

during his tenure; which is why the prisoner is sitting here now rather than being kicked unceremoniously back into the world like the rest of today's lucky few. Hunter has expressed contrition for his crime — the murder of a twenty-eight-year-old woman — and exhibited a sustained understanding both of the conditions and circumstances that led to the event, and ways to avoid such triggers in the future. He has said he's sorry and shown genuine awareness of what he is apologizing for. Nine years is an unusually long time to have lopped off a sentence, especially for a murder crime, and the warden feels proud on the man's behalf.

Meanwhile, the man sits in front of him. Polite, silent, immobile as a rock.

'Anything else you want to discuss?'

'No sir. Except, well, just to say thank you.'

The warden stands, and the soon-to-be-ex-prisoner follows suit. 'A pleasure. I just wish everyone in here could look forward to this kind of ending.'

'People get the endings they deserve, sir, maybe.'

The warden knows this isn't even remotely true, but he reaches out and the two men shake. The warden's hand is warm, a little damp. The other man's is dry and cool.

★ ★ ★

The prisoner is escorted along a series of corridors. Some are the pathways that have circumscribed his universe for the best part of

4

two decades, routes between mess hall and workshop and yard that echo with the shouts and cage rattling of men — thieves and killers, parole violators and pedophiles, carjackers and gangbangers anywhere from eighteen to seventy-one years in age — whose names and natures and varying degrees of moral deviance he has already started, with relief, to forget. A few call out as he passes. He ignores them. They're ghosts, deep in the caves. They cannot hurt him now.

Subsequent corridors are foothills of the route out, the freedom side of iron gates and multiple locks. As these start to predominate, the man experiences moments in which it is difficult to maintain a flatness of emotion that has been hard-won. To walk these halls is to feel as if you are making unexpected headway in the endless maze in which you have spent a third of your life; to sense you may finally be escaping the madness that had colonized every corner of your mind — except for the tiny, central kernel in which a soul has crouched, interred in time, for a period long enough to hold four Olympic games.

In Holding & Release Hunter signs papers under the supervision of correctional officers who treat him differently now, but not so very differently. To them, as to the world outside, this period of time will never quite be over. Once a criminal, always so — especially when your crime was murder. Murder says you are not like the rest of us, or so it comforts us to pretend.

A clear plastic packet of possessions is returned to him. A watch, a wallet holding seventy dollars and change, other trinkets of a former life. He is shown to a wire cage room where he changes back into the clothes in which he entered the prison, in view of officers and the other men who are being released. He is used to his every move taking place in front of other men, but he is looking forward very much to the moment when this ceases to be so. The clothes still fit. A pair of jeans, a long-sleeved black T-shirt, and a battered denim jacket. An outfit that is effectively timeless.

An officer escorts him down a set of stairs and into an open courtyard adjacent to the yard where he has taken his four hours of outside time per week. They walk across this space to a gate. The gate is unlocked for him.

He walks through it.

The world.

⋆ ⋆ ⋆

A cab is waiting forty yards down the road. The other prisoners released today will be ferried away in the back of a van. This man wanted real life to start right at the gate, however. He walks straight over to the car and gets in without looking back.

'Where to?' the driver asks.

Hunter names a nearby town. He rests back in the seat and stares through the windshield as the driver starts the car and begins the journey away from this place. He appears in no hurry to converse, and neither does he turn the radio on. For both of these facts, his passenger is grateful

— though he has no need to mentally rehearse what he is going to do next, or the broad strokes of how this first day is going to be spent. He has done that already, and so it's done. Hunter knows how important it is to keep his concerns and aspirations driving forward, leaving every yesterday behind. The past is the past, and inviolable as such. The only thing it can do in the present is drag you back.

Almost nothing that happened within the high walls now receding in the rearview mirror will be allowed to escape: the beatings; the early nights of abject horror; the two attempts, in the first month, to kill himself; later, the decisions over who to program with and how much or little to get involved in the prison's interior worlds in order to avoid being either called upon to do other people's time or winding up on some gang's Bad News list — an effective death sentence of infinite jurisdiction. That was then, and in there.

This is now. Out here.

The single thing he has brought with him, the knowledge that has sustained him throughout the years but that also cast shadows over his darkest nights and hours, is this: that he was innocent of the crime for which he was convicted. Ninety percent of men in prison make this claim, and pretty much all of them are lying.

This man, however, was not.

He didn't do it.

★   ★   ★

There are details still to be worked out — what to eat first, where to pick up some clothes that don't stink of confinement, where to stay the first night. The main business, however, is already laid out in his mind.

He is going to get hold of a gun.

And then he's going to start using it.

PART I

IMPERFECT CONTINUOUS

Every day, in every way,
I'm getting better and better.

— ÉMILE COUÉ

1

As I pulled around The Breakers' inner circle I saw that Karren White's car was already tucked into the better of the two Shore Realty slots — the one that gets shade in the afternoon and stops your vehicle from feeling like an oven turned to BURN when you climb into it at the end of the working day. She had parked with characteristic accuracy, the sides of her sporty little BMW exactly parallel to the lines, as if she'd put the car in position first and then sweet-talked Big Walter the handyman into painting the parking space around her (which, knowing her charm and forcefulness, was not entirely out of the question). I parked my own vehicle in the remaining space, with not dissimilar skill, and glanced at the clock in the dashboard. Eight twelve.

Hmm.

I logged the time in a utility on my iPhone. I'm not OCD about these things, you should know. The point of logging is merely to develop positive habits, reproducible patterns of behavior that can later be reallocated to tasks of greater importance. The point also was that Karren was at work before me on the third straight Monday, and doubtless thought this proved something, or might yield competitive advantage in the long run. She could not know that I'd already taken a working breakfast up at St. Armands Circle,

11

coffee and French toast and twenty-five minutes of light banter with someone who might, eventually, make me a lot of money. She would also not be aware that on the way over from my home in Sarasota I'd caught up on the weekend's brand-building and entrepreneurship podcasts (spooled from the Web onto the iPhone, and thence to my car's meaty sound system), sent five e-mails (drafted before I left the house, edited, and then dispatched while waiting at traffic lights), and updated the status on my LinkedIn, Facebook, and HollaBack pages. The early bird gets the worm, true, but Bill Moore doesn't mind dining second if the specimen of the phylum Annelida he snares is bigger and juicier as a result.

So, Ms. White, gather the better parking spot while ye may. We'll see who grows fat in the end.

I braced myself before getting out of the air-conditioned comfort of the Lexus, but the heat still came on like a middle-aged banker bracing a cocktail waitress. Six years in Florida hadn't yet accustomed me to the way humidity makes the place its bitch, already in position with insidious weight and heft before humans have even hauled themselves out of bed. As I locked the car I glanced at the sky above the sturdy two-story condo blocks all around me and was reassured to see clouds gathering inland. Sooner or later — maybe this afternoon, please God — a storm was going to break, and after that it would become more bearable for at least a day or two.

I strode over to Shore Realty's little hut,

12

noting that the picture of a recently listed two-bedroom condo had finally made it into the window. It was crooked. Once inside the cool and air-con-dry building, I righted this state of affairs, before turning to the office.

'Morning,' I said, a little louder than necessary — with an air of distraction, too, to make it clear I was not actually starting my working day but already well into my stride.

My voice bounced off the rear wall and came back to me without much to report. Shore Realty's lair in The Breakers is neither large nor bijou. It's the smallest outpost of a chain that has more impressive accommodation at the Ocean View Mall halfway up the key, plus additional locations in Sarasota, Bradenton, and Tampa. The bulk of my office's business comes from reselling units within The Breakers itself — though this was something I had been trying to change.

The working area is a rectangle perhaps eight yards by six (I've never actually measured it), with space for three desks: mine, Karren's — at which she sat, clattering away at her keyboard — and one for Janine, the assistant who spends her days performing support tasks like confirming meetings, misunderstanding basic computer functions, and putting properties in the window, never quite straight. Janine was nowhere to be seen, business as usual for this time of day (and other times, too).

'Back atcha, Billy-boy.'

Karren was sporting her standard getup — smart white blouse and a snug-fitting blue skirt that stopped above the knee, the better to showcase her tennis court-honed calves. Back in the day she'd been a force on the courts, by all accounts, had even considered turning pro. From what I'd seen — we're afforded complimentary use of the resort's facilities — she remained sharp at twenty-nine. Like, whatever. I play just enough tennis to hold my own when business demands and to lark around with my wife when she's in the mood. Winning at sports is not the same as winning in business, just like *The Art of War* is not a corporate how-to manual. You run that beat-up 1980s routine on me and I'm going to stomp you into the ground.

'And Janine is . . . ?'

'Doctor's. Kid's got the plague.'

'Again?'

Karren shrugged theatrically, causing her long dark hair to pool up on her shoulders. Just about the only matter on which we absolutely agree is that Janine is basically useless, and her kid actually defective.

'Says she'll be here by one, cross her heart and hope to diet.'

'I'll be out again by then. Got a meeting down on Siesta.'

Karren went back to her keyboard and failed to rise to the bait. Point to her, probably, or maybe she simply hadn't been listening.

When I got to my desk I saw something lying on it. This was easy to spot, as my working area is the tidiest in the Sarasota area, possibly even along the entire gulf side of Florida — though I've heard rumors of a guy up in Saint Pete who has nothing on his desk *at all*. Propped in the center of mine was a rectangular card, midway between business and postcard size.

I picked it up, flipped it over. Just one word on the other side: **MODIFIED**.

'Hell is this?'

'What?'

'Thing on my desk.'

'No idea,' Karren said without turning around. 'Came in the mail. Probably some viral marketing crap.'

'Viral marketing?'

'You know. Coming in under the radar. Keeping it on the down low. Advertising that's cool and hip and engaging and just so New Edge it makes you want to spit.'

I looked back down at the card in my hand. It was matte black on both sides, had just that one word in white letters and bold type across the front, and my name and the company's address on a laser-printed sticker on the back. The sticker had been put on perfectly straight.

'I'm not engaged,' I said, and dropped the card in the trash.

2

I got through a slew of e-mail, made a few calls
— Shore business only, anything else I do on my
cell when away from prying ears — and left the
office a little after eleven. The clouds were
bunching overhead, purple thunderheads that
promised an almighty downpour. The only
downside was that the air had become even
heavier in preparation, the earth offering up
every drop of moisture from its hot lungs,
anxious to have it purged in the upcoming
hammer of rain. It felt like if you were to reach
out and make a wringing motion, actual water
would drip down out of the atmosphere to steam
off the ground.

I hesitated, aware that this was precisely the
kind of moment when I would formerly have lit a
cigarette. I didn't do that anymore, however, and
this morning that felt like less of an imposition.
It was taking hold, finally, Mr. Nicotine
Addiction packing his bags. I paused to pay
homage to the fact. The author of one of my
favorite personal development blogs is big on
taking the time to mark good moments rather
than fretting about the bad — reprogramming
reality through altering focus to the positive.
Drive yourself and you drive the world. Plus, I
was running a little early anyhow.

From where I was standing you get a good
sense of what The Breakers is about. A condo

complex built in the heady days when throwing up blocks on the Florida coast was basically a license to print money, the resort had everything a family needed to beguile a couple of weeks in the Sunshine State. A hundred and twenty apartments, in blocks of six; said two-story blocks arranged in a pair of concentric circles around a central area holding eight tennis courts. (The Breakers prides itself on its facilities, and hosts the annual Longboat Key Tournament.) Palms, fern beds, and path decking lightened the effect and gave the blocks a little personal space. Each had a cheerful name, was painted a different shade of pastel, and, to the discerning eye, was beginning to look a little tatty.

On the ocean side of the inner circle stands a four-story administrative building holding the resort offices and reception, meeting/conference spaces, a gym, and — arrayed over the entire top two stories — the gargantuan living space of the resort's owners. The corresponding point on the outer circle is home to, in addition to the adjunct of Shore Realty's office, a little grocery market, a place to buy beachwear, Marie's Restaurant (small and poised, a pianist most evenings, nonresidents welcome, but shorts or flip-flops are not), and Tony's Bistro (the more casual dining option, child friendly, with a tiki bar and tables on a patio overlooking the pool area).

Beyond that, the beach — on which there are several four-bedroom bungalows, the pinnacle of the resort's rental cost ladder. Other buildings dotted around the complex hold a game room and an area where parents can dump their more

17

tractable children under semiexpert supervision for two-hour sessions, the better to sunworship in peace. There's a repair division, too, domain of Big Walter the maintenance man, but I've seldom needed to tangle with that side of things (or with him). He's a decent guy and a wiz at fixing things, but of large build and inclined to perspire freely.

My job was to take listings of condos of which owners had decided to divest themselves and sell them to someone else as quickly as possible. In many ways this was a sweet deal — a monopoly located right on-site — which is why I'd chosen to work there rather than at the mainland office over in Sarasota. The problem was that selling the properties was getting harder every year. Tony and Marie Thompson ran The Breakers with an iron fist, tight purse strings, and a management style that was beginning to betray its age as blatantly as the buildings were. All but three of the apartments were owned on a fractional basis, as is common practice. The owners were not allowed to do their own decorating, on the grounds that this led to regular guests developing favorites among the condominiums and demanding the freedom to choose, which would make it harder to allocate them with maximum income-generating efficiency. There's nothing inherently wrong with the system except it had been a few years since the buildings had been given attention, and this was beginning to show both inside and out. Everything worked — bar the occasional blatting AC unit or a toilet that needed unblocking on too regular a basis; it just wasn't looking what Karren insisted on calling 'supergreat and perfect.'

This meant in turn that the condos weren't getting the resale prices their location on the key warranted; thus I was neither making the commission I deserved for the hours and dedication I put in, nor shining in the community to the degree required to actualize my five-year plan (now already in its sixth year, which was bugging me no end) of being able to get the hell out of Shore Realty and set up my own shop, preferably in an office down on St. Armands Circle, candidates for which I had picked out some time ago. And *this* was why I had taken it upon myself to do what I was going to do next: meet with Tony Thompson to try to convince him to shake out a little cash to spruce up the place.

I went to my car, unlocked the trunk, and took out a shopping bag. Then I rolled my shoulders, muttered a couple of motivational phrases, and strode off in the direction of reception.

★   ★   ★

'This is quite a find, Bill.'

I stood sipping a glass of iced tea, looking down out of the plateglass window toward the ocean, while Tony Thompson peered with satisfaction at the bottle of wine.

'Heard you mention it a while back,' I said. 'I happened to spot a source, snapped it up.'

'You got a good memory.'

19

'Stuck in my head, is all.'

He looked at me suspiciously. 'Can't have been easy to get hold of.'

'Not locally,' I admitted, watching waves lapping at the concrete pier sticking out from the middle of The Breakers' section of beach, and on which a lone, picturesque heron was often to be found standing, as if hired by the management. About a third of the Thompsons' residence was taken up with a double height living area. From its vast windows you could see a couple of miles in either direction along one of the most unspoiled sections on this entire stretch of coast. When Longboat Key began to be developed in earnest during the early 1980s, there were already sufficient numbers of people singing the conservation song that a degree of tact and reserve held the day. This probably enraged the moneymen at the time, but in the long run there had been advantages. Were it not for a cluster of taller (and more recent) condos down at the south end, you would be able to see all the way to the wilderness at the end of Lido Key.

It was a great view. I wanted it.

'So how'd you find this one?'

'The Internet is a marvelous resource.'

'Yeah, I hear good things,' Thompson said, setting the bottle on the breakfast bar and leading me toward a sitting area with white sofas and a glass coffee table big enough to play Ping-Pong on, assuming you had really short legs. It was bare, aside from a fat book of Sudoku puzzles and an ornate wooden box. 'I got more than enough stuff to deal with in the real world.

mouth shut in the interests of a greater good. 'But I *will* tell you the chatter is not just coming from people who are looking to sell. With those folks, they're out of here already. Screw 'em, right? I'm talking about the families who are happy owning their corner of The Breakers, who want to stay a part of it.'

'You're really not going to give up some names?'

I hesitated again, this time to give the wily old fucker reason to suspect that, under *exactly* the right circumstances, I might spill a name or two.

'No can do,' I said. 'But you know the economic climate as well as I do, sir. Far better, uh, of course. It makes people twitchy. Everybody loves The Breakers. You built an amazing community here. Even the people I'm selling for, ninety percent wish they didn't have to let their properties go. But they also have expectations. You let the feel-good factor drift, and . . . It's a social network, old style. People sit around the pool and they talk. You need the core community to remain stable — and to believe it's being listened to and valued. Otherwise it all starts to feel random, and then someone says, 'Hey, that new place on Lido has got a bigger hot tub, and it's just a short walk from St. Armands Circle . . . ,' and people decide to vote with their feet. En masse.'

'Are you saying that — '

'We are not at that point. Not yet, sir, not by a long shot. But nobody wants that to happen, either.'

'What's your angle, Bill?'

'Sir?'

'Why are you telling me this?'

I went for broke. 'I want what you've got.'

Thompson's mouth opened, closed. He cocked his head on one side and stared at me. 'Say again?'

'What are you worth, sir, financially, if you don't mind me asking?'

'I surely fucking do.'

The skin on the back of my neck felt very hot, despite the frigid air. 'I respect that, sir, and I already know it's in the tens of millions. Depending on how it's accounted, and who's asking.'

One side of his mouth moved upward about a quarter of an inch. He looked like an alligator that was trying to decide whether to eat something right away, or if it might be worth watching its prey just a little longer, to see if it did something else funny.

'I'm listening.'

'I don't want to be manning a desk at Shore forever,' I said. 'Right now, I'm capital light. That means my focus is on assisting those who already *have*. Protecting their position and investments, getting them a little more on top. Sometimes a *lot* more. And that means The Breakers, most of all. The better you do and the happier you are, the better I look and the happier I will eventually become.'

The gator still didn't bite.

'The bottom line is that the talk I'm picking up is not Shore Realty's problem. Matter of fact, the more people who sell, the more commission my company gets. But I don't think I'd be doing my job if I didn't give *you* a heads-up that you've got a situation brewing here.'

I stopped talking. Not before time.

'The people you've been hearing this from . . . '

'Are not just the ones who whine about every damned thing, no. Otherwise I wouldn't be bothering you with it. You've been in this business a *lot* longer than me. It's your game, and you can play it exactly how you want. But if you like, I could talk to a few of the key players. Diffuse the chatter, press the pause button. Suggest it's worth waiting a little longer before getting too het up about the situation.'

He thought for a moment.

'I'll discuss this with Marie,' he said, standing. 'Not going to promise more than that. But that I will do.'

'Thank you, Mr. Thompson.'

'The name's Tony,' he said, reaching out to shake my hand. 'As you know. You may as well start using it.'

* * *

Fifteen minutes later I was standing at the end of the pier on The Breakers' beach, surrounded by the flatness of the ocean. I still had an hour before my appointment down on Siesta Key, in reality nothing more than a meet-and-greet and something to tweak Karren White with. I'd take the meeting, of course — a key tenet of the Bill Moore brand is that if he says he'll do something, it gets done — but right now it seemed very unimportant.

There were a few couples meandering up and down the water line, and a group of kids twenty feet away being encouraged to look for shells. Most people were indoors, out of the noon heat.

My hands were now still. For ten minutes after the meeting they'd been shaking. Sure, I'd planned to get man-to-man and cards-on-the-table with Tony at some point — but not today. The bottle of wine had been intended merely as an opening gambit. I'd logged the name and year, put out a notice on a beginners' wine board I found on the Internet. A guy got in touch, declaring himself able to supply one and to also be in possession of another vintage that was an even bigger deal and guaranteed to be a huge hit with anyone who was searching for the first. I'd quickly snapped up both bottles — at a cost I hoped my wife did not discover before I'd had a chance to capitalize on the expense — and had been intending to get serious with Thompson only on production of the second. I actually had very little to offer him at this point. I'd taken a degree of license when describing the level of owner dissatisfaction, too, and was aware that Tony was a golf-and-drinking buddy of Peter Grant, founder-owner of Shore Realty. The two went back to the boom years, had been to school together, and socialized all the time. I was a Shore employee. Implicitly offering to set that to one side in order to run interference for The Breakers' management was a very high-risk strategy.

And yet . . . it had felt like the thing to do.

Or I'd gone ahead and done it, at least, and it hadn't yet exploded in my face. If Thompson had gotten straight on the phone to his friend, there'd be a message on my phone telling me to clear my desk and go fuck myself from here to Key West. No such missive had arrived — which hopefully meant I'd taken a massive step in the right direction.

I wasn't even having a cigarette to celebrate, either. Behold the man, see how he grows.

There was a blarping sound from my pocket. It made me jump. I yanked out the phone and was relieved to see it was just a calendar reminder.

But then I swore — loud enough to startle nearby children and have their wrangler glaring at me — and ran up the pier toward the resort.

3

By nine thirty I was pretty drunk. This is something all the blogs and self-improvement gurus advise against, but I felt I deserved it. Not only had the day seen strides toward me becoming a bigger blip on Tony Thompson's radar, but I had reason to be relieved to be where I was — at a great table in a great restaurant, enjoying another big glass of Merlot and hiding the effects very well, I believed.

'You're pretty drunk,' Steph said.

'No. I'm just high. On the vision of outstanding natural beauty across the table from me.'

She laughed. 'Corny. Even by your standards. Still, twelve years together. Eight, postknot. Can't say we didn't give it a try, right?'

'You're still the one, babe.'

'You too.'

She raised her glass. We chinked, leaned across the table, and kissed for long enough to make nearby diners uncomfortable. She was happy, and so was I. I'd bought her something nice from her favorite jewelry store and also gotten huge props for fulfilling her primary request, securing a table on the upstairs balcony at Jonny Bo's. This is the premium spot in the place, with the (alleged) exception of a fabled private upper dining room, which no one I knew had even seen, and which I was ninety percent sure was a

28

suburban legend. Our table booking still had me a little mystified. I'd broken into foul language at the end of the pier because I realized I'd failed to make the reservation. I'd tried, a number of times, but the number had always been busy — I recalled muttering about this in the office a week or so ago (mainly, of course, as a way of bragging about the venue I was trying to book). And yet, when I'd called that afternoon on the slim chance of a cancellation, I discovered I *had* made a reservation after all. Obviously I'd got through at some point, become wrapped up in some other piece of business, and forgotten. Whatever. Today was evidently one of those days when the universe elected to throw me a couple of bones. Hence the extra glass of wine.

Our waitress appeared. She was a little older than most, late twenties, but otherwise standard issue: black pants, starched white shirt, black apron, capable-looking ponytail in blond or brown. This one's was midbrown.

'Can I interest you fine people in the dessert menu?'

'Hell yes,' Steph said. 'Thought you'd never ask.'

I declined, picked up my glass, and looked down over the Circle. Dessert selection is a serious business with Steph. It can take a while.

It was the other side of twilight, and the streetlights looked pretty. The storm — smaller than I'd hoped, but effective — had burned itself out, and the air was comfortable. The Circle lies in the middle of St. Armands Key, providing the entry point to Lido and Longboat. It is, as the name suggests, a circle, holding a small park with palms and firebushes and orange blossom in the center and exits at the cardinal points. It's lined with chichi stores plus a Starbucks and Ben & Jerry's, and eateries including an outpost of the stalwart Columbia chain — and now also the bracingly expensive Jonny Bo's, high days and holidays favorite for well-heeled locals over the last two years. There are still a few T-shirt and tourist stores to leaven the mix, but they're in decline, and the Circle represents some of the highest-priced retail space on the gulf. With all the redevelopment happening over on Lido Key — which can only be accessed via the Circle — that situation was only going to improve.

But fifty or a hundred years ago?

Where I was sitting had been nothing but a dusty crossroads on a chunk of sand and scrub back then, holding orange groves, a shack or two, and little else except wading birds. Back in the 1920s Sarasota itself had boasted a population of only three thousand, with nothing to say for itself beyond agriculture and fishing. What I saw beneath me had been just another piece of speculation, in other words — like The Breakers, the huge Sandpiper Bay development on Turtle Key, or the new condos going up to replace the old family motels along Lido Key's southwest shore.

Making money out of land is all about time. Understanding it, using it, knowing what to do when. Some guy spied a location and thought — Hmm . . . what if?

I could be that guy.

Steph had made her selection and was watching other diners at the candlelit tables inside. 'Isn't that the sheriff?' she said.

I looked and, sure enough, saw Sheriff Barclay making his way across the restaurant from the direction of the restrooms. He's a big guy, both in height and front to back, and not hard to spot. He saw me, too, raised his chin about an inch. We've run into each other at business functions, charity events. I saw a couple of other people clock the connection between us, and smiled inside. They weren't to know we'd barely exchanged a hundred words in total; they just saw a guy with good contacts.

'I just realized,' I said, 'I'm about the same age Tony was when he started to build The Breakers.'

'It's 'Tony' now, is it?'

'At his specific request.'

'Call-me-Tony did start with a preexisting construction business and a few million dollars cash, though, right?'

I sighed theatrically. Healthy skepticism on your wife's part is appropriate, however. As focus groups go, they don't come much more focused than the woman who stands to lose whatever you lose.

'True,' I said. 'Plus, he had a wife with drive and determination and a good honest faith in her man. But, you know, what I lack just makes me stronger.'

She grinned and flipped me the bird, just in time to be witnessed by the waitress as she returned.

31

'I'm so sorry,' the girl said. 'I do hate it when I interrupt a special private moment.'

'Nah, business as usual,' I said. 'You know any *nice* women, give them my number.'

We all laughed, Steph made a concerted start on the complex confection on the big square plate she'd been brought — Steph doesn't screw around when it comes to dessert consumption: she's all about shock and awe — and as the waitress walked away, she glanced back and looked right at me. Which was nice. It always is.

But being in love with your wife is nicer.

★ ★ ★

Steph drove us home over the bridge across the bay and out the south side of Sarasota to Longacres. Longacres is a gated community of thirty artfully mismatched minivillas around a small private marina to which our house does not have direct access — as we don't care enough about boats to have made the dockage price hike worthwhile. The houses are dotted along a meandering drive, and though you never feel hemmed in, you have the comfort of neighbors, of seeming like you're living somewhere in particular. Those neighbors are all people like us. Most had a child or two already, however. We do not. This had started to become a topic of discussion, a recurring item cropping up, low down on the agenda, but no longer just Any Other Business.

It had not come up tonight, thankfully. I want a family — of course. I want to make sure I've got my goals on a roll, however, before a row of gynecological *forces majeures* start directing the run of play.

I went and sat out by the pool. Steph disappeared indoors, leaving me time to think back over the day and be pleased with progress. Your life is your real job — and you're being lazy and dumb if you don't make the best of it. One of the reasons I believe this, I guess, is my dad. Don't get me wrong, he was a decent guy. He was patient and generous, not overly bad-tempered, and could make you laugh when he had the time and inclination. He sold paint for a living — the kind you use to decorate your house. He kept up with the fashionable colors and finishes and accessories and tools. He was cheerful and friendly and he'd help carry your goods out to the car if you were old or female or simply looked as if you could do with a hand, and if it turned out you'd bought too much paint he'd cheerfully take back the excess and try to sell it to someone else. He did this for thirty years and then one day went out back to get something for a lady who wanted to finish the basement of the house she'd just bought — and he bent down to pick up a pair of gallon cans of brilliant white, and never came back up.

He died of a heart attack at the age of fifty-nine, seven years ago, and though people in town were content to say it was the way he would have wanted it — right there in his store, in the act of being helpful — my mother privately expressed the view that my father would have preferred it to have happened many years later, possibly in Aruba. She was joking, in the way you do around a death, and I knew by then that Aruba wouldn't have been where he'd chosen. When I was a kid I'd started to notice that in my dad's den (and dotted around other bookshelves, in low-prestige spots) were a lot of books on French history and culture, all of them ten or fifteen years out of date; annotated grammars and vocab books, too, with studious jottings in pencil, in a version of my father's handwriting that looked exotic to me — a tighter, earlier style than I was accustomed to seeing in shopping lists or reminder notes on the fridge. I don't think I ever heard my father say a single word in French, but when I looked at those grammar books for the last time — when I was at the house in the week after he died, helping my mother make sense of what was left behind — I realized they were pretty advanced, and that the marginal notes said this was not a guy who'd just been looking at the pictures.

I'd asked my mother about all this one day, way back when I was around thirteen. She shrugged, said my father had been on long family vacations to France as a child and liked the idea of spending more time there. I took from this observation, and the offhand manner in which it had been delivered, that moving to France had been a dream of my father's back in the pre-Bill era of the planet. Something he'd thought about, talked about, probably kind of bored her with over the years . . . before the ship of his dreams ran aground on the sandbank of lack of dedication, becalmed by a slowness to act.

In the aftermath of his death, reconsidering him with the vicious perspective that comes when someone has committed their last actions and has nothing else to say — I realized that my assessment had been correct, but only up to a point. Half-correct, but also halfwrong and naive and cruel — in the heartless way children often measure the worth of the adults they are here to supersede.

There are men who would have made their dream happen without reference to how inconvenient it was to others. Patriarchs who would have put their foot down, made their love a hostage, and turned their family's lives into a living hell until they got what they goddamned wanted. My father was not that guy, and as the years went on, I came to realize how it had more likely been. That the money was never there. That my mother would have gotten herself involved in events around town, part-time jobs, school jamborees — never mission-critical, but enough to stay the hand and compromise the ambition of a man who loved her, and valued the things she did, and wanted her to be happy. That there was a kid in the house who had friends and a community nearby: and there's always some marker, some birthday or test or rite of passage that seems essential to pass on home soil, some relative who might not last the year. Something to clip the wings.

But there was also the fact that my dad was

fundamentally an abstract noun, and not a verb: a feeling word, not a doing word. It was sad he didn't get what he'd wanted, but it was not Mom's fault or mine or the world's. He was a nice guy and I'm sure he had nice dreams, but we're only asleep half the day, and dreaming is therefore only half the job. Nobody gets points for living in a conditional tense.

Dad lost his cherished future by himself, dropped the ball one night in his sleep, and probably didn't even realize it until it was too late. Maybe he *never* realized it. It could be that on the day he bent to pick up those two big old cans of paint, part of his mind was still noodling around the perfect little French fishing village, and how to convince his wife that now — finally, the kid having left home — was the time to make the move.

But I doubt it. Dreams are immortal, fickle, self-possessed: the cats of the subconscious. Once it becomes clear that you're not going to step up to their demands, they desert you and go rub up against someone else.

I had no intention of letting mine do the same.

Bill Moore is not that kind of guy.

Bill Moore is a verb.

Believe it.

* * *

Steph returned carrying a couple more glasses of wine. She'd changed out of her dress in the meantime, put her long blond hair up in a ponytail, and was wearing a thin robe and nothing else. She looked tall and slender and beautiful.

'The day just keeps getting better,' I said.

'Don't make any promises you can't keep,' she said, smiling as she handed one of the glasses to me. 'You've not stinted on the wine already, tycoon-boy.'

I stood, meaningfully. 'You ever known me to break a promise?'

'Actually, I have not,' she admitted, coming closer.

Afterward we cooled off in the pool, not saying much, content to float around in each other's orbits and look up at the moon and stars.

Suddenly it was late. Steph headed upstairs to the bedroom around one thirty. I went through to the kitchen to get us a couple of glasses of mineral water. As I poured them from the bottle in the fridge I noticed a small manila envelope propped against the coffee machine.

'What's this?' I called.

After a pause, Steph's voice came down from the gallery. 'What's *what*, dearest? Damned telepathy's still cutting in and out.'

'Thing on the coffee machine.'

'I have no idea,' she said. 'Came in the mail after you'd left. Oh, and will you get me copies of the pictures you took at Helen's party? She's baying for them. I need a CD, or can you at least throw up a Web gallery so she can pick the ones she likes?'

'Will do,' I said.

'Really, this time?'

'Really.'

I picked up the envelope. Tore it open, and found a black card inside. I flipped it over.

On the other side, there was a single word: MODIFIED.

4

He waits in a car. He has been here three hours already. He doesn't know how much longer it will take, and it doesn't matter. It has taken John Hunter three weeks to get this far. He bought the car a hundred miles away, dickering about the price just long enough to remain unmemorable. By the time he left the lot, steering the car accurately into midmorning traffic, the salesman would already have been hard-pressed to describe him. For the last four days he has been staying in local motels, a single night in each. He pays with cash earned during a two-week stint of manual labor in another state. He behaves at all times in a manner so unexceptional that no one has any reason to mark his presence, or his passing.

He has spent his time watching a man.

Hunter has observed this person leaving the house in the mornings, and then been a distant, unmarked presence on the periphery of his every waking hour. He has seen him take meetings and supervise work on two building sites, watched him drive between venues in his understated but expensive car, and observed him enjoy lunches on the terraces of upmarket restaurants. The man drinks red wine with clients but switches to beer as soon as they've gone. He laughs, shakes hands, remembers the names of spouses and children. He is a little overweight, fleshy, with the confidence to ignore the zeitgeist's strident views on body mass indices. He is a normal, unexceptionable man . . .

Except in all the ways he is not.

Several times Hunter has passed close enough to overhear his quarry on the phone. One of these conversations did not concern business. The man's voice was quieter this time, more conspiratorial, and he half-turned from other patrons outside the unnecessarily expensive café where it occurred. He asked if a meeting was to go ahead and sounded pleased when it was confirmed. The audible pleasure was there merely to flatter the person on the other end of the line. He had known the meeting would take place as planned. He was used to people doing what he wanted but smart enough to occasionally let them think it had been their choice.

The man's fate was already determined. The overheard call only helped Hunter choose a convenient when and how.

Two nights later, the man drives to a midscale neighborhood on the northeast side of town. As he parks outside a private residence, his shadow drives past, stopping fifty yards up the street.

And there he has waited.

★   ★   ★

At a quarter after two the door of the house opens and the man comes out. He says good-bye to the woman standing in a robe in the doorway, and strolls away to the curb. He unlocks his car with a cheery electronic *blip-blip* — forgetting or

40

not caring that she might prefer him not to be observed by neighbors who know she is married. She retreats inside.

Hunter waits until the other car has pulled away from the curb, then starts his own engine and follows. He does not bother to tail his target closely. He knows where they are going.

Twenty minutes later the other man pulls off the road and up a driveway. Hunter parks his car a hundred yards farther along the highway, in the rear lot of an Italian restaurant closed for the night. He has already established that any car lodged here cannot be seen from the road. He walks back to the man's property and up the curving path to the house. He stops at the gates and takes a pair of surgical gloves from his jacket. He snaps them tight, then removes a set of tools from another pocket, along with an electronic device bought on the recommendation of a kid he befriended in his final year in prison. The kid knew a great deal about new technology and was very grateful for the protection of an older and more experienced inmate, especially one who didn't want to have sex with him.

Hunter works methodically, following instructions gleaned from a seedy corner of the Web. He knew about the Internet before he got out, of course. They have it in prison, along with — should you wish to consult it — a rolling, 24-7 master class in how to do just about everything that people are not supposed to do.

Twelve minutes later the entry pad has been disabled. He opens the gate wide enough to slip inside. He walks across the paved area beyond, a space large enough to hold several cars in addition to the one presently in position, its authoritative German engine ticking in the still, dark warmth. Hunter does not concern himself with the security camera that observes this space. All it will record is a person in dark clothing moving purposefully toward the side of the house, his face angled away. The man inside will not be watching it, and by the time anyone else has cause to do so, it will be too late.

Hunter makes his way around the house, skirting the well-tended palm trees, past a frosted window that runs along the side of the house's epic kitchen area. He can hear a radio or CD player playing within: orchestral trivia, of a style favored by those who do not like or understand classical music but would prefer other people to think they do.

One of the glass doors at the rear of the house has been slid wide, to let in the sound of the waves — celebration of the house's position and, implicitly, its cost. This is the major failing of security systems. The owner hands up his or her safety to a technological higher power. In common with all such agencies, the protection it affords is imaginary. Higher powers don't care if you drink. They don't care if you have a shitty day. They don't even care if you die.

Hunter slips inside the house. He walks into the center of the room — which is large, carpeted in a camel color, and luxuriously furnished. The lights are low. After a moment's pause, he continues toward the kitchen. Once there, he pushes its door open wider, and waits.

The music is louder here, but no better. The house's owner is doing something noisy with ice cubes. After a couple of minutes he happens to turn in the direction of the door, and does a decent job of not looking startled.

'What the *fuck*?'

He has relinquished the steel blue Prada trousers — too tight around the gut for comfort now that there's no longer anyone around to impress — and changed into nice clean gray sweatpants. He has undone his lilac shirt to the waist. He is holding a heavy cut-glass tumbler. A bottle of single malt stands on the counter behind him, next to a set of keys.

He grunts, presumably a laugh. 'This a robbery?' He takes a gratuitously long sip of his drink. 'Wrong house, my friend. Wrong house, wrong guy, and you are about to enter a bad, bad phase in your life.'

Hunter's facial expression doesn't change.

The man in the sweatpants hesitates then, finding himself susceptible for a moment to a tremor of disquiet, as if dusty neural pathways — or the vestigial sliver of an older, better soul — are telling him to beware.

And also . . . that he might have met this man before.

Hunter sees this flash of recognition, and takes a step into the kitchen.

The other man starts to back away. 'You are so — '

The bullet enters his right thigh just above the knee. The gun is fitted with a silencer and makes less sound than the mangled shell when it exits

43

the man's leg and thuds into one of the kitchen cabinets. Hunter is at the man's side before he's even made it down to the floor. The second half of the descent is more a tumble than a fall, and involves a crash against a side cabinet.

Hunter waits for the body to reach a temporary point of rest, then brings the butt of the pistol down on the back of the other man's head.

★　★　★

Later he takes the set of house keys from the kitchen counter. He locates the heart of the CCTV surveillance system in the office space on the first floor, establishes that it spools what it observes — both inside the house and outside — to hard disk. He removes the drive. So long as the next part goes smoothly, he has effectively never been here.

He leaves the house via the front door, locking it behind him after he has propped the man's unconscious body against it. An injection has ensured that the man will not be waking any time soon.

Hunter reopens the main gate and fetches his car from the restaurant parking lot. He loads the comatose body into the trunk, reenables the gate's entry pad, and rearms the security system. Then he drives sedately back out onto the highway.

Within half a mile he has become a ghost who was never there, and never did anything at all.

5

'You're sure?'

I shrugged. 'Hazel, I'm not sure, no. Like I said, this is an overheard conversation — which I wasn't a part of — and I'm keen that you not jump to any conclusions. I just thought I should let you know what I'd heard.'

The woman opposite me frowned. Hazel Wilkins, midsixties, widowed owner of three prime beach-view condos within The Breakers. She was dressed head to toe from boutiques around the Circle, some doubtless visible from where we were sitting taking this midmorning coffee — the sidewalk table outside Jonny Bo's streetlevel café. Hair once blond was shot with gray, but she was still a good-looking woman.

'Tell me again. Word for word.'

I really didn't want to go through it all again. Partly because, despite forty dire minutes in the gym, my head still felt fragile from all the wine the night before. Mainly because the conversation I was alluding to was entirely fictional, and I couldn't remember exactly what I'd said the first time.

'The play-by-play isn't important,' I said airily, as if keen to keep things on an elevated level. 'Bottom line is that he and Marie look like they're holding to the no-improvements-this-season rule. As they have for the last few years.'

'Tony's an extremely self-centered man,' Hazel

said briskly. 'And she's worse. Dangerously so. Neither is capable of being happy unless they're pushing other people around. I'm tired of it and I'm tired of them. I've been an owner here right from the start. They ought to respect that. They ought to respect *me*.'

'I'm sure they do,' I said, holding my hand up to attract a waitress. This meeting had gone on long enough. I needed to be somewhere else. Somewhere out of direct sunlight. 'They have their own way of doing things, and progress comes hard to people. There's comfort and convenience to the status quo. Everyone needs a compelling reason to change.'

I might have kept quoting random self-improvement mantras forever, but thankfully a waitress arrived with the check, though not the waitress who'd been serving us previously. It was, as a matter of fact, the girl who'd waited on Steph and me the night before. She evidently saw me noticing the switch.

'Shift swap,' she said. 'Or maybe Debbie just exploded. You never know. Hey,' she added, belatedly recognizing me. 'Back so soon? Should get you a loyalty card.'

'Is there one?'

'Not really. But I could make a prototype, maybe. Out of a serviette and, like, drawing our logo on it.'

'What would the rewards be?'

'Well, I don't know,' she said. 'But the card itself would be an awesome thing.'

I handed over my personal Amex. She went back indoors.

'You come here often, Bill?' Hazel asked, one eyebrow lightly raised.

'Last night,' I said. 'Stephanie and I had a great meal on the balcony. That girl was our waitress.'

'You must be on the up if you're making a habit of hanging out at this place.'

'Hardly a habit. It was our anniversary.'

She nodded, her eyes vague. Phil Wilkins was six years dead, but it didn't take a genius to work out that his wife still missed him hard. I'd met Phil a couple of times, soon after we moved to Florida, and even when hobbled with advanced cancer you could tell he'd once been a man of compelling character. Hazel still presented well, but there was an air of pointlessness about the performance. She was keeping her end up because that's what you did, not because she especially wanted anyone to notice, or cared what anyone still alive thought of her. It was as though her husband had told her to stand to one side and wait for him while he fetched the car, but then had never come back to collect.

Her hands lay together on the round metal table as if they had been mislaid by someone else. I put one of mine gently on top of them.

'Look,' I said, as if the idea had just come to me. 'You want me to try to have a word with Tony?'

'Could you do that?' Her gaze came back to the here and now. 'I don't want him to know it's coming from me. I'm only looking to sell two of the units. The other I'm going to keep until the day I die, and then the kids can fight over it. The

47

Breakers is in my life, and I never want to lose that. I just want to be able to make some changes, you know? I love it that I can still see Phil there. But I think maybe . . . I need to see him just a little less.'

She looked away. 'Sometimes when I try to go to sleep at night, it's like I can feel him standing by the bed, looking down on me. And that's nice in some ways, but if he can't climb in and get beside me, then I think maybe I could live without it. Do you understand?'

'Sure,' I said, feeling uncomfortable. I sat back in my chair, bringing my hand away with me.

The waitress returned with my card. She seemed to sense that Hazel was having a moment, and backed away again discreetly and without comment.

'Anything I can do, I'll do,' I said. 'I promise.'

Hazel smiled. 'You're a good guy, Bill,' she said.

* * *

By the time I'd parked outside the office I'd shrugged off the encounter. Refreshing dissent among owners at The Breakers remained a sensible tactic. I hadn't been expecting that Hazel Wilkins's issue with the decor would be quite so personal, but that was all to the good. Business concerns come and go and ebb and flow. Personal beefs are permanent. If someone who'd known the Thompsons for that long was prepared to start trusting me as go-between, it was going well. I didn't actually

48

care if she got what she wanted.

Karren's desk was unattended when I walked in. Janine was in position bending over hers, laminating something. Personally, had I been born and bred a Floridian, I might have made the effort not to be fat when I grew up. In this weather and humidity, it's simply not the thinking person's choice. Janine cleaved to some other vision, however, and when stuffed into bright blue stretch pants, her rear end was another thing that Karren and I were at one in finding less than supergreat and perfect.

'Hey,' I said.

Janine let out a squeal and turned around. When she saw it was me, she rolled her eyes and fluttered a pudgy hand over her heart. She did this every single time anything happened that hadn't been exhaustively trailed via radio, television, and public service announcement. How she'd managed to make it to twenty-six without a heart attack, I had no idea.

'Oh,' she said. 'It's you.'

'Live and in color. Who did you think it might be?'

'Well, you just never know.'

'I guess not. How's . . . ' I struggled and failed to come up with the name of her spawn. 'Feeling better?'

This was not something I cared about in the least, but that morning a Danish positivity blogger had suggested going out of one's way to attempt to get inside other people's lives and minds, however small and unappealing they might appear, as a thought experiment in connection building.

'A little,' she allowed cautiously. A cynical person might have wondered whether the kid, whose name I suddenly remembered — Kyle — was in fact this morning so very healthy that he was being held up by pediatricians as an example to others everywhere, but that his mother was withholding this information in case she needed to come in late another morning that week.

'That's great. Great.'

She smiled suddenly. 'And so how was your dinner?' There was a strange inflection to her question, as if I was being upbraided for being coy.

I frowned at her, confused.

'At Bo's, silly,' she said. 'Was it great? I've always wanted to go. But of course it's *way* out of our range. It's on my list. One day.'

'It was fabulous,' I said. 'As always. But how did you know I was there?'

Now it was her turn to look baffled. 'Well, you asked me to make the reservation,' she said. 'You sent me an e-mail, end of last week.'

'Right, right,' I said. That was one minor mystery solved at least. 'Of course. Thank you for sorting it out. We had a lovely evening.'

'That's so cool.'

'Where's Karren?'

'You know, I don't actually know. She left about half an hour ago. I did ask her where she was going, just out of interest or in case you needed to know, you know, and she was all, 'To meet with a client.' So basically, I think that's what it is, probably.'

'Okay then,' I said.

* * *

I discovered where Karren had gone as soon as I logged on to check my mail. She'd sent me a note explaining that a man called David Warner had called midmorning (while I was sitting listening to Hazel zone out over her dead husband), asking for me and wanting advice on selling his house up the key. He'd wanted to get onto it right away, her e-mail said with judicious reasonableness, and I hadn't been there, so she was going to take the meeting instead. She hoped that was okay.

'Bitch,' I muttered.

She knew damned well it wasn't okay. Warner was a guy I'd met at a bar on the mainland a couple of weeks before. He had an eight-million-dollar house on Longboat about three miles north of The Breakers, and selling it should have been my gig. I'd done the groundwork. I'd met the guy and started the fire.

'Excuse me?' Janine said.

'Just clearing my throat.'

I sent a clipped e-mail to Karren saying how *delighted* I was to hear she'd been there to get onto meeting Warner's needs, and that I looked forward to working with her on it. Then I hesitated, and did a little editing, making it friendlier and backing off the irony a tad. Thinking about it, David Warner had struck me right off the bat as a high-maintenance vendor.

51

He was hefty, bluff, black hair flecked with gray and swept back, a man who had clearly supped long at the font of self-confidence: local boy made good (in the sense of 'wealthy'), and convinced he could outthink and outexperience everyone on every goddamned thing — and sell his house better and faster and more lucratively himself, moreover, were he not too busy being so very rich the whole time. The more Karren had her hands full over the next few weeks, the less likely she would be to notice what I was doing with Tony Thompson.

I sent the e-mail, feeling satisfied. I'm all for being in the moment, but sometimes you have to take the longer view. Had I been Janine, for example, instead of bovinely accepting that Jonny Bo's was out of my range, I would have saved for weeks or months to get in — and Steph would have been there with me, taking the chicken and drinking iced water and skipping dessert. You move forward in life by throwing a foot up onto the next rung, then hauling the rest of you up after, time after time.

There wasn't much other mail to deal with. A couple of no-whats (as in 'No, I'm not looking to sell my condo right now — what, in this market, are you *insane*?'), general crap and updates from the main office, plus a notification from Amazon that some order of mine had been shipped. I couldn't even remember what was in it, so that hardly qualified as headline news.

I gave Janine a few pointless things to do and then left for a walk around the resort. Since the advent of cell phones, e-mail, and push notifications, sticking to your desk is a sign not of diligence but of inertia. I took a notepad with me and jotted down every single little glitch, snag, and imperfection I could find.

★　★　★

Two hours later I was sitting outside The Breakers' market with an iced coffee and a head full of half-formed plans, when I saw Karren's car coming round the circle. She parked, saw me, hesitated, then walked over.

'Thanks for picking up on the Warner meeting,' I said. 'Glad you were there to do it.'

She glared down at me, then reached into her little briefcase and pulled out a pad. She ripped off the top few pages and dropped them on the table.

I leaned forward and peered at them. Notes on a house, in Karren's tidy hand.

'He . . . ' She bit her lip.

'Yes?'

'He thanked me for taking the time to come out,' she said coldly. 'And said that he looked forward to dealing with you over the actual sale.'

I leaned back, being careful not to allow any hint of expression to make it to my face. 'That sucks,' I said, reaching for my phone. 'You want me to give him a call? Put him straight on what century we're living in?'

'Fuck you,' Karren said, and stormed away.

I managed to hold back the laughter until she was back in the office, but it was hard.

Boy, it was hard.

★   ★   ★

I'd just climbed into the car at the end of the day
when my cell rang.

'Mr. Bill Moore?'

The voice was young, female, professional.

'That would be me. How can I help?'

'I'm Melania — David Warner's assistant.'

Melania? Was that even a real name? 'What
can I do for you, Melania?'

'Mr. Warner was a little disappointed that you
weren't able to make the meeting today.'

'Whoa,' I said. 'Let's hit pause. Not my bad,
okay? He called the office — after I had told him
my cell was the best way of getting hold of me
— and said he wanted a meeting right away. He
agreed to meet with my colleague. Who he
managed to alienate more than a little, if you
want to know.'

I didn't give a crap about Warner having
pissed off Karren (and had savored the idea
more than once in the meantime, as a matter of
fact), but you have to make it clear to other
people's minions that you're not down on their
level, and are not available to be bossed around.

There was a slight pause. 'He can be that way.'

'Yep. It's how they roll,' I said, making my
tone a little more friendly, implying that men
(and women) of a certain age, and of a certain
wealth, seem to think that their possessions act
like spells, empowering them to behave toward
others without fear of resistance or reprisal, most
of the time.

She understood what I was saying.

'And we love them for it.' Her voice sounded a little warmer now, too. 'Okay, well, the bullet point is that Mr. Warner would like to pursue matters. Could you meet with him at nine this evening?'

'Nine? That's kind of late.'

'I know. He has a dinner engagement ahead of that. But he really wants to get the ball rolling.'

I was tired, and the wine hangover had come home to roost, despite a few fistfuls of aspirin. Steph would be mildly pissed at the late notice, too, more as a matter of form than because it would materially inconvenience her. An eight-million-dollar house is an eight-million-dollar house, however, as I believe it points out in the Bible somewhere.

'No problem,' I said. I noted down the address of the property when she reeled it off. Then I called my wife and told her I wasn't going to be back until late.

'What's up?'

'Remember I told you about a guy I met in Krank's? Couple, three weeks back? Might be wanting to sell a house on the key?'

'No,' she said. 'It must have slipped my mind.'

'Well, I did. And he does. Wants to talk about it this evening. I'm going to take the meeting. Wouldn't normally, but it's a big house. Could go up to ten mil.'

'Can't Karren do it? She's single, right? Surely she can take the evening shift.'

'Not really,' I said. 'Less I want her to take the commission, too.'

'She going with? To the meeting?'

55

'No. This is a solo flight.'

'Well, grab something to eat in between, because the fridge is empty and the situation will not have improved by the time you get back.'

'I'll do that.'

'And be good, tycoon-boy.'

Then she was gone, leaving me wondering what that was supposed to mean.

6

I got home at a little before midnight, and by then — if I hadn't been so tired — I would have been pretty mad.

After talking to Steph I drove down to the Circle and killed half an hour shooting the breeze with Max, the guy who looks after a lot of the commercial property there. He had no new listings, and answered the inquiry with a slight smile. I'd been talking to Max for over a year, looking for the kind of place that might work for Bill Moore Realty when the time came. Previously he'd been enthusiastic — he didn't handle residential, so there'd be no conflict of interest — but this time I got a strong hint of 'yeah, right,' in the way he dealt with me — as if he was starting to get the idea that me setting up on my own (as he'd done ten years before, also after a period working for Shore) was a dream that was becoming more insubstantial by the month. I kicked against this by dropping hints that I was on the verge of big things Any Day Now, which left me feeling exposed and vulnerable and something of an ass.

He also asked whether I was sure I'd got the right name for the business, given that Bill Moore could be heard as 'bill more,' which is not what you want in a Realtor, or indeed anyone in a service industry. Annoyingly, he had a point. Having spent the last six years getting myself known around town as Bill rather than William, however — Bill being much more direct and personal and can-do — it was too late to change. I put a pin in the problem and set it aside.

I thought about getting a sandwich but couldn't get the idea to generate any traction and so I wound up going to the Ben & Jerry's instead. The area inside had the air, as usual, of having recently withstood a concerted attack by forces loyal to some other ice cream manufacturer. I noticed a girl I hadn't seen before, standing behind the counter.

'Hey,' she said as I wandered up.

She was skinny, early twenties, curly black hair in goth/emo style. Drapey black clothes under the corporate apron, a stud through her nose. The effect was not unattractive, though had I been the place's manager I might have wanted the staff to look like they'd be dishing out fresh dairy products full of organic, carbon-neutral goodness, rather than bat wings sprinkled with toad's blood.

'Hey,' I said. 'I'll take a . . . '

I trailed off. I actually had no idea what I wanted. Maybe nothing. The conversation with Max had pissed me off more than I'd realized, and I was struggling to pull my mood back up. I wasn't sure if I even wanted ice cream or if I was just in here to get out of the tail end of the afternoon's heat.

'I know what you need,' the girl said.

'You do?'

'You bet. You want to take a seat outside? Oh, and give me six bucks. That allows for the generous tip you will wish to confer upon me, after the fact.'

Slightly bemused, I did as she asked. Five minutes later she emerged onto the sidewalk with a bowl of something pale orange in color. I peered at it.

'Hell is that?'

'Mascarpone Mandarin frozen yogurt, with a twist.'

She stood there pertly while I took a tentative mouthful. It was refreshing and yet not too tart, and actually very nice. 'Good call,' I said. 'I'm liking it.'

'It's supposed to be called Multimazingmagical Mandarin Mascarpone Madness, for your future ordering convenience. Only, saying all that makes me want to kill myself.'

'I'll remember it. You nailed me.'

'It's my superpower. One of several, I might add.'

'I thought people were only allowed one superpower.'

'Nah. That's just the story they put around.'

I reached my hand up. 'Bill Moore. I work up at The Breakers, on Longboat. For Shore Realty.'

She shook, a smart up-and-down motion. 'Cassandra.' She slowly turned about the waist to point back at the ice cream parlor. 'I work . . . here.'

I ate the yogurt slowly, but the process still filled up less than half an hour. Toward the end the server girl came back out again, divested of white apron and carrying a long black coat.

'Have a good evening, Mr. Moore.'

'You too.'

Halfway to the corner she stopped and turned around. 'I never asked. What's *your* superpower?'

I was slightly dismayed at not being able to come up with a smart answer right off the bat. I shrugged, rolled my eyes, as if to suggest it was *such* a long story that I didn't know where to start, but it was weak.

'Aha,' she said, however. 'You've yet to discover it. How *exciting*.'

She winked, and disappeared around the corner.

★ ★ ★

I got to half past eight largely by catching up on blogs on the phone and updating my Facebook profile with links to the best of them, and then drove back across to Longboat Key. I continued past The Breakers and a succession of similar developments to the upper half of the island. The southerly end of Longboat holds condos on the gulf side and a few communities on the other, bay side — the latter not dissimilar to the kind of place where Steph and I lived, except every house had access to the waterway and they all cost about three times as much as ours. The top half of the island gets a lot narrower and holds larger private dwellings. While they don't reach the heights of the real glamour compounds down on Siesta Key, there are few that don't fall into the 'price on application' bracket. The address I had been given lay about midway along this section, gulf side.

I slowed as I got into range, peering at the properties I passed. For the half mile coming up to Warner's place, everything looked swish and expensive and cool. No minicondos, nothing in danger of being pulled down and noisily rebuilt, nothing overgrown on account of a diminishing and cantankerous oldster inside, a relic of the premodern phase of the key, who might raise lunatic enviro-hippy objections to your plans for six additional tennis courts. All good.

I pulled into the driveway, which curved through a piece of landscaped and watered gardens. About forty yards from the highway it revealed a set of gates hidden from the road within a small grove of palms. Also good.

I stopped in front of the gates, wound down the window, and jabbed the buzzer. Nothing happened. I waited a couple minutes and then pressed it again. Nothing continued to happen, or happened again.

I gave it five minutes and a couple more presses. Then I got out of the car and walked up to the gates, wondering if Warner was waiting in the driveway space beyond. There was no sign of anyone. A few lamps were lit around the area, but the house itself looked dark.

I went back to the car and pulled Karren's notes out of my folder. A quick look was sufficient to confirm I was at the right house. I got out my phone, then realized I didn't have a number for Warner. He'd taken mine, but deftly circumvented my attempts to get his. I searched back through my call history until I found incoming from just before six that evening.

It rang for quite a while before anyone answered.

'Bill Moore,' I said in a clipped voice. 'I'm supposed to be meeting with David. Right now.'

'I don't work for him twenty-four-seven, you know.' Melania sounded tetchy. I could hear the sound of a television in the background.

'Neither do I,' I said. 'It remains to be seen whether I work for him at all. My point is I'm at the house, he's not, and it's after quarter past.'

'Christ,' she muttered. There was a pause. 'Oh god,' she said then, contrite. 'I'm *so* sorry. I just checked the BlackBerry. His dinner is running late so he asked me to see if you could meet him in Sarasota, around ten?'

It was on the tip of my tongue to tell her to inform her boss that he could meet me during office hours at Shore, or not at all. It seemed dumb to blow it when I'd already sacrificed the evening to the cause, however, and I'd be driving that way home anyhow.

'Am I meeting him anywhere in particular? Or is guessing the venue an exercise for the Realtor?'

'Krank's,' she said quickly. 'I think you met him there once before? Look, Mr. Moore, I'm *really* sorry. He's *got* your phone number, right? I don't know why he didn't just call you himself.'

Because that's *also* how these people roll, I could have told her. The big house and the money are not enough. That's just cash wealth — and existential wealth is what counts. You've got to make it clear to everyone, every day, that your life is different, that you don't have to jump through the conventional hoops, that politeness is for those who cannot afford to behave otherwise. That you rule. That you're god.

You learn this within days of starting in the luxury real estate business, and I looked forward very much to behaving this way myself.

As a start, I ended the call without saying anything more. If she had any sense, Melania would have realized that I now had a choice over whether I revealed that she'd failed to pass on her boss's message. Which meant she owed me, which in turn meant that being jerked around would wind up playing to my advantage in the end. If you're sharp enough to see through the games people play, you start to pull ahead. Bill Moore understands this.

Bill Moore is fit for purpose.

★ ★ ★

Except . . . the asshole didn't show up there, either.

Krank's is a newish bar/restaurant on Main in Sarasota at the intersection with Lemon Avenue (the street name a remnant of the days when the town was only here to grow and ship citrus), the kind of zeitgeist-crazed trend pit where you have to be ever vigilant in reminding yourself that you are not there merely to kowtow to the whims of the staff. I parked with ten minutes to spare. Being inside the bar was like being punched in the face with music, so I got a bottle of Ybor Gold and took it onto the terrace out front instead.

I drank the beer. Twenty-five minutes later, Warner hadn't arrived. I got another Gold. I drank that one, too. Warner still didn't show. The beers were, however, doing what beers do the night after too much wine: making me feel a lot better.

So I had one more. By the time that was done it was coming up on eleven o'clock, and I was done, too. I considered calling Melania again but dismissed the idea. All that would achieve was showing that her boss had no compunction about standing me up again. The blogs all say that people take you at your own estimation, and that's true, but people sure as hell take you at other people's estimation as well. Melania didn't need to know I'd been stood up a second time — not from me, anyway.

I paid my tab and drove carefully home.

When I got to the house, the lights were on Steph's I've-Gone-to-Bed setting. I stood for a moment in the living room, wondering whether I'd gain any material advantage from having a swim. I decided not. Instead, I gently let out the burp that had been building since the last beer and caught a tiny hint of mandarin on my breath.

I went to the kitchen to get a couple of glasses of water for the bedroom — Steph never bothered to do this for herself, but liked it when I did — and tramped upstairs. She was still awake, propped up in bed reading.

'Hey, babe. Success?'

'No. He didn't show.'

'Really?'

'Really.'

'So what have you been doing all this time?'

'Waiting.'

'Where?'

I got into bed beside her. 'Outside his house, then at Krank's — where his assistant said he'd be.'

'Kind of a busted evening, hey.'

'Say that again.'

She turned out the light, and rolled onto her side.

7

His abductor has only one question. The man understands perfectly well what it means. He gets what the guy wants to know. He also realizes that once he answers the question, he's probably going to die.

And so he hasn't answered it.

Yet.

★ ★ ★

He woke several hours before. Consciousness crept upon him slowly, as if unsure how good an idea it would be to get reinvolved. Eventually it stabilized. His eyelids seemed broken, too heavy to lift, and so initially he left them closed. His head felt stodgy, as if after a long evening of turgid red wine. He was aware of businesslike alerts from various other angles of his body, as if they'd collided with something hard. He was not hungry. He was very warm.

These impressions came to him in an orderly procession, as if presented on burgundy-colored velvet cushions held up by tiny, deferential servants. For a moment, in fact, he believed he could actually see these minuscule helpers bowing and scraping in the dark corridors of his mind. Then they fled, all at once, darting chaotically to either side to clear the way for bigger news, as it suddenly declared itself.

Somebody had punched his right thigh, above the knee. Either that, or hit it very hard with a hammer.

This hadn't occurred recently — it didn't have the raw edge of the this-just-happened — but the pain was still very large. It was large in a measured, I-can-keep-this-up-forever style.

It was large enough for the man to feel it was probably time to open his eyes.

★ ★ ★

The first thing he sees is his own lap. His head has, he realizes, been lolling forward. He sees blurred images of gray sweatpants, now mottled, and the crumpled front of a lilac shirt. He recognizes these. They belong to him.

He pulls his head up, dislodging drops of sweat that had been hanging off his nose. His head whirls. After a moment of confusion, things start to fall into place. He sees the bare walls of some octagonal space thirty feet across. There are four blue patches, like windows — except you can't see through them. Tarpaulins. Around the edges you can see the outside world, where it is bright and very sunny. A flapping sound from the tarps says there's a light breeze outside, but it's not reaching the inside. The man can also hear, distantly, the sound of the sea. A standard concrete cinder block, eight by eight by sixteen inches, lies against the wall.

He looks back down. He sees now that an area of his sweatpants above his right knee is stained reddish brown. In parts this stain is very thick, and hard, suggesting that a lot of blood was involved.

Ah. He remembers now.

He was shot.

The wound feels like some eternal moment of impact, but he understands that it maybe still hurts less than it should. It seems likely he's on some serious kind of painkiller. Possibly he's also coming out of a dose of something used to knock him out, a narcotic presumably.

None of these are reassuring ideas, especially when the third and most salient detail of his situation finally announces itself. His wrists are tied to the arms of a very heavy wooden chair. They are bound by thick canvas straps. So are his ankles. There's a similar strap around his waist, and another around his shoulders.

They are all very tight.

He tries to pull himself forward in the chair, but he cannot move more than half an inch. This is enough for him to notice, however, that someone has chalked a question on the gray concrete floor in front of him. The letters are about a foot high, and the chalk is red.

There are just two words:

Who else?

He tries shouting. His voice is thick and coarse, barely loud enough to rebound off the walls. After a few minutes he's able to get up to a good loud bellow. Nothing happens except that he gets hotter and starts to panic.

He stops, takes deep breaths, evaluates what

68

he knows. He's been brought to a building — either a private house or a condo — in the early stages of construction. He gets the feeling he's on a second or third story, because when he gets a momentary glimpse around the edge of one of the tarps, it only shows sky. The building has been mothballed, otherwise they wouldn't have bothered to tarp the window gaps in a building that hasn't got to first fit stage. The structure has been built out of cinder block that was given a quick cement render. The man in the chair knows about these things, having been involved in many a development in the last decade.

This doesn't enable him to work out where he is, however, as he's aware of at least six big condo projects currently in hibernation, waiting for the market to get more frisky. He's a stakeholder in two of these himself, but he knows this building isn't in one of those. He'd recognize it. He might be able to work out a little more if he were able to move, but the strapping is irrevocable. If a point comes when he needs to relieve himself — it hasn't yet, but that might be a temporary aftereffect of whatever drug he was given — he's going to be doing it where he sits.

The chair is very heavy. He tries rocking from side to side. He could probably *just about* get it to tip over to the left or right. There are two problems with that plan of action, however, even assuming he doesn't bang his head on the way over. The first is that he's just going to be strapped to a chair lying on its side, which doesn't really represent an improvement in his situation.

The second, as he's now realized, is that though there's floor space in front of him — where the two-word question is written, for example — there's none to either side. This octagonal space is evidently intended as an observation lounge, designed to be accessed by a showy spiral staircase from below. That staircase isn't in place yet. From what he can make out, only half the octagon has a floor. The chair has been placed on a stubby rectangular platform that juts out into a space not much larger than the footprint of the chair itself.

Causing the chair to tip over to the left, right, or backward will make it fall at least one story, to crash onto a concrete floor.

So he's not going to do that.

★ ★ ★

He sits, occasionally building himself up into a few minutes of increasingly hoarse shouting, for many hours. The flickers of sky that make it past the tarps start to soften, and the bright blue of the sunlight hitting the cloths themselves starts to darken. In the end the stuffy heat allows him to dip into a shallow drowse.

He opens his eyes after an indeterminate period. The painkiller has begun to wear off. It's clear that the discomfort in his thigh has a lot more to give. His ass hurts from prolonged, unmoving contact with the chair seat. All his joints hurt, too. He tries not to think about this, as he knows the feeling of being trapped will make it even worse.

70

He raises his head. The room is dark now, though sufficient moonlight creeps through the gaps to keep it three-dimensional through glints of gray and silver.

There's someone in there with him.

A figure leans against the wall directly in front. He's dressed in dark clothing, but in this light, that's all you can tell. He says nothing.

The man in the chair finds his mouth is suddenly dry. He asks the bottom-line question. 'What do you want from me?'

'You had plenty of time this afternoon. The reading matter I left you was only two words long.'

'You really think I'm going to give you names?'

The other man seems to consider the question. 'Yes,' he says, 'I do.'

'You're wrong.'

'I guess we'll see. I'd guess also it's been a long time since you've been hungry, though. Plus, you've had no liquid for eighteen hours. Feeling thirsty at all?'

The man in the chair suddenly realizes just how parched he feels. Not just dryness in the mouth — that can be temporarily salved by running his tongue around it — but in his throat, and in his head, which feels desiccated and tight.

'Nope,' he says nonetheless.

'Keep telling yourself that. If it gets boring, though, there's something else to think about.'

The man pushes himself up from the wall and walks over toward the chair. The seated man realizes that Hunter is holding something in either hand.

Hunter slowly raises his left hand, and it becomes clear that his fingers — displaying a disquieting level of strength — are gripping the cinder block that has lain by the wall all afternoon. He raises this block to chest height, moves his hand until it is over the other man's right leg, and drops the block.

The man in the chair screams.

The pain is so enormous that he bucks in the chair. The other man reaches out, unhurried, to prevent it from tipping over.

'Steady,' he says.

The seated man can barely hear. His teeth are clenched, his eyes clamped shut. He feels the block lifted off his lap, hears it thrown back into the room. Something else lands on his leg, but it weighs next to nothing and he doesn't care about it or anything else. His leg feels as if someone is hammering a huge rusty nail up along the bone, again and again and again.

★　★　★

It is ten minutes before he has control of himself and opens his eyes. Hunter is no longer in the room. How he left, the man in the chair has no idea. He also has no clue how he is now going to prevent the idea of thirst — and increasingly, its reality — from moving front and center of his every thought. He knows he ought to look down at his leg but believes it unlikely that will achieve much except make him feel worse.

Nonetheless he does so — and what he sees drives, for a moment, all thoughts of thirst from his mind. The thing Hunter dropped on his lap is a woman's robe.

The man in the chair recognizes it. It belongs to a woman called Lynn Napier, the one he spent the evening with the night before.

A voice floats up from the level below.

'Who else?' it asks.

There is the sound of footsteps receding, and then silence.

8

'Is this from you?'

'What?'

'This.' I turned from the counter toward the kitchen table, where Steph was swiftly eating breakfast while absorbing local nonnews from the small flat-screen in the corner. She put her head on one side, causing still-wet hair to slide across her face. When she clocked the jacket of the book I was holding she gave a snort.

'That would be a supersized no.' She laughed. 'With a side of 'Dream on, my friend.''

I looked back at the book, which I'd found propped outside our front door, in corrugated packaging, when I got back from the gym. It was large and heavy and apparently retailed for eighty bucks. It was published by a European house I recognized as purveyors of lavish coffee-table tomes, and featured a retrospective of the work of a photographer I'd never heard of.

A quick flick through confirmed that, as the cover implied, said snapper was all about honoring the timeless beauty of the female form, in fetishized states of undress. An immaculate airline stewardess bending over a meal cart, skirt hitched up to reveal tattered, cheap underwear. A secretary dutifully typing at an old Underwood, unaware of how very close her besuited boss — seen only from the waist down, complete with self-evident bulge — was standing behind

74

her. A female doctor, adrift in a lamp-lit ward in the dead of the night — the patients asleep in their beds — wearing only high heels, garters, stockings, and a stethoscope, gazing with apparent melancholy at a clipboard she held in one hand.

'Really?'

'*Really*,' she said.

'This isn't some guy who's going to have an exposition here or something?'

'Ex*hib*ition, not exposition, dear,' Steph said around a mouthful of high-spec granola. 'And no. Sarasota has come a long way, but it ain't New York. Or even Tallahassee. The art-porn market still falls outside what local folks will countenance in a public gallery.'

I frowned down at the Amazon delivery note. 'Well, that's weird.'

'Does it *say* it's a gift?'

'No. It was bought on my account.'

'Hon,' Steph said, 'it's okay.'

'What do you mean?'

'If you ordered this, I don't mind.'

I stared at her. 'Why would I even open the package in front of you if I had something to hide?'

She shrugged. 'You're cruising around the site, see the book, accidentally click BUY IT NOW instead of ADD TO BASKET. Forget all about it and then bang, here it is. And in front of the wife. Whoops. No biggie.'

I spoke slowly. 'I did not order this book.'

'So send it back,' she said, grabbing her car keys. 'I got to go, hon. Big day of prep for the

Maxwinn Saunders powwow tomorrow.'

'Steph, listen. I didn't buy this.'

'I believe you,' she said with a wink, and then she was gone.

* * *

First thing I did when I got to work was to e-mail Amazon, briskly requesting the procedure for returning a book sent in error. I'd already checked the shipping notification e-mail I'd received the day before. Paying more attention when it came in wouldn't have achieved much — by then the book had already been on its way. It was Steph's response that was nettling me most. It wasn't as if the book was hard-core. Two seconds with a search engine would have flooded my screen with pictures that would have made Henrik Myerson (creator of the images in the book stowed in the trunk of my car) blanch. But that wasn't the point. The *point* was that the book's arrival had made me look like the kind of person who wanted to own this kind of thing. I have dedicated a lot of time and effort to assuming control of my personal brand. I'm not going to stand for random misinformation muddying the waters.

That was the first point, anyhow. The second was a broader one. I grew up in Pennsylvania. My mother's sister lived in South Carolina, and from time to time the family would migrate down to spend a week. Aunt Lynn was a recovering hippie and big on producing her own food. This included a series of impressive chili

76

plants that grew along a fence in the backyard. The fruits of these were fascinating to me. There's something so ripe and eye-catching about a chili when it's ready to pick, a plumpness that bellows 'eat me' to the untrained eye. My parents had firmly instructed me not to do any such thing, and I was in general a well-behaved kid.

Imagine their surprise, therefore, at coming out into the yard one afternoon to discover that the eight-year-old child they'd left peaceably playing was now in paroxysms of agony, unable even to come indoors, apparently caused by having eaten one of these chilies.

They were comforting, and supportive, and fed me ice cream to dull the burn, all the time managing to refrain from saying they'd told me so. I said I *hadn't* eaten a chili, and they didn't explicitly call me on it, but smiled when they thought I wasn't looking. But the thing is . . .

I hadn't eaten a damned chili.

All I'd done — and this hadn't been explicitly disallowed, and children need explicit instruction because they are not good at expanding from the specific to the general — was to reach up and touch one of the swollen, bright red chilies. I'd marveled at how hard it was, how powerful and fecund, then turned my back on the forbidden fruit and got on with something else. I'd evidently also accidentally brushed those same fingers across my lips, however, bringing the freakish power of a Scotch Bonnet to bear upon skin that still thought of American mustard as wantonly aggressive.

The pain eventually subsided. What did *not* fade was the sense of injustice — the injustice wrought by someone being kind and forgiving over a sin that had not been committed. Steph shrugging off the book's arrival this morning felt the same way — and the worst of it was that there was no way back. I could go home at the end of the day clutching proof that I'd returned the book, and she could interpret this as me going out of my way to maintain the pretense of not having ordered it in the first place. Even if she eventually believed me, the instant in which she'd thought otherwise remained alive in time.

I was still fulminating over this when there was a *ping* to indicate I'd received an e-mail. It was the Amazon help desk, with guidelines for returning a book if you had ordered it in error.

Suddenly I was even more angry. I *hadn't* ordered it in error. *Their computer had fucked up.* I knew the response I'd just received was itself computer generated, and that made it worse: a computer telling a human how to unscrew an error made by another computer, making me a pawn in some ludicrous glitch-generated scenario I hadn't asked for in the first place.

I scribbled a note for Karren's desk — saying I was headed out to a meeting, and in the process also demonstrating I'd been at work before her — and stomped out to drive to the post office at Ocean View Mall.

★ ★ ★

After I'd mailed the package back I felt better. I took a twenty-minute time-out with an iced Americano before driving back to work, taking myself through some positivity exercises. It didn't take long to work out that what had really bugged me was the feeling of loss of control. I'd quickly regained it, and so — big deal. By the time I was done with the coffee I'd gotten to the point where I was emboldened to drop an SMS message to Steph, reiterating that I hadn't ordered the book but saying that if it had given her any ideas, then I was all ears and would be at her disposal tonight.

Two minutes later an SMS came back, saying she'd bear the offer in mind, with a winking smiley and a kiss.

Job done. Steph could think what she liked about whether I'd ordered the book. So long as it turned to my advantage, what did I care?

On the way back across the lot to my car I noticed a dapper figure walking along in front of the drugstore. He was listening to someone on his cell phone. I slowed, gave him time to end the call, and then took a side step to put me in the man's field of view.

'Morning, Mr. Grant.'

Peter Grant, owner-CEO of Shore Realty, frowned. 'There's no meeting up here today, is there?'

'No,' I said, thinking on my feet. 'Just met with a potential client. I'm heading back to the office now.'

He nodded, evidently glad to have cleared the mystery up. He was dressed in an understated but wildly expensive suit, and his silver hair seemed to have been spun from the finest thread. He looked distracted, however, slowly replacing his phone in his jacket.

'So . . . how are things down there, Bill? I see the figures, of course, but it's been a while since we've had a chance to catch up man-to-man. Too long.'

I wasn't sure if Grant had ever taken the time to 'catch up' with me. 'Quiet,' I allowed. 'But we're working at it. Putting our ears to the ground, keeping the clients happy. If they're on our side, it's all win.'

'Very true,' he said, and for a moment seemed to look directly at me, as if seeing me in a particular light. 'That's a positive attitude. It will serve you well.'

'Only way to beat the world, sir.'

'Absolutely. Okay, well — don't let me keep you, Bill. Keep up the good work. And good luck.'

'Good to talk to you, sir.'

'You too, Bill,' he said, as he turned to head back into the building. 'You too.'

As I climbed back into the car I was feeling a *lot* more chipper. Spurred by my off-the-cuff excuse to Grant, it even occurred to me to wonder if my straight-to-the-nukes reaction to the photo book was down to lingering annoyance at the blowout of the night before. I pulled up to the highway, hesitated, then turned right instead of left, to head up the road to David Warner's house.

He wasn't there, and a call to Melania's

number dead-ended in voice mail. I didn't leave a message. I took out one of my cards instead, and jammed it in a crack in the buzzer mechanism — after jotting the words 'Call me when you're ready to do business' on the back.

Now feeling two hundred percent better, I drove back to The Breakers.

★   ★   ★

When I got out of my car I had a sighting of the resort's rarest fauna — Marie Thompson. She was talking to Big Walter, dressed in an immaculate white trouser suit, the perfect outfit to showcase an evident dedication to the maxim that you can never be too rich or too thin. As had been the case on most occasions I'd seen her, she was giving someone a hard time. Word was that Marie was from old Sarasota money. It was evident from her body language toward Walter (one of the very blackest black guys I've ever met) that she had yet to receive instruction on modern modes of interacting with people of color.

After a final jab of the finger to underscore whatever dread point she was making, she turned on her heel and stalked into the main building.

Walter watched her go, then turned to look at me. I shrugged. He shrugged back. That made me feel cool.

As I reached for the handle on the door to the Shore office, I heard someone guffawing inside. I knew who it would be. Janine had a very distinctive laugh, one of those plain-girl cackles — bubbly, raucous, and strange. It's the kind of laugh that grown-ups who find themselves unable to compliment a child on her looks may favorably comment on instead, causing the girl to carry what is in reality rather an annoying sound into her adult life.

Sure enough, I walked into the office to find Janine at her desk, hand in front of her mouth, grinning inanely at something on her screen. Buoyed by recent successes, I decided to play nice.

'S'up?' I said.

She giggled, as if we'd been caught in some collusion. 'It's kinda bad,' she said. 'But I like it.'

'What is?'

'You know. What you sent.'

I bent to look over her shoulder. An e-mail from me was open on her computer screen, with a joke. It was a mildly funny joke, assuming you were prepared to overlook the fact that it was markedly off-color and somewhat racist, too.

The only thing was that I hadn't sent it.

Not to her, or any of the other people on the list.

9

I had a late lunch of an egg salad sandwich, sitting in the shade outside the grocery store a few doors down from the office. It's something I do once a week, a little ritual — they make it with a little dill and a touch of Dijon mustard, and it's very good — but either the bread was a bit stale today or I just wasn't in the mood.

Karren had received the e-mail, too. So had a couple of private contacts and a few nonwork friends. Only one person on the list had responded, expressing surprise that I'd forwarded something that had nothing to do with realty, as I never normally did that kind of thing.

Well, right. True statement.

I'd stayed at my desk for a while, looking like I was taking care of business. I quickly established that the e-mail was not in my SENT MAIL folder, nor had it been filed. I'm very organized about keeping everything I receive and send. Big or small, even if it's merely a 'Great meeting!' or (god forbid) an 'LOL!' everything gets given a sensible home. In realty you never know when you might wish or need to demonstrate exactly what was said, to whom, and when. In reality, too, I guess.

The original e-mail was nowhere to be found. Setting that aside, there was the question of who'd sent it out in my name. Clearly not Janine. That left, of course, Karren. But when

Karren had walked into the office five minutes after me, and found the e-mail, I'd seen her frown. She read it again, then looked at me.

'Well, it's technically comedic,' she said. 'Ha and, I guess, ha.'

'Forwarded it by accident,' I said. Janine had popped out of the office, thankfully.

'You can do that?'

'If you're dumb,' I said, going into a prepared spiel. 'Meant to pass on a property listing, evidently selected that so-called joke by mistake.'

She nodded. 'Figures. Doesn't seem like the kind of thing you'd send to the world on purpose.'

'Well, right.'

'You're normally far too worried about what people might think of you.'

She turned back to her work, leaving me smarting. If I'd been entertaining suspicions about Karren sending the e-mail from my computer — laughing an evil laugh as she hit SEND — they were dispelled there and then. I had no doubt she was smart and bold, but it would have taken big balls indeed to wrap an unspoken denial in such a blatant diss.

When Karren went to the bathroom twenty minutes later I darted over to Janine's machine. The e-mail was still sitting there in her in-box, together with about seventeen million others. I forwarded the joke back to my own address, taking care to remove the evidence from her SENT MAIL folder when I was done.

Back at my own machine I established that the original e-mail had been sent at 9:33 that morning — when I'd been standing self-righteously in line at the post office waiting to mail a package back to Amazon, thus tying two small, inexplicable things together in a knot.

A book I had not ordered.

An e-mail I hadn't sent.

★ ★ ★

I'd made no sense of either by the time I drifted out to lunch. As I was sitting outside the deli, fingers drumming on the hot metal of the table, I saw Tony Thompson emerge from the reception block. He noticed me and started to head over.

My stomach did a little flip. Tony's address had been on the distribution list of the e-mail. As he walked down the ramp toward me, I took a slow, deep breath.

'Funny e-mail, Bill,' he said, before I could even get started. 'Laughed my head off. You got more like that, send 'em right along. Marie and I are going to have a talk about the matter we discussed, by the way. Probably tonight.'

I shut my mouth, smiled, and didn't say a thing.

★ ★ ★

'No way of telling,' the geek said. 'Bottom line is it could have been anyone in the world.'

'That's it? *That's* your professional opinion? How much you get paid for this level of insight?'

I was sitting with him outside the ice cream place at the Circle. It was coming up on seven in the evening but still warm, and getting heavier.

He took a lick of his chocolate sugar cone. 'A lot less than you, dude. Plus, no commission. Not to mention I spend all day sorting out shit where the root cause exists between the computer and the chair facing it. By which I mean, you know, the user.'

'I got the joke. I'm laughing inside.'

I'd had the idea of calling the company's tech guy by midafternoon. It had taken him three hours to extricate himself from the IT needs of the main office, and forty minutes to check over my computer. Getting him to do this without yakking on and on about what he was doing was the hardest part, but luckily by then I was the only person left in the office. As soon as he'd pushed himself back from my desk, I'd nonetheless encouraged him to carry on the conversation elsewhere. Sitting with a spindly midtwenties guy in a tatty Pearl Jam T-shirt was not helping to resettle me, especially as his phone kept beeping at irregular intervals: a single, echoing *ping*, like sonar. He tilted his head to check the screen every single time this happened, but did not pick the phone up or do anything, and this was beginning to get on my nerves.

'You got two issues,' he said, squinting against the slanting remains of the day's sun. 'First is this e-mail. Simplest explanation is someone sat at your machine in the office. This is hardly an exploit of legend.'

'An 'exploit'?'

'It's what they call a hacking triumph.'

'Who are 'they'?'

'Hackers.'

'Assholes with no life, you mean.'

'It's a point of view. Anyway, an exploit is *not* what that scenario would constitute. Even newbies and script-kiddies would think it beneath them. You'd be amazed how many people leave their computers unattended, though, with their e-mail accounts lying open.' He looked pointedly at me.

'I'm a Realtor,' I said irritably. 'I work in a tiny office with two people who are employed by the same company, one of whom has to be reminded how to set the alarm, even though it boils down to pressing four buttons and then another button and has been covered about a zillion times via memo and the spoken word. Concerted campaigns of cyberespionage are not one of my fears. I'm at DefCon Minus Five.'

The guy shrugged again, as if this was the kind of naïveté he encountered all the time — though I was confident his occupation consisted largely of crawling under people's desks to check that cables were plugged in. Meanwhile, he slurped another mouthful of his ice cream cone. Although the girl who'd introduced me to it was not working, I'd ordered the mandarin mascarpone again, and it was the only part of this encounter I was enjoying.

The geek's phone *pinged* once more. 'Look,' I said. 'Why is it making that noise?'

'The social network never sleeps.'

'You want to turn the sound off? It's really getting on my nerves.'

He pressed a key. 'You're kind of tense, dude.'

'Yeah, I am,' I said, 'because, according to you, someone snuck into my office this morning and, in view of at least one of my colleagues, forwarded an e-mail that I've never seen. Then trashed all evidence from my computer. And snuck back out. Right?'

'Actually, no,' the guy said. 'The e-mail could have been set up anytime in the last weeks or months.'

'You can do that?'

'Yep.'

'Oh.' I didn't like the sound of this. I'd preferred it when it had simply been impossible for me to have sent the e-mail at the time it claimed to have been sent. That gave me a concrete conundrum — and a specific time frame — to grab hold of and shake. This new idea untied the knot and had the potential to pull the event, and thus the intentions of whoever had done it, back in time.

'Except that probably wasn't what happened,' the geek said smugly.

I stared steadily at him. I very much wanted a cigarette. He coughed and sat up straight.

'Okay,' he said. 'Someone with skills *could* have dropped below GUI level and triggered it from underlying OS. I couldn't find any sign of that, though, which brings me to Issue Two. You'll recall I said there were two issues, right?'

'You did. How are you still alive, by the way?'

'This Amazon delivery you mentioned. Could be the two are unrelated, but . . . Occam's razor, right?'

'What are you talking about now?'

'Medieval logician guy. He said if you've got two competing explanations for an event or situation, always choose the simplest, at least as your starting point. Point is, you have this weird e-mail, plus this morning you receive a book you say you never ordered.'

'I didn't,' I said tersely.

'Your login for the Amazon account is your e-mail address, I assume? Like half the frickin' world?'

'Yes,' I admitted.

'But there's a password, too, right?'

I opened my mouth, then closed it again.

He nodded. 'Right. Anyone can find your e-mail address. You probably bandy it about more than your actual *name*. But your password? That's not for sharing. So this is where it starts to look concerted. Where do you keep a record of this password?'

'Nowhere. I just remember it.'

'Tell me it's not something like your name or your wife's name or date of birth.'

'It's not. There's no way anyone could guess it.'

'Excellent. So . . . how *does* someone get hold of it? Simplest way is a keystroke recorder. A piece of code that sits on a computer, makes a record of every single thing that's typed on its keyboard, saves it to disk, or covertly e-mails it to someone out there in the void.'

'Is there one of those on my computer?'

'No. What tech do you have at home?'

'Two laptops. One for me, one for my wife.'

'You use public wifi much?'

'No. The machine stays at the house.'

'You have wireless there?'

'Yes.'

'How close is the nearest house?'

'About thirty yards.'

'Perfectly feasible for them to be piggybacking. Or else someone could be war-driving past your house.'

'Which means?'

'Cruising around with a laptop in a car, scoping out wifi networks, taking data snapshots.'

'Are you kidding me? We live in a gated community. You can't even get *in* unless you're a resident or a certified guest.'

'Doesn't rule it out. So you got three options.' He counted off on his long, slender fingers. 'Human engineering — like glancing over your shoulder at work, or in a café, when you're using the Web. Two, a keystroke recorder. Three, someone scanning your home wifi.'

'I don't like the sound of any of those.'

'Don't blame you,' he said, wiping his hands on a napkin. 'Whatever way you cut it, someone's on your case.'

'So what do I do?'

He stood up. 'Check your laptop — see if there's anything that you don't recognize. If you want, bring it in tomorrow and I'll check it out. Meanwhile, change every password you have.'

'I will,' I said. 'And thanks . . . '

'Kevin. No problem. I'll drop you an e-mail later with hints on how to look for black hat wifi, okay? I gotta go now, though. There's a Chronicles of Dunsany's Kingdom fragfest waiting for me in Bradenton.'

'I have no idea what that means, but good luck with it. Kevin.'

He sloped off, leaving me with a bowl half-full of melted yogurt and a head completely full of questions.

I was confident 'human engineering' was not the answer. I'm not a freak, but I do have a clearly defined personal space. I'd have been aware if someone had been invading it sufficiently to visually eavesdrop on what I was doing on my phone. That left two options. Home laptop, home wifi. Both featured the word *home*, which I did not like. Being fucked with out in the world is one thing. Someone doing it where you live is another matter.

As I stood up, I heard someone speaking.

'Hey hey,' the voice said.

I turned to see the goth/emo girl I'd met a couple days before, walking along the sidewalk toward the shop.

'Glad to see you slipping into Mascarpone Madness again, Mr. Moore,' she said. 'Hope you didn't give Craig as big a tip, though. I'm sure he won't have served it with anywhere near as much panache.'

'He did not,' I said, forced into a smile. 'I thought you worked afternoons . . . ' I racked my brain, and then added 'Cassandra,' just in time for it not to sound like too much of an afterthought.

'I like to mix it up,' she said, appearing pleased

91

I'd recalled her name. We like being singled out, most of the time. 'You never know who's watching, right?'

I didn't say anything, and her face turned serious. 'Sorry — did I just touch a nerve?'

'It's fine. Really.'

'Okay. Just, you look as if you bit into a lemon. And not in a good way.'

'Long day,' I said, and walked away to my car.

*   *   *

I drove home slowly, taking the time to run a detailed damage appraisal in my head.

The Amazon incident was done and dusted, and might even pay out, if Steph rolled with her response to my SMS of the morning. The e-mail didn't seem to have materially offended anyone, had even hit the right note with Tony Thompson. It could be that this intrusion into my life might actually lead to improvements.

Conclusion: *minimal negative impact sustained*.

That didn't mean it was okay.

By the time I pulled into the driveway, I had my ducks in a row. Step one, check for weirdness on my laptop. If I found some, throw it off. If I drew a blank, then I had to look into someone stealing stuff out of the air. I'd got the sense from Kevin the Geek that this was going to be a lot harder, but hoped the promised document would point me in the right direction. Either way, I could reset the minimal number of passwords in my life, keep a low online profile for a few days, and see if that killed the problem.

I parked and got out, full of purpose. As I was locking the car I heard the house door opening, and looked round to see Steph storming down the path.

'You okay?' I asked.

She slapped me hard across the face.

10

I don't know if you've ever been slapped by your wife, but it's not a great experience. It hurts, for a start, especially when delivered by a woman who plays her tennis old school, with a fiercely single-handed grip.

'You *loser*,' she said. It wasn't a shout. It was throttled way down, rasping deep in her throat.

'Steph,' I stammered. 'What the *hell*?'

'Inside. Now.'

She turned on her heel and marched back up the path. I followed quickly, casting a glance down the drive to see if any of the neighbors happened to be in view. I couldn't see any, though that didn't mean there wasn't someone in one of the three houses visible from our yard, standing beyond a window that had just turned into a screen featuring an intriguing new TV show. Shocked and nonplussed though I was, I still found a second to worry about whether the incident had been witnessed by others. That was part of it. But I realized I was also wondering if someone might be watching us.

Or watching me.

★　★　★

Steph turned back to face me the moment I'd shut the front door. I'd had time to wonder whether she'd received the joke e-mail — I

94

couldn't recall whether she'd been on the list or not — and if this was a weirdly extreme reaction. Steph's not a prude or too obsessed with being politically correct, but that was the only thing I could think of. Her face destroyed whatever minimal credibility the theory/hope had. She was furious, but there was something else in her eyes. They weren't hard enough for it to be anger alone. There was the softness of hurt in there, too.

'Honey,' I said, reaching for the voice I used with clients when a deal had gone belly-up and the world needed making right. 'Tell me what's going on.'

'The sad thing is,' she said, her voice still at the reined-back snarl that I found more worrying than shouting, 'I'm actually slightly relieved. In a bizarre way. I'd thought there might actually be something going on between you two. Okay, I didn't *think* it, but the possibility had entered my mind.'

'Between who?'

'Oh *shut up*. You really think that's going to play now? Don't insult me.'

'Steph,' I said, disconcerted at how hard my heart was beating, 'I have not the slightest clue what you're talking about. Really.'

She started to say something, and this *would* have been a shout, but the words collided in her mouth and canceled each other out. Instead, she shook her head and marched off in the direction of the den. I followed.

The den, or family room (if you've got a family), is on the other side of the kitchen, a continuation from its open-plan cooking/eating area and sharing its view out onto the pool area. As I entered I saw that both of our laptops were lying open on the L-shaped sofa.

I stopped in my tracks. 'What are you doing with my computer?'

'What *you* said you'd do two weeks ago,' Steph snapped. 'And *again* a couple of nights ago. Pulling off the pictures from Helen's birthday party. Remember?'

I started to protest, but I had nowhere to go with denial or selfrighteousness. I had said I'd do those things, and it was also long-established practice for us to access each other's computers as and when required. Why not? Neither of us had anything to hide. But it felt like an intrusion nonetheless, especially today.

I watched as Steph stormed over to my machine and banged a key. This caused the blank screen to blink back into life. Steph tried to say something, but once more it died in her mouth. She gestured at the screen instead.

I bent over the back of the sofa and looked. At first I couldn't make out what I was seeing. A picture of some kind, but oddly framed: a skewed, multicolored oblong surrounded by near black, a short series of numbers in orange down at the bottom right.

Then it snapped into sense, and I realized I was looking at a photograph taken at night, through a window. The colored area showed the inside of someone's house. A small, blurry blue-gray section was presumably a television screen. A portion of a blood-red sofa — which is what broke my first half-assumption, which was that the picture had been taken through one of *our* windows, of our den. Our sofa is pale blue.

The other thing that had broken it was the figure visible a third of the way along from the right side of the window. Also blurry, but flesh-toned, apart from a black bra. The hair that hung down almost as far as its horizontal line was a very dark brown.

'What the hell is this?'

'Bill, please. Spare me.'

I reached out and hit the cursor key. This brought up another picture, which was similar but in better focus. The edges of the objects within it were still fuzzy, suggesting that the photograph had been taken twenty or thirty yards from the window, using some kind of zoom. It was, however, sharp enough to tell both that the woman had removed her bra, and that she was Karren White.

There were twelve photographs. In all but four, the identity of the woman was clear. The others caught her from behind or at a nonrevealing angle, before and after she had removed her clothes and put on a terrycloth robe. They began and ended what was evidently a sequence taken from some vantage point near Karren's apartment. I knew the building, near the bay at the north end of Sarasota, having sold an apartment there several years before.

'I have no idea how these got on my laptop,' I said.

'Yeah, right. I mean, for god's *sake*. How lame

do you have to be to do this? Never *mind* the lying.'

'Lying?' I said, confused.

'Good lord. You don't even realize how clearly you've screwed up, do you?'

She jabbed her finger at the screen, where the last of the sequence of pictures — a relatively innocuous one, showing Karren in the process of leaving the room via a door — was still in view. I saw that Steph was indicating the sequence of numbers in the corner.

09•14•2011

A date, of course. The fourteenth of September. Yesterday. So the lie had been . . .

'*Steph, I've got to see a client,*' Steph snarled, seeing the penny had dropped. '*Steph, it's so cool, I'll get the commission. Oh no, honey* — *Karren won't be there.* And of course, she actually wasn't — except via what you could see through your putrid lens.'

'Steph,' I said. I was mirroring how she'd just spoken, but couldn't help it. I was starting to get angry, but defensively assuming the offensive. 'I don't even *have* a zoom lens. I've got a three-hundred-dollar compact. You know that. You bought it for me.'

'Sure, I bought *that* one,' she sneered. 'But who knows what other gadgets you've picked up in the meantime? From Amazon, maybe? Your favorite online retailer, from what I gather.'

Having done the head work over the book earlier in the day, I knew the corner I was now

98

in. I could suggest she search the house, and she could choose to believe I'd stowed the camera elsewhere. I could demand she look through the last year's credit card statements: she could laugh in my face and ask me how hard it was to get a couple hundred bucks out of an ATM and take a quick drive to the Bradenton Outlet Mall. Every time I set up one of these barriers for her to knock down, it would just make me look more and more as if I was not only lying, but doing it with malice and forethought. The harder I tried and the better I argued, the more it would look like I had my story straight, and that would just make it worse.

And anyway, the camera wasn't the point.

I said all this. Steph agreed. She agreed all too readily. She agreed that the *real* point was that I had snuck around to Karren White's apartment — on the pretense of being out at a meeting that (surprise, surprise) hadn't materialized and thus *couldn't be checked*. The *real* point, she was happy to see that I'd grasped, was not only was I obsessed with my coworker, but that I was enough of a loser to take stealth pictures of her naked, instead of having an affair like any normal person.

'Hold on,' I said. 'Whoa. I'm *not* obsessed with Karren. What are you talking about?'

'No? So how come you're always mentioning her?'

'*What?*' I couldn't help being distracted by each untruth as it arrived. 'Of course she crops up — we work in the same office. I know the names of everybody *you* work with at the magazine. I know the names of their *children*. Karren's an operator, you know that. I only bring her up to say how I'm trying to get around her, to get *my* thing going, to build *my* rep.'

I took a step toward her. She stepped back, making a sound like a can of soda being opened.

'Don't even try it,' she said.

'Steph, listen. Something else happened today. An e-mail.'

'You *e-mailed* her?'

'Just *listen*. When I got back from returning that book to Amazon, Janine was sitting in the office laughing at some joke she thought I'd sent.'

'Yeah, you sent it to me, too. It wasn't funny.'

'That's just it — I *didn't send it*.'

'What?' Steph looked angry at being derailed.

'I didn't send it. To you or Janine or anyone. Somebody else did, using my e-mail account. The reason I was late home this evening — before you even *start* speculating about that — is because I was talking to the IT guy from Shore, trying to work out what happened, how the e-mail got sent.'

She snorted. 'Why would I believe that?'

I yanked out my phone. 'His number's top of the outgoing call list. Call him right now, Steph. Ask him if we just sat and had ice cream outside the parlor on the Circle. Ask him if he had a chocolate sugar cone. Or do you think I've gone so far into the heart of darkness that I'd recruit some random patsy to lie about my whereabouts?'

She didn't say anything. The expression on her

face remained lodged in a mixture of anger, hurt, and disgust.

'Wait one second,' I said, and sent up a prayer to whatever tiny god looks after Realtors who are in serious trouble not of their own making. I leaned over the laptop and fired up my e-mail app. Five e-mails came straight in. A couple of positivity newsletters, two from clients . . . and one from Kevin the Geek. Thank god.

I opened the e-mail. 'Look.'

Reluctantly, Steph bent forward and read what was on the screen. A reference to the meeting I'd just described, a page of complex instructions on how to check for a keystroke checker, and an introduction to Wifi Spying 101.

She wouldn't look at me. 'So what does that prove?'

'Someone's messing with my e-mail,' I said. 'They ordered a book from Amazon in my name and this morning sent out a dumb, racist joke.'

'Even if this is true, how does it have any bearing on you taking pictures of Karren?'

I took a deep breath, then let it out. She was right, in fact. It didn't. With the photographs, we were into new and uncharted territory.

Which we then set about exploring, at length.

11

Nothing had become clearer or more positive by the time Steph went up to bed. We'd gone round in circles until the momentum of tiredness pulled her out of my orbit. I didn't follow straightaway. Steph and I have had very few full-blown rows in our years together, but I knew time was needed to deflate this, time and the space it would give for common sense to prevail. You don't tell an angry person they're wrong to be angry. You have to wait for the emotion to diffuse.

Before that, following the instructions in Kevin's e-mail, I'd checked my laptop. There were no strange apps hidden among my login items, no windowless background processes chugging away — at least as far as I could see. Kevin had reiterated in his e-mail that there were more hard-core possibilities, but that any attempt by me to establish their presence would almost certainly result in my computer being 'borked.' I didn't know what that meant, but it didn't sound good and I didn't want it. My life felt 'borked' enough already.

'Right,' Steph said, when I told her I'd drawn a blank. 'So no supersecret spy software. How *weird*.'

She was sitting stiffly at the extreme far end of the sofa. She'd worn through some of the initial fury, but retained the air of a volcano that could wipe the hell out of town if it so chose. I guess she'd assumed that, presented with what she'd thought was incontrovertible evidence, I would cave immediately, throwing myself on her mercy. I hadn't. In fact, while I'd been running the tests on my laptop, I'd been simultaneously delivering a point-by-point recap of the true events of the previous evening (which did not include amateur night soft-core pornography) and offering her my cell phone (again) to call Melania, Warner's assistant, for confirmation.

Her refusal to consider doing this weakened her position — even though, yes, I could still technically have driven up to Karren's apartment regardless of whether a real meeting had been scheduled — but I took care not to belabor the point. Steph was genuinely upset, and with good reason. It didn't matter how firm my defense — or whether she eventually came round to believing it — she'd still spent time believing something different. You can't unthink a thought. Your mental patterns, your perception of someone, has been changed. That can't be undone, only superseded by fresh and concrete evidence — which so far, I didn't have.

'So it must be someone scanning our wifi,' I said, looking across the room to where the unit sat, close to where the cable feed entered the house.

'Oh, definitely,' Steph said acidly. 'I *wonder*: will it be the Jorgenssons or the Mortons?'

She had a point. Quite apart from the basic absurdity of our neighbors wanting to screw with my e-mail, there were practical issues. The

Jorgenssons were Longacres' token oldsters, in their midseventies: healthy, golf-obsessed, surrogate grandparents to half the kids in the community — and no one's idea of cybervillains escaped out of The Matrix. On the other side we had the Mortons. Again, nice people, and moreover a family who cleaved to a genteel subdivision of some Christian faith that had a downer on the Internet as a whole — source, as it is, of unwholesome images and concepts and ways of being. I remembered being apprised of this a while back, during an affable but interminable dinner party. They didn't even have cable.

I sat back from the screen, baffled. 'It's not going to be the Smiths opposite, either. *I* had to install Microsoft Office on their computer for them.'

Steph chose not to reply. She just sat there looking at me, her right foot twitching up and down.

'It could be war-driving,' I offered weakly.

I was surprised to discover she knew what that meant. She poured scorn on the idea, but eventually conceded that someone's kid in the community *might possibly* have the hardware, know-how, and adolescent assholeness to have cruised by the house, taken a snapshot of what was traveling through the ether, and snatched my e-mail and Amazon passwords from it.

The pictures remained harder to explain. I tried to tidy this away by harping on about the wifi conundrum, but Steph wasn't buying. She asked how some kid could even *know* about

Karren in order to take the pictures. I didn't know the answer. All I could do was say what *hadn't* happened. I denied taking the pictures, denied all knowledge of how they'd ended up on my machine. Denied it loud, denied it long. There was nowhere else that the conversation could go — nowhere, at least, without the fade down and back up of sleep.

Her anger had burned down to embers by the time she went to bed, but her eyes looked hollow. There was no parting shot before she went upstairs. She merely looked at me as if wondering what she was seeing, and then went. Maybe I should have gone up with her, but it didn't seem like the right course.

Instead I went and floated around the pool for a while. I was thinking about the photographs, mainly, and eventually found myself opening doors that hadn't occurred to me earlier — preoccupied as I had been with the clear and present danger, with dealing with the emotional firefight in front of me.

There was another thing to consider, I realized, something I hadn't mentioned to Steph. Partly because I hadn't noticed it at first, but then, once I had, because I didn't know what it meant, and there was enough incomprehensibility between us. I hadn't thrown the pictures of Karren away, though that might have seemed an obvious thing to do ('Look! See! I throw them away! Ugh!'). Steph had insisted that I should. She'd even tried to do it herself, shoving me aside and skating her fingers across the track pad during one of the more heated portions of the discussion. I'd used her own tactics back at her, asking what the point would be when I could have stashed copies on the net or on the memory card of this alleged camera that I didn't own. I'd argued that I needed them to try to get to the bottom of where they'd come from. It was just after preventing her attempt to throw them away that I'd noticed this final thing — the fact that finally got me to climb out of the pool, cold and tired and confused.

I got out to check the folder on the computer once again, to make sure I'd seen what I thought I'd seen.

★ ★ ★

When I opened the door to our bedroom, the lights were out. I could hear Steph breathing in the darkness, however, and it didn't sound to me like she was asleep.

She said nothing as I carefully slipped into bed. I didn't say anything, either. I lay there on my back, thinking about what I'd confirmed. The pictures of Karren were all in a folder together on my laptop's desktop. I keep as tidy a virtual desktop as I do in the real world, and knew I hadn't created this folder. Someone else had, somehow, before filling it with these photographs.

The folder had been called MODIFIED.

12

Hunter returns, eventually. This time the man in the chair knows he's coming. He hears the clatter of a distant door being opened and re-secured. It sounds like something temporary, a piece of hardwood with a padlock on it.

He hears the measured tread of footsteps approaching along the concrete of the floor below. These cease, beneath where he is sitting, to be replaced by a difficult-to-interpret sequence of noises that culminate in Hunter pulling himself up onto the half floor of this level. He does this with disconcerting ease, like a man hoisting himself out of the shallow end of a swimming pool. The man in the chair cannot know how much of this strength and agility comes from exercises Hunter performed, day in, day out, in his cell; alongside regimens in the yard and further programs during the twice-a-week free-weights sessions prisoners were allowed if they wanted. When he's up, he dusts his hands off. He appears to ignore the other man, walking over to one of the tarps, pulling it aside, and looking out.

'Beautiful day,' he says. 'You possibly found it kind of warm, though, maybe.'

The man in the chair says nothing. Hunter has been back before, he knows. The man woke from a fractured drowse not long after dawn to see that a cool bottle of spring water had been placed in the middle of the floor, next to the chalked words saying 'Who else?'

Not very subtle. But effective.

Were it possible for the human mind to move physical objects, the bottle would no longer be there, but instead in the man's lap, and empty. It isn't. It's still standing next to the chalk letters. And it's still full.

Hunter sees him looking. 'Oh, right,' he says. 'You saw that? The water? Looks good, huh?'

'Fuck you.'

'Want to know what I had for breakfast? Or lunch? Man, I am enjoying getting some proper food again.'

'I refer you to my previous answer.'

Hunter tells him anyway. The man tries not to hear. His head feels like it's in a vice. Every swallow is bleakly memorable. He is finding it hard to think in straight lines, relying upon stitching together moments of clarity occasioned by surges of pain from his leg. It's been bleeding intermittently ever since Hunter dropped the cinder block, and the muscle has started to feel heavy, thickened, right up into the thigh. He hopes part of this is merely related to the low, throbbing ache present in most of his body, dehydration, and having been forced into the same position for such a long time.

It says something for the magnitude of this discomfort that the man welcomes the distraction of wrenching twists of hunger when they come. He is a man whose needs are used to being met before they have to even raise their voice. His body is becoming shrill now. His body is getting *concerned*. Trying to think about

108

abstract matters is the only tactic at his disposal for muting its visceral anxiety.

He has spent all day focusing on what to do, therefore, and finally thinks he has a plan.

* * *

It formulated late. Sleeping isn't easy when you're strapped to a chair, and his night was rough — not least because a series of short thunderstorms kept waking him up. He zoned out for a while in the early afternoon. Remembering stuff. Some recent memories, others from way back. He has tried to think only of good times, but he has learned a lesson, a little late. When you act in the world, consider that at some point — on your deathbed, or in your death *chair* — you may find yourself looking back. The ratio of good to bad within your personal story is shown in a very harsh light under these circumstances. Time can flatten out, too, making your early teens seem as present as the day before yesterday.

A small group of men, standing around a woman.

That time when he and Katy hitched a ride down to Key West and got burned to crap watching the rays swim in the harbor and then watched the sun go down and he didn't mind feeling like one of the crowd for a while.

A half-naked woman, drunk on martinis, her hand raised to a young boy.

When he nods back into full awareness, he's already accepted that he is going to have to give someone up. Everything about Hunter and the way he is conducting himself says he isn't about to go away. That decision's made. Done. He's got a choice of only three, or so he thinks at first — and given that he'd already started to move against these people himself, he could not care less. The only question is whether the selection he makes will have any influence on his own chances of survival.

But then he realized there was another option, a name he could reveal that would *not* appear to involve betraying decades of trust, and that might even send a message that could bring help. The idea felt like a draught of cool water flowing briefly through his mind. Even strapped to a chair, shot and dehydrated, the icicle in his soul schemed how best to provide.

He thought it through and decided the new plan was good. He'd spent his life making judgment calls. On this, his judgment said yes. So it became a matter of timing.

The how, and the when.

Back to now, in the hot, late afternoon, and Hunter is standing closer, looking down.

'I don't want to hurt your girlfriend,' he's saying. 'Lynn, right? Partly because she's innocent, except for the adultery. Mainly I'm just not convinced you care about her. So it could be a waste of effort. And a waste of a pretty woman, and god knows there's little enough beauty in this world. I just dropped by her house when she wasn't home, picked up that robe to show you I'm serious.'

The man in the chair says nothing.

'But now, time's moving on. I don't have any experience in this so I don't know exactly how long you can last. I Googled it, though, and it sounds like forty-eight to seventy-two hours is when the really bad stuff starts to kick in. You look like shit already, though, to be frank, and they're saying tomorrow's supposed to be *real* hot for this time of year. So why don't you just tell me who else I need to talk to, and we'll see where we can go from there?'

The man in the chair remains silent. He can tell that Hunter is making an effort to keep his temper down but that he's finding it increasingly difficult. Silence is a risk, but one he has to take. He looks up at Hunter and winks, for good measure.

Hunter takes a couple of steps toward him. 'You're beginning to piss me off.'

The man in the chair smiles.

Hunter looks at the man's right shin. He sighs, and gives it a kick. The man in the chair takes a sharp breath, grits his teeth, and waits for the stars of white pain to fade.

'I don't like doing this stuff,' Hunter says, sounding strangely sincere. 'I stopped being that guy long before I ever even met you. But I've made it clear what I need, and you're just not cooperating. You see how that makes things hard for me, right?'

The man in the chair raises his head. 'You know what you sound like? You sound like the kind of father who's going to hit his kid, hit him hard, who *knows* he's going to do it, and for no good reason except he's hungover and an

111

asshole, but wants the kid to take the blame.'

Hunter opens his mouth, but shuts it again — so fast and hard you can hear a click.

'Ring any bells?' the man in the chair asks. 'Take you back at all?'

Hunter cocks his head, and the man in the chair realizes he's hit home a lot harder than he meant to, and possibly in the wrong direction.

'You're talking to me about kids?' Hunter says quietly. 'Because of you, I don't *have* kids. Because of you, I spent sixteen years in jail for the murder of the woman I wanted to have children with.'

'Just as well. You're a loser, and she was a whore. The world doesn't need more of that in the genetic stew.'

Hunter kicks out again, and this time he does it hard. Hard enough to cause the man in the chair to cry out, something halfway to a scream — and to make the chair rock back on the concrete promontory.

'You want another?' Hunter asks, his voice thickening. 'How many more kicks before a chair leg goes out over the edge, do you think?'

Light-headed with pain, suddenly unsure if this is such a great idea after all, the man nonetheless looks up at him. 'You're not going to send me over, asshole. Do that, and you got nothing.'

Hunter looks at him, breathing hard.

'You're smart,' he says finally, and his voice is calm again. 'Course you are — else you wouldn't be such a success in life, right? I really do not want to have to push you over yet, it's true. But that leaves me in something of a pickle. It limits the range of the threats I can make — and you, smart boy that you are, have got right onto that. Hmm. Oh wait, though, I just thought of something.'

He turns and walks back to the far wall, where he stoops and picks up the cinder block.

'I found some comfort in repetition and ritual during the years I was in jail,' he says. 'When time started to weigh on me, it was things happening in the same way and at the same time each day that helped. It turned it into a long dark dream, so that sometimes I could pretend it wasn't happening to me at all, but was some weird shadow turning over and over itself in one endless night. Maybe you'll find the same.'

He walks back until he is standing in front of the chair. He raises his hand slowly, lofting the block high over the other man's knee again.

'Let's find out,' he says softly.

And that's the point at which the man in the chair decides he's waited long enough and he's wound the guy up sufficiently and it's time to end this *right here and right fucking now.*

He says a name. Blurts it quickly, says it three times, the syllables tripping over themselves.

Hunter freezes.

He looks down at the other man for a long moment, the arm with the cinder block held out, perfectly still.

'Really?'

The man in the chair nods, feverishly.

'I guess I can believe it,' Hunter says, lowering

his hand, his eyes already elsewhere. 'Mother-
fucker. I kind of looked up to that guy, too. Well,
thank you. That's a start. You done good. I hope
we can keep things moving along this more
positive road in the future.'

He takes the block back to the wall and puts it
down. 'I'll leave that there, though — just in case
tomorrow's session doesn't go so well.'

He picks up the water bottle. He returns to the
man in the chair and drops it in his lap. 'You be
thinking about some more names,' he says. 'And
maybe next time I'll even let you drink some of
that.'

Then he steps over the edge of the floor and
disappears, like a bird of prey dropping out of
the sky.

13

Steph had left the house by the time I got out of the shower. I knew she had some big-deal meeting, though I couldn't recall who it was with. As I trotted down the stairs toward a kitchen that seemed larger than usual and preternaturally empty, I was aware of how strange this was making me feel. Our lives are meshed at root level. I'm normally very aware of Steph and her movements, her doings and concerns. Not this morning. She was out, meeting someone somewhere. Not a big deal, yet a big deal. Life felt different on the back of it.

She'd gone early, too. It was still only seven fifteen. I put a pot of coffee on and fetched my laptop — now destined to be looked over by Kevin at his very earliest in/convenience — and my phone. I copied the folder of photographs off onto a USB thumb drive and deleted the original from the laptop. If Kevin was going to geek all over my computer, the folder clearly couldn't remain in place. Then I picked up my phone and found Melania's number. My finger was a quarter inch from tapping it when there was a knock on the front door.

I swore irritably and went to open it.

Outside was a man in a police uniform. He had short brown hair and was about the same height as me, but with the trim, fastidious-looking build that comes from working out with free weights. His upper arms looked, in fact, as though he'd come straight from doing bicep curls.

'Mr. Bill Moore?'

'Yes,' I said. 'What — '

'Deputy Hallam,' he said, showing me his ID. I blinked at it. He stowed his badge and held something else up. 'This yours?'

It was one of my Shore Realty business cards. 'Yes,' I said. 'But what are you doing with it?'

'Can I come inside? I'd like to talk with you.'

'What about?'

'A man called David Warner.'

* * *

I took the policeman back through to the kitchen and offered him a coffee, which he declined. I poured one for myself, feeling as if I was acting a part.

'I should tell you straightaway,' I said, 'that I don't know the guy well.'

Hallam held my card up again, this time flipping it over to show me the other side.

Call me when you're ready to do business.

'I found this wedged into the entry system of Mr. Warner's property,' the cop said. 'Is that your handwriting?'

'I called round yesterday morning, on the off chance. He wasn't there. I left my card.'

'The message could be interpreted as threatening, sir. Snippy, at the very least.'

116

'I was feeling snippy,' I said. 'I was supposed to meet with the guy. He gave me the runaround.'

'How?'

'We arranged I'd view his property at eight o'clock on Tuesday evening. But he wasn't there. The meeting was rearranged, for a bar in town. He didn't show up to that, either. So I bailed. Got home at midnight, a couple beers down, which did *not* make me popular with my wife.'

The cop didn't respond to this attempt at guys-together chumminess. Either he didn't have a wife or being unpopular with her was business as usual.

'Next morning I happened to be near the guy's house, so I stopped by in the hope we could talk. He wasn't there. I left my card, went to work.'

'You arranged these meetings with him direct?'

'No — via his assistant, on the phone. What exactly is the problem here, Officer?'

'The problem,' the cop said, returning my card to the pocket of his short-sleeve shirt, 'is that David Warner seems to have disappeared.'

My stomach turned over, as if I was in a plane that had suddenly dropped five hundred feet.

'What do you mean, 'disappeared'?'

He cocked his head. 'That's a word most people have a ready understanding of, sir. You really need help with it?'

'Pardon me?'

'I apologize,' he said, his gaze flicking away. 'Mr. Warner is an extremely wealthy person, and my boss is all over this. Warner was supposed to be having lunch with his sister yesterday, but didn't show up at the agreed place and time. It's under twenty-four hours, in which case normally we wouldn't be paying any attention. But with Mr. Warner, evidently we are.'

'At what point did he, uh, stop being where he was supposed to be?'

'That's what I'm trying to establish.'

'I know my colleague Karren White had a meeting with him late morning, day before yesterday.'

'What time was that?'

'Not sure. But she was back at the office around lunchtime. So I don't know, maybe one thirty? I mean that's when she got back.'

'And she'd come straight from seeing him?'

'Far as I know. Then evidently Mr. Warner was out meeting *someone* Tuesday evening — he missed my appointment because a dinner engagement ran late.'

'Time?'

'It was a little before half past eight, I think, when we rearranged. I waited fifteen minutes before I called his assistant. Though . . . his message to her had come in a little earlier, so I don't know when exactly.'

The deputy noted all this down and asked if I had any idea who Warner's dinner had been with. I said I did not. He asked for any information I had on Warner's assistant, and so I got my phone off the counter and — without really knowing why — made it appear as though Melania's number wasn't already sitting there on the screen, ready for me to call. I spent a few seconds looking as if I was going through different screens before I read out her number. He noted this down, too, then flicked back a couple of pages in his little pad.

'That's different from the one I have.'

'I believe there's more than one line of communication,' I said. 'When I was on the phone to her she talked about having a BlackBerry, too.'

'Oh, okay.' He stowed the pad, then handed me a card of his own. 'If this guy gets in touch with you again, will you do me a favor and let me know right away?'

'No problem,' I said, leading him back out through the house toward the front door. 'But probably he's just not picking up his phone, right?'

'Or he doesn't want to talk to his sister,' the policeman muttered. 'You have a good day, sir.'

I watched him stride pugnaciously down the path to his vehicle, thinking that were I Deputy Hallam's boss — Sheriff Barclay, presumably — I might want to have a conversation with him about not wearing his heart so evidently on his sleeve.

14

When I got to The Breakers I was relieved to see I was the first to arrive. The mere act of speaking Karren's name to Deputy Hallam had made me feel odd. I didn't want to have to deal with her in person right away. As soon as I got to my desk I called Melania's number. There was no reply. It was early, but I got the sense David Warner's assistant was used to being at his beck and call.

I left a voice mail asking her to call me back. Then I e-mailed Kevin the Geek, thanking him for sending the instructions the night before and saying I'd like to take him up on his offer to give my laptop a sweep. I offered to buy him lunch at his choice of venue. Finally, I sent an SMS message to Steph, saying I hoped her meeting was going/had gone/would go well.

I felt extremely jumpy, and lack of sleep wasn't helping my mental clarity. The arrival of the police officer that morning had complicated matters in ways I hadn't yet been able to quantify. One of the doors I'd seen while floating in the pool still hung open in my mind, however. Finally, I walked through it.

Someone, somewhere, was fucking with me — seriously, with malice and forethought.

The photographs on the USB drive were not tied to me, in the sense that it couldn't be proved that I'd taken them. They couldn't be, as I *hadn't taken them*. Therefore, whoever was responsible for the images had linked them to me by association. First, by causing them to be discovered on my laptop; second, by causing the camera to date-stamp each picture. It was this second link — pinning the event to an evening when I hadn't been at home, and so could feasibly have done what I was purported to have done — that seemed far more important, and had kept me awake half the night. It *proved* it was a deliberate setup, one that had been planned. It might not to Steph, but *it proved it to me*. If enough odd things happen — inexplicable little events, one after another — after a while you start to question yourself. The date stamp on the pictures got me out of self-doubt jail. On any normal evening I'd have been at home, or out with a friend (or Steph), who could have been a witness to my whereabouts. On Tuesday night I'd been out on what had proved to be a wild-goose chase . . . and perhaps deliberately so. Whoever took the photos *knew* I wouldn't be at home, either because they'd observed me being out or — probably far more likely — because they'd engineered me to be where I was in the first place. And who could have done that?

I only had one answer.

David Warner.

He'd called the office midday, got hold of Karren instead, and so played along — but then insisted it be me who turned up for part two of the negotiations. He'd had his assistant call and set up the meeting . . . to which he didn't show. Having committed me to being out, he then *kept* me out by rearranging the time and place via his assistant (even though, as she'd mentioned at the time, it would have been easier for him to call me direct). Using Kevin the Geek's technique of Occam's Razor, you only need one guy to make all this so.

But why the hell would Warner do this?

I didn't even *know* the guy. I'd met him just once, that chance encounter in Krank's — and it wasn't like I'd latched on to him and got feral Realtor upside his face, hustling him to the point where I deserved some kind of comeuppance. I was in the bar with Steph and a couple of her colleagues from the magazine. They were all over some minor work crisis, and so I'd wound up chatting with a stranger about the Reds' chances in the state league, as two men leaning on the same bar will sometimes do. It was *Warner* who'd brought up his house, not me. So why on earth would he meet Karren on Tuesday, think, 'Hey, here's a pretty girl, here's some leverage, let's stir things up for the asshole Realtor . . . '

Why?

I heard footsteps approaching the office, and froze. The door opened and Karren walked in. There was nothing different about her, but she looked different.

'Hell happened to you?' she asked, as she dumped her purse on her desk.

'What do you mean?'

'You look like a bad passport photo. Late night?'

'Couldn't sleep,' I said.

She winked. 'Doesn't surprise me.'

'What do you mean?' My tone was a lot sharper than I'd intended.

'Whoa,' she said. 'Just a pro forma dig, okay? The 'How do you *sleep* at night, dude?' routine. Not that I'm implying you have anything to . . . Look, whatever, you know? Call off the dogs. Relax.'

'Sure,' I said, forcing a smile. 'Sorry.'

I was finding it hard to look away from her. Once you've seen a picture, you can't forget it, and I had seen pictures I should not have seen. Being in her presence wasn't turning me on, however. I felt . . . protective, perhaps, which was not something I'd ever have expected to feel about Karren White, a woman I believed had chosen to spell her Christian name in a nonstandard fashion purely to give her an excuse to spell it out to clients, the better to lodge it in their minds.

I felt that I should warn her about the photographs. But you can't just pipe up with 'Hey! I've got a dozen seminude pictures of you on a USB drive in my pocket . . . ' unless you have a very innocent and convincing second half to the sentence, ready and waiting. I did not. Maybe I could do it when I had an explanation for how the pictures had ended up on my machine, but not yet.

'When you met with this David Warner guy on Tuesday,' I said instead, making it sound casual. 'Anything strike you?'

'Apart from him being a sexist asshole? Not really. Why?'

'I didn't tell you. He arranged to meet me that

evening, to see the house.'

'Good for you.'

'Uh, not so much. He blew me off. Twice.'

'Huh,' she said, a little less tart. 'Seems like he's prepared to piss off Realtors regardless of their race, creed, or gender.'

'An equal opportunity asshole, for sure. You get a number for him?'

'No,' she said, looking sheepish. It was appealing because of its rarity value. Karren did not make unforced errors. 'Forgot to take a note of it off the log. Duh.'

Indeed. One of the first rules of the job is to get a potential client's phone number. I smiled and said something about it being no great loss.

As she settled down to bash out e-mails, I picked up one of the office handsets and scrolled laboriously back through the log of incoming calls. I went more slowly once I got back to Tuesday morning, knowing that what I was attempting would likely be hard — as we get a lot of calls, almost all with local codes.

I was about to give up when I saw a number I thought I recognized, however. I cross-checked with my phone and confirmed it. When I'd been sitting with Hazel outside Jonny Bo's, a call had come into the office from the number I had stored for Melania's cell phone.

'Karren — he called the office himself, right? Warner? Not his assistant.'

'It was him.'

'And not a pass-through? A 'Got my asshole boss on the line, will you take a call from Planet 1970s'?'

124

Karren actually laughed, unaffectedly, a sound I hadn't heard before. 'Nope.'

I didn't know what to make of that.

* * *

Kevin the Geek was a cheap lunch date, professing himself a big fan of some grilled sandwich on offer at Starbucks. I met him at the one on St. Armands Circle and left him at a table with my laptop while I ran a few errands. I performed these with about a third of my mind. The bulk was taken up with trying to work out whether to try calling Steph, and with wanting a cigarette, pretty badly. I didn't call her, though I sent another SMS. I didn't buy any Marlboro Lights, either.

'What's the deal with the word 'Modified'?' Kevin asked, when I returned.

I stiffened as I sat down, horrified that I'd somehow screwed up throwing away the pictures, and the folder was still there on my desktop. 'Why do you ask?'

'You got about ten, twenty folders called that. Plus, it's what you named your hard drive, right?'

'No,' I said, concerned that I hadn't even noticed this the night before. 'It was called, well, whatever the default is. Hard Drive, HD . . . I can't remember.'

'Well, I'll add that to the Pile of Strangeness, but I'll warn you it's a very small pile. You got nothing on here that raises a red flag. No keystroke recorders. Nothing unusual when it

125

comes to wifi. Built-in firewall operating as it should, no suspicious ports open. Your machine is clean, basically, and your desktop as tidy as any I've ever seen. I have given it a gold star.'

'So what does that imply?'

'One of two things,' he said, looking a little uncomfortable. 'Either someone is cruising your gated 'hood — a person who can grab passwords and whatnot out of the air and also tunnel back through a firewall to change folder and drive assignations.'

'How hard would that be?'

'Reasonably hard.'

'So what's the *or*?'

'Physical access to your laptop. It's by far the simplest explanation. Sending e-mail is a formality. Your browser will have saved a cookie, which means ordering off Amazon is easy, too, unless you log out every time, which no one does. And renaming folders and disks is *far* more explicable if someone's just sitting at the machine.'

'There's only one person who'd have access to my laptop,' I said. 'My wife.'

Kevin didn't say anything. He just looked a little more uncomfortable.

★ ★ ★

As we walked out of the coffeehouse, someone called out Kevin's name. We turned together to see Cassandra the ice cream girl coming along the sidewalk.

'Oh my lord,' she said. 'What cataclysmic

online dating accident brought *you* two together?'

'Hey, Cass,' Kevin mumbled. In the presence of a Real Live Girl his geekiness trebled in intensity. 'What's up?'

'Well, you know, you know,' she said, pausing to light a cigarette, her hands cupping around it in the process, as if to protect against a strong wind. 'Still bathing in the glory of having kicked your ass.'

I presumably had the air of a human question mark. The girl blew out a mouthful of smoke and smiled. I watched the smoke dissipate into the hot air.

'Me and Kevs — or Lord Kevinley of Benjamin's Estate — lately hang in the same gaming crowd,' she explained. 'We were both at a meatspace meet-up last night for some convivial Dark Ages fragging fun. Lady Cassandra of the Eternal Lurid Flame — that would be me — proved *far* too tight a strategist for this gentleman and his rat-punk accomplices.'

' 'Meatspace'?'

She held up her hands to indicate the universe in general. 'This hot, smelly place that some do call 'The Real World' and in which we are constrained to hang out. At least some of the time.'

Kevin chuckled appreciatively, and I realized he didn't mind losing at whatever this dumb game was, at least not to this girl — and that her presence in the much-maligned Real World probably had a lot to do with him playing the game in the first place.

'Gotta head,' Cassandra said. 'Kevs, see you in

the chatterverse, stat. Mr. Moore, I'll be dishing the frozen cow squirt later, should you wish to drop by.'

Kevin and I watched her go, like a cool breeze departed, and then got into my baking car.

★ ★ ★

I dropped him back at the main Shore premises up at Ocean View, then drove thoughtfully back down to The Breakers. As I parked I saw that Karren was sitting at a table outside the deli. She glanced at me when I got out of the car, and then back down at her hands.

I walked over. 'You okay?'

'Kind of. The police are on their way.'

'Why?'

'They think David Warner might be dead.'

15

They arrived twenty minutes later. I was still sitting with Karren, whose take on the situation boiled down to: it wasn't like we'd really known the guy, but, you know, wow, freaky shit. My own take was more complicated. So complicated, in fact, that I was glad to have Karren's to listen to instead. The police car finally came around the loop and parked in front of our office. Deputy Hallam got out the driver's side, Sheriff Barclay the other. I'd often thought, somewhat dismissively, that if you wanted to cast a typical good old boy sheriff, Barclay would be perfect. Over six feet tall, big hands, broad shouldered, that gut. As he walked over toward our table, however, he didn't look like someone you should dismiss in any way at all.

'Morning, Mr. Moore. And you're Karren White?'

We agreed that was who we were.

'You want to take this into your office?'

I shook my head. 'Here's good.' I didn't want to be taken inside. It would have felt as if I had something to hide from general view.

Barclay gestured at Hallam, who pulled over a couple of chairs. 'You know why we're here?'

'Karren told me. So . . . what's happened, exactly?'

'We knew that, we wouldn't be here. Or we'd be here differently.'

Karren spoke sharply. 'What's that supposed to mean?'

'Don't get me wrong,' the sheriff said. 'I don't think either of you has anything at all to do with David Warner's disappearance. I mean, from what Ms. White told me, you were hoping to sell his house.'

'That's correct,' I said.

'Right now we're not sure what happened, or when. Two hours ago we entered the Warner property. We discovered evidence that he may have been abducted, and could also have been either injured or even killed.'

' 'Evidence'?'

'The digital record from his security system has been removed. CSI found traces of blood in the kitchen, and something that looks like a bullet impact site. An initial workup says the blood is likely Warner's, but until we get confirmation, we're freewheeling. My deputy and I are trying to fill some gaps in the meantime.'

'Okay,' I said. 'Deputy Hallam was pretty thorough this morning, though. I don't know if there's anything I can add.'

Karren turned to look at me. 'I got a visit before I came into work,' I told her, trying to make it sound on a level with a visit from the pool cleaner. 'I didn't mention it because . . . well, the guy had been missing less than a day.'

She nodded, but I could see her thinking: *Maybe so — but nonetheless, you brought Warner up the minute I walked into the office. Which is odd, right?*

She looked at her watch. 'I just realized I have an appointment,' she said to Barclay. 'Okay if I head back to the office, make a call to postpone it?'

'Sure,' the sheriff said. 'We'll drop by when we're done speaking with Mr. Moore.'

'Here's the thing,' he went on, when Karren had gone. He put a sheet of paper on the table. It looked like a blown-up photocopy of a page from a notebook, with additional annotations in a firm hand. 'I've got a record of what you told my deputy, and we've got an issue to resolve with some of that information.'

'What kind of issue?'

'You were supposed to meet with Mr. Warner on Tuesday evening, right? He didn't show, and rearranged through his assistant. That's what you said.'

'Yes,' I said.

'Okay. Well, she says that didn't happen.'

'What? Which part?'

'Any of it. We spoke with, uh, Melania Gilkyson, an hour ago. She denies speaking with you on Tuesday evening or at any other time.'

'That's bullshit,' I said angrily, pulling my phone out. 'It's right here in my call record.'

'Thing is,' the cop said, 'that's not Ms. Gilkyson's number.'

'Well, that's the number she called me on. And I called her back on it, and got hold of her at' — I checked the record — 'eight sixteen.'

'Not according to her.'

'But . . . why would she *say* that?'

'That's what we're wondering,' Barclay said.

'Hold on a moment,' I snapped. 'I'm sure I can straighten this out.' I jabbed my thumb onto the number. The two cops watched impassively. The number rang, and rang. And rang. 'No reply,' I said, killing the call. 'Not going to voice mail, either.'

'That's what we found,' Barclay said. 'Ms. Gilkyson says she's never seen the number before. She showed us their records and it doesn't show up on them, either. She also assures us that her boss had no intention of selling his house. Mr. Warner's sister confirms that he hadn't mentioned it. He built that place himself, when he came back to live in the area. There's no evidence at all that he was looking to divest himself of the property.'

'I don't understand,' I said. 'You talked to Karren on the phone, right? You know *she* met with him over the sale, too?'

'That's what she told us, yes.'

'So that's evidence, right? Maybe he just hadn't gotten round to informing the women in his life. His sister and his assistant.'

'Except you say the latter was responsible for setting up the meeting with you on Tuesday night. To which you admit, however, that he didn't show up.'

'It doesn't make a lot of sense, I know.'

The cops just looked at me.

*   *   *

I stood up when they left to go talk to Karren in the office. I remained standing after they were

132

inside. I wasn't sure where to go or what to do.

Just then a man in a jacket, black jeans, and a white T-shirt walked around from the direction of the highway. He was looking casually up at the condos, and it looked altogether possible that he was in the market to buy one. Normally I would have been all over the possibility — going up to the guy, introducing myself.

This time I turned away. I didn't feel like a Realtor right now. I felt like a man whose problems had just gotten far more complicated in ways he didn't yet comprehend.

David Warner was AWOL.

Fact.

Until the conversation I'd just had, part of my brain had been fighting the reality of this information. Okay, someone tells you someone's missing — but that doesn't mean they're actually *missing*, right? Karren could have got it wrong, or been . . . Yeah, okay, of *course* it was bullshit, but I'd been in denial, anyhow. That fight was over. Once you've sat with policemen while they not only confirm that a person's vanished, but make it clear they don't like anomalies in the information you've given, the reality kicks in. It kicks especially hard when one of the cops is the sheriff with whom you've exchanged pleasantries on a number of social/civic occasions.

Less than three hours ago Warner had been my best — my *only* — explanation for the photos on my laptop, patchy though the who, when, and why of the scenario had been. Now I had nothing. Warner could still have been behind the pictures, but I was barred from talking to him, either for confirmation or to find out why he'd done it. His assistant had turned into a dead end, too.

Then, like a bolt from the blue, I realized that was okay.

I froze for a moment as my thoughts tried to catch up with each other and swim in the same direction. Then my feet were in motion, taking me down the path that led around the restaurant terrace and past the pool toward the sand.

If Warner *was* the guy behind the pictures, it was likely that he wasn't going to be screwing with me anymore. Whatever game he'd been playing was over — especially if it turned out he really was dead. He was not around to either confirm or deny anything I might say to the only person it concerned, apart from me — Stephanie. I had a culprit, in other words. It didn't *matter* if I understood why he'd done it. It didn't actually even matter if he *had* done it.

I just had to paint a picture that made it look that way.

I stopped before I stepped out onto the sand. There was still no reply to any of my earlier SMS messages to Steph. I decided to call her instead. I got transferred to voice mail, however. I didn't know what message to leave, so I ended the call. It was almost three o'clock. That was a *long* meeting. A very long time for the two of us to be completely out of contact, too. I thought about it, and then selected Steph's office number.

Her assistant, Jake, answered.

'Oh, Billiam,' he sang. 'How wonderful. And how *are* you on this so beautiful day?'

'Peachy,' I said, knowing Jake wasn't on drugs or anything but just always talked this way. 'I wanted to check what time Steph's meeting ends.'

'Meeting? Oh, the biggie with Maxwinn Saunders.'

'Right,' I said. 'She going to be done soon? Seems kind of an epic.'

'Done? Honey, that was dusted *hours* ago.'

'It was?'

'Lord, yes. They rolled out of there at eleven thirty. Happy smiling faces all around.'

'And then?'

'And then *what*, my love?'

'Where did she *go*? Stephanie. Is she in another meeting now?'

'Oh, no. Not one I know about anyway. She left the office straight afterward, and . . . da-da-da . . . let me check . . . nope, Miss Stephanie got white space in the diary. Nothing the whole rest of day, lucky thing. You want me to take a message, case she returns?'

'Just tell her I rang, would you?'

'No.'

'What?'

He laughed. 'Yes, of course I will, silly. You have a gorgeous afternoon.'

Two text messages sent, and by the sound of it I'd sent the second one after the meeting had finished. No response. She wasn't picking up her phone, either — at least not to me. I wasn't liking the look of this.

Steph and I love each other. A lot. She is, if I'm honest, the only person whose company I genuinely prefer to being on my own. In addition to this, we're on the same team and facing in the same direction. She even started working at the magazine in the first place because she knew it would get us access to an upper circle of locals — the art and gallery crowd, and those with the money to be their patrons — who it would have been hard to tap into otherwise. We send the occasional shot across each other's bows if someone's getting excessively cranky, but there's never been anything anywhere *near* as blunt as ignoring the other's attempts to communicate for half a day. It was like having half of my mind lopped off. I hadn't worked out how I was going to spin Warner's role in the photographs, but I had a strong sense it would be a good idea to get Steph and me around the same table as soon as possible.

I called her cell again. This time I left a message, cheery, saying I'd gotten to the bottom of something and would like a chat at her earliest convenience. I should have asked Jake if Sukey, Steph's key ally on the magazine, was out of the office, too. If so, I could have sold myself on the idea that they were off somewhere sinking glasses of celebratory Pinot, having successfully achieved . . . whatever the damned meeting had been about.

I couldn't face talking to him again, though, not least because I knew it would look weird that I couldn't geolocate my own wife.

I called the house instead. It rang several times, and I was about to give up when I heard it pick up.

'Oh, hon, there you are,' I said, trying to sound confident and upbeat instead of just terribly relieved. 'You're a hard lady to pin down today. Didn't you get my text messages?'

She didn't say anything.

'Okay,' I said. 'I know, I know. Last night was weird. But I promise I was telling the truth. And more stuff's happened today. I think I've worked out what's going on.'

She still said nothing, though I could hear her breathing. 'Come on, Steph,' I said, now merely trying not to sound like I was pleading. 'Let's talk about this properly, 'kay? I'll come home. Or we could meet. Get a coffee or something, grab a beer. Sounds like your meeting went well, right? Let's celebrate.'

Silence. I fought the urge to fill the gap with more words, knowing that I needed *her* to speak next, to commit to dealing with me, to reopening lines of communication that I hadn't realized had become so fragile. But after what must have been a full thirty seconds, I couldn't keep it up. 'Steph? Come on, honey. Talk to me.'

There was silence for another few seconds, and then a female voice said a single word, very clearly.

'Modified.'

The voice was not my wife's. There was a soft laugh, and then I heard the phone being put down.

PART II

PRESENT TENSE

There are heroes in evil as well as in good.
— FRANÇOIS DE LA ROCHEFOUCAULD,
Réflexions

16

It's the afternoons that drag.

In the morning you wake up, and bang — there you are, back in the world: and Hazel has gotten used to doing this in a bed with no one in it but her. She opens her eyes and stares up at the ceiling while she waits for reality to settle upon her. It is not a reality of her choosing, but it seldom is, despite the promises of the self-improvement industry. She's read her share of the earnest books available on bereavement and guilt. None has helped, regardless of the hectoring assurances of whichever airbrushed robot graces the cover. They're all the same. Snake-oil sellers in a hope industry.

She eventually gets up and puts on a robe — Phil liked the AC ferociously high, and it's a habit she hasn't gotten out of, and never will — and pads into the living room. At one end is the kitchen. It's small, so as not to dominate the space (and also because The Breakers has two restaurants that would appreciate your custom, so why make cooking any more attractive a proposition than necessary?). She brews a cup of Earl Grey tea. She showers. She dresses. She fixes her makeup and hair.

On her way out of the condo she glances at the calendar on the inside of the door. This tells her how long it is until the next chunk of her life begins, before she goes to stay with one or other child. This morning the calendar tells her that it is three weeks until she goes to Klara's house over in Jupiter, and gets to be grandma (and free babysitter, and occasionally tolerated advice giver) for a spell.

Three weeks.

Twenty-one days.

She spends her mornings wandering around a mall or taking a look in the (only, and not great) downtown bookstore, occasionally lunching with a friend. These are people she has met in the last few years, since Phil died and her life stopped being wrapped up in what she now thinks of as 'the club.' Her friends are kind to her, and they meet up and talk and laugh, and Hazel finds it hard to understand why the world nonetheless feels as though someone had turned the volume down to zero. Maybe, she thinks, precisely because of the club years. Their entertainments go on, she supposes, but without her, like so much else. It is one thing to know the world will continue when you're gone, another to observe it doing so while you're still around.

Once in a while she will do something off the beaten track, like taking coffee with that handsome but smug Realtor the day before. She knows full well that he is using her to gain advantage in what passes for his career — knew it the moment he came strolling toward her with his hand outstretched — and she doesn't care. She wants to redecorate, and has known the Thompsons long enough to understand that it would be easier to levitate than to influence their behavior. Phil could do it, having known them longer and better and being no stranger to bloody-mindedness himself, but Phil ain't around no more.

So fine, let the boy wonder Realtor see what he can do. Hazel doubts he'll achieve much. At his age, Tony and Phil were already very wealthy, men of action and result. It might be amusing to watch Tony Thompson wearing the little asshole down to dust, however, dust that Marie will then disperse with a single smoky exhale.

It's something to do.

And maybe, Hazel realizes, she's still playing games after all — albeit small and lonely ones of her own.

The evenings aren't bad. She'll take a glass of wine in the bar and eat something. A little television, a spot of reading, and early to bed. The evenings, oddly, are okay, possibly because the essence of the evening is the promise of the end of the day.

It's those endless afternoons . . .

Hazel has fallen into the habit of spending them in the condo. In high season, because it's hot and humid outside and the resort is too busy and she finds she no longer enjoys being among groups of people. At other times of year . . . perhaps because she fears, below the level of conscious choice, that if she spends too much time in the world, there'll come a day when she's used it all up. Better to mete it out. Doing nothing of consequence feels less like defeat than deliberately doing something arbitrary, to fill the time.

She reads. She watches boxed sets of TV

shows. She enjoys a few rounds of Sudoku, so long as she can stop herself remembering how pointless it is. She and Marie discovered the craze together, back in the old days, though Marie was always much better at it. She chats with the maid who comes in every other day.

The afternoons do pass, in the end. There has never been one yet that hasn't eventually come to a conclusion — though there have been a few that felt like they might not, as if time had actually stopped and might never start again — leaving her alone forever, sitting in her chair, in a dry, cool room.

But they drag. They *really* drag, which is why, when Hazel hears the knock on her door at a little before three, she's happy to get up and go answer it.

* * *

A man is standing outside. The walkway is much brighter than her room, and he's initially presented to her in silhouette.

'Afternoon, ma'am,' he says.

His voice is polite, deferential. He's dressed in dark jeans and a new-looking shirt. Trim build, broad shoulders, short hair touched with gray in the temples. Hazel alters her position against the glare and sees that he's kind of good-looking, with a nice open smile.

Once in a blue moon Hazel feels the shallowest of stirrings when confronted with a good-looking man: it has to be an unexpected encounter, as if to bypass her mind and go directly to the biological core. It's not something she's ever going to act upon, but it's pleasant to experience all the same — a reminder that only one of the Wilkinses is actually buried in the ground, so far.

'Afternoon,' she says. 'Can I help you?'

'I hope so. Looking for a man called Phil Wilkins.'

And just like that, her mood collapses. 'You're too late,' she says, not a woman, merely a widow again.

'Too late? What time will — '

'Six years too late. Phil died.'

She's looking at the man's face as he receives this information, and it's as if his eyes go flat, matte, like a pond icing over. It's fanciful, but she catches herself thinking that this is a man who also knows what it is to wait, and who has just discovered it isn't over yet.

Welcome to my world, she thinks.

'Dead, huh?' he says.

'Yep.'

'I'm sorry to hear that.'

'You and me both.'

He nods, looking pained. Rather too late, it occurs to Hazel that he looks familiar, as if he's someone she saw in passing once or twice, long ago.

'Then I guess it's you I need to talk to,' he says, stepping inside.

★ ★ ★

An hour later Hunter is sitting in his car. His door is open. He has driven to a location at the northern end of Longboat Key. When he last saw it the place was nothing more than a couple of acres of scrubby woods, swampy in parts, a reminder of the true nature of these half-sea, half-sand islands — an example of the kind of wilderness that still exists down at the southern end of Lido Key. He discovered it by accident when he came to live in the area. For someone raised on the alien plains of Wyoming, there is an endless fascination about this borderland between water and land.

It is no longer how it was. Some developer has bought and cleared it, cutting down the trees and carting off their carcasses, filling in the boggy parts, laying down swatches of crabgrass until it looks like a golf course. Anything that was natural has gone. Even the ocean now lies in an artificial relationship to the land, its edge trammeled, made convenient and beautiful according to the values of leisure development. Somewhere, perhaps in Sarasota, maybe New York or Houston or Moscow, someone owns this land. Hunter wonders if they think of it, beyond seeing it on a balance sheet with the words *Not Yet* scribbled next to it by an underling. He wonders if God keeps these kinds of records, too, and how many people have those same words noted by them.

He feels tired and dispirited and angry. He has spent a portion of every day for the last decade turning down the static of thought and character, letting a simpler John Hunter simply be. It has been far harder since he's been back out in the world, but he had been holding steady.

146

But now, today, he has broken the spell.

He has Hazel Wilkins's keys in his pocket. He will have to return to her apartment after dark. Before that, he needs to focus, regroup, and gather himself. He does not want to make any more mistakes.

He doesn't want to break anything else.

He sits staring out through the windshield at a place made anonymous and dead. After a time he stops seeing this and sees it instead as it was, hears the laughter of a woman he used to come here with, and feels the ghost of her hand in his.

He is not aware of the tears as they run down his face, and by the time he returns to the present, they have dried away in the heat.

★ ★ ★

As he is driving back down the key, he sees something on the side of the road that interests him. He pulls over, into the front parking lot of the Italian restaurant.

He watches for half an hour. He sees two police cars arrive, along with an unmarked white truck. He sees a third car leave, and then return.

It seems unlikely to him that this level of activity can relate simply to a missing person.

He drives away, knowing that his life is getting more and more complicated. That he must be strong, and fast, and that time is already running out.

147

17

I got home in twenty-five minutes. You can't do it quicker than that, midafternoon, no matter how fast you're prepared to drive — and I drove *fast*. I parked in the street outside the house — or stopped the engine and jumped out of the door, at least — and ran up the path.

The front door was locked. The interior of the house was also exactly as I'd left it. I ran around calling Stephanie's name. I checked the ground floor first, then went through the whole of the upper floor. Nobody there, nothing that looked any different from the way it had when I'd left. I came back down, heart thudding. When I reached the living room I turned in a circle before suddenly finding myself in motion again. We had a portable phone, naturally, but because we both have cell phones the handset generally lives on the kitchen counter. I saw that's where it was now, next to the base. I couldn't remember whether it had been there when I'd left. It didn't matter. Whoever had been in the house had evidently been standing *right there*.

I had a sudden thought and turned to look through the window out at the terrace and swimming pool. Nobody there, either.

Resisting the urge to pick up the phone handset was easy. Would there be fingerprints? Possibly. Would there also be a small black card with the word MODIFIED hidden somewhere in the house? Also possible.

Either would be a distraction from the main point, which was that someone had come into the house with the aim of screwing with my life. It wasn't David Warner.

So who?

* ⋆ ⋆

At five o'clock I was still standing at the counter, or rather standing there again. In the meantime I'd searched the house more thoroughly and found nothing. No little black cards, and no missing suitcases or clothes. I hadn't seriously believed that Steph would just take off, storming down the path like something from act one of a romcom (trials and tribulations lie ahead, constant viewer, though expect reconciliation/ redemption before the credits roll). But people do actually do that kind of thing in real life, apparently, and I was very glad not to see any evidence of it in my own home.

I'd thought about calling the cops, of course. I'd thought about it every thirty seconds since hearing the woman's voice on my phone. I hadn't done so, because I found it too easy to imagine what the response would be.

Your wife is a grown-up, sir. It's still within business hours. Plus, you had an argument last night. So, uh, what's your point?

I also felt that if I was going to talk to the cops for a third time in one day, then I needed to feel on firmer ground. A nonlocatable wife wasn't enough. An alleged voice on my house phone line wasn't enough, either. It could have been a wrong number, a mishearing, or I could have made the whole thing up for motivations of my own — which could only be suspicious, strange, and of possible terrorist intent.

Did I *have* any other evidence? There were the cards I'd received. Had I kept any of them? Of course not. I'd thrown each away as it arrived, dismissing the baby steps of chaos until it was too late.

He didn't *know* that, of course — whoever he was, the person behind the cards and behind whatever was happening to me. I could have kept the cards. I also had a laptop in the car with folders — and a hard disk — that had been renamed to the same word. I had a copy of the e-mail sent out in my name, and a photocopy of the delivery notice for the book from Amazon. And, it finally struck me, there might have been something else, too: the booking at Jonny Bo's for our anniversary dinner. Janine said I'd e-mailed her about it. That wasn't inconceivable — I often gave her jobs when she was looking even more unoccupied than usual — but I couldn't actually recall doing so. Someone had evidently been digging around in my digital identity even before this week, in order to place the Amazon order. The same person *could* have sent Janine the e-mail asking her to make a booking at Bo's.

So it was *possible* I should add that to the pile, though doing so would mean accepting the idea that someone had a pretty in-depth knowledge of my habits. Why hadn't I paid more attention to this at the time? How could I have been so wrapped up in my machinations at The Breakers that I'd let this stuff just flow by?

As I listed these pieces of evidence in my head I was also aware of how trivial they sounded — how easy they were to let roll by when your mind was on higher things. That was probably the whole point. Every one of them was like a tiny little chili that was not only perfectly possible for me to have eaten but seemed too small for someone else to have bothered with.

Except the pictures of Karren, of course.

That was a bigger deal, harder to organize, and came with a heavier payload. They might be deemed worthy of being taken seriously. *But* . . . I could just have taken *those* myself, too. My 'proof' that I'd been deliberately kept out of the house that evening — in order to set up the pictures — had disappeared the moment Melania told the cops she'd never spoken to me. Claiming otherwise now just made me look like a liar as well as a fantasist.

'*Shit*,' I shouted suddenly, the whole mess spilling out of my head to bounce off the walls.

The house said nothing. The house felt alien, like a friend you happen to glimpse from a distance one afternoon, sitting outside a café with another member of your crowd, some rendezvous to which you were not invited. No injury has been done to you. Yet something about the sight — as you stand becalmed on the other side of the street, traffic making a river of difference between you — demonstrates that you are not at the center of creation after all. The house was just a house, and a life was just a life. Both might feel like they belonged to me, but there were gaps in its fabric, and gaps mean entrances, ways for strangers to get inside. Life suddenly felt like a random series of events and people connected only by accident and happenstance. So your friends are out for a drink, and you're there, too, and maybe it's even your birthday: does that mean it's actually *about* you? No. It could have happened by coincidence, or to watch a ball game. You could slip away midevening, and after five minutes of bemusement they'd buy another beer, close the circle, and it would be as if you'd never been there. You could die. Within weeks the same thing would happen.

You're not the cause, the be-all and end-all, of anything. There's no house. There's no life. There's just you. A point in space and time.

I shook my head violently, trying to break the train of thought. Of course it wasn't the house's fault that someone had been inside it. Everything was whirling around my head too fast. I knew the only way I was going to be able to regain control was by talking to someone about it. But Steph wasn't here to talk to.

That was the whole point.

18

Five thirty found me perched on a chair out by the pool. I had the sliding door behind me open — the one leading to the living room rather than the kitchen — so I'd hear the instant a key was inserted into the front door. I had my cell phone on my lap. I had the house phone on the table — I'd carefully carried it through, holding one corner with fingers protected by a piece of paper towel, feeling absurd but telling myself I'd feel far worse if it turned out I'd fucked up a set of fingerprints, if it came to that. Which it wouldn't. Of course. My wife was not home yet, that was all. And had lost her phone. Or her battery had run down.

Or something.

There had been a whole lot of somethings in the last half hour. I had discovered in myself a vein of wild inventiveness that, when my life got itself back on track, I was determined to apply to my career. My current obsession was trying to convince myself it had actually been *Stephanie* on the phone when I called the house. That she'd said the word *modified* in an unusual tone to wind me up (the most convincing version of this fantasy had her frisky with drink, mischievous with the triumph of her morning's meeting) and was now out shopping hard, to rub the point home. I could *just about* get the idea to work if I made myself believe she had a reason to know

153

the impact of the word — but that was tough: she only knew about one of the cards, and I hadn't made a big deal of it at the time or since. I was finding the story hard to let go of nonetheless, because as time went by the alternative explanations felt less and less appealing.

I'd put Deputy Hallam's card next to the phone on the table. I'd also given myself a deadline.

Six o'clock.

★ ★ ★

At six thirty I hadn't made the call. It was still only an hour after the point when Steph would normally be home, and I'd by then semiconvinced myself that were it not for all the other things that had happened I wouldn't be worrying. I'd be checking blogs or refining the six-and-a-half-year plan or listening to podcasts while getting virtuously upside an extra gym session. It's amazing what you can get yourself to believe, briefly, if you really put your mind to it. I'd also changed out of my suit into jeans and a shirt, presumably in the belief that looking smart-casual would help in some way, I don't know.

Suddenly my cell phone rang. I saw immediately that it was the Shore Realty office number.

'Who's that?' I asked cautiously.

'It's Karren. Look, I'm still at work.'

Normally I would have asked why, of course.

Right now I couldn't care less. 'Okay, so?'

'The cops have been by again,' she said. 'I think they were kind of looking for you.'

'Why? Why would they be looking for me?'

'They didn't say, but I got the sense something's happened with the David Warner thing. They made me go through my entire meeting with him *again*, play by play. They seemed very serious. Where are you, anyway? You just blew out of here and didn't come back.'

'I came home.'

'Okay. Um, why?'

I had to say it to someone. 'I don't know where Stephanie is.'

'You supposed to be meeting her?'

'No.' Already I regretted saying anything. 'She's just . . . I can't get hold of her.'

'At her office?'

'At her office, on her cell, anywhere.'

'Oh,' she said, and I stopped regretting. There was a marked lack of irony in her tone. 'That's weird. You guys are attached at the hip, communication-wise.'

'Well, yeah. We are.'

'She mad at you?'

I hesitated. 'She may be.'

'That means yes. You want womanly counsel on the matter? That what you're hoping for?'

'No. I didn't realize you even had womanly advice to dispense.'

'I don't put everything on show, my friend. The good stuff stays in the drawer for special customers. For this phone conversation only, you qualify.'

'Okay.' I felt nervous, not knowing what she'd be likely to say, or how I'd wound up in a position where I was listening to Karren White's opinion on anything.

'If she's real mad, then she's going to want to come back, slam the door, read you the riot act with the volume up. There is no point trying to circumvent this process, so just tie yourself to the track and wait for the rage train to run over you. Meanwhile gird your loins for saying 'sorry' about ten times more often than you think you can bear.'

'Then what?'

'After that, I got nothing. I know it probably seems like we chicks are all the same, but actually each of our kind is slightly different. It's your job to know what Stephanie's going to need to hear next.'

'No,' I said tersely. 'I didn't mean that. I meant . . . what if she *doesn't* come back?'

It felt strange to be talking to Karren in this way, but less odd than I might have expected. Maybe because of the pictures I'd seen (with their fake but effective message of connection). A part of me was also aware, however, that if Steph *did* march into the house and find me on the phone with Karren, she'd be marching straight the hell back out again. This call needed to end soon, however helpful Karren was trying to be.

'She doesn't come back by midnight, tell the cops,' Karren said. 'Matter of fact, you might want to mention it early, give them a heads-up when they arrive.'

'What do you mean, 'arrive'?'

'Crap, sorry — didn't I make that clear? They're on their way to your house. Right now.'

'You've been a great help, Karren. Thanks. I'll have a talk with the cops, get everything straightened out.'

'No problem. I've — '

She probably said more, but I'd cut the connection. I walked back into the house. I poured a tall, cool glass of water from the fridge and drank it in slow, measured gulps. I put the glass in the dishwasher. Turned back to face the room. All that was fine.

But then I did the dumb thing. I'm not even sure why. Could be that waiting in the house for so long had put me on a hair trigger. I knew I hadn't done anything wrong. The prospect of having to explain that *again* caused a spasm of spastic motion — and the idea of sitting in the house waiting for cops to arrive is no one's idea of a fun time. Either way, a section of my consciousness centered not in my head but in my guts said: *Nah, not going to hang around for that.*

I went to the den and got a pad. I wrote a message:

Steph — please call me! I'm really sorry. But I really need to talk to you — now. I love you, Bxxx

I put the sheet on the counter next to the phone.

Then I left the house.

19

'Guess you thought that was real smart, huh.'

Warner is startled by the sound of Hunter's voice. He'd been listening, alert for sounds, and yet here the bastard is, back again, unannounced. That's worrying. It has become increasingly important to believe his senses are working correctly, that he can accurately discern between what is real and what is not.

He raises his head and sees Hunter leaning against the far wall, watching. He is motionless. It seems inconceivable that there can have been a process that brought him here from somewhere else. He must always have been here somehow.

'Is that you?'

Hunter just stands there with his totemic face. He does not look happy.

Warner looks wearily from Hunter toward the tarpaulins that have been his only windows for nearly seventy-two hours. At first he hated that they obscured the view, but he has come to realize that this enables him to see whatever he wants. The light they filter is fading again now. It's beautiful what twilight does to the sky in Florida, the soft unfurling of the sunset as darkness wanders in from the ocean. The colors may be a little lurid sometimes, but what's wrong with that? Life is lurid. Life is big.

Live it, do it, turn it up.

He traveled earlier in life, wound up on the

West Coast, which is where he made his money. But after he sold the company he came straight back to Sarasota, never considering anywhere else. He is aware that the rest of the world nurtures a pissy little caricature of the Sunshine State. Tourist trap. Cracker country. God's waiting room. He is of the opinion that if you're sitting at the right bar with a cold beer and a fat Cuban smoke and the right companion, however, there's nowhere in the world that comes so close to heaven. He even likes Jimmy Buffet, for crissakes — why would anyone not? — and he would literally kill for a cheeseburger in paradise right now.

He feels he should be making a rejoinder to what Hunter has said. Zingers have been a stock in trade all his life. Right now, he's got nothing. Holding his head upright hurts, but he knows that letting it drift back down would hurt, too, and look weak. He is not weak. He has always been one of the strong, a player, someone in charge of his destiny, one of the people behind the veil. He *owns* the fucking veil. He *built* the veil. It takes more than strapping a man to a chair and starving him of food and water to rob him of his character — though it does make his life a lot more difficult, and means that people can come find him.

Come find him in the night.

★ ★ ★

He has no idea what time it is when he wakes. It is very dark. Over the last couple of days he has tried to gauge the hour by listening for the distant sound of traffic. There is none, and so he assumes it's somewhere in the small dead hours of the night. His throat feels like someone was making deep, slow nicks in it with a salty knife. The wound in his leg lets off a dark siren once in a while, but otherwise feels ominously dead. His mind is a network of dried-up creeks, and as he nods back to what passes for consciousness, he actually tries a piece of New Age bullshit he withstood Lynn chattering about, lying in her husband's bed a couple weeks back.

He imagines rain falling in his head. He imagines a cloud gathering under the bones of his skull, growing pregnant and blue-black-purple, then bursting with a thunderclap. He imagines water falling into his thoughts and starting to flow through those arid riverbeds, at first a trickle and then a fast, gurgling stream.

All it does is make him thirstier. It also makes him hate Lynn, briefly, with a bright and almost sexual intensity. This is not because he suspects her of collusion in his abduction — he's decided Hunter likely needed no such assistance — simply because he knows that right now she will be lying in her bed, asleep and with a full belly, without a care in the world. They are often not in contact for weeks at a time, and so she won't realize he's missing. Would she even care? Up until recently he would have said yes, of course. But now he's not so sure. They had fun, and she dug hanging out (discreetly) with a man of his wealth. But was he also just a thing she found herself unable to stop doing? Might his passing actually occasion her relief?

He abruptly decides that visualization just ain't working for him. He opens his eyes instead, and sees a girl sitting cross-legged in the middle of the floor.

He closes his eyes, opens them.

The girl is still there. She is wearing old, torn jeans and a vest in a pale color. It is not Lynn. Lynn has short hair. This girl's hair is long, styled out of fashion. Her arms are hooked around her knees and she is looking to the side. The moonlight picks out features that are soft and pretty. Features he knows.

'Katy?'

She doesn't move, or even acknowledge him. In a way this is no surprise, as he knows that Katy is dead and has been for some time. But she's there now. He can see her. And so he says her name again, more loudly.

She stands, slowly. She is still not looking in his direction, however. As she stands a faint odor is unfurled. He can't put a name to it. He senses he doesn't want to, either. It is not strong. But it is not good.

It takes too long for her to reach an upright position. Finally she turns her head to look at him. The entirety of her irises is black. The skin of her face is pale and slack. She has no fingernails.

She speaks:

'Do you remember that time when you said you had an idea in a dream and it was that people would be able to see all the people they'd ever met or hung out with and see if they'd

161

thought you were hot or if they wanted to have sex with you and it was like a 3D graph or something, and all these people would be standing around you in circles, and the closer they were to you meant the more often they'd thought about it or the more dirty they'd done it with you in their heads?'

Her voice is the soft, one-note drawl of the stoned or exhausted. The movement of her lips is slightly out of sync with the words, and continues for perhaps three seconds after the sound has stopped.

'I don't remember that,' he says.

'You don't remember anything you don't want to.'

'Maybe I did say it.'

'Yeah, maybe.'

She walks toward him, her left leg dragging behind. She walks past on his right-hand side, over the edge, but she does not fall. She is still at the same level when she disappears out of sight.

He sits in the chair, his hands gripping the arms. A quantity of urine he would not have believed he still possessed has leaked out into his pants. He knows that he cannot just have seen her, but . . . is she going to return?

She does not.

But he doesn't sleep again, either.

★   ★   ★

Back in the here and now, he gives up on finding a smart reply and instead asks the question in his head.

162

'What did you do to Hazel?'

Hunter looks a little sour. This doesn't seem like gamesmanship.

He evidently does not want to talk about it. So Hazel is probably dead. Warner can remember what she was like twenty-some years ago, when he first met her. The wife of one of the big wheels of the local set he was sliding his way into. A good-looking older woman. Someone who he more than once thought had been looking at him in a certain way, though probably not — she and her husband had been very tight. That whole group had been, long before he joined, and you don't mess with that kind of bond for the sake of random couplings.

'I remember Wilkins,' Hunter says. 'He seemed like an okay guy. Was he really a part of it?'

'A part of what?'

'You know.'

The man in the chair summons his strength. 'I do. But I think that *you* still don't get it.'

'You care to enlighten me?'

'Nope.'

'I guessed not. So I'm going to leave you to it for another while. I got work to do now. Cleanup. And that's your fault. Another dumb game you played, right?'

The man in the chair looks at him.

'Yeah,' Hunter said. 'She talked.'

As Hunter levers himself up from the wall and prepares to go, the man in the chair feels panic.

'I have friends, you asshole. Other friends, not the old folks' club here. Friends without limits. I pay my dues to them. They owe me. They'll bury you and set fire to your grave.'

'Been there,' Hunter says. 'Being buried is no big thing. Pour as much earth as you want over people, they have a way of climbing back out.'

'And so what if they do? You'll always be trash. And I'll always be who I am.'

'That's true, my friend, and it must be a source of *great* comfort to you right now.'

Hunter walks over and looks down at the man in the chair, and Warner is confused and disconcerted to see something in his eyes that looks like compassion.

'You're old school. But even people like that learn new tricks once in a while.'

He picks the water bottle off Warner's lap, twists the cap. He takes a drink from it and the man in the chair thinks yes, of course — that was only ever going to be about another way of taunting me. But Hunter holds the bottle down at about the level of Warner's mouth.

Fearing — knowing — that this is just going to be a trick, but too desperate to resist, Warner leans his head forward hungrily. Hunter holds the bottle to his lips, gently tilts it. A slow, steady stream of water courses into his mouth. He can feel it as it travels down his esophagus and finally into his stomach. Hunter keeps the bottle in position, gradually changing the angle to keep the water coming, until it is completely empty.

Then he scrunches it up and puts it in his pocket. He heads over to the portion of the ledge where he climbed up the day before.

'You have a good night, David.'

Fighting a feeling of nausea, Warner looks round at him. 'She gave you someone else, didn't she.'

Hunter smiles. 'I'll be back.'

He sits down on the edge and is about to drop over it, but then stops, as if struck by a thought. 'One thing, though,' he adds. 'Driving down Longboat, I saw something. Don't know what it's about, but you might. Seems like the cops are taking an interest in your house. Saw four or five cars. Plus a CSI wagon or two. Seems like a lot of hardware for some guy who's gone missing, no matter how rich he is.'

He winks, and then he's gone.

★   ★   ★

The water has made a difference. His thoughts have clarified. Warner knows the effect is temporary, and for some reason the image that comes into his mind is that of a faithful dog, locked into a house with its old, dead owner, lapping at the body's blood, biting a hole, snuffling and chewing at what's inside. Great, in the short term. A meat bonanza. But when it's gone, it's gone.

He feels okay. His thoughts are more able to restrict themselves to the positive, to the golden hours and days. His thoughts are like strong hands, lifting moments up in front of his mind. He can hold them there, turn them, look at the past from every angle. In the past this would have been associated with pinpricks of guilt and doubt. But now? There's no need, no space, and no time. He can be who he is and has always been.

He stares straight ahead, eyes open. After a time they start to smart, and collude with the oncoming twilight to make the edges of the room shade away.

When the women arrive, he knows they are only in his imagination. He's still not sure about Katy, but he knows that the figures that start to appear now around the periphery of his vision are nothing more than the product of his memory. He remembers then that he *did* come up with an idea something like the fantasy index Katy's ghost told him about. He knows that's what his mind is serving up, except that the figures that are coming to share this space are not those who were attracted to him. He had a very different role in their lives, and there are many of them. He'd never realized quite how many.

He's not afraid.

But he's not a fool, either.

When he's ready, he holds the ends of both arms of the chair with his hands. He anchors down with the balls of his feet. He closes his eyes and pushes, raising the front legs just a little.

Then he throws his back against the chair, hard.

The chair rocks, once, twice, and then tips slowly backward over the edge.

20

I didn't go far. After I'd made it onto the main road without being confronted by a cop car, I calmed down a little. I knew what I was doing was not smart, but also that it wasn't a CNN-worthy Bronco debacle either. How was I to have known that the cops were on their way? Well, okay, because Karren had told me — but they didn't *know* that (yet). And they should have called ahead, right? You can't just assume people are sitting around with nothing better to do. I had business to attend to. I had a client to meet, a dentist's appointment, a brand-building encounter group and astrology 'fragfest' up in Bradenton. I had to do . . . whatever the fuck.

So I wasn't home. So sue me.

I drove into downtown Sarasota and developed an idea on the way. It was a small idea, but it was the only one I could find, and some form of positive and direct action seemed like a good plan right now (and a great excuse for not being at home, too).

I parked on Felton Street and walked the extra block to the offices of *Not Just a Beach*. I could see through the big glass doors that someone was still behind the desk, but when I tried to open the door, it was locked. The girl looked up from her computer and shook her head with the god-given authority of receptionists everywhere.

We be shut. It de law.

167

I went through a mime show to indicate that I knew it was after six and they weren't open, but that I was desirous of communicating with her anyhow — and not likely to give up any time soon. She took her time interpreting this, or maybe just wasn't too smart. In the end she pressed a button and the door clicked.

'We're closed,' she said primly as soon as I'd set foot inside.

'I know, and I'm only going to keep you a second. I'm Stephanie Moore's husband.'

The girl upped her respect level by about twenty percent, Steph being senior editor of the magazine. 'Oh, okay, hi.'

'I've had my phone crash on me. I'm supposed to be meeting Steph but I can't remember where. She texted me the place, but I can't access my calendar. Can't reach her on the phone, either. She didn't mention where she was headed this evening, anything like that?'

The receptionist diligently consulted various bits of paper strewn across her desk and stuck around her computer monitor. 'Sorry, no.'

'Okay, last resort — you got a number for Sukey?'

This was something I'd tried to establish back at the house during my phase of searching the place, but the number wasn't on Steph's laptop.

'I'm not allowed to give out that information.'

'Of course.' I grabbed a pen and a slip of paper from her desk and started scribbling. 'But this is my cell, okay? Will you do me a favor, e-mail or text Sukey that number, ask her to give me a call?'

I walked back onto the street. I wasn't confident she'd do as I'd asked, and it probably wouldn't make much difference. So what now?

As I walked back to the car, I caught sight of a bar sign in the distance and thought: *That's* what now.

* * *

Krank's was slammed with the after-work crowd and I didn't bother to even try to get a seat in the air-conditioned interior, instead grabbing one of the tables on the terrace. With a beer on the way I tried Steph's number for the three millionth time. Getting voice mail again had me gripping the phone about as hard as its tough little case could handle. I didn't bother to add another message. I did, however, notice that my battery had taken a thrashing over the course of the day and was already down to half a charge. This gave me a twist of additional anxiety that I didn't need. Though, after all, I could charge it when I went back to the house, right? It wasn't like I was on the run or anything. I'd be home real soon. Exactly.

I also didn't need the fact that three women sat at the next table and immediately started smoking their heads off. If you've never tried to give up cigarettes, then you don't know what that shit is like. You can be months down the road, over the addiction and dealing only with the tendrils of habit: then one afternoon you see someone happily sucking away on a cancer stick and find yourself knocking down children and

169

old people in your rush to buy a pack, dully knowing that this moment was always here in front of you, waiting for you to plod your way toward it. The guy behind the counter takes your money and moves on to the next customer, not realizing the momentous event that has occurred, the edifice of effort, internal dialogue, and self-denial that crumpled in his presence.

Maybe *all* the types of pain and disappointment we find in our lives are there just because we invite them, because we have the receptors ready and waiting.

Maybe I should just have a fucking smoke and be done with it.

I turned to the ladies. Got halfway to asking one of them if I could bum a cigarette. But didn't.

I turned back to my own table, feeling no triumph, just a thin and vicious sense of lack. Luckily my beer arrived and I swallowed half of that instead. The other half followed quickly, so I got another on the way.

And so it went, and still Steph did not call.

★ ★ ★

An hour later I was starting my fourth beer and realizing this had better be the last. The sun had started to dip but the air was getting heavier. The terrace had cleared in the meantime. The smokers nearby had gone, too, which had helped my clarity somewhat — leading me to remember something Kevin had said at lunchtime. He'd said that physical access to my laptop would be the easiest explanation for everything that had happened; that, by implication, there was a person who could very easily have gained access to my passwords and/or account.

Stephanie. Of course.

The idea broke with the photographs. Sure, Stephanie *could* have put them on my laptop. She could even *maybe* have taken them in the first place.

But why? What would be the point of going nuclear on me over something I hadn't done? David Warner engineering the event was inexplicable enough. Steph doing it was plain incredible, and without evidence . . . though it was hard to imagine how Warner would have had the opportunity to put the files on my computer, either. I didn't understand enough about the tech to know how likely it was for someone to be able to dump files on my machine from without. That made me realize just how little I understood the capabilities and limits of the technologies to which I'd merrily handed up control of my life. In the old days identity meant your face, or your signature at the very least. Now it was a collection of passwords, each chosen with less thought than you'd use to name a pet. Know my passwords, be me — functionally, at least — and we are what we do or appear to have done.

I couldn't believe I was even *considering* this about my own wife. The alcohol was making me tired and tetchy and miring me in anxiety that was uncomfortably like panic. There was no point sitting here any longer, not least as I had

171

the car and was already over the limit. I called for the check and headed inside to the john.

As I walked back through the bar afterward I tried Steph's number yet again and received the same lack of response. It was half past eight. As I cut the connection I abruptly made a decision. I was going to follow Karren White's advice. I'd call the cops — saying I'd heard they wanted to speak to me. And when we met, I'd mention the fact I hadn't heard from my wife all day. Their reaction — which I hoped would be low-key — might settle me a little.

I nodded to myself, glad to have made a decision, and reached for my wallet to find Deputy Hallam's card. I happened to glance up, and saw a waiter placing a tray with my check on the table where I'd been sitting.

Behind him, on the other side of the street, I saw a man walking by.

It was David Warner.

21

I went from immobility to sprinting in two seconds flat. As I went hurtling out of the terraced area I heard the waiter yell something, but paying my check wasn't anywhere on my mind.

David Warner was walking down the other side of the street. He was even wearing the same jacket from the time I'd met him in the bar, pale green and wide-shouldered, the kind that cost a thousand bucks from somewhere on the Circle. He was alone, wandering with the relaxed, heavy roll of someone who knows he could own the whole damned street if he wanted.

'Hey!' I shouted, as I darted into the road between cars. Somebody honked. Warner kept walking. I realized he was probably not accustomed to being addressed in this way, wouldn't for a moment imagine that some guy bellowing in the street could possibly be relevant to him. He was heading toward a car parked twenty yards away, and I picked up the pace.

When I was finally in range, I lunged out to grab his shoulder. He recognized me right away — I saw it in his eyes.

'What?' he said, however. 'Who the hell are you?'

'It's Bill, Bill Moore.'

He stared. 'Who?'

'Bill Moore. The Realtor. We met in Krank's a few weeks back? You're selling your house. You had a meeting with my colleague on Tuesday.'

'I've no idea what you're talking about.'

'Bullshit.'

He started backing away. 'I don't know who the hell you are, but get away from me or I'll call the police.'

'I've *talked* to the police. They came to see me. They think you could be dead.'

A couple of passersby were now taking an interest. Both sported vests and tattoos, the kind of guys you see propping up bars on the highway out of town. David Warner glanced at them, meanwhile stuffing a hand in his pants pocket.

'Guy's a wacko,' he said. 'Never met him before.'

'Don't think you should be making threats,' one of the men said to me. He sounded like he wanted an excuse to hit someone.

'I'm *not* threatening him. I'm just saying — '

But now the other man had stepped up, and had gotten between me and Warner, who was moving with purpose toward his car.

'Come on, guys,' I said, trying to keep it light. 'This really isn't any of your business. I have to talk to this guy, that's all. He *knows me*.'

'Never seen him before,' Warner said, as he got into his car. 'Thanks, gents.'

He slammed the door, had the engine running within seconds, and started to pull away immediately.

'*Assholes*,' I screamed. I turned on my heel and started to run the other way. I'd barely gone

174

ten feet before I ran smack into the waiter from Krank's.

'Don't try to run out on me, sir,' he said. 'You owe — '

I yanked out my wallet and threw a bill at him. I have no idea how much it was. The other two guys were advancing quickly toward me now, having decided I'd done enough to validate some recreational violence, even though the original catalyst had taken himself off.

Warner was meanwhile nosing out into traffic.

I'm pretty fast, it turns out. Seems all that time on the running machine had not been wasted. I took the corner about thirty yards ahead and got my keys ready. I ran straight into the road — narrowly avoiding being wiped out by a passing truck — and to the driver's side. Once inside, I flicked central locking on and both guys started to beat on the roof of the car with their hands out flat, sounding like metal thunder. I slammed my foot down and fishtailed out backward, leaving the men off balance and shouting, then slammed into drive and hurtled straight out into the street, cutting off the corner that would take me into the road past Krank's against a stop light. I could see Warner's car down at the end of the street, waiting to make the right out onto the boulevard.

There were too many cars between us for me to be sure of making the turn in the same set of lights, so I hung a hard right instead and cut off the block. It felt counterintuitive to lose sight of him, but I knew it made sense. I took the next

175

left and swore hard and loud when I saw what the traffic was like on First. There was nothing I could do except nose the car out into the stream and hope.

By the time I got down to Tamiami I'd almost given up, so when I saw Warner's car clearing the intersection and heading out toward the bridge I shouted again, this time in something like animal triumph.

I jammed my foot down before the lights changed — flying across the intersection and over onto Ringling Boulevard. I nearly got taken out by another truck in the process, just before I realized I knew where the guy was most likely going — his house — and so I didn't have to kill myself for the sake of it.

★ ★ ★

Except he didn't take the turn.

I followed him over the bridge and across Bird Key and all the way to St. Armands Circle, expecting him to then take the right that would lead him over the water onto Longboat.

Instead, he went left. I was caught out by this and slammed on the brakes far too late. Warner must have known I was following him, because he sheered straight round the island and hammered away into the side streets.

I know those roads well — have sold more than one house there — but I still lost him.

I drove up and down the grid for fifteen minutes, but he'd gone, somehow. Doubled back on me, most likely, headed back over the

176

bridge to the mainland. Eventually I started to run out of steam, and the slower I got — and as the adrenaline started to leak out of me — I realized I was actually pretty drunk. Shouldn't have been, after only four beers, but I hadn't eaten that evening — or at lunch or breakfast, now I came to think of it. In fact, I worked out doggedly, the last thing I could remember ingesting had been half a bowl of frozen yogurt . . . yesterday afternoon.

Abruptly I pulled over to the side of the road. I was half a mile from the Circle, in a street of studiedly nonidentical but still similar properties in the $950K — $1.2M bracket. A man stood in the yard of one of these, watering his plants. He saw me sitting, staring straight ahead as if I'd been unplugged.

He bent down to the window. His voice was kind. 'You okay, bud?'

'I'm not sure,' I said. 'But thanks for asking.'

I backed up, did a careful U-turn under his calm and watchful eye, and drove slowly up toward the Circle.

* * *

I meant to just have coffee. But when I sat down at a table outside Jonny Bo's café, the waitress — not one I'd seen before — happened to mention beer among the products on offer. I knew it was a bad idea, and I had no exit strategy for being ten miles from home with a car and excessive blood alcohol levels, but sometimes you just have to go ahead and do the dumb thing. Today was evidently that day.

My phone was down to twenty percent charge. This meant its battery icon had started to glow orange. I wish they wouldn't do that. I *know* the battery's low. One bar left out of five is a message I can understand. So leave it green, for god's sake. Changing it to a warning color is just liable to stress people out. There was, of course, no voice mail from Stephanie and no text message, either. It was now nine o'clock, and I was getting scared.

While I waited for my beer, I did what I'd just started to do back in Krank's. The phone rang and rang, but then finally picked up.

'Deputy Hallam,' he said, as if distracted.

'It's Bill Moore.'

'Where are you?'

'He's not missing,' I said.

'Who, sir?'

'David Warner. I've just seen him.'

'That doesn't seem likely, sir. Though we would like to talk to you about him. We came out to your house a little while ago, matter of fact.'

'I'm not there.'

'We're aware of that. Where are you?'

'Up in Saint Pete,' I lied. 'At La Scala. Business dinner.' I fluffed the name of the restaurant, crashing 'La' into the second word.

'Uh-huh. Have you been drinking, sir?'

'Not really any of your business, Deputy.'

'It is if you're intending to drive back.'

'I'll get a cab. Look, fuck the DUI tutorial. Why are you pretending Warner's missing, when he's not? I just *saw* him, half an hour

178

ago. I *talked* to him. He jumped in his car and booked it.'

'Where was this?'

'Felton Street. I tried to talk to him, to, uh, tell him people were worried, but two passing assholes got involved and he got away.'

'That sounds like an interesting encounter. I'll look forward to hearing more about it. The sheriff's definitely going to want to talk to you tomorrow, sir. You want that to be at your office or at your house?'

'Why aren't you listening to me?'

'I am listening. Listening hard enough, in fact, to know you're lying about your current location, because there's no way you could have gotten from downtown to Saint Pete in half an hour, especially the way traffic is on the Tamiami right now.'

'Deputy, okay. I'm sorry. You're right, I'm not in Saint Petersburg. I'm in town and I'm *freaked out*. I cannot find my wife and I swear to God I really did just see Warner. He knew who I was but denied it, and then he ran away. He is in good health. I don't know who got shot in that house but *it was not him*.'

'How long has your wife been missing, sir?'

'Only a day, and I *know* that's not enough. But it's *not like her*. We're usually in contact the whole time. We had an argument last night, but this isn't right.'

'What was the argument about, sir?'

'Stuff.'

'Okay. We generally require a longer absence to open a file. But I'll check the reports, just in case. If she's still missing when we meet tomorrow, we can get much more serious about it.'

I knew that was as good as I was going to get from him — that in fact he was being decent. 'Thank you. Let me give you my phone number.'

'It's right here on my screen, Mr. Moore.'

'Right. Of course.'

'My advice is that you cease drinking and get yourself driven home, Mr. Moore. Will you do that?'

'I will.'

'Great. Matter of fact, when you *get* to your house, why not give me a call. That way I'll know how to get hold of you real quick if I hear anything about your wife.'

I said I would, but ended the call convinced that if I went home, a cop car would be pulling up outside real soon.

I ordered another beer instead.

It wasn't a plan. It was just what I did.

22

When Warner woke this time, he could tell that a lot of things were different. *Seriously* different. Gravity seemed to have altered, for a start, to be pulling him in a different direction. The rigidity of his position had changed, too, and felt less implacable. In addition to the pain in his thigh, to which he'd become horribly accustomed, there were now deep veins of discomfort spreading from his left arm and hand, the back of his head, and the small of his back.

Then he remembered why all this might be.

He'd tipped himself backward off a twelve-foot drop onto concrete while strapped to a heavy chair.

Astonishingly, he wasn't dead.

Not yet, anyway.

★ ★ ★

He peered up into the near darkness and confirmed that his view was now of the underside of the half floor where he'd spent the last couple of days.

He turned his head to the right, and then all the way to the left. It hurt a lot, but he could do it. He tried moving his arms. They were both still constrained, but less tightly than before. The chair was broken.

How about that.

He took his time. He rotated his right arm around the shoulder and then started to pull the hand up. It caught hard around the wrist, but ten minutes' patient effort worked it free.

He held it up in front of his face, turning it slowly around. He had his hand back. Slowly, he started to laugh, a dry whistle in the back of his throat. He made this sound until he believed he was going to be sick. His head spun. But he wasn't stopping now.

He reached across his body and started working at the canvas tied around his other wrist. That arm of the chair was more badly broken, and his left hand took only five minutes to free. He reached both hands up together and tried to determine how the canvas around his neck had been fastened. After twenty minutes or so he'd made no progress — but then a chance movement revealed that the upper cross-panel on the chair had been broken, and a sideways movement of his head pulled it free. The canvas band stayed around his neck, but he could live with that. In a world where his fall hadn't killed him, he was prepared to be accommodating on the details of survival.

He planted both hands on the ground and pushed backward, trying to gauge how badly damaged the lower portion of the chair was. It inched along with him, which suggested it wasn't damaged enough. With a little more shoving and a series of slewed and twisted movements, however, it started to come apart. The process was made easier by the fact that he could feel very little in his right leg. That was likely bad in the long run, but for now it made things easier, and sometimes you have to be all about the now, after all.

He pulled. He wrenched. There was a slow, whirling sensation in the back of his head, which probably didn't augur well. He sobbed from time to time, and was eventually sick, a sequence of wretched dry heaves. When he'd done with that, he went back to work.

After about forty minutes, he was free.

He rolled onto his stomach and pulled himself along the floor until his feet were no longer tangled in the remains of the chair. When he was close to the wall, he laboriously looked back.

It was pretty dark, but the pile of broken wood in the middle of the floor picked up enough ambient light to look like the aftermath of a conjuror's trick, some Copperfield showstopper. Once there had been a man tethered in the center of it. Behold, now he was gone.

The escapee hurt, however. He was bleeding from a number of places, two fingers on his left hand looked and felt broken, and his head kept swirling, slowly, permanently, as if his consciousness was trying to exit via a blocked drain. He hurt *everywhere*, with a messianic, third act, this-may-not-be-fixable density of sensation.

But he was alive. So what now?

His aim had been straightforward. He'd gone through with it, too, attacked it with commitment. Only to find himself out the other side.

Death would have been simple. His current position was not.

He slowly stood up.

He made his way through the ground floor, supporting himself for much of the way by leaning against the walls. By the time he got to the padlocked door to the outside, his right leg had called off the pain amnesty. So had his memory. He'd recalled the full detail of why it had seemed reasonable to try to take his own life.

If the cops were digging around his house, then more than one system had failed, and his old life was over.

He couldn't go home.

So where?

Even a week ago, he knew he could have called upon other friends. The club that he'd been a part of for nearly twenty years. After three days out of the loop, however, he had no idea what had happened there: what they knew, what they'd guessed, how mad they'd be, and what they'd be prepared to do to get back at him.

Getting in contact with them could be like handing himself up to a pack of dogs. Old, fading dogs, yes, but dogs all the same.

There was a pile of pallets close to the door. He gingerly lowered himself onto it. His pelvis didn't like the arrangement, but he needed to rest. He needed to think. He gently patted the pockets of his gray sweatpants, now blood-and-sweat-and-urine-stained beyond recognition. No phone. Hunter would have taken that, of course. No money, either. No nothing.

Just him.

He was suddenly aware that he smelled really bad. On the upside, he noticed that the padlock on the big slab of hardboard was hanging open. Hunter must have broken it. He could have replaced the lock with one he'd purchased, of course, but evidently that hadn't occurred to him. With his captive tied to a chair, why bother?

Because, you loser, some men are made of stronger stuff.

His survival was an accident, of course. But you make your own luck, right? Even now, even in these late days, even with the world as very badly screwed as he knew it to be . . .

Game not over.

He flipped the padlock off. It fell to the floor. He only realized how weak he actually was when he tried to move the makeshift door. He barely managed it, and nearly fell over backward to land with the thing on top of him. Finally he edged it far enough to one side that he could squeeze through the gap.

Once through, he found himself lurching down in a flat, muddy area between the shells of two five-story condo blocks. He shambled into the middle, stopped, turned around. It was fifty yards square, a few tarp-wrapped pieces of inexpensive machinery parked neatly over to one side. If you listened real hard, you could hear the sound of the ocean.

'You're kidding me.'

He looked back the way he'd come.

Yeah. Once you were oriented, there was no question. This was the Silver Palms development on Lido Key. Small, by recent standards. Not a

185

career maker, just one of those journeyman projects you'd walk away from with a few million — assuming you hadn't been shut out of the deal by a trio of ancient assholes who'd decided to turn their backs on you. It was the very resort, in fact, that — when Warner had discovered that the others had edged him out — had caused him to unofficially and covertly resign from their dumb little club and start having some fun with the old fuckers on his own account.

Hunter couldn't have known this, of course. It was merely life playing itself out like the big cosmic joke it was. Ha ha. Very funny.

Slowly Warner began to make his way up the slope, to try to find a public phone. He could think of one person he could call. Another if it *really* came down to it — though that would really have to be a very last resort. Neither of these people was Lynn. He was beyond any form of normal life now, and knew it. Lynn was back in the shadows of before-life-in-the-chair.

He knew also that his ghosts were still behind him, Katy closest of all, following him up the slope.

Let them come.

He was screwed, but he wasn't dead yet.

23

I was sitting looking at my phone, and no, I was not back at the house. I'd just called Steph's number again — leaving yet another message, and remotely checking those on the machine (finding none but my own thirty-second slabs of ramping anxiety, a jump-cut graph of my state of mind since midafternoon). I was sick of the sound of my own voice, both inside my head and in messages apparently destined to go unanswered. My phone battery was down to ten percent, and the icon was firehouse red — which meant it could go splat at any moment, probably within seconds of starting to receive an actual phone call.

I knew I should be getting myself the hell back to base. Hallam had told me so (and I did feel a measure of relief, or at least a sense of having done the right thing, having mentioned Stephanie's not-being-aroundness to him). Karren had told me that was the best place to be, too, if I wanted to get a jump-start on placating my wife. I knew it on every other level, including that it simply wasn't a great idea to be seen getting drunk on the Circle, one of my key areas of business.

I'd known all these things when I ordered the previous beer, however. I wished I'd simply gone home after the first drink at Krank's, sat in a chair, and waited for my wife. I would have been in the right place, possessed of righteousness: here I am, ready and willing to sort things out — and where the heck have you been, my love? Now I was in the *wrong* place, and drunk, and apparently intent on paddling myself further and further up a side creek of wrong action.

'Is that one of those phones where if you stare at it hard enough you can get it to explode? Because that would be cool.'

I looked up, startled.

At first I thought someone at one of the nearby tables must have spoken. Then I saw a slim figure ten feet away, just out of range of the bar's lights.

'Who's that?'

She stepped forward. It was Cassandra. She was carrying a paper grocery bag crooked in one arm.

'Oh,' I said. 'Sorry. I was miles away.'

'Without a map, by the look of it. May I join you?'

She sat neatly, the bag perched on her lap like a well-behaved little dog. 'So what's up, Mr. Moore?'

'Up?'

'Just wondering why you might be here all by yourself. And glaring at your phone like that. As if it was a really *very* naughty phone indeed.'

'Battery's nearly dead,' I said. 'And I'm . . . It would just be good if it didn't run out right now.'

'You want a charge?'

'You can do that?'

'Well, duh. Do I look Amish?'

I stared at her owlishly, wondering how exactly

she could achieve this outside a bar. She laughed.

'You would need to take a short walk back to my apartment. Where I have a USB charger cable for a phone such as yours, along with many other technical goodies and gewgaws.'

'Is it far? Actually, I have a car with me.'

'I'm sure you do. But — and please don't take this personally — I'm thinking some foot-based locomotion would be a smart tactical choice for you right now. Certainly before attempting to steer a large chunk of metal back to the mainland.'

I thought for a moment. Okay, weird idea, but she was right — I was too drunk to drive, however slowly and methodically. Short walk, charge phone, get car, head home. That could work. It even kind of rhymed.

'That would be great,' I said.

I went indoors and found my waitress, paid. I caught a glimpse of the other waitress, the one from our anniversary night, on the other side of the room. She recognized me and gave a small, distracted nod. I thought about making my way over and asking if she'd seen my wife — you know, the woman I had dinner with upstairs the other night — but the room was crowded and I knew it would look drunk and strange, so I did not. I thought I'd got the drunk/strange look nailed pretty well already, without going to any extra effort.

Cassandra was standing on the sidewalk under a streetlight. She looked like the cover from some 1950s novel about an innocent in the big city, or would have if the Circle looked even slightly urban, and if they'd had emo chicks back in those days.

'Follow me, sire,' she said.

* * *

We walked up the road onto Lido Key. From there it was a long straight stroll along Ben Franklin Drive, past the car park for the beach and the looming hulks of condo developments. Lido is small, intimate, with a crescent moon of white sand beach about half a mile in length. At the far end, the key abruptly becomes much wilder, acres and acres of trees, bush, and near swamp around a couple of large, natural (and hence flybown and unattractive) stretches of water. One day the whole key would doubtless be covered in opportunities for fractional ownership, but for now the southern quarter wasn't that much different from the way it had been when dinosaurs roamed the earth.

It was dark, but the air felt soft and warm. At one point, halfway along the drive, I stopped for a moment, frowning. I turned around. I almost always did this when I came along this way, but had never been able to work it out before.

'Aha,' I said, however, feeling a flip of recognition deep in my gut. 'This is it.'

'Yeah, I heard they kept the secret of life along here somewhere. So you found it, huh?'

'The Lido Beach Inn,' I said. '*That's* where it was.'

'Excuse me?'

I turned to look at her, feeling old. 'We came to Florida a couple times when I was a kid,' I said. 'We always used to stay on Lido Beach. Back then this key wasn't so developed, in fact it was the budget option — though it had been a big deal in the distant past. There was a huge old hotel back on that last corner, where the Sun Palms is now, but it was abandoned all the years we came. And along here . . . '

I indicated the row of finished and nearly finished developments that now lined this stretch. 'I think there were already a couple of smaller condos back then, but it was mainly old motels. They're all gone now, but every time I've been along this road since we've lived here, I've tried to work out where the Lido Beach Inn was. And I've finally realized, it's here. Or it was.'

I pointed into the heart of a small, upscale development, and suddenly I could actually *feel* it, situate myself on the planet and in my memory and know this was the spot that had held a scruffy old U-shaped motel where you drove under an awning and turned right or left to park in front of two parallel blocks of rooms. There were perhaps a dozen rooms on each of the two levels, a swimming pool in between — and a walkway that led out to the beach. The motel had a laundry room, a Ping-Pong area with a table whose net never stood up, and whirring ice and soda machines. No restaurant, no bar, no store, no child-care facilities or concierge service. Just a place for families to hang out while they soaked up some rays (back in the days before it was determined that

191

sunlight was cancerous poison and to be avoided at all costs). For a moment it all seemed totally real, as if those family vacations had been only a year or two ago.

I saw, however, that the building that had replaced the Lido Beach Inn could itself do with a lick of paint, a chunk of render missing up on one side. The next generation was already getting old. I recalled, too, that only two days ago I'd been caught up in lobbying Tony Thompson to refresh The Breakers, and found it hard to remember why. I knew I would do so again, at some point, but right now it seemed far less important than the fact that a gangly kid with my name and DNA had once passed over this stretch of sidewalk without realizing that twenty years later an older version of himself would be weaving there, drunk, missing a wife, his life in disarray. It seemed strange that we can do this, stand in a place and not be able to feel the breeze of a future self walking past. We wouldn't be coming *back*, after all, had we not been there before — so the events must be conjoined. How had *he* not been able to see my shadow standing here? Had he not happened to look in the right direction? Or not listened hard enough? Or *had* I in fact caught a glimpse, and was that why I was back here now, to try to find my way back to that self? I thought about asking something like this out loud, but guessed I probably seemed drunk enough already. I let my hand drift back to my side.

'Come on,' Cassandra said. She stepped closer

and looped her arm through mine. 'I think you need to sit down for a while, big guy.'

* * *

It was only another ten minutes' walk, down at the far end of the drive. Just before the road abruptly downsized to a single lane before winding off into the palms and scrub of the undeveloped part of the key, there was an old and dilapidated apartment block, a little back from the road on the nonocean side.

Cassandra led me through the metal gate. The building was three stories high and arranged in a horseshoe, an empty water feature in the middle with a long-dead fountain at the center. It was all straight lines and semicircles and looked like it might have been kind of a big deal in the 1930s. Giant grasses were running riot around the courtyard now, obscuring it from the road. Patches of once-white render had fallen off, revealing a pinkish layer underneath. I'd vaguely noticed this place many times before, assumed it was derelict and waiting a wrecking ball under the control of one of the local developers. Most from that era had already vanished, including the old Art Deco casino that older locals still spoke of with pride.

'You live *here*?'

'For now. It's mainly empty, which is cool. Nice and quiet. Got kind of a vibe, too.'

'It's an abandoned ship, is what it feels like.'

'Adrift, and far from home.'

She led me up some spiral stairs at the end of the right arm. As we came out onto the top floor,

I tripped on a chunk of plaster that had fallen off the wall.

'Sorry,' she said, as she got out her keys. 'The maid hasn't been in a while.'

'Maybe the rats ate her.'

'The only major rodents I've seen are roving packs of developers — wondering if the time is right to pull down something fine and throw up something cheap and profitable in its place.'

'Touché.'

Feeling seedy, I followed her along the balconied walkway to a door halfway along the arm. I peered down into the overgrown courtyard as she undid the three separate locks in the door to apartment 34.

'Welcome,' she said, as the last one gave a *thunk*.

A short corridor beyond led onto a living room. Cassandra flicked a switch and three small lamps came on, shedding yellow-orange glows in the corners. There were two doors on the right-hand side of the room, a frosted glass one at the end. A single bed had been pushed against the other wall and piled with cushions. There was a desk fashioned out of cinder blocks and an old door, a set of shelves made of bricks and short planks. The walls had been painted some dark color. There were a lot of computing books and magazines and bits of computer hardware and in general quite a lot of *stuff*, but it would be hard to find an object that looked out of place or as if it wasn't designed to go exactly where it was.

'You're . . . tidy.'

She set the grocery bag down on the table, momentarily seeming awkward about having a stranger in her space. Despite her poise, it probably wasn't very long since she'd been living in a room in her parents' house. She looked around. 'Well, I guess. Do I win a prize?'

'It's just that women aren't, always. I thought they would be, but you live with a few and find it ain't so.'

'Well, then, Bill — if I may call you that — I'm pleased to have restored your retro faith in my kind.'

I felt myself coloring. 'I didn't mean women *should* be tidying the whole time.'

'Well, no, indeed. Then whenever would we have the time to cook and sew?'

I decided to shut up, and went to the bathroom. This was small but also tidy, and smelled of other people's soap. Compared to Stephanie's stash in the bathroom at our home, there was a notable lack of Women's Bathroom Stuff, and I realized Cassandra probably just didn't have the money for it. It was a long time since I'd been in the company of a woman who didn't have the money for Stuff. I splashed a lot of water on my face, which made my head feel colder but no more clear. The towel I used had a hint of mildew, which made me feel nostalgic and affectionate, too. I think it was the towel I was feeling this toward, anyhow.

Back in the living room I saw that Cassandra had opened the frosted door at the end, revealing a minuscule balcony. She'd also taken off her coat, and was holding a white USB cable in one hand and a bottle of red wine in the other.

'One of these you need,' she said, jiggling the cable hand up and down. She was wearing black jeans and a close-fitting, multilayered top made from black lace, with a scooped neck and sleeves down to her wrists. 'The other, not so much. But, like, it's your call.'

'A small glass, maybe,' I said, businesslike. 'While the phone charges. Then I'd better head home.'

She efficiently connected my phone to the battered laptop on the desk and waited until it had chirped to confirm it was getting juice. 'All systems operational. All we can do now . . . is wait.'

She poured me half a glass of wine and a full glass for herself and sat down on the edge of the kinda-sofa.

'So, my friend.'

I felt lumbering and awkward, an untidy older man in a young woman's just-so room. 'So . . . what?'

She looked up, glass in her lap. Her face was open, very pretty, and unlined. 'We've got a little time. You totally don't have to, but . . . do you want to share?'

24

An hour later, to my surprise, I'd told her quite a lot. About the e-mail with the joke, about the book from Amazon, about the fact that the police were claiming David Warner was dead when I had the evidence of my own eyes to prove he was not. We were sitting on the floor by then, our backs against the kinda-sofa, and I had been informed that, should I wish, I could call her Cass. In my defense, I'd tried both the house phone and Steph's cell again, twice. It was now well after eleven, and the world felt like it was teetering in the balance. Midnight is a feasible time to get back: I'd returned home around that time after the evening trying to meet Warner. Midnight can happen if the evening gets away from you just a little. Much later than that, however, and either you're trying to make a big and serious point, or . . . I couldn't complete the thought. That *or* led in directions that tangled and became poisonous.

'Okay, well, that's pretty strange,' Cassandra said, after thinking about what I'd told her. She poured us both another glass of wine. It was not the first refill. 'Weirdness-wise, you can tick the box.'

'Yeah.'

'But what I don't get is why your wife is so mad at you. I mean, a salacious photo book, even if you *had* ordered it . . . not such a big deal,

197

right? I'm not getting the impression she's notably uptight or a total vanilla wife, so why the spat?'

Red wine on top of beer, I'm not sure what it was . . . but I reached in my pocket and pulled out the thumb drive. 'Last night,' I said, 'I got home, and she'd been on my laptop looking for pictures I took at a friend's party. Instead, she found what's on here.'

I had been intending to describe the images, in very vague terms. Cass grabbed the stick from me, however, and was on her feet and up at the desk, slipping the drive into a port on her laptop, before I'd had time to react.

'Hang on,' I said, struggling to my feet. By the time I got there, however, the first of the images was already on-screen.

'A bad photo of a window, at night,' Cassandra said. 'Yeah — I can understand why that would . . . Oooh, oh, I see. Gotcha. La-di-da.'

By the time the fourth picture was up — the first showing Karren White with nothing above the waist — I was standing beside Cass. 'I didn't take these,' I said, about as embarrassed as I had ever been. 'But they're dated to a night when I was kept out all evening.'

'Kept how?'

'Chasing the meeting with Warner, which his assistant now disclaims all knowledge of.'

The next picture came up. 'Who's the pretty lady?'

'Her name's Karren. She works in my office.'

Then the next picture, frontal, in better focus. I was uncomfortably aware that I was standing

198

close to a young woman while we looked at pictures of another woman, in a state of undress.

'So how did these end up on your machine?'

'I have no idea.'

'And this is why you met up with Kevin?'

'I didn't tell him about the pictures, only that it seemed like someone had gotten remote access to my machine.'

'What'd he say?'

'That it was possible. Though he liked the idea of physical access better.'

'Is the woman aware of her starring role?'

'No.'

'You didn't tell her?'

'I thought I should wait until I had some clue about how to explain the pictures being on my laptop,' I said, aware of how lame an excuse this was.

'Hmm,' she said, and then ducked her head closer to the screen. 'This interests me.'

'What?'

Her hands flashed around the keyboard for a few seconds, causing small, semitranslucent windows to pop up and disappear almost too quickly to see. 'You mind?'

'Mind what?'

Then the first picture was back up on-screen. A couple of finger taps, and it jumped in size — first to fill the entire screen, then twice as large again. Cass used a diagonal movement on the track pad to scroll to the bottom right-hand corner of the image, and leaned back, cocked her head, squinted.

'Yep,' she said. 'I *am* as cool as everyone says.'

She closed the window and opened another from the folder, apparently at random. A three-quarter view of Karren was treated in the same way. 'Again. See?'

'See what?'

She tapped a key combination and the image popped down a level in resolution. She caused the cursor to circle around the date and time stamp in the corner. 'Examine the edges of those numbers.'

I looked more closely. 'I don't get it.'

'They're not real.'

'Not real?'

'The way date- and time-stamped numbers appear on digital photos is pretty distinctive. These look off. The edges are too sharp, don't have the halo. Could just be the camera in question, it does vary from brand to brand, but I don't think so. Let's check something else.'

Another key combination, and a long thin window popped up next to the image, filled with orderly lines of text. She ran a finger down it, humming to herself.

'Aha.'

'What's all that?'

'The EXIF data for the image. Let me check another.' She reopened the first image, and the side window filled with similar data. 'Bingo. My awesomeness abounds.'

'I don't understand what you're showing me.'

'E-X-I-F,' she said, spelling out the letters as if to an illiterate cat. 'That's Exchangeable Image File format to you. A way of storing metadata about a picture, in the file itself. When a digital camera takes an image, it injects pieces of information into the JPEG or TIFF, where it can be accessed by any viewer application. It will typically store the aperture, shutter speed, focal length, and ISO setting — and some will even log geolocation data in there, too.' She placed the slender tip of her finger near the top of the data window. 'And of course, basic, it will log the time and date when the picture was taken.'

I looked at the date next to her finger. Then at the numbers in the corner of the image itself.

They were different.

'Hang on,' I said. 'The numbers on the picture say it was taken midevening on the twelfth, Tuesday. But the EXIF data says the eleventh. Which was Monday.'

'That would be my point.'

'But wait . . . *wait* a minute,' I said, as it dawned. 'On *Monday* night I was out with Stephanie. All evening. From before dark. So if these were taken on Monday, then it *couldn't* have been me, and she would know that.'

Cassandra tipped her hand like a seesaw. 'Don't get *too* excited. The EXIF data relies on the camera's settings as much as the old-school time/date stamp would. If someone set the camera to the wrong date or time, the EXIF stamp will be wrong, too.'

'But I set the date and time correctly.'

'I'll bet. But you can't prove it. You could have changed it to take the pictures, then changed it back, for some fell purpose of your own. You can't use those numbers to actually *prove* when the picture was taken.'

'But *something*'s hinky with them — because either way, the two dates should be the same. Right?'

'Yes. Someone faked the date and time onto those images to pin it to a specific day and time. Which — '

She stopped talking abruptly, mouth hanging open. Slapped herself upside the head. 'Well, duh.'

'What?'

She appeared pained at her own stupidity. 'What's the word you keep seeing? *Modified?*'

'They modified the dates, I can see that, but — '

'No no *no*. Not only that, my friend. It's not just one thing being modified, or even a bunch of little things. It's an actual *mod*.'

'What the fuck is a mod?'

'Rewind. I play games, okay? Computer games, online. This has been established in prior conversation. Recall?'

'Yes.'

She looked perplexed. 'You *really* don't know what a mod is?'

'No.'

'Okay. In gaming terms, a mod is what it sounds like — a modification — but actually it's more than that. It's ontological, world changing. It's a file or patch you deploy in a computer game that alters a player's circumstances — or the world — in fundamental ways. It's an old-school idea — been around since people were playing Middle Earth text-based games back in the 1960s.'

'Alters them . . . how?'

'Depends. A weapons mod might mean that a character in a fantasy medieval universe suddenly has access to unlimited arrows, or even a gun. An environmental mod could mean anything from castle walls turning rainbow colored, to there being no trees or horses or gravity. You see?'

'I still have gravity and I do not have a gun.'

'But some things *have* changed, right? There's people who feel differently about you because of a joke e-mail you never sent. Your wife thinks you ordered a book of arty porn — not just that, but lied about it — and *not to mention* thinks you might have gotten Peeping Tom around a coworker. People see you differently, behave differently toward you, and your world ends up different as a result, in a snowball effect, and you have to play catch-up.'

I was getting there, albeit slowly. 'But who the hell would be doing this?'

'That's the question. Old college buddy? Drinking pal? Some friend who's close enough to know your life?'

'I don't really . . . have friends. Not like that.'

'*Really?* You can't think of anyone?'

I could not. I had colleagues. I had contacts. I had blogs I followed. I came up short after that.

'O-kay,' Cass said. 'You might want to get onto that. Friends, well, I hear good things about the concept.'

I was feeling tired, confused, and drunk. 'I've got to get home. Right away. I've got to show this photo thing to Steph, tell her about all this.'

203

'You do. Going to be a long walk, though.'

'Only twenty minutes to get back to the car.'

'Dude, driving-wise, you are in even worse shape than when you got here.'

She was right, of course.

'You got a number for a cab firm?'

She grinned. 'Let me ask my good friend Mr. Google.'

And she did, and got a number, and I called it, and they said they'd send a car.

In the meantime, we had another glass of wine. It was probably a kind of fuzzy jubilance that eventually had us sitting close together on the floor: mine at discovering actual evidence that I was innocent and that someone was absolutely, definitely, and for sure fucking with me; hers at having helped me get to this point.

It gets foggy after that.

I remember a call from the cab firm saying the driver had broken down or been abducted or something, and another would be sent at some point. I recall an additional bottle of cheap wine being opened. I remember trying all available phone numbers for Steph yet again. I remember — for god knows what reason — talking up my plans for clawing up the property ladder; perhaps because I thought Cass would disapprove, and I seemed to have started to care what she thought of me. She appeared to feel that my ambitions did not make me the devil incarnate.

I remember her phone ringing, and her looking at the screen and not taking the call. I asked her if it was the cab firm, and she said no, it was Kevin.

'He, uh, he likes you,' I said. I was drunk enough to think I was sounding avuncular and man-of-the-world. 'I think he likes you a lot, in fact.'

'I know. But it's not going to happen.'

'You don't want to talk to him?'

'Not right now,' she said, and settled back next to me, perhaps a little closer than before.

I remember, but by then it's getting patchy, flash images fading in and out as if illuminated by a failing strobe light of recall, getting to a point where she was leaning against me, my arm was around her shoulders. I remember her smoking, and I remember looking down as she took a drag on her cigarette, and looking not just at her hand, but at two small, pale shapes just beyond.

'Mr. Moore — are you looking down my shirt?'

'Sorry,' I said.

She looked up at me, and smiled. 'S'okay.'

'It's not, really.'

'You see me moving away?'

'I'm . . . married. And older.'

'True, both. But I'm not, like, an actual infant. I can do up my own laces and everything.'

'I know,' I said (though now I felt very ancient indeed), and tightened my arm around her shoulders, to show that I was taking her seriously.

We didn't say much more after that. I sat, content to be wreathed in her smoke, her body warm against my side as it got darker and darker in my head, and her breathing got shallower, and

205

eventually she fell asleep.

I sat there, supporting her meager weight, a still point at the center of the world.

* * *

Some time later, having half woken, she smiled drowsily at me and hauled herself to her feet. She stumbled off in the direction of the bedroom, pausing just long enough to glance back at me from the door.

I drifted back to sleep for a while, before waking again to find myself on the floor, her pack of cigarettes close to my face. Without giving the idea a second thought I took one, lit it, stuck it in my mouth, and dragged on it deep. I don't remember whether it felt good or not, or whether I even finished it.

25

At two o'clock in the morning Hunter walks into the sleeping condominium complex and lets himself into the apartment on the second story. Everything is as he left it. He walks to the couch, lowers himself down, and sits in the darkness. It is very quiet. No one is awake at this hour. Through the sliding doors at the end of the living room he can see across the central area of tennis courts. There is a light in one of the condos opposite, but it is dim, most likely there to comfort and guide a child should he or she need the bathroom in the night. Hunter watches for ten minutes and sees no one. A child sleeps on, undreaming, unaware.

He turns back to look across the room. On the wall is a canvas. Pieces of coral and seaweed have been stuck to it, along with some shells. In the darkness they look like blots of black ink against shadow. He wonders how long ago Hazel Wilkins undertook this project, a quiet and earnest celebration of where she lived, while a now-canceled TV show played in the background. These things of the ocean, once alive and in transit, are now so still they seem to deny the very idea of change, dismantling continuation and breaking the world into an infinite series of present moments.

They're there.

They're still there.
They're still there.
And so is he. He closes his eyes, and there is a flash of noise and movement in his head. He lets his skull tip slowly forward, and holds it in his hands.

★ ★ ★

He stands over the shape on the bedroom floor. This is where she ran. He is not yet sure what he's going to do about the result. He steps over her and goes to the closet, pulls the doors open. From the interior comes the smell of perfume worn on other days. Dresses, blouses, jackets hang all in a row. There is a sufficient number that most touch the next in line, but it seems to him that if he were to take each item to a different town in the country, or even the world, they could not feel farther apart from each other than they do now.

He has never been responsible for someone's death — not so directly anyhow. If it hadn't been for Hazel Wilkins, he could have told himself everything was going better than planned. He broke this woman's neck with his own hands, however, and he feels bad about it.

He turns from her closet and kicks her body, hard.

★ ★ ★

He goes into the kitchenette and makes himself a cup of instant coffee. He drinks it standing at the

208

doors out onto the balcony, far enough back that — should anyone look over — they will see nothing but shadow. It is cold in this apartment. The body in the bedroom would likely not announce its presence for a couple of days, by which time he hopes it will all be done. Hunter doesn't know how often the maid service operates, however. It could be that at 8:00 a.m. sharp tomorrow some poorly paid Mexican woman will be opening the door to this apartment. Her response to a dead body is unlikely to be restrained.

Hunter worked out pretty quickly why Warner had given him Phil Wilkins's name. Partly as the real target was already beyond his reach, but also because Warner hoped a confrontation between Wilkins's widow and Hunter would send a message to the real people Hunter is here to find. He was ready to sacrifice Hazel, in other words.

Unfortunately, Warner was right — or he will be, if people find out what happened in this condo that afternoon. It doesn't surprise Hunter that Warner would have been prepared to sacrifice someone, and he feels he owes it to Hazel Wilkins that her death not be a matter of fulfilling someone else's plan. She cannot just be David Warner's Post-it note or ploy, and so he needs to come up with some other way of letting this play out.

Which means he needs to move her body.

But first he needs to check if there is anything here in this apartment, anything from which he can learn.

It soon becomes clear that, wherever the bulk of this woman's stuff is, it isn't here. Either she's divested herself of a lot of the past, or it's stored elsewhere.

He checks the shelves, the drawers, the closets. There's nothing except the big framed photograph of her and Phil, holding cocktails and grinning on the balcony of this very apartment on some long-ago sunny afternoon. He saw the picture on his previous visit. He recognized Phil Wilkins, recognized him as someone he'd thought of as, if not a friend, then a more than casual acquaintance. Realizing that this had been a lie, even so long after the fact, was part of what led to the unraveling of his discussion with the widow. Given how many lies we tell other people and ourselves, it's funny how much those of others hurt.

On the upper story of the duplex — a small adjunct up a narrow stairway, holding a second bedroom and bathroom — he finds a storage area. This is home to nothing but a couple of suitcases, both empty. It's beginning to look as though all he's going to come away with is the names she gave him that afternoon. She tried to give them early, too. It needn't have gone the way it went, that was the worst of it.

Except . . . once he had pulled down the neck of his T-shirt, saw her read the signs and come back with recognition in her eyes, it had already been heading down a one-way road. She'd started trying to talk, to tell him things, to name

210

names, as if to unburden herself. He'd stopped listening, however.

He can still hear the sounds in his head, remember the frenzy of movement. There were a couple of moments when it seemed like it was another woman in front of him, just as old but fatter — a woman whose heart gave out. Memories leaking sideways, as they sometimes do.

At last, as he tramps back down in the living area, he spots a ruffle in the valance of the sofa. He reaches underneath and finds a laptop. Not hidden, merely stowed out of sight, Hazel having been of an era that regarded computers as machines — like a vacuum cleaner or ironing board — to be brought out, used, and returned to steerage, not tolerated as part of a room's decoration.

Bathed in the screen's dim cold light, he soon realizes that, though the pickings may remain slim, this is how the woman stored her past. There are a lot of photographs, some child having been diligent in digitizing Mom's visual history for her. He sets his back against the wall and starts to go through the files.

★　★　★

By 4:00 a.m. he has only one image pulled aside. It is a shot of David Warner with both Wilkinses, taken in some bar on an evening many years before, and it seems to Hunter that Hazel doesn't appear entirely comfortable. Warner has his arm around her shoulders and is grinning like a shark. The older woman has a fixed smile. This picture is not much help, though, as everyone in it apart from Warner is now dead.

Then he comes upon a final photograph. This has more people in it, and by the time Hunter has absorbed the content, his hands are trembling. He closes the laptop, but it makes little difference.

The image burns in his head like a flare. The photograph was taken, presumably, by the woman lying dead in the bedroom. She's not in it, at any rate, though her husband is. It shows a table in the sidewalk area of the Columbia Restaurant on St. Armands Circle. The cloth is strewn with plates of half-eaten food and jugs of half-drunk sangria. Candles and lamps are lit — it's midevening, middinner. Phil Wilkins is in the center, next to a young-looking Warner, with another two women and two men, most of whom Hunter half recognizes. They look happy and full to the brim with confidence and joie de wealth and circumstance, their shared grins, teeth, and tans impregnable as a fortress: except the couple in the middle, whose smiles look a little forced, as if there's something on their minds.

Behind and to one side of the table, at the edge of the range of the camera's flash, is another man. He's looking down as he locks the battered car he's just arrived in. He's totally unaware of the Kodak moment twenty feet away. The man is John Hunter.

At the moment the picture was taken, they didn't even know he was there. He remembers the night, however. About thirty seconds after

212

this picture was snapped, he noticed Phil Wilkins at the table, and Phil stood up and — in retrospect — took care to come over to Hunter rather than let it happen the other way around.

They had a brief conversation. Though Hunter knew a couple of the others by sight — and had met Warner a couple of times — none appeared to pay him any attention. His mind had been on other things in any event. He was keen to go meet his woman. He waved vaguely at the table and hurried away. He arrived at a much cheaper restaurant on the other side of the Circle to find that his date hadn't arrived yet, and was relieved.

He was less relieved when, an hour later, she still hadn't shown up. He eventually left alone.

Yes, he remembers this night. It was his last as a free man. It was the night before the cops found the mangled body of the only woman he'd ever really loved, and blamed her murder on him.

26

I woke with a cricked neck and a head that felt very terrible. I was sprawled on the floor, face pressed into the rug, forcing my head at a right angle to the direction it usually faced. My neck had clearly been unhappy about this for a while, and got straight onto announcing the fact now that I was awake. Opening my eyes made everything much worse immediately. The room was full of morning light streaming from the glass door onto the balcony. It smelled of ash and wine.

I blinked and focused and saw my phone lying on the floor near my head. The screen said 7:35. The panic this induced had me sitting upright, very suddenly.

Cassandra's bedroom door was shut.

I had time to feel a beat of relief that I hadn't made a *total* fool of myself by trying to follow her in there in the dead of night.

Then I noticed that the bathroom door was closed, too, and that there was now a word on it. The word was scrawled in letters that had dripped and run like spilled red wine.

The word was MODIFIED.

Someone was banging on the front door.

⋆ ⋆ ⋆

I scrambled to my feet, pushing myself upward via the sofa, meanwhile stepping on the saucer

214

Cassandra had been using for an ashtray, flipping it over, and spreading ash and lipsticked butts everywhere.

I grabbed my phone. I lurched over to the bathroom door. The letters there had not been written in wine, of course. Wine would have simply run, leaving nothing but a faint residue. These letters had dripped more slowly, viscously. The red was browner, matte where it had dried. It was blood. It had to be blood.

I pushed the door open. 'Cass?'

Just the bathroom. The shower cubicle. Water dripped from the fixture slowly. No one there.

More banging on the front door. I turned toward the bedroom. My head was pounding and I could feel sweat popping out all over my body and scalp.

I pushed the bedroom door. It opened six inches, showing me a strip of the far wall.

'Cass? You in here?'

There was no response, so I said it again, fighting against the climbing volume of the hammering coming from the front door and against the knowledge that I was going to have to go into the bedroom.

'Cassandra?'

I pushed the door farther, and took a step.

The smell of whatever perfume it was Cassandra wore. A bed, empty. The comforter thrown back. Everything covered in blood. Just so *much* blood.

There was no sign of a body, but I knew Cass could not have lost so much blood and still be alive.

All the perspiration on my body turned to ice. I stumbled back into the main room. It seemed clear I was going to have a heart attack and I didn't care. The front door was beginning to splinter around the lock. I stumbled in the opposite direction, toward the frosted glass door.

Out on the balcony it was very hot and very bright. The balcony was three feet deep, four feet wide. A rusting railing, broken brown tiles underfoot. A couple of stories below lay a patch of waste ground, once landscaped but now overrun with scrub and tilted palm trees and discarded household items dropped off the balconies on this side of the building. Those either side of Cassandra's were too far for me to hope to get to. I leaned over the railing, feeling it shift and squeak beneath me, and couldn't see how I could hope to get down without breaking my neck. This was a dead end. There was only one way out of the apartment. I stepped back into the room just as the front door finally flew open.

A woman burst in. She was wearing jeans and a black T-shirt, brown hair tied in a tight ponytail. She clocked the word daubed on the bathroom door.

'Where *is she?*'

I must have glanced toward the bedroom. She ran over, ducked her head through the door — and swore violently, in a voice that sounded close to cracking.

When she came back out I realized I'd seen her before, dressed differently. She was the waitress from Jonny Bo's. The one who'd served us on Monday.

'What . . . what are you — '

'Come with me,' she said, grabbing my arm and driving me toward the front door with enough force to almost throw me over. 'Come now. Or you're going to die.'

★ ★ ★

She herded me in front of her along the walkway toward the spiral stairs. I stumbled down them, round and round, my head splitting, and I didn't start to resist until we got down to the courtyard at the bottom, and she started to trot toward the gate.

'Who are you? Why are you — '

She stopped and turned in one fluid movement, and before I knew it had her hand at my throat, thumb and fingers gripped around my windpipe. She looked me directly in the eyes and tapped my cheek lightly — tap tap tap — with the tips of two fingers of her other hand.

'No questions. Do what I say, and do it *now*, or I'll leave you here and that will be the end of it.'

She let go of me and ran off toward the gate. I followed. I didn't know what else to do. There was a battered pickup parked in the street outside. I went around while she opened the driver's-side door. I'd barely got my ass on the seat before she stamped on the gas and yanked the vehicle in a hard fast 180-degree turn and accelerated off up the road.

After thirty yards she slammed hard on the brakes, however, staring intently through the windshield up the long, curved road that passed the condos I'd walked by the night before with a girl who . . . whose blood had since been used to write a word on her own bathroom door.

'Shit shit *shit*.'

The woman jammed the truck into reverse and pulled a long, fishtailing U-turn to hurtle back the way we'd come. She bumped up over the curb as she completed the turn and sent the side of my head cracking into the window frame. I crashed back down into my seat and grabbed the seat belt as she kept the vehicle accelerating along the last fifty yards of the two-lane.

At the end was a low gate between two short metal poles, and I'm glad the gate was open, as I don't think she would have stopped.

She swerved through the space and bounced onto the pockmarked single lane that cut away into the scrub and into the swampy woods beyond. Before long the bushes were crowding in, and the dirt road twisted back and forth to follow the contours. She'd either driven this way before or believed she had no choice, and kept going faster and faster. I saw a couple of faded and tilting real estate signs, indications that someone had tried to develop this part of Lido's southern nowhereland at some point in the last decade and given up, but otherwise nothing more than the sight of branches whipping past the window.

After a couple of minutes the road broadened a little and the trees fell away on the right to reveal the banks of a flat, overgrown waterway. I got a flash memory of a fuzzy, long-ago afternoon: of a place you could walk to if you were intrepid and had a lot of time and started from outside the Lido Beach Inn and went the long way around the shoreline, past all the motels, past the point where man had trammeled and honed — but I have no idea if that's what I was seeing now. In a flicker of trees it was gone, and then we were back into the woods.

Thirty seconds later the truck decelerated suddenly. There was a patch of dried mud by the side of the road ahead, home to old tires, an ancient mattress stained brown, and strewn with pieces of rusted metal. The woman pulled over onto this and wrenched around in her seat, staring intently back up the way we'd come.

I opened the car door and was sick.

I was glad of the acrid smell. It anchored me to the here and now for a moment, though what slopped out of my mouth onto the ground was the color of the red wine Cass and I had drunk together.

I'd barely finished before I was hauled back into my seat by the neck of my shirt, the woman's arm then pushing past me to pull the door closed.

'You done?'

Then we were in motion once more, bouncing onto the dirt road and following it farther into the wilder part of the island, the acres of scrub and forest and moss and occasional flash glimpses of stagnant water through the trees. She was still driving fast, but without quite the dire urgency of before.

The flickering of the early morning sunlight was making me feel broken and sick, and so I closed my eyes. I found it was no worse inside my head like that than it had been with my eyes open.

So I stayed that way for a while.

27

It was one of those dreams you get where you wake to find you're in the same kind of place in reality as where you'd just been in your sleep. Warner had always hated that kind of dream. They seemed to carry a message that there was no respite, no way out.

He had tried to escape his coding, many times. Drink, drugs — which work for a while but come back to bite you; business had been a form of escape, too, and that at least had made him rich. Playing the executive, playing the boss, playing the computer-games visionary, every role easier than real life — personas he strapped on every morning before he left the house. Women, too (the endless variety of their shapes, textures, and smells) ... you could escape into them sometimes.

There were the ones who went okay and ones ... who went the other way. There were different kinds of women, after all. He'd been able to keep them in separate pens in his mind. Usually. He'd long ago accepted that in reality there isn't any escape, however ... in which case what else is there to do except play your hand out?

In his dream he'd been lying on sand, his head shaded, legs out in the morning sun. The sky he could see beyond his feet was a featureless blue, and from close by came the rustle of waves running up ashore, then trickling back across broken shells. A mangy black dog walked up, turned its head to look incuriously at Warner, and then carried on past.

At first that was all, and it was a restful kind of dream, but then he realized that this was not a dream at all but a memory. He knew this beach. It was on the Baja coast near Ensenada, and he'd been there at the end of a two-week road trip across Louisiana and the vast bulk of Texas and then into dark Mexico. Many, many years ago. A trip with a female friend, a look-how-grown-up-we-are-now expedition that spiraled away into the dark.

Yeah, that trip.

He realized also that he did not feel good in the memory. His fists hurt. There was guilt, and a vertiginous feeling of 'what happens next?' Most of all there was the relentless, gnawing knowledge that he'd done something he ought not to have done: but an accompanying certainty that it had been an event that had been building within him, unavoidable.

In some people, anger dissipates. It rises from the spring and then flows gently away via gullies and streams to the ocean. In others it sinks back into the earth, finding its way back into the source, bubbling and biding its time underground before reemerging even more concentrated than before.

It never, ever goes away, and sooner or later it's going to be spent upon someone. That's just how it goes.

Was there a feeling of relief, too, then, that the event had finally come to pass? More than that

— an excitement, dark and lurid, a *breathless* excitement, a sense of a door having been opened that could never be shut again — now that you'd finally glimpsed what lay on the other side, you knew normal life was never again going to be enough?

The bulge in the front of his jeans said yes.

He let his head fall back onto the soft sand of a beach that lay thirty years back in time. But it was the beach, too, that he'd laid his head on every night ever since. It didn't matter where the pillow was, or whose, or how expensive the cotton . . . really, it was that beach on which he laid his head.

★ ★ ★

When he woke — for real this time — he realized he wasn't wearing jeans at all but blood-stained sweatpants, and remembered also, in the small hours of the night, wading out into the sea to try to get some of the mess out of them. He'd crouched there for some time until it simply got too cold. Then he had come lurching back up the beach and gone to sleep.

As he sat up he was confronted by a small child. Five, six years old, in a pair of yellow swimming trunks, a long-handled spade in one hand, a red bucket in the other. The colors seemed very bright.

The child said nothing, just stared at the adult beached here on the sand. In his gaze was a look of frank appraisal and lack of morality that

223

Warner had spent a lot of time learning to hide in his own eyes.

Yes, you look cute enough now, Warner thought, *but I bet your parents know different. I'll bet there are times indoors when you set their hands shaking with held-back violence. A six-year-old on the warpath — with its lack of care or understanding for either punishment or incentive — shows you why our prisons are full and bodies are found buried in the woods. In our hearts is a love of breakage and chaos for which society is only ever a failing brake.*

'When I was your age,' Warner said to him, 'I trapped a bird. I broke its wings in my hands and watched to see what happened.'

The child started to cry, and ran away.

Warner tried to massage life back into his face. The skin there moved, but it felt slack, dehydrated. The swirling sensation was still there at the base of his skull. It seemed miraculous now that he'd been able to make his way out of the half-built condo and to the sea. His leg felt so dead it seemed unlikely he would ever be able to move it again. Though the trip into the ocean had removed some of the smell of sweat, it had done nothing to the odor that had begun to come from the wound. There was bad shit happening in there. Someone needed to come for him, soon.

In addition to his wander out into the ocean, he had made several calls from a battered public pay phone he'd discovered around the back of the next condo along the drive. He'd been shambling slowly around the resort for what seemed like hours, a one-man zombie movie, when suddenly he'd turned a corner and found a phone attached to a wall, glowing in a pool of light.

He'd made two calls, collect.

The first had gone unanswered. As he didn't have a watch or a phone, he wasn't sure what time it was. Late, certainly, possibly very late — but the intended recipient was a cop, someone who didn't live by normal hours. So now what? He was trapped here. His leg was too badly injured for him to go anywhere under his own steam. But he couldn't stay here, either.

There was the other number he could call, but he didn't want to do that. He really didn't want to.

The panic in his guts started to grow. He had even, for a moment, thought about calling Lynn instead. He knew this was born of nothing more than desperation, however. She was just a chew toy, part of a long and complex program of self-distraction, a way of proving to himself that he could live as others did. He knew that. She could be of no help to him now, and it puzzled him that he'd considered it.

He wondered for a moment then, as he held himself upright with one hand, the handset gripped in the other (the two broken fingers in the left making it hard to hold it properly), whether he'd somehow got it all wrong. Whether he could, in fact, have led a normal life.

Too late now.

Too late by years.

Too late to be anything else.

And so, finally, he'd called the second number.

After five rings, it had picked up. Perhaps this was because the guy was on the West Coast, and three hours back in time. It seemed equally possible, however, that he just never slept. Warner had met this person three times over the last few years, and though he understood himself to be a bad man, he had immediately realized that this person was on a whole other plane. The man had been polite, even friendly at times. He had nonetheless scared Warner badly, as you might be by an alien who looked exactly like a human, and yet was something else.

'Who's this?' the voice said.

'David Warner.'

'And?'

'I've got some serious . . . problems.'

'I'm aware of that.'

'You . . . how? How do you know?'

'Why are you calling, David?'

Warner had tilted forward until his forehead rested on the rough, pebbled wall above the phone. He used a sentence he had never previously uttered in his life.

'I . . . need help.'

He explained his situation. He explained his injuries. He explained why he could not go home. Though he knew it was probably a mistake, he mentioned the heavy financial dues he'd paid every year.

The man on the other end told him what to do. He gave him a phone number, told him to leave a message as to his whereabouts, and then to keep out of sight.

226

Warner started to thank him, but realized the phone had already been put down. He called the toll-free number he'd been given, left the message, saying he would be on the beach in front of the unfinished Silver Palms development. It seemed as safe a place as any. No tourist was going to recognize him.

He put the phone back on the hook and shambled out toward the beach.

* * *

He didn't know what time it was now, but if children were up and about and looking for shells, it had to be coming up for nine. Maybe later. He hoped they'd come for him soon. He really didn't feel very well.

'I saw her face,' said a voice.

It came from behind, a point about six or eight feet up the gentle sandy slope. He recognized the speaker. He didn't turn. No point turning to face the dead.

'I saw it every night when I lay in bed. I saw how it looked when she realized how drunk you were.'

Warner let his head drop, and answered to the sand between his knees. 'She was a bar slut. A whore. She'd seen drunk gringos before.'

'But not like you. Not a man who'd get her into the back of a car, with me there in the passenger seat so it looked safe. Not someone who'd drive her way out of town and then pull off the road and stop the car.'

'Shut up,' Warner said.

'And I was just too high to do anything. Too drunk, too many joints. And fuck, David, *I was only seventeen*. So were you. How should I have known something like that was going to happen?'

'I didn't know, either.'

'Yeah, you did. I'd always thought there was ice in you, but . . . *fuck*, Dave. Do you *remember* the way her face looked afterward? What you did to it with the rock?'

He remembered. He remembered waking the next morning, on the beach, miles from the mess he'd hidden in an abandoned house — he'd tried to get Katy to help, but she was too screwed up and drunk and crying too hard. Remembered feeling sick, remembered the sense of horrified awe at what he'd done.

Remembered the erection, too.

He heard Katy crying behind him, here on Lido. He'd heard her on that beach in Mexico, too, the morning after his life changed.

Poor dead Katy, who'd looked a little like Lynn did. Katy, who he'd known since they were five years old. Katy, who if things had turned out differently could have been by his side in a totally different kind of life.

'I loved you,' the voice behind him said.

'I know that now.'

Warner knew whose fault his life was. But who do you blame, when you're the one? Who do you take it out on? You can't punish yourself — at least any more than you already do by turning your life into an endless dark carnival. So you hurt others. Not always intentionally, either. Sometimes you just lash out. Things get out of

228

control. You watch your hands act. Verbal warnings turn into violence, beatings turn into a bloodied mess.

And your dick gets hard.

Gradually, the sound of crying faded out. Not as if she'd stopped — Katy would never stop crying now — but as if something had slowly dragged her away.

★ ★ ★

Half an hour after that there was a tap on his shoulder. At first he thought it was Katy come back again, but then he realized the tap had hurt. Physically, in the real world.

He looked up and saw someone standing over him, a silhouette blown into soft-edged white by the sun.

'I've come to help,' it said.

28

Forty minutes later we were back on the mainland. When I started taking my surroundings in properly again, I saw we were heading south on the Tamiami Trail, a chunk of anonymous urban sprawl twenty minutes from downtown. Office supplies, perfunctory restaurants, copy shops, places to get your exhaust fixed, and the single-story DeSoto Square Mall. The woman was driving with negligent skill, as if this were a video game she'd played every day of her life. She appeared to be looking out for something.

'Where are you taking me?'

'Here.'

She swerved off the highway into the parking lot of a Burger King — and drove straight toward a space on the far side, decelerating only at the last minute. She snapped off the engine and rubbed her face in her hands. She rubbed hard, as if her face had done her wrong. I stared out through the windshield at a brick wall.

When she was finished rubbing, she yanked open the glove compartment and pulled out some cigarettes. She took one and tossed the pack into my lap.

'I don't.'

'You didn't. If you haven't started again yet, then you're a stronger man than I thought.'

I looked at her, nonplussed.

'You haven't noticed?' She lit up, blew out the first lungful of smoke. 'God, you're slow. Not even the table of women at Krank's last night? I forgot to cancel them. Of course that was when you were supposed to be there with your wife. The big reconciliation drink, destined to go badly wrong. And yet you wind up taking yourself there anyway. Funny, huh.'

'Who the hell are you?'

'Jane Doe, to you.'

'What's happening? *What is going on?*'

'Well, that's the question right there. Everything was laid out. Lines were drawn, walls put in place to stop it spilling too wide. The walls have not held, and this has got *way* the fuck out of hand.'

There was a word fighting for attention in my head, but to get at it I had to fight past a double image of Cassandra's upturned face. My mind hadn't caught up with the implications of what I'd seen in her apartment, and insisted on presenting her to me as she'd been in the night — cute, happy to be drinking wine and hanging out and talking about computers or whatever it was we'd been discussing when my brain had taken that snapshot. Then — *bam* — the other image dropped down like a lead curtain.

A door. Dark. A bed full of blood.

I got the word out in the end. 'Modified.'

'Yep,' the woman said, rolling down her window to let out the smoke. 'You have been.'

'By who?'

'Me. Among others.'

'The e-mail? The photo book?'

'Both, with a little help. I was also Melania Gilkyson for a couple of phone calls.'

'That was you?'

She cocked her head, and altered her voice slightly. ''I don't work for him twenty-four-seven, you know.''

'But *why*?'

She didn't answer, just stared with a flat kind of unhappiness across the lot.

'Why *have you done this to me*?'

'Because it's my job.'

'Where's Stephanie? Have you done anything to her? If you have . . . '

'No.' The woman shook her head, a concise back-and-forth movement, as if economy of motion ran deep in her bones. 'That's not on me. I have no clue where your wife is. That is one of many things that have gone badly off-script in the last forty-eight hours.'

'Were you at my house?'

'When?'

'Yesterday afternoon.'

'No. Why?'

'I called, trying to track down Stephanie. A woman picked up the phone. She said the word 'Modified.''

The woman rubbed her forehead with her fingertips and looked pained. 'Not me. Christ.'

'But you have *been* to my house. Right?'

'Why do you think that?'

'Because when I asked, you didn't deny it. You just asked when I was talking about.'

'Shit. I must be tired,' she said. 'Yes. I was

there Wednesday morning, to put the pictures on your laptop.'

'*You* took those?'

'Not me. Someone I know.'

'How did you get in?'

'I have keys.'

'*Why?*'

'Why what? There's a lot of whys here. You need to be specific.'

'Why plant the pictures?'

'Why do you think?'

'To make my wife believe I'd been spying on Karren.'

'Duh.'

'Did someone pay you to do this?'

'Maybe you're not as dumb as everyone thinks, hey.'

'Who? Why would anyone do that to me?'

'I'm not at liberty to — '

Suddenly, and without warning, I lost it. I've never raised my hand to a woman in my life, but I wanted to pull this one's throat out, break her nose, do anything and everything that would hurt forever. I needed to be sure, absolutely sure, that this woman didn't know where Stephanie was and hadn't hurt her in any way. I snapped around in my seat and lunged toward the woman's neck.

I didn't even see her hand move from the steering wheel, but then suddenly there it was, clamped around my wrist, arresting the forward movement in my arm so fast that I felt my shoulder joint twist.

'If you want,' she said, looking at me with cool

blue eyes, 'I can drag you out of this truck and do you in the lot. Right now. And I'm talking flamboyant, crowd-pleaser, playing to the gallery. Broken bones, rib kicks, with my hair down and chest stuck out so everyone sees it's a girl busting you apart. What do you say? Want to press start on that?'

I tried to pull back, but she was too strong. Her eyes held mine, unwavering. The muscles in her face and jaw were hard planes of intent, and I could feel the long bones in my forearm being pushed together. I had no doubt that she could — and would — do what she'd threatened.

I've also been in many meetings in my time, however, sat face-to-face with a lot of people who aren't revealing everything they know. I've seen what humans look like when they're trying to hide something, to present only one side of a deal, when they're playing poker with a guy they think is just a dumb-ass extra in their lives.

'You're scared,' I said.

She blinked. 'Excuse me?'

'You heard.'

'You know what, I *am* going to do it. I'm going to kick your fucking ass.'

'Not scared of *me*. I get that you're tougher than I am, okay? Big deal. But you're scared about *something*, and blowing up at me isn't going to help you solve that.'

The grip on my wrist got even tighter, then she abruptly dropped my arm. She looked away, at the brick wall in front of us. The middle fingers of both her hands moved to press against the opposing thumb. She held them there, pushing hard for a few seconds, and then let go with an audible exhale.

'I need something to eat,' she said, as if the last conversation had not happened, as if she was a friend of a friend who just happened to be in the same car this sunny Friday morning. 'Probably, so do you.'

The idea made me feel ill.

'Suit yourself.' She shrugged. 'But you need rehydrating at least, or today is going to get worse and worse for you. And trust me, your baseline of expectation should already be set very low.'

She opened her door. 'Are you coming, or what?'

⋆   ⋆   ⋆

She directed me to a table in the corner of the restaurant, sweeping the detritus of the previous eater's meal onto a tray with an oddly prissy movement before marching over to the counter. As she waited in line, she got out a cell phone and pressed a speed dial number.

The place reeked of fries and ketchup and sounded like an experimental station called 'Radio Human': people chewing, bawling out kids, talking on phones, belching, breathing, existing. I don't come to burger joints very often, for the same reason that I *do* head to the gym and read positivity blogs. Because we're supposed to. Supposed to eat right, think right, act right by the planet: the endless series of secular rituals intended to keep others thinking well of us, or keep us thinking well of ourselves. People rag on about God, how lucky we are to be getting shot of him, but He at least would throw the occasional bone, handing down a good harvest or ticket to heaven once in a while. The internal taskmaster we're working for now doesn't believe in fripperies like motivation. He/she just wants you as his bitch.

Steph and I have a ritual, though. Once in a blue moon we'll come out to an UltraBurger or Kingdom of Fries — though usually it's a McDonald's — and slum it, showing the world that we're bigger than the zeitgeist, that we can make our own choices. I suddenly realized we hadn't done this in months, however. I had been getting deep into the program. We both had. Time had been patiently breaking Steph and me, turning us into everyone else.

But now the program was breaking down, too, and the only thing I cared about was finding my wife and putting things right.

As I sat watching the woman getting closer to the front of the line — she'd finished on the phone now — I recalled how convincing she'd been in Jonny Bo's, both on the night of my anniversary dinner and the time I'd had the coffee with Hazel (who I suddenly remembered I owed a call, though I couldn't imagine when that might happen). In Bo's this nutcase woman had been slick, professional, the consummate waitress.

She could act, in other words. This got front and center in my mind and stayed, enough to make me raise my head and watch her properly, and start asking questions.

What did I actually know? I knew this woman had been involved in getting pictures of Karren onto my computer. Maybe she'd even e-mailed Janice to ask her to get a booking at Bo's, the restaurant where she'd been working, presumably as a cover. A cover for what, I didn't yet understand. So . . . I knew *some* stuff.

But I didn't know what had happened to Cass, who'd killed her, or — for the love of god — why. I didn't know where Steph was — though I hoped it had nothing to do with all of this. I didn't know why this other woman had happened to turn up — how she'd known I'd be in Cassandra's apartment. I didn't know why, after starting to drive one way, she'd turned around. Had there really been someone up the road — or was that another piece of acting, to convince me a pursuit was under way at exactly the point where I was starting to get my breath back and question why I was allowing myself to be dragged out of a building by someone I'd never properly met before?

How could I tell what was the truth?

She'd admitted she'd been involved in screwing up my life. Why should I believe that she now had another goal? Wasn't it more likely that this was another roll of whatever dice were being used in this . . . What? Game? Did she *really* not know where Stephanie was, or was she faking ignorance to bond me to her? When she came back to the table was she going to tell me truth, or more lies? Would I have any hope of being able to tell the difference?

I realized that I would not, and there were only two things that I needed to do right now:

Find my wife.

Talk to the police.

Neither involved this woman.

She reached the head of the line. The server stared at her with bovine insolence. The woman's eyes flicked up to the menu boards, as they always do, even if you know what you want. She was occupied, for a few moments at least.

I stood up. I walked at a steady, even pace to the doors. I opened them, went outside, and when my feet made it to the sidewalk I started to run.

29

What screwed me was trying to be clever. While I was sticking to sensible and semismart, I did okay. Clever was a step too far. I trotted down the sidewalk — and I was starting to get my shit together quickly, because though I wanted to sprint, I didn't, as who the hell goes haring down the street at nine o'clock on a Friday morning without evident quarry, unless they're running away from something they've done? So I trotted instead, as if in a vague hurry but no more — no need to stare, people, nothing of interest happening, just a guy doing something, going somewhere a little fast. Move along.

Soon as I could I ducked around a corner, however, and then I *did* ratchet up the pace. I'd like to say this was a conscious decision to put distance between me and the woman before she noticed that I'd gone. It wasn't a real decision, however. It just happened. I started to run because I was scared. *Really scared.* Scared of what I'd seen in Cassandra's apartment. Scared because I didn't know what was going to happen to me, or where my wife was. And scared perhaps most of all by the fact that the woman I was running away from was frightened, too. If the person who knows more than you do looks freaked out, then you'd better be freaked out even more, on principle.

Eventually I had to stop. I staggered to a halt,

gasping for air, and glanced back along the street. I'd been jacking back and forth through the blocks for ten minutes, and there was no sign of the woman on foot or in her pickup. It probably hadn't occurred to her that I would up and run, that someone in my position would turn down assistance in a time of need. Probably it was an outlandishly dumb thing to do. I didn't care. Getting away from her felt like the first sensible or active thing I'd done since my first beer at Krank's the night before — and maybe for far longer than that.

I ran a quick inventory, bent over on the corner as trucks and cars belted past me. I had my phone, with nearly a full charge (courtesy of a dead girl, but let's not think about that). I had my wallet, credit cards, and around sixty bucks in cash. That was all good news.

I was wearing a creased shirt and battered chinos, drenched with sweat. The lower sections of both pant legs sported red wine stains that dated to when the stuff had been coming back out of me rather than going in. I had a mind-fucking headache, tremors in both hands that weren't solely due to exertion, and a whole-body nausea that was getting worse by the second. This was all less good.

Then I realized I'd left my USB drive in Cass's apartment — a disk that had both the pictures of Karren on it (my only proof that I was being fucked with) and copies of letters and documents featuring my name and address — and so could be tied to me in half a second.

Things were actually worse than I'd realized.

I finally convinced myself I wasn't going to throw up, and started to move again in a ragged half trot. Halfway along the next block I found a minimarket. I bought a bottle of cold water and a pack of industrial-strength painkillers. I washed a handful of the latter down with half of the former before I'd paid for either. My stomach tried to revolt, but I kept it down.

Back outside I considered my options, keeping an eye on the street and sidewalks in case 'Jane Doe' had been merely biding her time. I couldn't get my thoughts to run straight, and the thing that kept popping up with the brightest and shiniest sign was the fact it was now coming up on nine thirty. That meant Karren would be at her desk, wondering where the hell I was. I didn't care about this from the point of view of ambition, not this morning. But still, I was supposed to be there. Insanely, I couldn't let this fact lie.

'Karren,' I said, when she answered the phone. My head was pounding so loudly I was afraid she'd be able to hear it down the line.

'Hey, you,' she said affably. 'Was wondering where you'd got to. Noticed you weren't at your desk. Turns out here you are instead, on the phone.'

Her voice was like an audio postcard from better times, bittersweet enough to make me want to cry.

'Yeah. I've, uh, I've been held up.'

'No big deal. It's like the grave here this

241

morning anyhow. You sort out your problem?'

I didn't know what on earth to say. Then I remembered that our last conversation had been about Stephanie and the mystery of her whereabouts. 'It's ongoing,' I said. 'But I have hopes of progress.'

'That's excellent. We like progress, right? So when should I expect you?'

'Little while yet,' I said, cupping the handset to mask the sound of heavy traffic. 'Got a meeting in a half hour, might as well head straight there, I guess.'

'Oh yes? Anything exciting?'

'Nah. Same old same old. I'll see you later.'

I ended the call, hearing an echo of what I'd just said. *Same old same old.* I realized I had two choices now, that two roads led from here.

Keep running . . . or not.

Either mark myself out as someone who'd done wrong — when, in fact, *I had not done anything at all* — or stick to the same old same old, in the meantime doing what I could to work out what the hell was going on — and try to stop it. Go undercover in my own life, effectively.

I was immediately sure which option made the most sense, and it had been talking to Karren that had driven it home. As far as *she* knew, my life was business as usual, the same old podcast: Longboat Key's Most Promising Realtor, Bending the World to His Will. She knew nothing about the rest: she wouldn't magically be aware of what I'd woken to that morning, just because it was smeared all over my mind.

The same applied to everyone else I knew

242

(except for the lunatic stranger I'd just escaped from). The only modifications that had taken, so far, were the ones in my own head. To the outside world, everything about the Bill Moore Experience remained cool — as other people's lives always are, from the outside, until some crisis blows the lid off and they're forced to reveal that the program's breaking down too badly to be papered over with bright smiles anymore.

My phone rang.

I didn't recognize the number, but I hoped against hope it might be Steph calling from some unknown location, as if my reaching the act-normal realization had somehow been enough to immediately realign the spheres and kick-start normality.

'Good *lord*, that was dumb,' another woman's voice said, however. 'You should win an award for stupidity. Why on earth did you run?'

It didn't surprise me that 'Jane Doe' had my number. 'Seemed like a good idea at the time,' I said. 'Still does, as a matter of fact.'

'Why?'

'I have no idea who you are,' I said, peering up and down the street, in case this call was supposed to distract me while she crept up from some unseen angle. 'Or what you've done, or whether you'll tell me the truth about anything at all.'

'Why would I lie to you?'

'That's just it,' I shouted. 'I don't even know the answer to *that* question. Without that, it's hard to judge *anything* you might say.'

There was a pause. 'That's a reasonable observation,' she said. 'But there'll come a time when you realize you have no other option, that I am your best and only hope. When you get there, call me. No guarantee I'll answer. But I might. You never know.'

The phone went dead. I decided to start right then and there on the second item of the short To Do list I'd developed while sitting in the Burger King.

I dialed Deputy Hallam. It went to voice mail. I cut the connection, hands shaking, realizing only then that I'd been intending to dump everything on him — to tell him about Steph, Cassandra, the whole nine yards.

Good idea? Bad idea? I didn't know. But I couldn't do it to a machine.

I called back and left a message saying that I'd like to talk to him as soon as possible, like right *now*. Then I crossed the road and trotted along the highway toward the DeSoto Square Mall.

30

Going home actually made the most sense, of course. What put me off that was the idea that Hallam might not be answering his office phone because he was currently sitting in a patrol car outside my residence with a huge butterfly net. I did wish to speak to the guy, but under circumstances of my choosing. I did not want to be shouting at him from the back of a cruiser into which I'd been forcibly shoved, head down, in that way you see all the time on *Cops* and that does not look cool.

I thought about calling the neighbors — at least one of the Jorgenssons should be at home — and asking if there was a cop car outside, or if they'd seen Steph, but the idea conflicted badly with the notion of trying to keep my life rolling under the Business As Usual banner.

One question kept jammering away at me as I hurried around the circular and cool and calm interior of the DeSoto Square Mall, looking for a men's clothing store.

Someone killed Cass while I was sleeping, then took her away, leaving only blood.

What kind of person does that?

My mind kept serving up flash frames of Cass standing pertly behind the counter in the ice cream store, or looking up at me and not minding I'd been glancing down the lacy front of her shirt, deep in the shadows of the small hours.

I don't know why it continued doing this. Maybe in the hope I might be able to help, to sort the images into a better order and undo what it had experienced since. I couldn't, not least because so much of my brain was occupied with worrying about where the hell Steph was, and hoping desperately that she was okay.

I went through the doors into the cool mall and headed straight into Eddie Bauer. There was no one else in the store, and clerks of both sexes converged on me in a pincer movement. I knew I must look a wreck and smell like I'd bathed in cheap wine, but both affected not to notice after it became clear that I had a charge card and was determined to use it. Six minutes later I had a replacement outfit — a classic, sober ensemble in which to turn up to work and pretend everything was okay.

I stood withstanding inane chatter from the male clerk as he bagged my purchases while the girl rang them up.

Someone killed her. Killed her, but not me.

'Excuse me?'

'What?'

The clerk was looking at me warily. 'I thought you said something, sir.'

'No,' I said. What he'd heard was an uncontrolled intake of breath, a flinch against another onslaught of internal images — and against the sudden realization that . . . I could have been killed, too. Somehow this hadn't even occurred to me before. I'd been asleep (okay, unconscious) on the floor, so out of it that I hadn't heard anything that happened. They could have sawed my head off and I'd have known nothing about it until I turned up in heaven ten minutes late.

I could be dead now. So why wasn't I? Why had someone killed Cass, but not me?

The girl behind the till made a tutting sound, eyes on the screen.

'System's real slow this morning,' she said, holding up my Amex. 'Going to try it over at the other register.'

'I'm in kind of a hurry,' I said.

'I appreciate that, Mr. Moore. I'm right on it.'

I waited, trying to keep my breathing even, trying to look like just any other normal guy. The male clerk finished packing my clothes in unnecessary tissue paper, and then stood waiting, too. There was no one else in the store to serve, and he evidently felt that abandoning me before the end of the purchasing event would be in some way inappropriate. We had nothing to say to each other. We stood like two dumb robots waiting for further instructions from higher up the chain of command.

Outside the store, women pushed babies in strollers around the interior marble walkway, looking for something to buy or to sip, disinclined to leave the air-conditioning and reenter the stretch of another featureless Friday morning of maternity. A young black guy strolled by with a mop.

Time passed, and then suddenly broke.

I should have got it earlier. I should have realized that if the card-checking system's slow, it's slow. It's a global variable within the store.

247

Putting it through another register three feet away isn't going to make a difference. And had the clerk picked up my surname just because she was an accomplished clerk, or because it flashed up as a detain-this-person-in-the-store?

A police car pulled up in the parking lot outside. I wasn't sure what was happening until I glanced back at the female clerk. She looked smug and correct: confident that the world would never turn against her, that she would always be a spectator in events like this and never the subject. As, until very recently, had I.

'Give me my card.'

'I'm advised to retain it, sir.'

It wasn't worth fighting for. I ran out of the store and hooked a hard right. Having killed plenty of time in the place over the years while Stephanie overturned Banana Republic, I knew that the mall had four sets of external doors, equidistantly placed around the circle. Would the cops have sent more than one car to apprehend someone whose charge card had been flagged? I didn't know.

About halfway round the mall I slipped on the mopped floor and careered into a stand geared to quick-sell Verizon contracts. The guy manning the kiosk had fast reactions and dealt me a smack around the ear, but I ploughed on, my head ringing.

Shoppers watched with mild interest but no more; as if I were an unusual car passing in the street, someone else's poorly behaved child. As if I were unexpected rain.

I came banging out of the back doors and into

248

the lot, to find no police car waiting. So then I was running again, as fast as I possibly could this time, and not caring how it looked — flat-out sprinting, dodging over hot asphalt between cars and sparkling windshields.

I didn't know where I was running to. Sometimes you don't have to.

You just run anyway.

31

The worst of it was that Barclay had known at the start, from day one — the first time he ever met the guy. He hadn't known it would amount to *this*, but he'd known Warner was at the wheel of a Bad News Express and sooner or later it was going to pull into a station. You could call it cop savvy — he'd been Deputy Barclay for three years by the time Warner arrived back in town — but he didn't believe it was that complicated. It was basic chemistry. It was what animals have to keep them safe among predators. It was a red-flashing-light-and-siren combo broadcasting on a silent, invisible wavelength.

It said: *There is something wrong with this man.*

And there was, though the others had never seen it. Well, they *saw* it, kind of — Hazel in particular had said things, a couple times, way back — but they didn't pay attention. They knew he wasn't the same as them, but they'd never understood just how big the difference was. Barclay hadn't, either, not until he'd got the call from one of the CSI guys late that morning.

He'd been standing outside the house having a cigarette, wondering what to do — and what to be *seen* to do — about the apparent disappearance of one of the richest men on Longboat Key. The tech team had been getting ready to ship out, having found nothing more than that single splash of blood. The senior tech said the trace was indicative of a larger quantity, inexpertly cleaned, and thus was suggestive of foul play, but no more. In those amounts it *could* just have been the result of a finger nicked while cutting a drink-bound lime. Barclay was sure it was going to amount to more than that — which is why he'd held a presence there for so long and insisted on having every tech he could lay his hands on, and the full CSI wagon outside — but for the time being, there wasn't what you'd call proof.

Then one of the younger techs had come out of the sliding doors. 'Uh, Sheriff?' he said, and Barclay noticed how the boy — previously cocky, 'Look at me with the science stuff' — looked awkward. He reached up and pushed his sandy hair back. 'We found something. It's, uh, dunno . . . you probably want to come and see.'

Barclay dropped his cigarette to the deck, thinking: *Here it is, at last.*

★ ★ ★

He followed the tech through the living area. He'd been to this house before, though the tech wasn't to know. It was a perk Barclay had received for doing his job. Not his actual job. His *other* job, the role he'd been playing for twenty-five years. Since Phil Wilkins had died, most of the group's enthusiasm had waned — not least because everyone was getting older. Life starts to seem complicated enough without screwing with the basic rules. But not Warner.

251

He wasn't going to give it up, and that was the problem. He was by far the wealthiest of them. Grew up locally, left and founded his computer-games company on the West Coast, sold it at the right time. Moved back to Sarasota, started dabbling in condo development, turned out to be good at that, too. Good at money, good with women. Good-looking. Broken inside.

Every year Barclay had said it was time for them to quit. It had been Warner who'd turned him around — just like he'd turned around the others. Not through reasoned argument, either. Barclay couldn't even claim that in his defense, though Warner was a very convincing guy when he put his mind to it. No, he'd been compromised by simpler means. Cold cash, sometimes. Also, getting invited to the kinds of events a cop wouldn't normally get near — not to mention being introduced to the kinds of women who could be encouraged to attend that style of house party, for whom the proximity of wealth (and a big bowl of cocaine) operated like an access-all-areas skeleton key. Warner's house operated a strict what-happens-in-Vegas policy. It was actually kind of amazing what a couple of nineteen-year-old girls would countenance with a grizzled middle-aged man with a gut, and when you knew the girls had been flown in for the event and would be on a plane back to Hicksville the next morning (never having learned anyone's names, and not caring), it was easy to indulge yourself. Everybody has a price. It's never so very high. It's always paid in the same currencies.

The tech led him along a wood-paneled corridor and through a door that led to a set of stairs. Barclay knew where they went — a large, temperature-controlled wine cellar built into a concrete bunker excavated beneath the house. When they'd tramped down the stairs, Barclay saw the other two techs and Hallam standing to one side.

Barclay noticed that a section of the limestone floor had a sheen to it, as if it had been recently cleaned. Hallam detached himself from the group and went to a bank of the racks on the far side of the room. He took hold of a section loaded with expensive-looking bottles and gave it a tug. It didn't move.

'Wouldn't have found it at all if one of these guys hadn't been going beyond their remit,' he said. He looked at one of the techs, a weedy, sheepish-looking guy. 'Got a little too interested in what vintages were in the racks, lifted a bottle. And dropped it.'

Hallam lowered himself to his knees, pointed at the lowest section of the rack. 'Mopping up the mess, he noticed a handle in here.'

He reached into a space that looked like nothing more than a gap for another bottle of wine, and Barclay heard a businesslike clunk, presumably a lever being turned. His heart sank.

Hallam stood back up, tugged at the rack again. This time it swung away from the wall, a four-foot section pivoting soundlessly.

There was a wide metal door on the wall behind, with a recessed handle. Hallam looked at his boss, evidently feeling that Barclay would want to take it from here.

Barclay wasn't sure he did. He believed, on balance, that he'd rather walk back up the stairs and get into his car and drive somewhere else. Maybe Key West. Or Brazil. He stepped forward, however. That's what being a cop is about. You're the guy who has to take that step, who has to open the doors that all the other people don't even want to know exist.

Behind the door, however, was another door. This was nearly a foot back from the first, suggesting a very thick wall. Barclay turned the handle, and was relieved when it didn't open.

'Locked,' he said, but he knew that wasn't going to be enough. He knew they were now into a period where they tried to locate keys for the door, and couldn't; tried to establish whether the lock was tied into the security system and under its control; and eventually wound up bringing in someone with the equipment to cut through this barrier with brute force.

We've all got that door inside. Behind it we keep the things that are personal, and what's personal to us may not be good. Either way, Warner wasn't here to stand in the way of this door now.

'Get it open,' Barclay said.

Then he tramped back upstairs toward fresh air and sunlight and somewhere private to make a telephone call to a man he'd met once at one of Warner's parties, a man who'd taken him to one side and given him a card and told him to call if — and only if — there was a problem that threatened to get out of hand and become public. All the sheriff knew about this man was that his name was Paul, and that he'd have been happy never to speak to him again.

But Barclay figured that if there was ever a day to make that call, this was it.

32

I ran/walked/lurched back into Sarasota, under skies that were beginning to cloud up fast. I took a chance and went to an ATM when I got to downtown, reasoning that if it refused me or set off a siren, I could be long gone before anyone could drive to the area to detain me. In fact, the machine simply gave me two hundred bucks, without backchat or prevarication — the process feeling magical, unforeseen.

I took the money to a nearby Gap and quickly bought new chinos and a shirt, then made another stop at the Walgreens three doors down. I changed in a Starbucks restroom, giving myself a wash-toothbrush-antiperspirant makeover and dropping my old clothes into the trash. I walked straight back out past the baristas without allowing myself to check whether they'd noticed the transformation. People seldom do, too wrapped up in their own concerns and neuroses to even notice yours. That's the kind of thing the positivity blogs yammer on about all the time, and evidently they're right. Nobody knows about your hell. They don't care. They're too busy cooking in their own.

I hailed a cab and went to St. Armands Circle. I chatted with the driver about property prices on the way like I always did with anyone. After he'd dropped me off I walked over to where I'd left my own car the night before.

I turned the AC on full and waited until it was working. When it finally got cold I started to feel slightly better, despite the fact that from where I was sitting I could see the table outside Bo's where I'd encountered Cassandra the night before. At some point in the last hour a thin film of protective scar tissue had started to build around what had happened since. Along with this had appeared something else, however: anger. She'd been a nice girl. A good kid. I didn't yet have any real understanding of what was unfolding or breaking down all around me, but I knew that it had brought about her death. And for that, someone was going to pay.

That was in the future, however. The next step in my plan — and it was a plan that had no aspirations beyond taking one step at a time and hoping I didn't fall on my face straightaway — was driving to The Breakers and dropping back into my role. Chatting with Karren, getting e-mails done. If I was 'just that guy,' then any bad things becoming associated with my life would be judged according to character. The character I wished to project. The real me, whoever that was.

Then I could get on with trying to find out where the hell Steph was, making sure she was okay, and not ungovernably pissed at me.

Before I set off, I tried Deputy Hallam's number yet again. Still no reply. I didn't leave a message. Dismissing the idea gave me another, however, and I called our home number. No reply, but I entered the key combination that allowed me to remote-access messages on the machine. I listened again to my previous messages. In the cold light of day I realized they would serve no purpose, and the last few sounded very drunk. The undertone of increasing moral indignation would also not sit well with my own lack of return to base overnight. I deleted them one by one.

But then, right at the end, I found another message. It had been left early that morning, and this time it was for me — but it was not from Steph or Hallam or anyone else I knew.

It was from the hospital.

*　*　*

Sarasota Memorial is a big white modern building with a sweeping approach and nice trees. Without the flag and the signs it could easily be a major condominium development. I ran into the main entrance and established that the ICU was on the third floor. I found an elevator. Stood in it, blinking, twitching.

I burst out into a big waiting area, sparsely occupied and decorated in the colors and shapes of expedience and calm. I went to the desk, said who I was and who I was there to see. The instant recognition this gained me just made me even more scared. The nurse said that someone would be right out, and got on the internal phone.

I pushed back from the counter, breathing deeply, trying to keep it even. I noticed a nervous-looking midtwenties guy on one of the benches, hands clasped. I was suddenly sure that he was waiting to hear about his wife, a pregnancy, an oncoming child. Maybe he had some superbad reason for being here, but I thought not. Probably everything in his life was going okay.

I wanted to be him instead of me.

A man in a white coat appeared at the entrance to a side corridor, and the station nurse pointed me out. I hurried over before he'd started in my direction.

He led me down the corridor and into a further side area, without saying anything. Toward the bottom was a portion where sections of the walls were made of glass, to allow people to see what was happening inside. He led me to one of these. I looked through.

Lying in a bed, eyes closed, and with plastic tubing going into her, was Stephanie.

* ★ *

Her skin was pale and seemed to hang off the bones of her cheeks and wrists. Her eyelids were lilac. She did not look like my wife. She looked like Steph might look like to herself in cracked mirrors glimpsed in bad dreams.

'To be honest,' the doctor said, 'we're not one hundred percent sure what we're dealing with. She arrived with vomiting, which was not a cinch to diagnose as she'd clearly drunk a lot. But then we discovered there'd been diarrhea, with blood, which switched us to looking at a bacterial infection. It seemed like this was heading into hemolytic uremic syndrome and kidney failure, which kind of made sense, though it'd be unusual given your wife's age and state of health — and there's no previous indicators of renal problems, correct? But then we started to see drops in organ function overall, to the point where we're running a slew of new tests on everything from E. coli to a couple of rare seafood biotoxins.'

He finally left a gap, as if for me to speak. I couldn't think of anything to say, and with my hand clamped over my mouth as it was, he wouldn't have heard the words anyway.

'It could be E. coli,' he said, as if that was in some way reassuring. 'We're pumping antibiotics and fluids into her and we're putting out the other fires as best we can. At the moment that's all we can do.'

She looked so pale, so broken, and very far away.

'Is she conscious?'

'Intermittently. She was awake up until about forty minutes ago, now seems to be drifting in and out.'

'I have to go in there.'

'Not right now.'

'Well, when?'

'I don't know. Maybe soon. It depends.'

'How long has she been here?'

'Since 3:00 a.m.'

'But . . . how come the first I hear of this is a message at eight thirty this morning? Why did nobody call me right away?'

The doctor glanced at his clipboard. 'The notes say your wife requested you be contacted as soon as she was admitted. Her brother said he'd get hold of you.'

I turned to look at him. 'Her brother?'

'Right,' he said, still reading. 'He brought her in. I don't want to be critical, you've got enough to process as it is, but she'd evidently been deteriorating for several hours before the guy thought, okay, there's a situation here, let's get to the hospital. You might . . . want to talk to him about that.'

'Oh, I will,' I said. 'Though I'll need to discuss a couple other things with him first.'

'Excuse me?'

'Like the fact that my wife doesn't have a brother.'

The doctor looked up from his notes. I could see him making a decision that this wasn't his problem.

'I'll be ten minutes,' I told him. 'And then I'm going to want to talk to my wife.'

When I got back out to the waiting area the guy was already trying to escape. The corner where he'd been sitting was empty. I saw the back of someone heading fast down the corridor toward the bank of elevators.

'Hey,' I shouted.

He started to hurry. I ran faster.

I got to him as he was jumping into the elevator. I shoved him in ahead, turned, and stabbed the button for the basement. He started to say something. I grabbed him by the neck and smacked his face into the wall of the elevator. I'd never done anything like that before, but it came easy and it felt good. His head bounced off the paneling and snapped back hard.

I put my face up close. 'Who the fuck are you?'

'Nobody,' he stammered.

I threw him back into the corner. 'Are you with them? Are you with that woman? Jane Doe?'

'I don't know what you're talking about.'

He looked scared now — but more than that. Wary, on alert, as if I was the guy in the wrong.

'Look . . .,' he said, but he had *guilty* written all over his face, and he didn't know where to take it from there. I smacked his head into the wall again. There was a loud *ping* and the elevator doors opened behind me.

I hauled the guy out into a subterranean corridor that was hot and semidark and smelled of chemicals, and shoved him backward, pinning him against the wall.

'Tell me,' I said. 'And make it the truth, or I'm going to hurt you as badly as I can.'

'I brought her in. That's all.'

'Bullshit.'

I pulled my fist back. I hadn't punched anyone in a long, long time — there's not a lot of call for it in professional realty — but I figured I could remember the basics if I had to.

He jerked up his hands, started to stammer.

'I don't *know* what happened to her. We were at my apartment. We were . . . just talking. Hanging out.'

Suddenly something clicked. 'You're . . . Nick,' I said. 'New guy at the magazine, art department. Golson, right? I met you at a party

262

about a month ago.'

'Right. I'm Nick. Exactly.'

He nodded enthusiastically, as if saying his name to the best of his ability was going to get him out of this situation. I smacked him back against the wall again to let him know how wrong he was.

'What the fuck was my wife doing at your apartment?'

'It was, look, seriously, it was nothing. They had this meeting in the morning. Her and Sukey, they went out afterward, celebrating. I ran into them downtown, after work. They were pretty . . . you know, they'd been in the bar quite a while by then. Sukey got a cab. Steph, uh, Stephanie, your wife, she . . . shit, I don't know. We had another drink. We wound up back at my place. I've got a studio in town. It was close.'

'And?'

'We were just talking. Magazine, work stuff. Had a couple more beers. Actually, she was drinking wine, but I only had beers. She brought the wine with her.'

'From the bar?'

'No. It was in her bag.'

'She was carrying a bottle of wine *around with her*? Are you *making this shit up*?'

'No! I don't know why she had it. But she, she got the bottle out as soon as we got to my apartment, seemed psyched about having it. Like it was 'score to her' or something. Wanted me to have some, too, but I don't like wine. And so she just kept knocking it back, and then after a while she started getting sick. I assumed it was because she was so bombed, but then she's, like, 'I need a paramedic.' I figured she'd plane out of it, but after a couple hours . . . *fuck*, dude, I didn't know what to do.'

The back of my neck felt cold. 'What wine was it?'

He looked at me like I was insane. 'I don't know — I know shit about wine. Like I said, I don't drink it. It had a fucked-up label. It looked old, I guess.'

'Where is it now?'

'My apartment. But it's empty. She finished it.'

'This ever happened before?'

He looked confused. 'Has what?'

'Have you two had a drink together before? You guys ever 'hung out' before? How often? Just how far does the 'just talking' go?'

He was absolutely still, and silent, and did not say 'dude' or fluster or try to deny anything. It could be a lot of prior hanging out and just talking had happened, it could be not. Either way he evidently realized that the next thing he said had to be right, and phrased carefully, and that was enough for me. I got my face up really close to his. I suspected this guy was too stupid and scared to tell me anything that was worth me knowing, but I didn't have time to prove that to myself. Maybe he was my wife's lover, maybe not. I could determine that from her. Right now I had a bigger problem.

'I'll be back for you,' I said. Then I hit him in the stomach, as hard as I could, and left him sagging down toward the floor as I got back in the elevator. 'Go home, get the bottle out of the trash, bring it here, and give it to the doctors,' I told him, as he crashed down onto the floor. 'Do it right now, or I'll come find you. Do you believe me?'

I saw him nod as the elevator doors closed. I stood, hands shaking, as the elevator shot back up.

33

The doctor didn't want me to go in. He made that clear. I made it equally clear that this wasn't an answer that worked for me, and in the end he said fine, but stay back from the bed and you've got five minutes max. He wanted to come in with me, but I dissuaded him. I could tell I was one step from having security called, but I didn't care. In the end the doctor stepped back, hands up, and reminded me about not getting too close.

I went and stood near the bed. I looked down. I didn't have a clue what to say, or whether she'd even be able to hear. After a minute, something dropped off my cheek and landed on the floor. I reached up and discovered that my cheeks were wet. I was feeling too many things to keep track of, and they were coming in the wrong order and out of sync. Maybe the asshole in the basement was something I should be angry or screwed up about. But for the moment there was just Steph, and she looked very sick.

'Honey,' I said gently. 'Babe, can you hear me?'

Something was making a dead, electronic noise near the top of her bed. It didn't sound like it was going fast enough, or sufficiently regular. I wasn't sure what was off about it. It just didn't sound right. It wasn't a noise you wanted to have marking your time.

'Steph? It's me.'

One of her fingers moved, and I took half a step closer. I wanted to reach down and hold her hand, but I'd heard what the doctor said. 'I'm here, honey.'

Her eyes flickered, then opened. They only made it halfway, and didn't do it at the same time or at the same pace. One started to drift back down, but she held herself together and it flipped slowly back up. She looked like a toy whose battery had run down.

'Lo, you,' she said.

Her voice was barely audible. She said something else, but I didn't hear it.

I bent closer. 'Honey — I didn't hear you.'

'Sorry,' she said. It was a mumble, still, but her voice sounded a little stronger and wetter than it had.

'For what?'

'Fucked up.'

'No you didn't,' I said, though I didn't know if this was true or not.

'Did.'

'It's . . . not a big deal.'

She nodded, or tried to, and now her gaze looked stronger. 'Is.'

'What actually happened?'

The corners of her mouth turned down, and she glanced away. She looked miserable, and my heart suddenly felt very heavy.

'Steph, it's all right. Whatever it is, it's okay.'

'Drank with Sukey. Celebrating, and I was still pissed at you, and . . . I just drank way too much.'

'And?'

'Didn't sleep with him.'

Somehow this denial made me feel worse. 'So what *have* you done?'

Her shoulders moved up a little, then back down. I guess it had been a shrug. I nodded. She watched me nod.

'It's okay,' I said. 'We'll talk about it. We'll . . . we'll get it worked out. Everything's always fixable, right? But you're not well enough right now. And there's something I have to do.'

She looked worried, and I realized what she thought I had meant, and it hurt that she looked alarmed at the prospect. 'Not to do with him,' I said dully. 'I don't care about him. It's something else.'

'Doesn't mean anything. Nick doesn't.'

'I believe you,' I said, though I was not sure. When do these things ever mean nothing? However small, they mean something. You turn to face in a different direction from your loved one, however briefly, and when you look back, everything's changed.

I don't mind, Cassandra had said, in the dead of night.

'Love you,' Steph mumbled. Her eyes looked blurred.

'You too. Rest. I'll be back soon, okay?'

She sort of nodded, but she was more than half asleep again.

I looked down at her, then set off toward the door. I had my hand out to open it when she spoke again.

'Remember breakfast at McDonald's?'

268

I turned back. Her eyes were open again.

'Well, yes,' I said. 'Of course I do, honey. That's us. That's who we are.'

She didn't say anything else. She just looked sad.

★ ★ ★

I went back outside into air that was heavy and vile and waiting for what the clouds carried above. I drove back down the Tamiami Trail, and half a mile before I reached downtown I pulled over into the lot of a Chieftain grocery store. I bought a pack of Marlboro Lights and a box of matches. I smoked a cigarette leaning against the back of the car. When I was done, I got out my phone and called Tony Thompson.

'It's Bill Moore,' I said when he answered.

'Okay,' he said.

'You know that bottle of wine I gave you?'

'Yes.'

'Don't drink it.'

'Okay,' he said again.

'You don't sound surprised to be hearing from me, Mr. Thompson. You don't sound surprised at what I just told you, either.'

'I think you and I need to talk,' he said.

★ ★ ★

Halfway back to The Breakers the skies opened. It rained so hard and so violently that the wipers couldn't make any headway against it and I had to pull over. I sat listening to the hammering on the roof of the car and looking out through the rain into a world that was the color of wet twilight.

Stephanie and I met at college in Pennsylvania. We were not an obvious fit, and it was a while before we noticed each other. She came from money, kind of: she came from a place where it had once been, at any rate. Her father had been the CEO of some big-deal corporation that got fucked by the last recession, at which point he lost everything and his pile of stock options became worthless. He did not take it well. He drank. He fucked up. He eventually came back to the land of the living, but broken right down the middle. Some people can be happy making do, living some new and smaller story. This guy could not, and Stephanie had gone from having everything money could buy to being reminded every single day of what it did not, by a man who'd become one of the living dead. Meanwhile my own dad kept selling people paint, and the store made enough for the family to get by, but never a whole lot more than that.

Eventually our paths crossed at a party in our sophomore year. It was a slow build, unusual at a time and place where people hooked up at a moment's notice and forgot each other twice as quickly. Initially we annoyed the hell out of each other, in fact, and we were too young to realize what this likely meant. Finally, drunk to hell at another kegfest in a beat-up house mutual friends shared on the edge of town, we got it.

We watched the dawn together from the

backyard, shivering under the same blanket, holding hands. We walked back into town in gray light, and when it came time to part and go back to our separate houses I let her keep the blanket. She had it for a long time. She laid it on the bed on our wedding night, in fact. Maybe she still has it, though I have no idea where it would be.

We were together after that. In our final year Steph's dad left her mom and Stephanie — left everything, in fact. He went out one day and never came back. Yes, people really do that. Six weeks later it was her birthday. The one thing her father had kept up after he stopped making much pretense at caring about anything else was Stephanie's birthday. Throughout her teens he'd always make something big of it, and even in the first two years at college he and her mom would drive up from Virginia and they'd take her out somewhere for dinner and there'd be some significant gift, and although this became compromised in Steph's mind as she came to realize that his largesse meant the household finances would be hurting for months afterward, it marked the day and was part of the turning of each year. It was her dad's love for her made concrete. I was there on the second of these, and you could tell the guy was in a bad place, but you could also see the love he had for her. It glowed.

But now he was gone. There had been no calls in the intervening six weeks, no note, no e-mail, nothing — to either Stephanie or her mom. The guy just bugged out, disconnected the line, went 404. I spent the week leading up to the day knowing Steph still believed that, come her birthday, something would happen and this bad, sad dream would end. That there'd be a card in the mail, a gift — cheap, trivial, it didn't matter to her — maybe even that she'd be sitting in the window of the house she shared with four other girls and see his car pull up outside.

The day came.

There was no card. There was no gift.

She sat in the window, and he did not come.

I wasn't with her. We were both working through college, barely scraping by. At that point I had a submenial job helping clear out the basement of a local factory, and the guy wouldn't let me take the evening off. There were plenty of other assholes, he knew, who'd be happy to step into my shoes. I couldn't afford to lose the job, and Steph knew it and wouldn't have let me. I'd given her my gift that afternoon — an inexpensive necklace and a new copy of *Breakfast at Tiffany's*, a book she loved — but had to leave her after that.

I got off work at one in the morning and walked back into town as quickly as I could. It was January and beyond cold. I'd talked to the other girls in the house and they'd said they were going to throw her a party, but either it hadn't happened or she'd declined to take part. There was only one light on in her house, and it was Steph's. Her room was on street level, had this big window in front. I stood outside and saw her at her desk. She had fallen asleep with her head on her arms. She was dressed in the best clothes she had.

She'd waited, and he hadn't come.

I was young and didn't understand a whole lot about the world, but I knew that this was dark and bad and wrong and could not stand. I stood there for ten minutes, too cold to shiver, not knowing what to do.

Then I turned back and walked home. I entered a silent house and looked around for what I could find. I knew it wasn't going to be much, or anything like enough, but it was all I had and all I could do.

At six I walked back to her street and went up to her window. She was still at her desk, still asleep. I rapped on the window, quietly. She woke up. She looked over at the window, saw it was me, and her disappointment was only momentary. I gestured at her to come over.

She did, and slid up the windowpane. 'He didn't come.'

'But I did.'

'What are you *wearing*?'

The answer was the blackest jeans I had (sadly also the ones with a tear on the knee), a white shirt belonging to one of my housemates, and another's crumpled black jacket — plus I had a tie I'd made half an hour before, from a strip of dark T-shirt.

'It's Armani,' I said. 'Really. I wrote it on the collar with a Sharpie.'

She tried to smile.

'Come on,' I said.

She climbed out through the window. I took her hand and led her up the street. It was still night-dark and when we got to Main there was nothing open yet except the place we were going. I felt kind of dumb and knew this could land very flat, but I also knew it was the best I could do and that I loved this girl enough to take the risk of looking a fool.

Finally we were outside the place.

'Bill, why are we . . . here?'

'Because we have a reservation,' I said.

I guided her toward the door. Inside the McDonald's it was deserted, though it was technically open. Only half the normal array of lights were on. A pasty-faced server stood yawning behind one of the registers.

'Bill . . . '

'Shh,' I said. The manager came out from a side door, a guy called Derek, an older student and world-class dopehead I'd worked with at a previous job and who owed me for covering him a zillion times. When I'd called him at 4:00 a.m. that morning he'd been pissed as hell, but eventually decided he'd help.

'Ma'am,' he said, in a croak that sounded like a rook with a hangover. He cleared his throat, tried again. 'Your table is totally waiting for you.'

He gestured, and Steph turned to see that the corner table in the window had two candles on it. I'd found them under the sink in the kitchen in my house. I had no idea how many years they'd been there, and one was three inches longer than the other. They had been stood upright in a pair of wineglasses I'd brought from the same place. There was metal silverware laid out, also from the house, a little bent and tarnished.

We went to the table and sat opposite each other. Derek brought us food. We ate. We talked, and when Derek couldn't let the restaurant just be ours any longer and turned the lights and the Musak on, the first song that played was Shania Twain singing 'You're Still the One,' and sometimes that's just how the world works, and finally Stephanie laughed and it was the day after her birthday, and everything was kind of okay.

That was our breakfast at McDonald's.

Back when I was me.

★ ★ ★

I didn't notice when it stopped raining. I merely realized, slowly, that it had. I called the hospital and was told that Stephanie was sleeping, and her signs were stable. I wanted to turn around and drive straight back, wait by the side of her bed and will her to be well again, but I knew that wasn't what I had to do right now.

I pulled back out into the slow, postrain traffic, and drove on toward Longboat Key.

PART III

IMMEDIATE FUTURE

Let us depart, with a kiss,
for an unknown world.

— ALFRED DE MUSSET, *LA NUIT DE MAI*

34

Warner is in a chair again, but this time it is not a hard wooden chair but one that is padded and comfortable. He has no idea where the chair is, but it is pretty warm. He is running with sweat, though he is naked, and he can smell the smell of himself around him like a cloud. He can see the mess on his thigh and it looks terrible, like mangled meat left out in the sun. He has been given something — a *lot* of something — to make the damage fade away. It has worked. The pain got on a jet plane and flew to the other side of the world, business class. He doesn't hurt at all, anywhere, even though his poor broken fingers still do not work. He feels great. He feels fabulous. He is just so fucking okay with everything, and everything is fine.

He jerks himself upright, peers around. Tries to work out where this heavenly place of comfort is. Hotel room? Apartment? The drapes are shut. The lights are low. The floor has been covered with plastic sheeting. There's someone lying on it.

A woman.

And just like that, the pressure valve opens in his heart. It's a feeling he's known many times before. How many? He doesn't know. He remembers the first, of course — he's traced through that memory already this morning. But afterward? Who's counting? He's never kept souvenirs, though many do. Since he realized he was not alone and there was even an organization, he has met men — and a woman, once — who make marks on an internal stick, who keep a little something each time, who want to be able to go back in their minds to each occasion, to savor those bright stars one more time. Not him. Once it's done, it's done. You move on, keep walking, head on down the road.

There's a noise, which confuses him. Did he make it? He doesn't think so. It was a soft, low moan. It can't have been him. He doesn't feel like moaning. He feels like singing. He feels like shouting to the skies.

The sound happens again and he realizes it has come from the woman on the sheet, and he almost whiteouts with the surge of power inside his head, and his joy is unconfined. Oh praise be — *she's still alive*.

He tilts his head downward and looks at her properly. She's dressed in a black blouse and a long skirt. Her hands are fixed behind her back with a plastic tie, and she has been gagged. She starts to move, as if she has just regained consciousness and is rapidly realizing something bad is happening. Her head jerks up, and she sees him in the chair. Her eyes open wide.

His grin feels like it's going to split Warner's head in two. He doesn't care where the woman's come from. He just knows that this time the rancid bag of shit on the floor in front of him is going to split properly, and that it will finally lance the wound in his head that has been there

280

since the nights when someone who should have placed no price on their love started coming to him and shoving her vileness in his face, smothering him in the dark, and afterward pinning him down with her sweating bulk, her face inches above his, martini tears running down her face and dropping onto his terrified cheeks as she whispered again and again: *I love you, you know that, don't you? I love you. That's why I do this. Because I love you so very much.*

It's the face he always sees when the valve opens in his head and the dam breaks — that huge, sniveling face, a face that will be smiling and perfectly normal tomorrow morning, as if what happens in the darkness of her young son's bedroom in the night is just a dream: and when Warner has done his work, it's always been the faces of the women that have borne the worst of it, right back to the bar slut in Mexico. The face has to die hardest. That revolting disguise, the lie of love, the bitter mask women are taught to use to shine darkness into the world.

'You don't have a lot of time,' a voice says from behind him. It's not Katy's voice, but it is a woman's. It sounds businesslike.

'Who's that?'

'Never mind. Check on the bed.'

Warner turns and sees what's laid across the counterpane of the king-size bed to the side of his chair. Some knives. Some pliers. A rusty spatula. A hammer. Other toys.

The woman on the sheeting sees Warner pick

281

up the biggest of the knives. She tries to scream, but the gag is tight. She tries to get up, but her ankles are tied.

'This has to happen?' Another voice, a man's. It sounds familiar.

'It's writ,' the woman replies. 'Now shh.'

Warner isn't listening. Warner is wrapped in delight. Oh, look at the way she moves. Watch — no, *watch properly*. The hair, already matted to her face with sweat. The muscles in her legs, twitching, trying to run in every direction at once. See everything that is revealed when a woman isn't pretending to be graceful, when she's reduced to an animal full of shit and blood. Warner can smell her.

Oh, thank you, Lord, for putting such things into the world. For putting them there and for blessing me with the knowledge of how they can be enjoyed. I'm sorry I have questioned you occasionally. I apologize for pretending sometimes that this is wrong. It's not wrong. It is unbelievable. It's the point of being alive.

'Enjoy,' the woman says. 'It's the last time.'

Warner hears the two people leave the room and close the door. He gathers his will and strength, staggers to his feet. He's laughing, or crying, he can't tell which and he doesn't care. His injured leg gives out and he drops onto one knee beside the woman on the sheet, who is now absolutely still, rigid, terrified, eyes like full moons.

Supporting himself on one quavering arm, Warner leans over until his face is directly over hers, until his tears drop down onto her face.

'This is going to really hurt,' he tells her.

His voice is too slurred for her to make out the words, but he can see in her eyes that she's understood.

35

I parked outside Shore Realty. I had a choice of spaces. Karren's car wasn't there, and I couldn't tell whether I was relieved or not. It gave me time to plaster a grin across my face and pretend everything was okay. I also didn't have to decide immediately whether to say what had happened to Stephanie when Karren asked about her, which she would. Two hours ago my plan had been to present as business as usual. Now the idea seemed ridiculous.

Janine was inside, sitting at her desk, frowning at her computer. She jumped when I entered.

'Oh,' she said breathlessly. 'It's you.'

'Who did you think it would be, Janine?'

She blinked at me.

'Seriously,' I said. I felt light-headed, angry, and scared. 'We get a lot of psychos dropping by? You got a few sharpened stakes hidden ready in your desk drawer?'

'I don't understand.'

I took a deep breath. 'Never mind. Where's Karren?'

'Well, she didn't say. But she got a phone call a couple hours ago and went out to meet with someone, so it's probably . . . '

' . . . a client, yeah, okay.'

I walked past her, wondering if I should just turn around and get on with my real reason for being at The Breakers. With Karren at a meeting for who knew how long, there was no point me being in the office. Without anyone to pretend to, everybody's life feels dark and strange — the perpetual make-do chaos that exists in our heads — and I didn't care what Janine thought about anything. So what did I do? Leave? Wouldn't that look weird? Did I care? Would Janine even notice? As soon as you ask what 'acting like normal' involves, the question explodes in your face. I felt arbitrary. I felt lost. I felt like a player in a computer game who'd wandered off track into a subarea from which you could spend the rest of your life trying to escape — but which had never had any bearing on the overall mission. Whatever that was.

'You okay, Bill?'

I'd ground to a halt near my desk, and had apparently been staring at the wall. I glanced round and saw Janine's concerned, bovine face.

'Yeah,' I said. 'Monster headache, is all.'

This was true, and I felt a tiny bit bad when Janine dug in her drawer for some painkillers, and found some, and insisted on getting me a glass of water from the cooler. There was something nightmarish about the length of time she took over this, mangling the first paper cup, filling the second with extreme care but then spilling about a third of it on the way over. Sure, I could sweep past her and push my way out of the office — but if I did that, could I come back? Finally the water was accepted and given thanks for and drunk.

Then something struck me. 'Why are you even here on a Friday?'

'Oliver's taken Kyle out,' she said proudly. 'Like, a Dad's day? And I was at home and I thought, well, there's so much stuff I *still* don't have a clue about on the computer, why not come in and go through it? Friday's always quiet — could be I might get some stuff done.'

I was surprised. A couple days ago I might even have been impressed. I responded as if I was still that person. 'Good for you. By the way — you keep all your e-mails, right?'

'Of course. I mean, I lose a few, but you know.'

'Could you find the one where I asked you to make that reservation at Jonny Bo's?'

She looked wary. A lot of computer-related things made Janine look wary, or confused. 'Well, probably. But why?'

'I want to check a tiny thing. No biggie, just a technical issue. Could you find it, forward it back to me? Actually, to my home e-mail address?'

'Sure. I know how to do that now.'

'Great. Oh, shoot — just remembered something I gotta do. Back in ten, okay?'

★　★　★

I was kept waiting in reception for twenty minutes. In the meantime I called the hospital to check on Steph again and was told that everything was the same except her 'brother' had brought in the remains of the bottle of wine she'd been drinking. It had been sent for testing.

The thought of the guy brought a twist to my stomach, but I was glad he'd done it. I didn't know what I was going to do about that situation. Right now it wasn't my highest priority, but at some point it probably would become so. Real life comes due in the end. You can't just focus on work. You can keep scribbling on separate Post-it notes and shoving them in drawers, but sooner or later every real thing comes to its moment on the great To Do List of Life. Probably it came down to what this 'friendship' amounted to. I hoped it wasn't much and took solace from the fact that the guy had only been at the company for five or six weeks. It couldn't be *that* serious, surely. I didn't know whether to be sad or worried or angry. I didn't know how much of the situation could be laid at my door, either, for failing to provide some thing or things Steph felt she was lacking. It is a bitter shame we're so much better at imagining perfection than life is at providing it. The perfect evening, perfect weekend, perfect house . . . Our minds effortlessly serve these images up, and so we write fairy tales in our heads, and they're always so damned bright. The world meanwhile digs in its heels and prevaricates and stalls — yet we believe the universe is so much bigger than we are, bursting full of potential wonders, and so we'll denigrate and underuse the good things we have on the basis that there's better out there. There probably isn't. The best life you can have may be the one you've already got. This fecund imagination of ours is just The Dark One's voice, cajoling, promising. Some gods might fight back by giving us lives that run closer to what we'd like, but ours doesn't operate on the letter-to-Santa model. He wants our respect because he's God — not for being nice or merciful or any pansy-ass crap like that.

And as I sat there, I did kind of pray, something I hadn't done in a long time — since back when I thought of myself as William rather than Bill. My mother was a lapsed Catholic, and prayed once in a while. I know the tune, that's about all. I tried to hum it. I felt sick and light-headed, and Cass's face was still appearing in front of my inner eye on a regular basis. I was trying not to think about where her body might be and had given up attempting to imagine why anyone would have done it.

I kept remembering, too, that my thumb drive was still in her apartment, and each time this made my stomach flip as if someone was turning it with a red-hot fork. I shoved all this to the side as best I could, however, and sent up a prayer for Stephanie.

I have no idea where it went.

* * *

Finally the guy behind the desk nodded at me. I went over to the elevator and took it to the fourth floor.

I knocked on the door to the Thompson apartment, and it was opened by Tony immediately, as if he'd been standing behind it. It could be that I was judging everyone else by how I felt, but it seemed to me he looked a lot older today. Older and tense and deep-lined around the eyes. The eyes themselves were flat, and despite the speed with which he'd opened the door, he didn't seem in any hurry to invite me in. Behind him I saw Marie on the big white couch, arms folded.

Eventually Tony stood aside. The bottle of wine I'd presented him with was on the coffee table. It was unopened. Tony didn't sit, and didn't invite me to, either.

'So what's up, Bill?' Marie asked.

I'd only been directly addressed by Marie on a couple of occasions. I had always found the experience unnerving. She'd gone full-bore on the figure-over-face school, and the planes on the latter were harsh and unforgiving. Even in her youth it would have been a countenance to be admired rather than enjoyed: the bones were big and asymmetric, arranged as if to withstand impact rather than inspire attraction. On the other hand, I'd seen this woman in her sixties beat Karren soundly on the tennis courts in front of a small crowd, and I was pretty sure Karren hadn't been playing politics.

'I bought that bottle along with one more,' I said. 'Someone took the other from my house. They drank half of it. They're in the hospital and very sick. I don't know if there's a link. But it's possible.'

'Tony said you bought the wine on the Internet.'

'Yes. I heard him mention it, thought it might be nice to see if I could track it down for him.'

'To curry favor with us.'

You could have held the sneer in her voice in your hand. You could have fed it. You could have kept it as a pet. 'Yes.'

'How precisely did you get hold of it?'

'I already told Tony. I found a wine forum on the Web. Put up a post.'

'Did you use your normal e-mail address?'

'Of course. Why?'

Marie and Tony looked at each other. 'So that's how,' she said.

Tony nodded, with something that looked like relief. 'Which means it wasn't necessarily aimed at us. Just a throw-out. A random spike in his life.'

'Yes. Though . . . ' She had a thought, and turned back to me, frowning. 'What did you actually say in your post? Did you *say* you were looking for the wine as a gift?'

'Said I wanted to do someone a favor, which is why I was keen to track it down and willing to pay well.'

She took a long drag off her cigarette, looking at me through the smoke. Her eyes were the same color. 'That's . . . less good. Come on, Tony — who else could Bill have wanted to suck up to?'

'What's going on?' I asked. 'Can you just tell me?'

Neither seemed to hear. Both appeared deep in thought, gazing out of different windows. After a moment, a question of apparently trivial importance struck Marie.

'Who drank the wine?'

'Stephanie,' I said. 'My — '

'Wife,' Marie said. 'I know. Pretty girl.'

Something inexplicable happened to her face, and she pursed her lips together.

'What the hell was that?' I asked.

'Excuse me?'

'Seriously,' I said. 'I tell you my wife is in the hospital, and you have to bite down on a *smile*?'

'Rather her than me, don't you think?'

I stared at her, and I remembered something Hazel Wilkins had said when we'd met for coffee a hundred years ago: *Self-centered. Dangerously so.*

Tony picked up on how angry I actually was. 'Bill — I'm sorry to hear about your wife. Do they have any idea what was in it?'

'Not for sure,' I said. 'But they were talking about E. coli. The bottle's at the lab now.'

'How on earth would he get hold of E. coli?' Tony asked, but he wasn't talking to me.

Marie shook her head. She wasn't looking so pleased with herself anymore. I was brutally glad. 'Probably wasn't him,' she said. 'He will have tasked one of his little helpers.'

'Wouldn't one of them have said?'

'No. They're *his* helpers, not ours. Always have been. Which is why I said — '

'Who?' I said, infuriated at being treated as though I wasn't there. 'Who the hell are you *talking* about?'

The phone on the coffee table rang — the sound sudden and jangling and harsh. The Thompsons looked at it. It kept on ringing. Finally, after about six rings, Marie leaned forward and picked it up. Listened.

291

'Okay,' she said. 'Thank you.'

The change in her face was remarkable. She stared up at her husband, suddenly looking about eighty years old.

'Get rid of him.'

Tony took my arm and led me to the door. His grip was hard and strong. 'Look,' I said, but by then I was outside in the corridor. The door closed behind me.

I didn't walk away. A beat later I heard Marie's muffled voice.

'Hazel's disappeared.'

* * *

As I stepped out into the sun I saw Big Walter the maintenance guy standing in the middle of the lot. He had his cap in his hand. He didn't look right.

'You okay?'

He looked at me. 'Don't know,' he said. 'You know Mrs. Wilkins is missing?'

'I just heard. But she could just be out somewhere, right?'

He shook his head. 'I was just up there. Melda took me. I been in that apartment many times, fixing things. Tidiest damned condo I ever saw. Now it looks like someone was looking for something, got mad when they didn't find it. Clothes ripped, furniture on its side, everything broken all over.'

'Well,' I said, backing away. 'I hope it turns out all right.'

It was weak. I didn't care. I headed over to my

292

car. I was done here. I was going. I wasn't sure where. Probably back to the hospital.

As I was unlocking the car I heard footsteps and glanced up and saw someone heading quickly in my direction. He looked familiar, and I realized he was the guy I'd seen the day before, the maybe prospect who'd been wandering around looking up at condos.

'Hey,' he said.

Something happened that was fast and hurt, and then everything was red black.

36

My eyes were open. I found myself in a field of gray white space, every particle in slow, rotating movement, like a flock of pale birds in flight. This kept trying to resolve into something in particular but evidently didn't know what that might be. I blinked, and fell into myself with vertiginous nausea.

I could smell dust. Concrete.

I rolled onto my side. I was lying on something hard. And gritty. And gray. Some of the grayness was closer to my face, a flat plane stretching out from my cheek. Other parts were farther away, like blocks. The far side of these was a patch of different colors. A vivid, blurry orange, and a kind of pale beige. This gave me something to focus on. I blinked again, more deliberately this time, and concentrated on the patchwork. The colors wavered, and then abruptly snapped into something I could recognize.

Hazel Wilkins.

I sat up fast, and my head swirled away from me again, making my gorge rise.

'Easy,' a voice said. 'Take it slow.'

Hazel was sitting against a cinder block wall about ten feet away. She was wrapped in an orange blanket. She wasn't really sitting, though. She'd been propped. Her head tilted away from her neck. She looked gray, too. She looked small. She looked dead. I'd never seen a dead person before, but Hazel looked really dead.

I woozily jerked my head around toward the source of the voice. A man was sitting with his back against the other wall. He was the guy I'd seen in the parking lot of The Breakers, the one who'd said, 'Hey.' Dark hair, flecks of gray. His gaze was calm but attentive.

'So the name's William Moore, right?'

Arrayed on the floor in front of him were my phone, my wallet (the contents removed and lined up in an orderly row), my car keys, and the pack of cigarettes. These piles occupied four out of five points, a neat semicircle. The last was taken by a handgun.

I tried to speak and it came out as a wet click, like a foot being pulled out of mud.

The man reached to the side, picked up a small plastic bottle of water, tossed it in my direction. I got nowhere near catching it. My hand hadn't even made it off the floor before the bottle bounced past. I turned and saw that a few feet behind lay the remains of a broken chair in the middle of what looked like a patch of dried blood. A few pieces of canvas strapping were nearby. The water bottle had come to rest in the middle of all this. I decided I'd do without it.

I looked up. Above was half a floor, some big windows covered with tarpaulins. 'Where is this?'

'Lido.'

'How did I get here?'

'Pushed you into your car and drove you out. Amazed I got away with it, to be honest with you, but I guess I was owed one piece of luck this week.'

I couldn't not look at Hazel any longer. 'Did you kill her?'

He was silent. I thought that if he hadn't, he'd have been quick to say so, and so that meant the answer was yes. I'd never been in the same room as someone who'd killed someone. I didn't know what, once you've killed one person, there was to stop you from killing a few more afterward — especially if you're the kind of guy who props a body in the corner while you have a chat with a man you've just kidnapped in plain sight.

I didn't know, either, whether you talk to people just before you kill them. I really hoped not.

'Did you . . . did you kill Cass also?'

'I have no idea who that even is.'

'A girl.'

'Wasn't me, anyway. When did it happen?'

'Last night.'

'You know what time?'

'Not exactly. Very late.'

'She mean something to you? You two going out?'

'No,' I said, and we had not been — but the word collided in my head with the memory of us sitting on the floor, and came out wrong. 'Just someone I knew.'

'Right.' He looked at me, as if reconsidering something, then stood up and walked over. I was glad to see him leaving the gun where it was.

He squatted down in front of me, pulled something out of the pocket of his jacket, and held it out where I could see. It was a photograph, six by four.

'Know any of these people?'

The print looked very new, but the picture hadn't been taken recently. The colors and hairstyles gave that away. It showed a bunch of people around a restaurant table. I started to shake my head, but then I flashed on the location — one of the sidewalk tables outside the Columbia Restaurant on the Circle — and then started recognizing faces, too.

'Guy in the middle is Phil Wilkins,' I said. 'I think so, anyway. I only met him a couple times.'

I couldn't help glancing at Hazel as I said this. For almost all the time I'd been in Sarasota, she had been defined by her continued existence after the death of the man she'd loved. As of very recently, that was clearly no longer the case. I realized that this made her position propped against the wall look more peaceful than it might have done otherwise.

'Yes,' the man said irritably, 'I killed her. But it was an accident. I want you to know that.'

I stared at him, not knowing how much of this to believe, if any. 'Okay.'

'Got no reason to lie to you,' he said. 'So. The others in the picture?'

'No idea who the younger guy next to Wilkins is,' I said. 'But on the left, the man with the blonde, that's . . . I think that's Peter Grant. I'm pretty sure. He owns Shore Realty. Where I work. And . . . Christ, okay, yeah, the couple on the other side. I know them, too.'

'Tony and Marie Thompson.'

'What *is* this picture? Why have you got it?'

The man stowed it back in his pocket. 'Funny

297

thing,' he said, though all levity in his manner had disappeared. He looked tired, and pained, and not like a man for whom things were going well. 'Reason I picked you up is you'd just come from seeing the Thompsons. I figured you might be able to help *me* pay them a visit. We'll work on that. But now I'm thinking we may have a lot more in common than I realized.'

'What do you mean?'

He reached a hand up to the neckline of his T-shirt and pulled down the front. There, scrawled onto the top of his chest in letters that looked more like a series of knife slashes, was an old, amateur-looking tattoo. A single word: MODIFIED.

My reaction must have been plain to see. He grunted, let the material flip back up again.

'Woke up one morning to find that,' he said. He fetched the bottle of water, handed it to me. 'I'd been drugged, I guess. Couldn't remember anything about getting home the night before. I had bruises up my sides, scratches on my arms that looked like they'd been done by someone's fingernails. Long nails, like a woman's. I took a shower, put some peroxide on my chest, tried to get my head straight. Half an hour later, a police car arrived. You know a cop called Barclay? He still around?'

'Yes,' I said. 'He's the sheriff.'

'Figures. He was a deputy back then. He arrested me.'

'What for?'

'I said to them — look what's happened here, guys. Someone's tattooed a *word* on me. They were not interested. They didn't care when I said I'd seen the word before a few times in the previous weeks. Barclay accused me of starting up an insanity defense. Said I'd had the ink done myself. That was so ridiculous that I got frustrated and took a swing at him, and soon after that I was handcuffed in the back of the cruiser. Thing is, I'd met the guy before, and I knew he was a good cop and a decent guy. He just wasn't listening that day.'

'What did they arrest you for?'

The man went back to the wall, sat down. He picked up my pack of cigarettes, took one. 'You mind?'

I shook my head. I took a drink of water as I watched him light the cigarette.

He frowned, looked at the tip. 'Haven't done that in a long time,' he said. 'Not sure I like it anymore.'

'For what?' I asked him again doggedly. 'Why were you being arrested?'

He shook his head. 'Been and done and not your business. I want to hear what's been happening to *you*.'

So I told him. I didn't see any reason not to. I could have got to my feet and run, I guess. I wasn't tied up. I might have been able to find my way out of the building. He didn't seem to bear me huge ill will, and so he might not have picked up his gun and shot me.

But, you know, he might have.

Added to which, this was a man who might know something about what had been going on in my life. He'd already admitted he'd killed the woman in the corner, and so it seemed unlikely he was a cop. It didn't make it impossible — but it didn't make a whole lot of difference anyway. I hadn't done anything wrong. I had to keep reminding myself of this, but it was true. The weird thing is that if you know you've done nothing wrong but the bad stuff keeps happening, you're actually in a worse position than if you're a bad guy to start off with. If you *know* you're doing wrong things, then you can choose to stop. You *know* what to lie about, what to hide.

But how can you stop trying to be you? How can you put an end to living your normal life?

I told him about the cards I'd received. I told him how my e-mail account had been hacked and an online order placed in my name. I told him it seemed that someone had intercepted a shout-out on the Web for a bottle of wine, had obtained one, poisoned it, and sold it to me — maybe in an attempt to get at the Thompsons. I told him the cops wanted to talk to me because of weirdness over the whereabouts of some guy who'd vanished — although not completely, as I'd seen him yesterday evening, long after the cops had started investigating his apparent disappearance.

He seemed to react in some way at that part, but said nothing.

I told him that I'd woken up that morning in a girl's apartment (an apartment that, if he was telling the truth about our current location, could only be half a mile from where I now sat) to find a word scrawled in her blood on a

300

bathroom door. I told him that an unknown woman had then burst in, driven me away, and that I'd escaped from her soon after she started telling me a lot of stuff that didn't make any sense.

He listened to it all, his eyes never leaving my face.

★   ★   ★

Finally I stopped, not because I'd run out of things to say but because my head hurt and I'd lost track of what I'd already told him and what I had not.

'Don't know who the guy you saw last night was,' he said eventually. His voice was quiet and flat. 'But it wasn't Warner. That much I know. At that time he was still tied in the chair on the floor behind you.'

I swallowed, my throat feeling dry. I'd seen the bloodstains on the floor. This probably meant that Hazel was not the only person this man had killed. The disquieting thing was that he looked just like anyone else. You think there must be some kind of sign, a badge of darkness or aura of the killing kind. Evidently not. Some people have murdered other people; some people get overly pally with coworkers of the opposite sex; some people can read French fluently and while away their lives selling house paint. Unless you catch any of them in the act, you're not going to know. Our essence is the stuff other people don't know, the things we hide . . . which means that no one ever has

301

the faintest idea of what's really going on.

'Didn't kill him,' the man said, contradicting my thoughts. 'Had a mind to. He was the one person I was absolutely prepared to go down that road with. But . . . he escaped.' He held out the picture to me again. 'Guy you didn't recognize? That's Warner, right there.'

'That's not the guy I saw.'

'Can't help that. I blame myself. When I left him last night, I told him the cops were taking an interest in his house. I was just fucking with his head. Only thing I can think is he pushed himself off that ledge up there, still tied to the chair.'

I looked up. 'Christ.'

'Right. What's going to make a man do that?' He closed his eyes, rubbed them. 'Shit,' he muttered. 'I got to get my head straight. There's too much new information floating around. Got to integrate.'

We sat in silence for five minutes, interrupted finally by a buzzing sound. The man frowned. It took me a moment to realize what we were hearing, too. I only got it on the fourth ring, when I saw that my phone was starting to migrate across the concrete floor.

'It's on vibrate,' I said.

The man looked at the screen. 'Still not used to these things. Somebody called Hallam. Who's that?'

'He's one of Barclay's deputies.'

'You want to talk to him?'

'Are you serious?'

'I can trust you not to be unhelpful about discussing your whereabouts, right?'

302

He picked up his gun, watched my face to check I'd got the message, and brought my phone over to me.

I hit the answer and speaker buttons simultaneously, uncomfortably aware that the man was now walking toward a point where he'd be standing behind me.

'Hey, Deputy,' I said, acting out a role in a drama called *Everything's Okay, and a Man with a Gun Is Not About to Shoot Me in the Back of the Head, Probably*. 'Thanks for calling back.'

Hallam's voice came out of the tinny speaker sounding a little breathless. 'Where are you?'

When I'd tried to get hold of him earlier, I'd been about to tell him everything I knew. Now I decided to stick to facts of current relevance.

'On Lido.'

'I only just got your message. You sounded freaked out. Is your wife still missing?'

'No. I know where she is now.'

There was a pause, and I heard the sound of a piece of loud, grinding machinery being used in the background of wherever Hallam was. 'She okay?'

'She's fine.'

'Get yourself back to The Breakers,' he said, sounding distracted. 'Do it now.'

'I will,' I said. 'But you know the falling-down apartment block at the end of Ben Franklin Drive?'

He raised his voice against background noise. 'What? Yeah, I know it. What about it?'

'Go there. Look in apartment 34.'

'Why?'

'Just do it.'

I ended the call.

There was silence from behind me. I waited maybe thirty seconds — long, treacly seconds — before deciding that, if he was going to blow my brains out, I'd at least like to be facing him when it happened.

I turned slowly from the waist.

He wasn't there.

37

Hallam barely heard the last few sentences with the Realtor. Despite him flapping his free hand at the guy with the angle grinder, the asshole kept on cutting around the lock on the door they'd found in the Warner basement. Every other route had been exhausted, and after dead-ending in his attempt to talk to the sheriff, Hallam had given the go-ahead to move to quick and dirty solutions.

The noise from the doorway behind him abruptly changed in tone and pitch and then cut out, accompanied by the sound of something falling to the floor.

'We're in,' the guy said.

★ ★ ★

The second door was as heavy as the first, and Hallam had to lean his full weight against it to get it to move. It opened onto pitch-darkness. The air that seeped out was cool. He reached his hand around the side of the door frame and slid it up and down. No switch.

'Get me a flashlight,' he said.

He took a step into the space in the meantime. It remained colder than an enclosed space should be, which suggested it was as climate controlled as the rest of the building. It was almost perfectly odorless, too, although after a moment he detected something, a low, acrid note, and sniffed hard. The noise rebounded flatly.

'Here,' the remaining tech said, and Hallam took the flashlight and turned it on. At first all he could make out was rebounding white light. Once his eyes readjusted, he got that he was seeing tiles. He turned back toward the doorway and played the lamp along that wall until he spotted the switch, positioned an unusually wide distance from the opening. He flicked it, and three banks of fluorescent lights came on in unison.

'Oh,' said the tech, sounding relieved.

A low-ceilinged room, twenty feet deep by sixty feet wide. The ceiling, floor, and four walls were tiled in white, orderly rows of nine-inch squares. It was entirely empty, not a single object to be seen. There was something eerie and a little inhuman about the space.

Hallam didn't share the tech's assumption that this meant the matter was at an end, however. This space had been laboriously dug out of the sand and bedrock of the island prior to the house being built. You didn't go to that much trouble and expense just for this, nor did you temperature-control or ensure its cleanliness at some recent time with bleach — a process the tiling could have been designed to make easier.

'We're not done yet,' he said.

* * *

306

They walked methodically across the floor, a few feet apart, looking down. They did it in five passes. They saw nothing, no sign of suspicious substances, no splash of blood to echo the one discovered in the kitchen two days before. If Warner had been killed or wounded here, someone had cleaned up after himself very well.

At the far end they stopped. The tech had visibly started to relax. Hallam hadn't. His mind told him it was just the notion that you didn't go to this much trouble for a big white room. His heart, or stomach, had more to say. It could hear something. It was a sound he remembered from when his mother had taken him on a trip to visit relatives up in Canada. It was one of the few times he and his mother had spent quality time alone, and it was a happy memory but for one thing. They spent a week in a town called Colindale, a couple of hours north of Toronto. It had been cold in a way he'd never experienced before or since — wind chill taking it below minus ten most days. One afternoon, when cabin fever set in and Mrs. Hallam decided she either had to get away from her sister for a few hours or risk intersibling bloodshed, she and her son had spent a frigid afternoon trying to find something of interest on Colindale's short main drag. Eventually they'd wound up in the church, a hulk of architectural nullity that was distinguished that day by having a lot of oil heaters turned up high.

Hallam's mother wandered, arms folded, looking at the things on the walls and checking her watch. Her son, mollified by the promise that once they'd warmed up he'd be taken to eat a slice of pie in the diner, stood in the center of the church and waited fairly patiently for time to pass. After a while he realized he felt something. A sensation that felt like a sound. He turned, looked around. The only other person present was his mother, now at the far end by a notice board. There had been a priest around, but he was nowhere to be seen.

'Mom,' he called.

'Yes?' Her voice floated back to him as if from a greater distance than the building could circumscribe.

'Did you just hear something?'

'Only you.'

He stood it for five minutes longer, then gained permission to wait outside. It was cold as hell, especially after the stuffy warmth of the church, but he preferred it. Half an hour later, with feeling beginning to return to his fingertips and a big slab of chocolate fudge cake inside him, he would have been hard-pressed to say why the church had made him feel uncomfortable.

In the twenty years since, however, he'd recalled this feeling from time to time, almost exclusively when work or daily life caused him to be inside some kind of religious structure. He'd developed an explanation, electing to believe that it was merely what remains in buildings when people are quiet in them for long periods: the residual silence of prayer, an accretion of contemplation — and also of intense emotion in the process of being mollified, sidelined, shoved aside: the sound of all the voices that are trapped in people's minds. The power of grief, escaping like a heat haze from heads lowered in reverence before some putative god.

He'd never mentioned this theory to anyone, of course. But that's what he was feeling now, and it was much louder than he'd ever heard it before, and it did not feel like an echo of anything like calm.

★ ★ ★

He walked to the center of the room, glanced from side to side, got his bearings. Far as he could judge, this room went the width of the house. The plots along this stretch of the key were relatively narrow, which is why the houses were deep. So ignore the side walls for now. He returned to the back and headed to the far left corner side. The tech watched him, looking puzzled.

'Go to the other side,' Hallam told him. 'Right into that corner. Stand a yard back from the wall.'

'And then what?'

'Shuffle toward me, a tile width at a time. Keep looking at the wall.'

They did it together. After a couple of steps their movements locked in time, and it began to sound as if they were engaged in a slow dance in an empty hall, moving toward each other in a pas de deux. Hallam pushed this out of his mind as long as he could, but then heard the sound of the tech sniggering.

'Shh,' Hallam said, though he was half laughing himself. 'This is serious.'

That just made the tech laugh out loud. Then he stopped. 'Hang on,' he said. 'I think I see something.'

Hallam went over. 'Where?'

The tech ran his finger up a vertical line of grout between two columns of tiles. 'You see?'

'Nope.'

'Every other line I've seen is about the same. Like an eighth of an inch gap. This looks smaller.'

Hallam saw the guy was right — though he would have never noticed it himself. Guess that's why some people make good techs. He felt around the wall either side of the line. After a minute he started pressing harder.

A moment later, there was a click. A section of tiling slowly bounced back half an inch.

Hallam heard an exhale. He wasn't sure whether it was the tech or something else. He got his fingers around the edges of the door and pulled it back.

A corridor lay beyond, perhaps thirty feet long. Two doors on the left, a single one at the far end of the other side. They stepped into it together. They became enveloped in a silence so loud that they could hear each other breathe. They opened the doors, one by one.

The first held what could have been pieces of gym equipment, but for the straps. A short rack on the wall held a few tools that would have seemed more suitable to a workshop.

Screwdrivers, short saws, a hand drill. There was a long mirror on the side wall.

The next room held two sofas, positioned so as to be able to watch through the one-way glass, and a good deal of video equipment. They came out of the room together and went, slowly, to the door on the other side.

This was much heavier than the others, and when it opened a burst of freezing air escaped and a sound like the flapping of wings.

The tech made some kind of a noise.

Hallam stared past him at the things hanging from a hook in the center of the room. The plastic had a frosted texture, presumably from the refrigeration. They looked like body bags. All were empty, now.

He reached out and pulled aside the flaps of the one nearest to him. The inside was smeared with dry, frozen blood. He looked more closely and saw indentations in the plastic, at about head height. They looked like teeth marks.

As if someone had been hung in one of these things, not yet dead, and had tried to bite their way out.

'Okay,' Hallam said quietly, acutely aware that what he did now would govern the rest of his career. 'We need Barclay right away. I'm going to go find a signal and call him. You're going to stand at the doorway in the wine cellar and let *no one* pass. And we talk to *nobody* until the sheriff says so. Got that?'

The tech tried to speak, could not, nodded instead.

38

I waited an hour in the street outside the gates to Cass's building. Hallam didn't show. I didn't know what else he had on his plate, but I believed that what I'd said should have been enough to get most cops to come take a look. Maybe he just didn't give a damn.

A clot of pain was attached to the back of my skull, mingling badly with the lingering effects of the previous night's drinking. It was making the world hot and bright and unreal. I called the cop's phone but got routed to voice mail again. I didn't leave a message. Fuck him.

I noticed I had an indicator saying that three Facebook 'friends' had sent messages, presumably updating me on what passed for their news. Fuck them, too. The idea that I'd care about whatever was going on in their lives — that I'd ever cared, or pretended to — made me want to laugh out loud.

I'd sat absolutely still after finding he was no longer behind me, convinced he'd moved to some position I couldn't see, the better to pull the trigger in safety. I gingerly got to my feet. I took some tentative steps, still half believing they were going to be my last. I darted forward and swept up my wallet and car keys. I made my way through the half-built structure until I found a thick plywood door. I stepped out into the glaring sun and a mothballed building site, and

312

walked across it to the road. My car was parked there.

When I'd stood on Ben Franklin Drive for five minutes and watched vehicles drive past and a few tourists stroll by, I finally began to believe that the guy had simply gone. I limped along the road to the building where Cass had lived, and waited. In the meantime I'd checked on Steph and was told she was sleeping.

So now what? I realized suddenly that there was something I could do, and I should probably have thought of it before. I didn't *want* to do it, but it'd become clear that I was no longer living in a world where what I wanted counted for much. It would also be, in its own horrible way, the smart thing to do. For once.

I hurried over to the big metal gates, pushed them open, and went inside.

★ ★ ★

When I got to apartment 34, I hesitated. Getting my USB drive back, thus removing the evidence that I'd been in the apartment, was critical — even besides the importance of having copies of the pictures — so I could try to prove to the cops that something was going on. I was going in, no question. But still, I took a moment.

Then I turned the handle. I did so in a firm, even fashion — and pushed the door open, stepping out of sight as soon as I was sure it was on its way. Nothing happened. Nobody came running out, nobody fired a gun.

I cautiously stuck my head around. The door

313

hung open, revealing the corridor beyond, bleached out by the light from the glass balcony door at the end.

I walked down into the living room. Before I stopped in the middle of last night's cigarette ends, near the two empty wineglasses, I already knew something was different. We ignore smells a lot of the time. We're all about what we can see and hear. But before either of these cut in, part of my brain had caught onto something else. The place didn't smell like Cass anymore.

I looked at the bathroom door. It was a little chipped and could do with a lick of paint — but it no longer had a word daubed on it.

I turned on the spot, being careful not to knock over the nearest glass, and stepped carefully over to the bedroom door.

It was here that the loss of scent was most obvious. Whatever it was that Cassandra had worn, probably something cheap, it had gone. The bed had been made, too. Not excessively neatly, either, but exactly how it might have been made by a girl in a rush, setting the room vaguely to rights before hurrying out to a shift she was already running late for. I pulled the comforter back. The sheet underneath was white, a little crumpled. It could not have looked more normal. It was not soaked with blood. It was not suspiciously clean.

Back in the living area the effect remained seamless. A low-rent apartment the morning after two people had made a night of it. Only one thing had been erased from this space's experience — whatever had happened to Cass.

I'm not dumb. I didn't doubt my sanity for a second. I knew what had happened. Somebody had cleaned it up, removing all evidence that a murder had taken place — a murder that had been finessed and staged for my benefit.

Suddenly afraid that the cleanup had extended further, I went over to the desk. My thumb drive was still sticking out of the USB port on the side of the laptop, thank god. I stuck it in my pocket.

I took a few steps and sat heavily down on the sofa. I was relieved, terrible though that may sound. Cass was still dead — but I was now the only person who knew this. The evidence had disappeared. Whatever the world and its authorities might want to grill me over in the future, a murder scene was no longer one of them. I'd told Deputy Hallam to come meet me here, but now there was nothing to see.

I wondered — was that *why* he wasn't here? I couldn't imagine the cop being involved in what was happening, but . . . what if his absence hadn't been caused by his being otherwise engaged? What if he hadn't come *because he knew there was nothing to see?*

I shook my head. It didn't make sense. Or at least I had no evidence for it, and I needed to stick to things that I had some reason to believe or I was going to lose track of everything, including my mind.

I realized that there was actually one other person who knew what had taken place here, and I believed the time she had spoken of had now come. I got out my phone, found her number in the INCOMING log.

'So,' Jane Doe said, when she answered. 'Does this mean you're ready to listen now?'

* * *

I was waiting out on the walkway when I saw her pickup park down in the street. It was a little after five and the air was softening. I was out there watching in case Hallam turned up. I was out there to smoke. I was out there because being in Cass's apartment was making me feel wretched and confused.

The woman walked quickly across the courtyard below without looking up, and I heard her feet pattering up the spiral staircase. The rhythm was even and fast. When she arrived at the third story and strode up the walkway she wasn't even out of breath.

'Fancy seeing you here,' she said, though her face was pinched and she looked wired. 'What the hell happened to you? You didn't look great this morning, but now you truly look like shit.'

I turned and walked into the apartment. When we reached the living area I stopped and looked at her.

She looked back at me. 'What's your point?'

'Look in the bedroom.'

'No need,' she said. 'I trust the guys I put onto it.'

'Pardon me?'

'When you did your dumb split-and-run from Burger King this morning? This is what I was organizing.'

316

She stuck her head around the bedroom door, appeared satisfied.

'Her smell is gone,' I said.

'Solvents. Blood is a bitch to clean up. They did it right, though, if all you're noticing is a lack of something else. Seriously, what happened to you? You really don't look good.'

'I got hit on the back of the head,' I said. 'I woke up in a disused building within a few yards of a dead woman. There was a guy with a gun. I thought he was going to kill me, but then he disappeared.'

'What guy?'

'Don't know. Never offered me his card. He was very informal during the entire encounter. All I know is he killed a woman called Hazel Wilkins.'

'Fuck,' she said urgently, but not in surprise. 'What happened to him? Where'd he go?'

'Don't know that, either.' I remembered full well what had happened when I'd lashed out at her in the lot of the Burger King — otherwise I'd have done it again. 'Listen, is it *all* going to be on a need-to-know basis? If so we're heading quickly toward another parting of the ways. Either you talk to me or I'm leaving — because there's other people I want to speak to.'

'The police are not going to be able to help.'

'That's not who I meant.'

'The guy,' she said. 'What did he look like?'

'Slim. Strong in the upper body. Early fifties. Ed Harris with hair.'

'His name is John Hunter,' she said. 'I don't know what he told you, but you'd be wise to disregard it. He just got out of a stretch in jail for murder.'

'He's already killed again,' I said. 'So that doesn't tell me much I didn't know.'

'Look, I don't have the details, but I know he's a very bad man.'

'Says who?'

'One of the people who employed me.'

'Employed you to fuck me up? Why would I trust them? Or you?'

She pulled out her cell phone. Hit a few buttons, waited, and then held it out to me. 'Recognize this guy?'

I saw the face of a middle-aged man, not too slim, dark hair swept back. 'David Warner.'

'No. He's an actor. His name is Daniel Bauman.'

'Well, he's the guy I met in — '

'I know.'

I opened my mouth, shut it again. I realized that Steph and I were in Krank's pretty often — and it was all too possible that a stooge could have been told to go there, perhaps even night after night, and wait until a chance came to talk to me: at which point I could be lured on the promise of the sale of an expensive house. It was bait I'd be bound to take.

After which . . . everything else followed.

The actor calls the office. He gets Karren instead of me, plays that out for the initial assessment (about which he doesn't care), then insists on dealing with me direct. This appeals to my vanity and I'm ready to be convinced to come out to the house, prepared to be left

318

waiting and eventually stood up — setting me up for photographs that make it look like I've been peeping at my coworker . . . except that the photos hadn't actually been taken that night but several days before. In preparation.

'How do you know this guy?'

'I hired him. Have I just watched you work out why?'

'To pretend to be David Warner, to provide a window during which my whereabouts were unknown and in which I could have taken those pictures of Karren White.'

'Good for you. I'd get Bauman on the phone to confirm all that to you, but he's not picking up. Which is . . . worrying me a little.'

'Who are you? And don't give me more of the Jane Doe crap — I don't care about your name. I mean *what* are you?'

'I'm administrative support,' she said. 'Edge work. Cleanup where required.'

'Are you some kind of cop?'

She laughed, a short, sad sound. 'No. Ex-army. Left with skills that aren't valued in civilian life. I bummed around for a while, getting in trouble. Then I was recruited for this.'

'Which is what?'

'I get paid to provide a buffer between certain situations and the real world. Containment, and holding up the scenery. Once in a while I play a part, like being a waitress at some lame-ass restaurant for hicks made good. Have you *really* got no better idea of what's going on?'

'I got modified,' I said.

'Bingo.'

'Then what?'

'The plug got pulled.'

'And you don't know why that happened, or why Cass got killed or by who, and that's why you're scared.'

She cocked her head. 'Well, well. Maybe you aren't that dumb at all.'

'Oh, I'm dumb enough. But here's something else you don't know. The guy who coldcocked me? He showed me an old photo of a bunch of people. One of them is now dead. Tony and Marie Thompson were in the picture, too. He evidently wants to talk to them real bad. I think maybe he's on the way to do it right now.'

The woman blinked.

'Sorry,' I said, with bitter satisfaction. 'Should I have mentioned that before?'

39

Ten minutes later we were driving fast back up toward St. Armands Circle. She'd made me wait in Cass's apartment while she went out onto the walkway and made a call. I heard her raise her voice. I gave it another minute and went out. She was gripping the railing, looking down over the entropy spreading over the courtyard below.

'I don't need this shit,' she said. 'I could just vanish, right now.'

'So why don't you?'

'Expiation,' she said. 'Heard of the concept?'

'No.'

She smiled in a sour, unattractive way. 'Not much call for it in the condo-selling business, I guess.'

'You want me to Wikipedia the word? Or you could just drop the condescension and talk in straightforward sentences. We asshole Realtors can do that at least.'

'I'm done with this,' she said. 'I thought I'd be okay with it, but I'm not. It's wrong. And for that, and for other sins to be taken into consideration, I have not yet done what I should have, which is bug the fuck out.'

'So just tell me what the — '

'I'm not telling you shit. I'm going to kick you up the chain of command, and then I'm done.'

She parked on the Circle, in one of the spaces around the central park. She started to walk away, and I, good local citizen that I am, noticed that she hadn't remembered to pay for parking even though there was half an hour before restrictions ended. I told her so.

She smiled in possibly her most patronizing way yet. 'I have immunity,' she said.

I'd assumed that once we got here we'd be heading to the Columbia (perhaps because I'd seen the place in the picture the man with the gun had shown me), but in fact she set off across the central area.

'Jonny Bo's?'

She didn't answer. She strode across the road and straight over to the restaurant. She didn't enter the sidewalk cafe area, however, but went around the side, toward the staircase up to the restaurant — where Steph and I had our anniversary celebration what seemed like a month before. There was a young woman standing behind the welcome desk at the top. She appeared not to recognize the woman I was with, at first, and started fretting about reservations. The woman just pushed right past her.

'Hey — '

'Drop it, babe.'

'Hang on, shouldn't you be *working* here tonight?'

'I resigned. Didn't I say?'

It was early yet for the first sitting, and the restaurant was only half-full — couples looking at menus and trying not to whistle between their teeth at the prices. The person I still half thought of as a waitress, Jane Doe, whatever her name really was, wove straight across the room and into the corridor leading to the restrooms. She walked past both without slowing, however, making for a door at the end, which I hadn't even noticed before. There was no marking on it, not even a sign saying PRIVATE, which figured. Say nothing, and most of us are too dumb to question anything. There was a little keypad on the side panel, painted in the same color as the wall. The woman rapidly tapped out a six-figure number, and the latch clicked.

On the other side was a narrow staircase, turning sharply to the right. I followed her up, but abruptly stopped halfway when I saw her reach into the back of her jeans and pull a handgun out from under her shirt. Something happened to her posture, too, becoming looser, rangier, as if readying for sudden decisive action. I let her go up the last set of stairs by herself.

She got to the top, where the wall stopped, making space for a half-height divide in expensive-looking wood. She turned, looking into a space I couldn't see, holding the gun low in her hand where it couldn't be seen by whoever was on the top floor. She glanced down at me, gave an upward nod, and disappeared from view.

I went up the remaining steps, wondering if it wouldn't be better to turn around, go find my car, and drive back to the house to grab anything that seemed necessary to starting a new life somewhere else.

But I didn't want a new life. *I wanted my old one back.*

That meant I could not run.

At the top I stuck my head cautiously up over the divide. I saw a big open space that ran the length and width of the building. A handful of couches, shabby chic, angled for discretion. A few dining tables with pert little chairs. A couple of big skylights made it light and airy. Artfully battered floorboards, paintings that were well above the usual local standard. At the back was a waitress station, to one side a discreet dumb-waiter.

The fabled upper dining room, I guess. And at the far end, three people I recognized. The Thompsons and Peter Grant — my boss.

They turned to look at me as if I were a low-echelon waiter bringing an undesired check.

★ ★ ★

Peter Grant watched me walk up. A week ago it might have seemed cool, encountering my boss in this locale. The guy who would have found it so felt like a previous incarnation of me, however, one long dead and unevolved for the present circumstances.

'Sir,' I said.

His gaze was cool and unreadable. Not unfriendly, exactly. But not friendly, either.

'I still think this is a bad idea,' he said, not to me, and then left. Nobody said anything to cover the sound of his feet going down the wooden stairs.

Meanwhile the woman I'd come with took up a position on the side of the room. Her feet were planted apart, her hands together at her waist.

Her gun had gone back to where it had come from, but I didn't think it would take her long to retrieve it should the need arise.

'What does he look like?' Tony asked me.

'Who?'

'Don't play dumb,' Marie said. 'I agree with Peter. I don't think this conversation should be taking place. Rise to the occasion or we'll kick you out right now.'

'Fuck you,' I said.

'What does he look like?' Tony asked again. He appeared to have ignored the entire exchange.

'Assuming you mean the guy who hauled me out of The Breakers, he's . . . just a guy. Dark hair with touches of gray. When I saw him he was wearing jeans and a white T-shirt. Early, midfifties. But I don't know.'

'He's fifty-three,' Tony said absently.

'You know him.'

'Yes, we did.'

'He appears to feel more warmly about you guys. He actually seemed very keen to renew your acquaintance.'

'What did he tell you?'

'He showed me a picture.'

'A picture?' Marie's beady eyes were on me through a drifting cloud of smoke. The cigarette looked like it was held in a large bird's claw, but I noticed for the first time just how thin the wrist supporting it was.

I nodded through the big window. 'Outside the Columbia. You plus the Wilkinses and Mr. Grant. And David Warner. Looked like you were all having a high old time.'

Tony kept pushing methodically forward. 'Jane says he killed Hazel Wilkins. That you saw her body.'

I glanced back at the woman at parade rest on the side of the room. She kept looking straight ahead. 'She's really called Jane?'

'I have no idea,' Tony said.

'Yeah, he killed Hazel. He admitted it, though he didn't seem proud of it. He had the body there, in the corner. And he'd done something to David Warner, too.'

This had them both far more interested. 'Done what?'

'I don't know. The place where he took me had blood on the floor, and a broken chair. But he said Warner had escaped.'

'Did he mention anyone else? Names of the people he's working with? Accomplices or partners?'

'He didn't seem like the kind of guy who needed any.'

The Thompsons looked at each other.

'No,' Marie said firmly. 'It can't just be him on his own. He was a loser. Was then, will still be now. He can't be doing all this by himself.'

She turned back to me. 'Anything else? What else did he say to you?'

'Not much, but he showed me something. About his body. Someone had carved a word on it.'

'We're done here,' Marie said, turning away.

I was aware that Jane whatever-her-name-was had started to listen more closely.

'He woke one morning with no recollection of

326

what had happened the previous night,' I said. 'The night that photograph outside the Columbia was taken. And the cops turned up at his house soon afterward and arrested him for murder.'

'Take him away,' Marie said to the other woman. Jane didn't move. 'Did you hear me?'

'I heard.'

'So — are you going to do it?'

'No. I want to hear you answer his question.'

'He didn't ask one.'

'Yeah, he did,' Jane said. 'I'll repeat it for the hard of thinking. It went something like: 'What the fuck?''

'You're fired,' Marie said.

'Excellent,' Jane said. The gun was back in her hand now. 'That means I don't have to be polite to your beat-up old face anymore, or do what you say, or put up with you acting the grand Southern belle the entire time. And now that I'm here on my own reconnaissance, let's put it another way; *answer the fucking question, bitch.*'

'Jesus,' Tony said distractedly. 'Marie, we don't need this right now.'

His wife turned her head smartly toward him, but suddenly it was Tony who seemed the stronger of the two. Marie looked old and a little frightened.

Tony moved his hand out toward hers. It didn't reach, but something passed between them.

Marie blinked, disengaged from the argument with Jane as if it had never happened.

'Bill,' Tony said, 'we've got a situation. You've

gathered that. You're a bright guy. David Warner has been a, well, not a friend of ours, but an acquaintance, over a long period of time. Now he's disappeared, or is dead, and we're hearing disquieting things about a cellar under his house.'

'What kind of things?' I asked, aware that — wrongly, as it turned out — this was a house I'd thought I was going to help sell.

'It's not relevant,' Tony said. 'The key matter is that we're running a little scared.'

'Join the club,' I said.

Tony smiled thinly. 'I guess you've hit on it there.' He breathed out, rubbed his temples. 'I'm going to tell you this because I'm done with it, and because I think you're owed. It can't go any further. Understand?'

'Tell me what?'

'It was just a game.'

40

'Phil and I knew each other since we were kids,' Tony said. 'We were born here when it was known for fruit and Ringling and squat else. Phil went to college up in Tallahassee. I traveled, tried a bunch of different things before I went into construction. Phil became one of those management guys, always moving on, troubleshooting a company and then jumping onto the next thing. We kept in touch and would meet up every now and then and chew the fat. I came home before he did, started my business. Eventually Phil made enough money and headed back, too. Marie and I were getting initial development for The Breakers up and running. He helped put some of the financing in place, and he and Hazel decided that instead of getting some big house they'd buy into our resort. They bought three condos, and we started hanging out again. Peter Grant was an old friend, too, which is how he wound up handling sales. It tied together. We all made a lot of money. Then some night, I don't even remember when, we . . . started playing again.'

'Playing what?' I asked.

'We'd had this thing we did in high school, with bits of paper, leaving clues around the place. Telling a kind of story. Like those Murder Mystery weekends, where you go to an old house and some actors put on a show, with a script

329

that's part worked out ahead of time, part improvised, and the guests try to figure out who killed Professor Whoever in the library with a wrench. When we were all back in town together, it just kind of started up again. Marie would plan some scenario, see if the others could work out what was happening.'

'It was just a dumb game,' Marie said again. She sounded defensive. 'It would have stayed that way, too, except for that asshole Warner.'

'How does he fit into your group?' I said. 'He's much younger than you guys, surely.'

'He is,' Tony said. 'He grew up here, too, but none of us knew him from before. He'd been out West for ten years, came back with a lot of money, and started to push his nose into the condo business. We were always going to run into each other. He's not hard to get on with. At first. We introduced him around. He fit. And after a while we let him know about the game, and he was all about taking it to another level. It was him who had the idea of pulling the games off paper, changing it from being just a long bullshit session over bottles of wine into something that actually happened out in the world. He was the guy who made it real.'

'How can you make a game real?'

'By introducing real people. First time, we just messed with some guy a little — a nobody who worked in a restaurant we went to over in town. It's closed now. It was arranged that some cash went missing in such a way it could only be this guy. He lost his job. We put some other temptations his way. He took them.'

He saw me staring at him. 'Yeah, I know,' he muttered. 'David came up with ideas and we went with them without thinking too hard about the implications for the person whose life was being modified. We got too wrapped up in the game, even back then, the first time.'

'Plus, you know,' Marie said, 'it was fun.'

'Fun,' I said, staring at her.

'Yeah,' she said. 'I'm sure you've heard of fun. It's what people can do when they don't have to waste all their time worrying what everyone thinks of them.'

'It was just small, though,' Tony said hurriedly. 'After the guy started to spin out of control we pulled the plug, smoothed everything over. It was Hazel who bailed first.'

'Always thought she was better than the rest of us,' Marie said acidly. 'Had her moral high horse saddled up and ready to go.'

Tony held up his hand to head her off. 'I found the guy a job in my company afterward, much better paid than he had been before. He worked for me for seven years before he moved upstate to be with his kids. We let him know what had happened. He actually helped us out on a couple of later games. There was no harm done.'

'Really?' I said. 'Like there's no harm done if people think you've sent racist e-mails, or if wives think you've ordered porn or taken photos of coworkers.'

'There's . . . some harm done, I admit that.'

I walked to the window at the end of the room, looked down over the Circle. Every time

331

I'd done that in the last five years, I'd been looking at it hungrily, as a place I wanted a piece of. Right now it just looked dry and hot, a mirage on a barren sand bar.

'How does Hunter fit into this?' I asked. I couldn't fail to listen, but I didn't want to spend the rest of the afternoon on what was becoming obvious.

'We were playing a game a year,' Tony said. 'Each time someone would get their . . . well, they'd get stirred around. Hunter was just this guy on the fringes. He'd been in town about nine months. A handyman type, jack-of-all-trades. He did jobs for Peter on a few of the properties that Shore managed. Thing was . . . David had this old girlfriend. A woman he'd known when he was young, anyway. Did some waitressing, bar work. Smoked a lot of weed, drank too much — you know the type, the keys are full of them. I'd seen her around over the years, propping up this bar, serving behind that one, slumped over a table with a pitcher of beer — and I was real surprised when it turned out she and David had a connection. I was having a drink with him one time in Bradenton when she came in. The look she gave him was kind of . . . weird. But he went right up and said hi, and she was on the edge of the group after that.'

'Because you all wanted to fuck her,' Marie said.

'I did not want to fuck her,' Tony said mildly.

'This going to take much longer?' I asked. 'See, my wife's in the hospital. And I'm not enjoying being around you people.'

332

'Hunter and Katy met, somehow. David didn't like it. He started to stir us up over it, did a little digging. Eventually it turns out Hunter's not everything he appears. Ran with a bad crowd when he was back in Wyoming, was maybe involved in a few burglaries, including one where an old woman died. It was natural causes, apparently, but it happened under duress. He was never tried for it, and had straightened out his life since, but . . . he just seemed like a good target for modification. Or so David said. To get him out of town.'

Tony hesitated. 'But then one afternoon David told us something that was a lot more worrying. He said Katy was trying to blackmail him. Not just him, either — the whole club. She'd been around us for a couple of years by then, and this was back in the eighties. We were younger, played harder. Drank a lot, did a lot of cocaine, had parties where . . . stuff happened. We weren't as discreet as we should have been. Then one afternoon Katy buttonholed Marie.'

'She was drunk,' Marie said. 'She came right up to me on the street. She said she had tape recordings of the group talking about the game, had been carrying a Walkman around for the last couple months. That she also had photos of our . . . recreational pursuits. She thought she'd been real smart. She became abusive. It was very embarrassing. She evidently believed that we were going to bankroll her and her white trash boyfriend so they could go off and start a new life.'

'I said we should pay her off,' Tony said. 'Phil

and Hazel said the same. But . . . David had another idea.'

I turned from the window. Tony and Marie were standing at an angle to each other, as if to not hold some past event between them. Jane was watching now.

'We didn't say yes,' Marie said.

'But we didn't say no.'

'And Katy died,' I said, 'and it got pinned on John Hunter, and he went to jail.'

'David handled all that,' Tony said quickly, as if relieved not to have to recount the event itself. 'We had nothing to do with it. And this was *the only time* anybody died. Until then it had just been messing with people. Spreading rumors. Planting stuff, to see what happened. It was entertaining, that's — '

' "Entertaining"?' I said, feeling my fists bunching at my sides. I looked at Jane. She didn't meet my eyes, looking down at the floor instead.

'I know how it seems,' Tony said. 'And we all knew it was *wrong,* we all got that — but by then it was too late. Hazel talked about going to the cops, but we knew that couldn't happen. We couldn't go down for something we hadn't done. So we talked her out of it.'

'But you stopped playing the games?'

'For a while. But David . . . David just kept pushing. He loved the ones where we got inside someone's head. He got off on messing with people's lives.' Tony shut his eyes momentarily. 'David was fucked up, bottom line. It became more and more clear. That's why Katy had been

334

wary of him, and thinking back, I knew that's what the look she gave him in the bar that first time had meant. She knew him when they were teenagers, maybe knew things about him that we didn't. I didn't understand a lot of this until it was too late. We said there could be no more deaths. And there weren't. But David kept ramping it up, year after year. The games had become the main thing he cared about. And each time it happened, the games got bigger and more complicated. David started to bring in hired hands to run the show in the background, like your friend over there.'

I glanced at Jane again.

'She's not my friend,' I said.

'There were larger casts each time. Longer lead-ins. More and more ornate. It got . . . it got a little out of control. And . . . look, Bill, maybe you'd have been the same if you were part of the group. You're an operator, right? I've seen that in you. You know what you want, you're going for it. You're all about trying to bend the world to fit. You'd have enjoyed the games, too.'

'No,' I said. 'I wanted to be someone, yes, but I'm not like you. And so now one of the people whose life you *fucked up* decided to come back and make you all pay, right?'

'That may be so.'

'Good. I wish I'd known all this when I met him. I'd've shaken his hand. So — is that all? We done?'

Tony shook his head. 'It's not that simple.'

'You don't think you deserve what's coming to you?'

335

'That's not what I meant,' he said. 'There's a death on my conscience, always will be. Katy was a waster, but she didn't deserve to die. But I mean *that's not what's going on right now.* That bottle of wine you gave me, and the one your wife drank. How long ago did you buy those?'

'I can't remember,' I said. 'A month. Probably closer to six weeks when my post went up asking around about it. Why?'

'It wasn't part of the game.'

'What do you mean?'

'We don't know who set that up. We weren't even started on this year's game six weeks ago, and the scenario was always initially sketched out by Marie. You'd been picked as the target, but nothing else had been put in place. And a month ago Hunter was still in jail.'

I didn't know what to say to that.

'There's something else going on,' Marie said. 'As soon as David went missing, we pulled the plug. Called Jane, told her to cease and desist. But it didn't stop. Someone else is playing a different game.'

'Who?'

'We don't know. My guess is Warner.'

'Why would he? I thought you guys were close.'

'We were,' Tony muttered. 'But the last couple years, it seemed like he was getting tighter and tighter wound. I started to distance myself. There's a chance he found out about a big condo deal Peter and I cut him out of. Marie's theory is that he decided to pull us into the game ourselves, in revenge for going behind his back.

336

Personally, I think he just did it for . . . fun.'

'So who killed Cassandra? You or these alleged other people, the ones playing to Warner's new script?'

He frowned. 'Who the hell is Cassandra?'

Marie looked equally confused.

'You didn't tell me this because you think I'm owed, or because you feel bad,' I said. 'You told me because you're scared to death and you're wondering if I made an arrangement with Hunter, or Warner, to hand you guys up. This isn't about me. It's still about you.'

'Did you make a deal?'

'No. But why me? What did I ever do to you? I *worked* for Peter Grant. I was *selling* your condos. I wanted to be somebody, but I was making money for you guys in the meantime. What did I ever do to make it 'entertaining' to screw up my life?'

'I'm sorry it happened. We can work things out.'

'No. This game's over, Tony, and now someone's coming for you. I don't know who they are, and I don't care, but good fucking luck to them.'

I turned and stormed away.

I heard Jane's footsteps following. My legs were stiff. My head felt empty. I knew that if I didn't get myself out of there then bad things were going to happen. A lot of me wanted to stay and let them happen, but I knew my life was fucked up enough.

As we got halfway down the stairs, I heard a voice call out above.

'Bill.'

It was Marie. She was standing at the top.

'This isn't over yet,' she said. Her face was pinched. 'There is no limit to what Warner will do. None at all. Go back to your house, get what you need, and then go. Go as far as you can, and go fast.'

41

The door at the bottom of the little staircase was shut. I grabbed at the handle, yanking it, had started kicking and punching out at it before I realized I was losing control. Jane moved me aside, almost gently, and undid the catch. I tugged the door open and stormed across the restaurant. It had gotten much busier in the time I'd spent listening to Tony Thompson justify more than twenty years of breaking lives, and I bodychecked a waiter without realizing he was even there, upending a full tray of drinks and appetizers. He started to get on my case, but I shoved him out of the way, knocking him backward into a table of four.

I was halfway to the door to the outside when something — someone — caught my eye. There was a couple sitting over on the left, a two-top well positioned near one of the nice long windows that looked down onto the leafy side street. The woman had her back to me. I didn't know the guy opposite her, a chunky guy in shorts and a Bermuda shirt, big fat face and goatee beard, staring down at his menu as if it was in Sanskrit. I knew the woman, however, even from behind. I knew even before I heard her let out a big, weird laugh.

I started moving toward them. I heard Jane say something, but ignored it.

'Hey,' I said when I got to the table.

Janine looked up. She was wearing a print dress that actually looked okay, and well out of her price range. Her hair had been done since I'd seen her that morning.

'Well, *hey*, Bill. How's tricks?'

I had no answer to that. 'I don't think you ever met my husband.' She indicated her dinner date. 'Oli, this is Bill Moore. You know. My 'boss.''

'S'up,' he said, nodding.

'What are you *doing* here?' I asked.

'Having dinner, of course,' Janine said, selecting a juicy olive from the bowl in the middle of their table. The movement was dainty, precise. 'Oli's going to take the rib eye, I bet. I'm pretty sure I'm headed for the swordfish. But as regards appetizers, I'm not sure. Going to take my time working that out.' She smiled at me again, with an odd, gloating expression. 'But hey — you've been here a couple times, right? What would *you* recommend? From your wealth of experience?'

'What the fuck are you doing here?' I asked again, more loudly. Diners at nearby tables turned. 'There's no *way* you can afford this place. We even discussed it.'

'I got paid,' she said, and the smug contentment ratcheted up yet another notch. 'Really I should be thanking you, I guess.'

Jane had taken hold of my arm. 'This isn't going to help,' she told me.

'Hey, Jane,' Janine said, popping another olive into her mouth. 'Doesn't he know yet? I assumed he just got the big reveal.'

'Know what?'

'I actually understand computers pretty well, Bill,' Janine said. 'Better than you, probably. Funny, huh? Month back, Peter Grant popped into the office one day when you were out shoving your tongue up the ass of some poor client. Peter asked if I wanted to help play a joke. And I thought to myself, 'What? Help trick the slick fucker who looks at me every day like he thinks I'm some fatso who's not worth the time of day? And who never misses an opportunity to buddy up with his pretty, skinny-bitch colleague to patronize the hell out of me? Why *on earth* would I want to do that?''

She winked. 'I'm joking, of course, Billy-boy. I said yes *right away.*'

I was swallowing rapidly.

'I sent that joke from your account,' she said. 'I set up the recorder to grab your Amazon password, too, and ordered the nudie book. Set up a few other things, too, which you probably don't even *know* about yet. They'll come home to roost sooner or later.'

Her face suddenly hardened. 'Enjoy, shithead. But for now, buzz off. I'm hungry, and I'm ready to order now. I've waited a long time for this meal.'

I lunged at her, but Jane was faster. She yanked me away from the table, whispering the same thing over and over in my ear.

'Not worth it. Not worth it. This is not worth it.'

★ ★ ★

She dragged me out across the floor of the restaurant, ignoring my shouts and attempts to break free. She pushed me out the door and to the top of the stairs and kept on shoving until we were down at street level.

'Janine was in on it?' I yelled. 'You *know* her?'

'I don't *know* her,' Jane said. 'But yes, she was a piece. I'm sorry. There's nothing you can do about it now, and no good will come of trying.'

'Holy Christ,' I said. 'Who else? Karren? Was Karren White in on this? Is that why she just *happened* to be undressing in front of the window that night? Is Karren sitting somewhere right now counting her money, too?'

'Not as far as I'm aware,' Jane said. She grabbed my shoulders and held me still, and her voice was low and clear. 'I never had any contact with Ms. White. But here's the point, Bill. The guy who took those pictures? He's disappeared. That's what Tony meant upstairs about other things going strange. This guy was called Brian. He was an old friend of mine. We even dated for a while. He's ex-army, too, and he sure as hell knew how to look after himself. He vanished last night. He didn't turn up to meet me where he was supposed to. I can't get him on the phone. Someone has pulled the plug on this game at a higher level than the Thompsons have any clue about, and people are starting to fall off the board.'

'What do you mean, 'higher level'?' I said. 'They said it was just them. A club of rich fuckheads screwing with other people's lives. Who else *is* there?'

'I don't know,' she admitted. 'Maybe Warner, maybe someone else. I don't know. The Thompsons don't know, either, and that's why I am splitting right now. You want a lift out of town, I'll do it. I owe you that much for having been a part of all this. But then I'm dust.'

'I'm not leaving town,' I said petulantly. 'I live here. I'm going home.'

'I wouldn't do anything predictable at this point.'

'Why? What the hell *else* can happen?'

She strode away up the sidewalk and I stormed after her. I didn't care what else she did, but I wanted a lift back to where Hunter had left my car. In all the things I'd been told upstairs, only one had really stuck in my head as worth listening to. Marie's advice.

Go home.

Jane impatiently gestured for me to hurry up. She trotted straight into the traffic, darting between the circulating cars. I started to run after her, shouting her name. I wasn't sure why. I just needed to shout something. She headed into the park area in the middle, but a passing vehicle nearly took me out as I tried to follow — so I diverted to head around the parked cars instead, getting honked at all the way.

I got to the far side of the Circle before she did, and ran around the back of her pickup as she came out of the park, her keys already out.

But then I stopped.

'Get in,' she snapped, unlocking her door.

'Wait . . .'

'No,' she said. 'I'm done here.'

343

I had seen something, however. I stepped back. I didn't know whether the truck was hers or a rental, but it had seen some action in the last few weeks — not least in the breakneck drive through the woods at the far end of the key that morning. The rear end was dirty and dented. But there, in the dust, was a clean patch. Not so much a patch as a series of linked lines, letters, written the way passing jokers will sometimes scrawl CLEAN ME.

But that wasn't what this said. It looked fresh, and it was just one word and it began with M.

'Don't!' I shouted, just as she turned the ignition.

★ ★ ★

It wasn't a loud bang. It was tight, short, contained. I doubt people across the road even heard it. But I did. And I heard Jane's scream.

I didn't consider whether there'd be another explosion. I probably should have. I ran to the driver's side and found Jane pinned in the seat, bolt upright. She looked surprised and let down. There was blood on her shirt and face. She was staring down at her right hand.

'Oh Jesus,' I said. The device must have been tiny, hidden in the steering column. None of her fingers were totally gone, but she'd lost most of one and half of her thumb and a chunk out of the side of her palm.

'I'm okay,' she said. 'I'm okay.'

With a kind of eerie calm, she reached under the seat and pulled out a T-shirt. She wrapped it

344

tightly around her hand, blinking fast but steadily.

'It's all fine,' she said, but I don't think she was talking to me. She was breathing in a slow, controlled manner, as if counting the seconds between each.

She turned awkwardly in her seat, and I helped her down out of the truck onto the street.

'Come on,' I said. 'I'll get you to a hospital.'

She shook her head. 'I'm okay.'

'No, you're not. You're going to the hospital.'

'How? Do *not* call the cops.'

'My car,' I said. 'It's back on Lido. Come on.'

I took her by the arm and started trying to pull her across the street. Cars kept driving around us, looking for somewhere to park, the drivers' minds on their first cocktail or breaded shrimp or their chances of getting laid once the kids were asleep. Jane was hard to move.

'Seriously,' I said, trying to stay calm, or at least sound it. I looked up, trying to gauge a gap in the traffic to pull her through. 'Let's . . . '

Then I saw him. On the sidewalk, watching us. Hunter. He was standing with his hands loosely down by his sides, a point of stasis, a rock in jeans and a casual jacket. He looked like he could have been there forever, from before the Circle was built.

I tugged Jane harder, and finally she started moving, her feet stuttering into motion like a toddler being dragged toward something she'd already said that she didn't want to do. A big white Ford honked hard but stopped to let us through.

345

'Was this you?' I shouted at Hunter as we approached. 'Did you do this?'

'It's my present to you,' he said. 'As a fellow sufferer. One of the modified.'

'What? *Why* would you do that?'

'I listened to what you told me,' he said. 'Ask yourself — who was the first person to arrive when you woke up this morning? Who came banging on your door? Did she look surprised that your lady friend was gone? What did she do then? She got you running before you could get your bearings. Got you in that truck and drove away as if there was someone hot on your tail. But did you actually see anyone? Did you?'

I opened my mouth, but he'd already dismissed us from his mind.

'I'm just saying,' he said, and walked away. From the direction of his feet and where he was looking it was obvious where he was headed.

'He followed you here,' Jane said, between teeth that were clenched tight. 'He's going after Tony and Marie.'

She was right. Hunter trotted calmly across the road and headed straight for the side stairway of Jonny Bo's.

'That's fine by me,' I said.

* * *

It took five minutes to hurry Jane down the road and over the short bridge onto Lido, and another five to follow Ben Franklin Drive around to the condo complex where Hunter had taken me. My car was still there. Jane said nothing on the way.

Her face had become pale, and the T-shirt wrapped around her hand was soaked with blood. Even the blue of her eyes seemed to have become muted, washed-out. She was tough, though. At first I was supporting her, but by the end she'd started to jog along under her own steam, her sneakers padding evenly along the road surface, and her eyes had started to look clear again.

I opened the passenger side of the car and helped her in, then ran around the other side.

'We're not going to the hospital,' she said.

'Jane — '

'My name's Emily. Sometimes Em for short, if that helps,' she said, with something between a wince and a smile. 'Can see I've thrown you a little there.'

'You . . . just don't seem like an Emily.'

'I guess my mother didn't know what I'd grow up to be like.'

'Emily, Em, Jane, whatever. We're going to the . . . ' I stopped, remembering what my plan had been before the ignition in this woman's truck had blown apart, and what I might want to do after getting to the hospital, and who with. 'How bad is it?'

She gingerly started to unwrap the T-shirt.

'Is that a good idea?'

'Don't know,' she said. 'We'll find out, I guess.'

We could see blood and torn, raw meat. She turned the hand over, and I realized that though I'd thought she'd lost the whole of the tip of the thumb, actually it was just the fleshy part — the bone seemed to be in place.

'Fuck,' I said, nonetheless.

'Yep,' she muttered. 'Still, I've seen worse.'

'The hell you have.'

'You don't always listen so good, do you? I told you I was in the army. I was in Iraq Two. I'd show you a nice big scar I've got up my side, but we never got properly introduced. That was a disconcerting sight right after it happened, I'll admit. Looked like a slab of spare-ribs before the sauce goes on. Which I have never been able to eat since, as a matter of fact.'

'How come you're not in the army anymore?'

'Long story, and not a happy one,' she said, as she started to rewrap her hand. 'I'm not welcome there, bottom line. Not welcome many places, which is how come I ended up on this gig. Brian found himself a no-questions-asked job that sounded interesting. He knew I was low on funds and likely to get myself in trouble, so he pulled me in on it, too. Three weeks later I turned up for work at Jonny Bo's. I wondered how they'd squared that away, but evidently the Thompsons have pull there.'

'They own it,' I said quietly, realizing. 'They must. Them and Peter Grant, maybe.'

'You want to light a cigarette? I feel I deserve one.'

I lit two, put hers into her left hand. 'Who actually hired you? Tony? Peter?'

'No. It was mainly done by e-mail and phone, though I had one face-to-face with Warner. He is one creepy guy.' She shrugged. 'Whatever. I have now resigned. Let's go.'

'You *are* going to the hospital,' I said. 'But I'm going home first.'

'We'll discuss it later,' she said, leaning back in the seat, taking a long pull on the cigarette, momentarily closing her eyes. 'Let's just go somewhere.'

'One second.'

After getting out of the car and checking all around it, and then looking extremely closely at the ignition, and praying, I got back in and turned the key.

It started. We did not explode.

'You're learning fast,' she said.

★ ★ ★

As soon as we got close to St. Armands Circle, we heard shouting, and as I drove into it we saw people running down the stairs out of Jonny Bo's. Couples. Families. Wait staff. All very afraid.

I got out my phone. When Hallam answered he sounded as though he had his mind on other things.

'You didn't come,' I said.

'Mr. Moore, I've got a serious situation up here.'

'It's a big day for serious situations. I know who killed Hazel Wilkins. And I can tell you what's happening in Jonny Bo's right this minute.'

'You know for sure Mrs. Wilkins is dead? And what do you mean, what's happening at Bo's?'

'I'm watching people run screaming out of it.'

349

'What the hell — '

'I have to go home. Meet me there and I'll tell you everything I know. Otherwise, in an hour, I'm gone.'

'Mr. Moore, I can't just — '

'It's up to you,' I said, and ended the call.

A woman came stumbling down the steps from Bo's, screaming. Halfway down she lost her footing and fell, landing on her face at the bottom. The people behind just ran straight over her. Sadly, the woman was not Janine.

I stepped on the gas and hammered out the other side of the junction toward the bridge. That's the last I ever saw of St. Armands Circle.

42

It all goes wrong, but that doesn't surprise him. John Hunter's life has been going wrong since the day he was born and maybe even before. For a while he did his best to help it. He didn't study at school or listen to a thing anyone told him. He got involved in bad deeds, ran with kids he shouldn't — and joined them in becoming the kind of young man that no parent dreams of when they first dandle a hot bundle of possibility on their knee. And he was there, fully present and coated with blame, on the night when a fat old woman who found her house suddenly full of jeering teenagers intent on breakage and fun got so frightened that her heart gave out.

The other boys ran away as soon as it was clear that she'd died, but Hunter remained, trying inexpertly to revive her, wondering about calling the paramedics, or the cops. In the end he ran away, too.

The next day he did not turn up at the bar where they gathered, however. He did not return calls from them, which stopped coming pretty quickly. His former friends went on to savor death and prison and drunken obscurity. He did not.

That night had been enough.

★   ★   ★

He ran up the stairs on the side of the restaurant and pushed past the girl in the smart black pantsuit at the top. He looked around the dining room and saw no sign of the Thompsons. They were here somewhere, though, he was sure of that — it was the whole reason he'd let the Realtor go, to watch what he did next: the reason he'd shown him the photograph and lit a fire under his ass. He'd learned something about playing games.

He stalked around the entire floor, ignoring the curious glances of diners and waitstaff, until finally he heard one of the latter tell him that the restrooms were over there, sir.

He turned on his heel and went in the direction indicated. He'd looked everywhere else. He didn't bother to even check the johns but made straight for the artfully nonobvious door he spotted at the end of the corridor. It was resting on the latch, the last person through evidently in too much of a hurry to make sure it was properly shut. He pushed it open, silently, and found the narrow staircase on the other side.

He pulled out his gun and started up the stairs.

★　★　★

Ten years on the roads. Ten years as no one in particular, as that guy who was polite and deferential and pretty good at fixing things. Ten years in the wind before he found a place that was nice and warm and there was beach and soft air and where the people seemed friendly and relaxed and didn't know or appear to care about the kind of person he'd once been. He found work. He was good with his hands. He was eager to please.

He found Katy, too, or they found each other.

She told him later she'd been feeling especially down the night they met and had come out to the bar determined to drink herself into oblivion (not for the first time). Somehow they'd wound up talking instead. They weren't sober when they parted in the lot outside, but they were straight enough to exchange phone numbers — and not to lose them.

He found love.

You can do that — matter of fact, that's the way it always works. You can't create love, you can't cause it, it's not there to be forged . . . finding it is all you ever do; if you're lucky, and at the right place at the right time, and sometimes that means nothing more than sitting on the right stool on the right evening, an event so random that it makes the discovery all the more inexplicable. Love is out there like gold and precious stones and the end of all the rainbows, but it's rare and always hidden, and once you find it you have to grab it with both hands and never, ever let go.

Three months was all they had.

By the end of the second they'd already started talking about heading down to Key West together. Hunter liked it fine in Sarasota, but for Katy it had too many years of bad associations and worse hangovers, and she'd always wanted to make silver jewelry and thought maybe Key West was a better place for that, plus there was a

guy from her past she wanted distance from
— by coincidence, the very guy who'd recently
started to hire Hunter for the occasional piece of
handiwork.

John had no problem with the idea of moving.
Wherever she'd be happy, he'd be happy there,
too. They drove down to Key West one weekend
and scoped out cheap places to live, and as far as
he was concerned, by Saturday night he saw no
good reason to head back. She said there was
something she had to do, however. She wouldn't
say what it was, but she implied she was owed
money over it. John couldn't see how that would
be — or why she wouldn't have cashed in earlier,
if it was the case — but they came back up
anyway.

Two nights later she announced she was going
out to sort this thing. They arranged to meet up
afterward and have dinner. He dropped her
outside a bar at the daggy end of Blue Key. She
seemed nervous and keyed up in a way John had
never seen before. They kissed when he set her
down by the side of the road, and he asked if she
really had to do this. She said she did, and as she
walked away she looked back and winked and
said, 'It's just about us now.'

He never saw her again.

* * *

He entered the upper room to see them standing
there. Marie and Tony Thompson. They turned,
startled.

'It wasn't our fault,' Tony said immediately.

John barely recognized him. They'd only met once, and the man had changed. Twenty years ago he'd been a lion. Now he looked old, and afraid.

'It was only supposed to be a warning,' Marie said. 'I said we'd give her money to go away, and David agreed. He was only coming because he knew her better, he said, because he might find it easier to talk sense into her, get her to drop the idea of blackmailing us.'

Hunter walked up the middle of the room, gun held out where they could see it. 'But?'

'But David . . . It looked like it was going to go okay, and he convinced us to go talk it out somewhere private, but . . . something happened to him. He broke a bottle and pushed it into her face.'

Hunter didn't doubt that the reflection of old horror he saw in the woman's eyes was real, that she had suffered, a little. Not enough.

'That photo was taken *afterward*?'

'Phil and Peter didn't know about what had happened at that point. We . . . we came up with everything else later.'

'You all went to *dinner*?'

'It . . . was booked.'

'John,' Tony said, 'I know it was a terrible thing, and what we did was wrong. But it's a long time ago now. And we're wealthy, you know that. So's Peter. We've talked about it. We want to put things right.'

The first bullet took off the top of Tony's head. John saw Marie pulling the tiny handgun out of her purse, but he saw it just a little too late.

He kept on firing anyway.

355

43

It was after seven when we got to Longacres and the light was fading. As I drove into the community a phrase popped into my mind: *entre chien et loup*. I knew this was a French idiom for this time of day — 'between the dog and the wolf' — and realized that I must have heard my father speak the language after all. Muttered under his breath probably, in some long-forgotten twilight, scooped up by childish ears on the prowl for adult indiscretion to be parroted with eerie accuracy at the least opportune moment. I must have asked what he meant — hoping it was really rude — and he'd told me. Enthusiastically? Matter-of-fact? In the vain hope I'd be intrigued? I couldn't recall. We walk through an endless sandstorm of experience, but in the end our lives boil down to those few grains that happen to stick to our clothes.

I jammed the card against the access point across the private road, and it let me through, the gate lifting with its familiar slow confidence, the stolid gravity of an object performing a job for humankind. I was ludicrously relieved, as if I'd been expecting that even this part of everyday experience would have broken over the course of the day.

'Nice,' Emily said as we drove in.

I didn't say anything. I was busy adding to a mental list of stuff to take with me to the hospital, and then beyond. (Where? I didn't know. A hotel or motel, somewhere to sit tight for a couple of days before coming home again to a life that had been corrected in the meantime.) Discovering that even Janine had taken part in what had been done to me made it difficult to take *anything* for granted. Were my neighbors involved in the fun? Had someone knocked on the Mortons' door and made a donation to their church? Had sweet Mrs. Jorgensson been offered an envelope of used bills and thought, Well, seems like harmless fooling, and it would mean bigger Christmas presents for the grandchildren, so why not?

Did I know any of these strangers, really?

Did I know *anyone at all*?

'Nobody here is in the game,' Emily said, disconcertingly. 'At least, not that I'm aware of.'

'How did you know . . . '

'You think loud.'

Yes, I thought bitterly. Maybe I do, and maybe that's it. Perhaps it was the naive and brash self-evidence of my desires and ambitions that made me the perfect target for the game in the first place.

He's a wanter. He has designs above his station. Let's take that and twist it. Let's show him how things really work behind the scenes. Let's break his little dreams apart.

I parked in the driveway. 'You want to stay here?'

She shook her head. 'Think I'll come wash this mess up, see what I'm dealing with.'

357

'I'm taking you to the hospital regardless.'

'So you keep saying.'

The house was quiet and dark. I led Emily to the kitchen. My note to Stephanie was still on the counter there. The problems of the man who'd written it seemed trivial now. I pushed it to one side.

'What do you need?'

'Paper towels, antiseptic if you have it. Painkillers would be good. Got a home medical kit?'

'Somewhere.' I went to the big cupboard at the rear of the room. As I rootled through it, wanting to get Emily set up so I could run upstairs, she wandered away from the counter, looking around.

'Nice,' she said again.

'Is that irony? Just, I'm not in the mood.'

'No,' she said. 'You have a nice home.'

'You don't seem the type to want this kind of thing.'

'Everybody wants it,' she said. 'Just some of us know it's unlikely to happen in this lifetime. So we pretend the white-bread life sucks.'

I stalled, still shifting things around in the cupboard, trying to find the first aid kit. Was I really going to run from all this, even temporarily? Okay, I'd wanted more, bigger. But this was a nice house, and I'd earned it. Steph and I repainted it. She'd found nice things to put in it. It was ours. It was *mine*.

Was I going to let a bunch of assholes force me out, when I hadn't done anything? Running is a deep instinct, but isn't it better

358

to turn and fight, defend your corner? *No — I have a good cave, and no asshole is going to take it away from me, for even a day.*

'Christ, here it is.' I turned, opening the first aid box and pulling out a roll of bandages to see what else was inside.

'Bill.'

She'd walked to the far end of the room and was staring through the doors into the pool area. Her voice sounded strange.

'What?'

'Fuck,' she said. The middle of the word stretched out for a long time.

I went to stand next to her. There was something floating in the pool. Something else was lying beside one of the loungers. Emily reached behind for her gun, found she couldn't begin to hold it with her right hand. She got it with the left instead. It looked awkward, heavy. I opened the screen door.

We went together, Emily sweeping the gun from side to side. There was a rushing sound in my ears.

The thing lying by the lounger was a forearm. It had been hacked off at wrist and elbow. There was blood on the floor around it, but not much. Presumably because it had been cut off after the person was already dead.

My stomach rolled over. There was nothing in there but liquid, which splattered to the stone floor. I emptied my guts until it felt like they were going to come out.

I straightened and we turned together to look at the thing floating in the pool. It was facedown, tilting on the right, as if it would not be long before it sank.

It was wearing the torn remains of a long black skirt and a black blouse. I knew the blouse. It ended in lacy cuffs at the wrists. I knew the front fell down a little when the wearer leaned forward. I knew because I'd glanced down it less than twenty-four hours before.

Emily stowed her gun and went over to the pool equipment and brought back the long pole with a net on the end. She couldn't manage it, and gave it to me.

I reached it out and snagged the body's left shoulder. I pulled. The body moved, spinning slowly about the middle, but did not come any closer. I tried again, this time resting the loop of the net across the body's back and pulling more gently.

It started to drift toward us.

We watched it come. When it was resting against the side of the pool I squatted down.

They'd shaved Cass's head. Before, during, after? Hacked at her back and her arms and legs. Floating there, pale and waterlogged and as dead as anything could be, she looked larger than I remembered, life taking with it the anima that had lightened her progress across the earth.

I reached down, against my will, and took her upper arm in my hand. I turned the body over.

The damage to the front was far more frenzied, especially over the chest. They'd taken her face, too. Someone had gone at her face with instruments I couldn't imagine. An ax, hammers, a saw. There was nothing left but holes and insides.

Something changed forever inside me then. Hazel's body had looked strange but somehow okay, part of a story we never want to hear but that death is always going to whisper to us someday. *We die, it happens.*

Cass's body said more than this. It said God was dead, too, and that he'd always hated us anyway.

'Bill.'

Emily was pointing at the wall of the pool area, at a two-foot smear of dried blood. 'And there.'

Another smear, on the floor toward the side. This was what the forearm had been used for. Someone had held one of the cut ends against these surfaces and dragged a trail of evidence, to make it that bit harder trying to hide it all. Were these smears just down here? Or upstairs, too? Were they in the bed, under it? In drawers, in the roof?

Emily looked sick. Evidently even her experience in the Gulf was not enough to make this okay.

'This isn't a game,' I said.

'No. Nothing like this was ever in the plan, ever even hinted at. You think I'd *be* here if it had been?'

'That's not what I meant.' I had tears running down my face and appeared powerless to stop them. 'I mean, how could *anyone* think of this as a *game*? I mean, what kind of person could even *do* this?'

'Warner? From the sound of it he was someone with — '

'He's been AWOL since yesterday evening. Hunter said he was injured, and I saw the chair he'd fallen in, too. I was with Cass *after* that.'

'Right.'

'I know,' I said. 'You've only got my word for that.'

She shook her head. 'You were seen on the Circle last night with her, late — by me, remember? I'd started to realize things were fucked up by then, but I was still holding the role. When Brian failed to show later I got properly nervous, and then I was at her apartment first thing this morning. I know it wasn't you. You didn't have time, and you were the most freaked-out and bewildered man in the world. And you're . . . you're just not that guy.'

'What about the things Hunter said? Asking how much I actually knew about you?'

'I guessed that would come up again.' She held her gun in my direction, handle first. 'You want to take this?'

'Of course not. I have no idea how to even use it.'

'Just trying to show you can trust me.'

'It might not even be loaded, for all I know. So — did you come into Cass's apartment while I was unconscious on the floor, kill her, hand the body off to someone to do all this to it, and dump it here? Then fake the chase afterward to make me believe you were on my side?'

'No.'

'This isn't still part of the game? The script

362

playing out? You earning your final payout?'

She held up her mangled hand. 'Hard-earned, if so.'

'Yes, you got hurt, but Hunter was the wild card nobody expected. He's the thing that screwed up their game, and Warner's, too. You weren't to know about him, either — and that could be the only reason you got injured.'

She shook her head, and I thought I believed her — but part of me didn't know.

'Still hearing your thoughts loud and clear,' she said. 'The answer's no. But it strikes me that Marie Thompson went to some pains to tell you to come back here. Made it look sincere, too.'

That had just occurred to me. 'Maybe in the hope I'd be caught red-handed with the body.'

'We should go,' she said. 'Now.'

'Bandage your hand. I'm going to grab a couple of things.'

She headed back into the kitchen. I stayed a moment longer, wiping my face, looking at the sinking body in my pool, remembering swimming there with Steph late on the night of our anniversary, floating in the aftermath of sex and food and thinking how fine everything was.

Four nights ago. That's how long all this had taken.

'I'll get them,' I said to the body. My voice was thick, throttled, quiet. 'I don't know how, and I don't know when, but I will.'

44

By the time I got back into the kitchen, Emily was wrapping a bandage around her hand. I'd forgotten what had been on my list of things to take from the house, and doubted any of them had been important anyhow. The only thing that had merit was a set of clothes for Stephanie. Anything else could stay until the world had been sorted out and I could start living my life here again.

'Going upstairs,' I said. 'Two minutes. Then we're leaving.'

'Roger that,' she said, holding the bandaged hand against her chest as she tried to fasten it with tape. She was shaking. I thought it was unlikely this was from fear, or even from what we'd seen in the pool.

'It hurts, doesn't it?'

'It really kind of does. I've come around to the idea of going to the hospital. You're wiser than I thought.'

There was a knock at the front door.

Our heads turned together. The knock came again, loud. Then someone pressed the doorbell.

I whispered, 'What do I do?'

She had no advice. The doorbell rang again, and then we heard someone speaking loudly on the other side.

'Mr. Moore, it's Deputy Hallam. I came. So if you're here, open the door.'

364

Emily reached behind with her left hand and fanned out to the left. When I saw that she was braced up against the wall, out of sight, I walked across the living room and opened the front door.

Hallam stood lit by the lamp above the doorway. He was alone. His cruiser was parked down in the street. He looked exhausted and spaced-out.

'So, on the way I hear there's been a shoot-out at St. Armands Circle,' he said, with something like wonder. 'Tony Thompson is dead. Marie's on the way to the hospital, along with some other guy, the alleged shooter. She received three bullet wounds, but gut-shot him in the meantime. She's probably going to live.'

'I'm sorry to hear that.'

'You don't sound surprised by the scenario I've just outlined.'

'I know who the shooter is. His name's John Hunter. I know why he did it.'

Hallam caught sight of Emily in the shadows. 'Who the hell is that?'

'One of the two people in the world who I trust right now,' I said. 'You are not the other. So come in slowly, keep your hands where I can see them, and do not do anything that could look like screwing me around.'

* * *

He entered cautiously. Once the door was closed behind him, Emily moved out of the shadow.

'Take his weapon,' she said to me.

Hallam laughed. 'Are you kidding me? I still want to know who the hell you are.'

Emily moved her hand to where he could see her gun. 'Any cop with half a brain would have established that before he stepped over the threshold,' she said.

Hallam knew she was right, and he didn't like it. He put his hand on his side holster.

'Lady, I want you to understand something — '

'Her name's Jane,' I interrupted, before this could get out of hand. 'She knows a lot more than I do about this. Jane — this guy's okay. I think. So everyone just be cool and nobody shoot anyone, okay?'

His eyes still on her, hand there on his gun, Hallam stood his ground. 'Whatever it is you believe you have to tell me, Mr. Moore, you got three minutes max. I need to get to the Circle. The call's out to the sheriff but he's not there yet and he's going to be furious if he finds out I'm not, either.'

'I'll tell you what I know,' I said. 'But I need to show you something first.'

'What?'

'It's out back.'

'I don't think that's a great idea,' Emily said.

'He needs to know.'

Hallam saw me glance out through the glass doors to the pool. 'Need to know what?'

He leaned forward, peered into the gloom. 'What the hell is that?'

I led him out.

★　★　★

Hallam stared down at what was in the pool. He didn't say anything for a long time. He turned eventually, but his eyes found the forearm lying alongside, and so he kept moving his head until it came to rest on my face.

'Who is she?'

'A girl called Cassandra,' I said. 'She was murdered in the small hours of this morning, at the place I tried to get you to come to this afternoon.'

'Who did it?'

'I don't know. All I saw was blood. They moved the body and brought it here.'

'The crime scene still the way it was? The one at her apartment?'

'Not exactly,' I said. Emily looked away.

Hallam rubbed his mouth with the back of his hand. 'This is fucked up.'

He walked back into the house.

★ ★ ★

'So?' I asked him. 'You going to arrest me right now, or do I have a chance of standing my ground? Are they so in control that I have to get out of here for a while?'

'Wait. Who's 'they'?'

Hallam's eyes looked like he was still seeing what was in the pool. The body had half rolled back over in the water when he saw it, hiding some of her face — but he'd still seen more than enough. He looked as though he was trying to decide what to do first out of about eight possible choices, all of them well above his pay grade.

'Tony and Marie Thompson.'

His eyes snapped back to life and he laughed outright. 'The *Thompsons?* You're kidding, right? They murdered some girl, hacked her body to pieces, smashed her *face off?* I don't think so.'

'There are others in the group,' Emily said, 'who probably — '

'The group? What is this — the Manson family? What the hell is going *on* around here?'

'A collective of locals,' I said. 'The Thompsons, the Wilkinses — back when Phil was alive — plus a couple of others, I think. They've been playing some kind of reality game for decades. Messing with people's lives, using them like pawns, smoothing over the fallout with their cash, and then moving on.'

'What? Why?'

'Because they can. Because when your bank account's full you need something else to divert you. For the fun of it.'

'And this includes *murdering* people? Come on.'

'Not usually.'

'But ... and these people you've listed — these pretty *elderly* people, I should point out — are who killed that girl out there? And did all *that* to her?'

'Maybe. We don't know.'

'But ... why bring the body here?'

'To implicate me. I'm this season's guest star. I'm the guy who got modified this time around.'

'"Modified"?'

'It's a computer-game term,' I said, remembering all too well that it had been Cass who'd first

368

flashed on what was going on — too late for her, once I'd accidentally got her involved. I could blame other people as much as I liked, but the bottom line was that it had been me who'd put her in my pool. 'Alterations are made. Like putting a rat in a maze and moving the walls when it's not looking, or putting an electric current under its feet.'

Hallam's face was frank in its incredulity. 'Bullshit.'

'They admitted it, to my face. Jane was there — she heard it. According to Tony, it had just been a kind of fireside puzzle before. It was David Warner who took it to another level. He made his money selling computer games. That's all this is, but in real life. Augmenting reality with a cattle prod.'

'And they've been doing this to you . . . how long?'

'Several weeks in the background. It really got going on Monday, but I only started to work it out last night. My wife's in the hospital because she drank a bottle of wine I bought. It was poisoned. Tony claimed to me that wasn't part of the plan, he and Marie were the intended victims, but he has no idea who did it — unless it was Warner screwing over his former friends.'

Even as I said this I realized how lame it sounded, how insufficient a handle I had on what was going on.

Hallam evidently felt the same. 'Are you *shitting* me?'

'Deputy, I've got a . . . you've seen what's out in my pool. Nobody's shitting anybody.'

Hallam turned to Emily. 'And how do you fit into all this, exactly?'

'I was one of the people moving the walls,' she admitted. 'Not a player. A hired hand, helping run the scenario that had been roughed out ahead of time. I've been waitressing in Bo's this last month. I helped set up some of the stuff in Bill's life, but I was *not* involved in anyone getting hurt. The plug was pulled once it starting looking like something had happened to David Warner. Someone clearly hasn't got the message, though.'

'I talked with the Thompsons an hour ago,' I said, 'and they were *scared*. The guy who shot up Bo's is called John Hunter. He was a victim of the game twenty years back. Warner framed him for a murder he'd committed, some local woman called Katy, and — '

'Whoa, whoa,' Hallam said, holding up his hand. 'You have evidence that Warner killed someone?'

'Not actual evidence, but this is straight from Marie Thompson. Why?'

'We found stuff at Warner's house today. I'd believe that guy was capable of almost anything right now.'

Hallam's eyes glazed over, as if he was trying to add, divide, and multiply a long series of numbers in his head. 'I have to call this in,' he said, as if suddenly remembering that he was a cop.

'No, you don't,' said a voice.

45

It came from above. There was a man standing on the gallery upstairs. It was Sheriff Barclay.

Hallam gaped. '*Sir?*'

His boss started down the stairs in a slow, measured fashion, as if weighed down with the gravity of a serious situation. I was aware of Emily backing away, melting into the shadows.

'What in hell's name are you doing here, Rob?'

'I . . . I received a call from Mr. Moore, sir,' Hallam said, defensively. 'He said he had information pertaining to a situation developing in the Circle. Sheriff . . . I've been hollering for you on the radio for three hours. We've got . . . there are *many* things going on, not good things, and I have been trying very hard to contact you. Where have you been?'

'It's been a very busy day.'

'Well, yeah. You know there's been a shoot-out at Jonny Bo's?'

'Yes, I'm aware of that. There's four deputies on-site at this time, full medical support. It's covered.'

'We found some very weird shit at David Warner's house, too.'

'I know about that as well, Rob. It's okay. Don't worry. It's all in hand.'

'*In hand?* Sir, I don't . . . understand.'

Barclay glanced into the shadows behind me. 'Where do you think you're going, young lady?'

Emily had retreated to the entrance to the kitchen, gun down by her side. She said nothing. Just watched Barclay carefully. He smiled. 'Why don't you come back in here?'

'Do not trust this man,' Emily told Hallam.

I finally managed to speak. 'Sheriff — how did you get into my house?'

'Round the back, of course,' he said, as if this was a dumb question. 'Like a lot of folks in these communities, you don't always remember to lock up. Which is a mistake, I should tell you. Just because you're all part of the same club doesn't mean you can trust each other to the bitter end.'

'But what are you doing here?'

'A neighbor called in a report of suspicious activity. Said you arrived here at four this afternoon and carried a bulky object into the building via the garage doors. A couple hours later you left, without said burden. Driving erratically.'

'That's bullshit,' I said. 'I haven't been back since early yesterday evening.'

'So I thought I'd better check it out,' Barclay continued smoothly, as if I'd not spoken, as if he was telling Hallam a story. His hands were in his pockets. He looked so relaxed it was surreal. 'Your name has been cropping up all over town, Mr. Moore. Has been for a couple days now. You've always seemed like a normal kind of guy, but I wouldn't have been doing my job if I didn't come take a look.'

'Which of my neighbors made this alleged call?'

Could one of them actually have done this?

After being paid to by someone in the game? What chance did I have of convincing the sheriff of this, even if they had?

Barclay ignored me. He glanced at his deputy. 'You've seen what's in the pool, right?'

Hallam spoke carefully. 'Sheriff, it did not seem to me that Mr. Moore was likely to have been responsible for . . . what's out there. He took me straight to it. He did not present as the perp.'

'That's a judgment call, Deputy. And as such my department, thankfully. The evidence actually suggests that Mr. Moore spent a portion of the afternoon out there by the pool, doing what you've seen.'

'Don't listen to him,' Emily told Hallam. 'That's not what happened. You know it. There's nowhere near enough blood out there, for a start.'

'Rob, are you going to take that woman's weapon, or what?'

Emily took another couple of paces back, lifting her arm to point the gun. 'Don't even try it.'

'Deputy, now.'

Hallam turned reluctantly toward Emily and unsnapped his holster. 'Ma'am — you heard the sheriff. I'm going to need to have that weapon. Please.'

There was a quiet click as Emily did something to the gun, fumbling the action because of her injured hand. From the way Hallam stiffened, I assumed the sound meant something significant. Never having held a gun in my life, I couldn't be sure.

Emily's gaze was calm and steady. 'Seriously, Deputy. Not another step or I'll put a bullet in your boss. Everyone be very still.'

Hallam was caught halfway across the sitting room, hand on his holster, not knowing what to do. He looked at the sheriff. Barclay said nothing, did nothing. I saw Emily judging the angle and distance from where she stood to the front door. The cops blocked her path, Hallam in particular. There was no way she could make it to the outside world. At least not via that route.

She backed up a little farther. I did, too. To cover this, I acted as if I was trying to calm things down.

'Emily — just be cool. Let's explain everything to the sheriff. He's a cop. He can help us.'

'Are you kidding? He's *part* of this,' she said. 'He must be. You told me the police helped frame Hunter, right? He told you that.'

I couldn't tell whether she'd realized what I was doing — but we kept moving backward anyway, slowly.

'That was twenty years ago. Doesn't mean the sheriff's still part of it. He's a cop, for god's sake.'

Hallam tried to regain some kind of control. 'Sir, stay where you are.'

Emily spoke over him. 'Bullshit. They were always going to need a pet cop, to smooth over anybody who got riled at their life being screwed around — and to bury any illegalities along the way. If you're going to play those kinds of games, you have to own the board, the whole island.

374

That includes its sheriff.'

'I don't know what you're talking about,' Barclay said. 'But like Mr. Moore says — let's talk this thing out. That's the sensible route forward.'

'Screw you. Did you *really* leave your back door open, Bill? Or do you think maybe this guy has keys?'

She put a little bit of extra weight on the words *back door*. I thought about it, hard.

Could I have left the back door unlocked? If the answer was yes, we could *maybe* get through it fast enough to escape across the backyard and over into the neighbor's. If the door wasn't open, we'd be screwed, cornered in the kitchen with nowhere to go.

I took another step backward, glanced through the kitchen. The back door was shut, of course, or we would have noticed it before. The key was in place, in the lock under the handle. But was it locked? I tried to imagine how long it would take to run to the end of the kitchen. The lock was stiff. Steph had asked me to oil the thing more times than I could remember, but updating Facebook and plotting my rise in realty had taken precedence. Even if it *wasn't* locked, would we really be able to get to it in time? How likely would Hallam be to shoot?

Emily kept needling. 'I've got keys, after all — and this guy is being paid from the same source.'

Barclay said, 'Deputy, are you going to disarm this woman or what?'

I moved to put myself in Hallam's line of fire,

between him and Emily. I saw her take the chance to steal a look sideways, try to gauge the probability of getting to the back door. I decided I'd take my cue from her. She'd be more likely to get the decision right.

Hallam finally pulled his gun out, but irresolutely. 'Sheriff, I can't get to her without — '

'Do they have an actual leash for you, Sheriff?' Emily asked. 'A real one? Or is it just money? You got a bigger house than you should? Take longer vacations? Keep a hot young woman in an apartment up in Saint Pete?'

'I don't think you're in a position to judge me. Or anything else, from what I hear.'

Emily laughed jaggedly. 'That didn't sound like denial. I helped them play the game, sure. I didn't agree to cover up a murder. But you did that once before, and now you're about to do it again, right? You get an actual bonus for that? How much?'

'I won't be covering up your crimes, no.'

'*My* crimes? Screw you.'

'I spoke this afternoon to a local actor by the name of Daniel Bauman.'

'Interesting. Is that why he's not picking up the phone? 'Spoke' how hard to him, exactly? He another loose end that you've been hired to tidy up?'

'You're a very paranoid young woman. Mr. Bauman is alive and well. He claims that you hired him to impersonate David Warner, and I believe him. I further believe this is evidence that you were involved in the latter's death. And by extension, that of Hazel Wilkins.'

'*What?* You're dreaming, asshole. You *know* I had nothing to do with those.'

Emily's voice was too tight, too low. She needed to be focused on getting out, not getting pulled into a toe-to-toe with Barclay.

Two more baby steps had got me to the point where I could dodge right and take my chances with the back door. She'd be in the way of any fire, would operate as a shield for me. But I couldn't do that.

'I don't know that at all,' Barclay said. His voice rolled on and on like an unstoppable tide of unreason. 'I *do* know you were involved in violations of prisoners' rights while you were stationed in — '

'No!' Emily shouted. 'Whoever told you that, they lied. I stole, yes. I whacked a guy who deserved it — he was a rapist and an asshole. But I did *none* of that other shit. They put that on me to get me out.'

'Emily,' I said desperately. '*Ignore him.*'

The sheriff had shoved his hand right into her emotional guts and grabbed her, however, and Emily abruptly started to walk back into the living room. The gun was pointing straight at Barclay's head, but it was wavering. 'Fucks like you,' she snarled. 'It's *fucks* like *you* that have ruined my *entire fucking life.*'

'Emily,' I shouted. She wasn't listening.

Hallam finally assumed the shooter's position. 'Ma'am, step back. Right now.'

She kept walking.

'Ma'am, do *not* advance any farther.'

377

I moved quickly, threw my arm in front of her, trying to stop her. She was stronger than me, though, and hard to hold back. Her entire body was shaking. Her eyes were drawing down on Barclay like he was everyone who'd ever done her wrong. She kept her left arm rigid over my shoulder, the gun still pointing at the sheriff's head.

'Emily,' I said, low, a whisper. 'Listen to me. Please. Don't do this.'

Barclay smiled. 'She'll do something, Mr. Moore. Count on it. She's volatile. Unstable. That's why she's here. Though just so you know, she was right about one thing. I *do* have your house keys. Your back door is locked. I checked. You wouldn't stand a chance.'

Emily stopped trying to push forward against me and went very still. 'Guess it's Plan B, then,' she said. 'Cool by me. I like the sound of it better anyway.'

She shoved me away, lowering the gun to aim unswervingly at Barclay's chest. 'Good-bye, asshole.'

She pulled the trigger.

46

But Hallam fired first, and Emily jerked back as if she'd been standing on a rear-ended train. Her shot went wide. She lurched past me over the threshold into the kitchen, falling skewed, sliding on the tiles and smacking back into the oven, her bloodied hand caught under her back, the arm breaking audibly as she landed.

'About time,' Barclay said. 'Jesus, Rob, what the hell is *wrong* with you?'

I ran to Emily. The bullet had gone through her throat, punching a chunk of it out the other side and splashing blood and tissue across the floor tiles. There was a beat of rawness in her neck before blood started to pump up from inside like a storm wave.

I grabbed her bandaged hand, put it to the wound. 'Hold it there,' I said, hoping this was the right thing to do. 'Hold it tight.'

She stared up at me. Her chest convulsed, as if something was trying to push its way out of her heart. Not violently, but with firm intent. 'Oh,' she said.

It happened again, and with the jerk of her rib cage a gout of blood surged from the mess in her neck.

'Please, Emily,' I said. 'Hold it. Hold on.'

Her mouth was moving, but nothing made it out this time except wet clicking sounds.

'Call an ambulance,' I shouted at Hallam. He

stood frozen, gun still held out, aghast. '*Get the paramedics.*'

'All units are busy at St. Armands Circle,' Barclay said mildly, as if thinking about other things. 'Sorry. Bad break for your girlfriend.'

Emily looked confused. She looked scared. Her eyes were on mine. I thought her left arm was starting to go into spasm, but then realized what she was attempting covertly to do. I slipped my hand along her arm and started trying to prise the gun from fingers that had become locked.

Barclay knew what I was doing. 'Aha, now, guns,' he said. 'Glad you brought that up. First, there's no point you going down that road. You're not going to shoot me.'

I got the gun free from Emily's hand and stood up.

'Don't do that, sir,' Hallam said dismally. 'Sheriff, I'm going to call the ambulance.'

The weapon felt heavy. It was warm from the sweat and pressure of Emily's hand. Every single thing I knew about guns had been learned from watching television, and I couldn't remember any of it. I looked down, however, feeling its heft in my hand, knowing that really I just had to pull the trigger and everything else would follow.

Emily coughed, and made a sound like a rook some distance away in the night.

I looked back at her, but she'd gone.

I'd missed her dying. She went without me watching, without anyone seeing her go. She went alone.

I turned back toward Barclay and thought that

maybe I could pull a trigger after all.

'Don't feel bad,' Barclay said. 'Her life was going nowhere fast, trust me. Now, my second gun-related point.' He reached into his jacket. 'I found this in the bedroom.' He brought out something and held it out where I could see it clearly. It was a handgun.

Hallam looked at it, then back at me.

'I've never seen it before,' I said, straightening. 'Deputy, you have to believe me.'

'Hidden under the bed,' Barclay said. 'Which is poor. You got a lot to learn, my friend.'

I started to raise Emily's gun. My hand was shaking badly. Hallam swore, and drew down on me, dropping back into the shooter's position.

'Mr. Moore, don't do this,' he said. 'I've heard what you've said. We can talk about it. Come on. Don't make this situation any worse.'

'The situation's fucked to hell already. And she was right. This guy knew all about it all along.'

'Mr. Moore, please. Don't make me do this.'

Barclay raised the gun in his hand and pointed it at me. 'Two against one, Mr. Moore.'

'Big — '

I stopped, noticing far too late that the sheriff was wearing surgical gloves.

I moved my finger onto the trigger.

Barclay swung his arm to the side, and fired.

The shot hit Hallam full in the chest. He staggered backward. Barclay fired again, and Hallam fell down.

★　★　★

After a moment, Hallam tried to sit up. Tried to say something. Tried to roll onto his side. None of these came to fruition. He finally managed to turn his face up toward his boss, to start asking a confused question, but he fell back again. I think it took a few minutes for him to die, but basically he was done from that point.

'Are you insane?' I managed to ask, finally. 'What . . . what . . . ?'

'That one's your fault,' Barclay said. 'Rob wasn't the brightest firework in the box, but he was dogged. And honest. You opened the door on a lot of stuff he'd have been *far* better not knowing. You killed him. I hope you're fucking proud of yourself. I'm godfather to his kid, for crissake.'

I seemed to be in a room with a lunatic from a world in which logic ran at right angles to mine. I took a step backward, barely aware that I still had Emily's gun in my hand. The movement banged me into a table that Steph had insisted we buy during a weekend up in Cedar Key, the table on which each issue of her magazine was displayed for a week after publication. Last month's had been knocked to the floor at some point, and stepped on.

'Relax. I'm not going to shoot you, Mr. Moore,' Barclay said. 'Least, not unless I have to. I got three dead bodies now, and I need someone to carry the weight for them. That girl in the pool in particular — that was a job of work I don't want going to waste.'

'You did that? To her?'

'Of course I didn't. Warner's other friends put

that in motion. They're in control of this now — and they're who pulled the plug on this whole mess.'

'What friends? Who are they?'

For just a moment, Barclay looked less seamless, as if I'd pushed him to the edge of what he understood. 'Call themselves Straw Men, or something like that, but that's something I'm happy to say I don't have a lot of information about. A guy called Paul is in the driver's seat now. Kind of a disconcerting individual, and not happy that Warner's game had been going on in the first place. He'd like me to tidy up the loose ends for him. No exceptions. No sir.'

I raised Emily's gun. 'I'm going to shoot you.'

'Jeez, Mr. Moore — no, you're not. We've been over this already. Don't kid yourself.'

'I . . . will tell people. About everything.'

'You got nothing. Actually, you got less than that.' He held up his gun, turned it round. 'This was purchased four days ago in Boynton, using your credit card number — a fake cloned from information your dead girlfriend gave us, when she was working as a waitress at Bo's.'

I stared at the gun, remembering the morning with Hazel, when Emily/Jane/the waitress went inside to run my card.

'Course, I'll have to do some work to make it look like you killed her,' Barclay said. 'Though it could be Rob did that, in self-defense, when he and I got here together and found what you'd done to the other poor girl in the water. I don't know. Haven't figured that out yet. But there's already a shell from this gun in the head of that mess out there in the pool. So that part's done.'

'There's no way,' I said, light-headed. 'No way you can put all this on me. I'm just a Realtor. How is anyone going to believe I did all this?'

'Happens all the time. Man leads a normal life in some place you've never heard of until it's on constant rotation on the news. Before that, all his friends and neighbors assume the guy's on the level. Course, they're the *first* to say, 'Well, he did seem a little uptight. Maybe almost even *too* normal?' — when it all rains down.'

'No,' I said. 'People know me.'

'They thought they did. Plus, there's a few other bits and pieces of evidence hidden around this house, not to mention at your office at The Breakers. Like I said — it's been a busy afternoon. The set's dressed. You got a history now.'

I tried to think of a stronger piece of denial. He watched me come up empty, and smiled. It was a real smile, too. 'Run along, Mr. Moore. I'm busy. Got to make it all look just so.'

He watched as I backed toward the front door and opened it. Gave me an encouraging nod of the head, as if in reassurance. I stepped outside slowly, though I'd already started to understand that the man had meant what he said. He wasn't going to kill me.

Not enough fun.

But then something he had said came back to me. My heart dropped.

No exceptions.

* ⋆ *

I ran to my car. I realized I was still holding a gun, threw it onto the passenger seat, then started the car and jammed it in reverse. I had my phone to my ear at the same time as the car swerved backward into the circle road. I pulled the car door shut as I put it into drive and hammered toward the gates.

'Steph,' I said, when they'd put me through. I kept my voice as steady as I could. 'I'm on my way to see you, okay? And maybe you should get dressed.'

'Why?' She sounded befuddled.

'Just do it. Do it now, okay? I'll be there soon.'

I cut the call and drove straight through the gates.

47

The hospital entrance was ringed with ambulances. There were three news crews in position, too, with a reporter I recognized from WWSB standing to one side talking seriously to the camera. I swerved to avoid all this and drove into the main parking lot, finding a space on the far side. It was only after I'd turned off the engine that I processed the fact that my hands were covered in Emily's blood. My shirt, too.

I got my shirt off and wiped as best I could. It wasn't good enough. I wrenched myself over the seat, found a sweatshirt in the back, the one I used after the gym. I put that on and then tracked down a half bottle of old, warm mineral water under the passenger seat. Steph was always on my case about not remembering to throw the things in the trash. I was glad of it now. I got out of the car and deployed the water carefully, using the blood-stained shirt to scrub. Some blood had dried under my nails and I couldn't get it out, but I soon decided I'd spent enough time. Only then did I realize there was blood down my trousers, too. I seemed incapable of seeing anything that wasn't right in front of my face. And maybe not just recently, either.

I couldn't do anything about the pants. I'd just have to hope that no one noticed. I shoved the gun into the footwell and dropped the shirt onto it, folding it so the bloodstains didn't show. I knew I needed to get rid of the weapon, but also felt that I had to do it properly — it would now have my fingerprints on it, making it even easier for Barclay to tell bizarre lies about me.

Usually there's a crew of die-hard smokers ganged up around the side entrance of hospitals, but either Sarasota Memorial operated a shoot-on-sight policy or they'd migrated around the front to rubberneck current events. On the way up from the house I'd tuned to local radio news but learned little I didn't already know. One dead from gunfire, two seriously wounded, all other injuries sustained while members of the public tried to escape from danger that would never have even come their way if they'd just sat tight. The police were not yet releasing the names of the dead and wounded. I wondered who was holding the fort down there, with Hallam dead and Barclay focusing on a different business. I considered calling the news station and telling them to send someone to my house, but threw the idea away. I didn't care what happened about all that. I cared only about the woman inside the building I was running toward.

The ground floor was in barely contained chaos. More newspeople. More paramedics. A lot of people who were presumably friends or relatives of either long-term or recent inhabitants. Raised voices, lots of people talking on cell phones. I dodged into the thickest part of the crowd, hoping the bodies would cover the state of my clothes, trying not to look like the only person with a clear mission. It was slow going, and when I finally got close to the junction near where the bank of elevators stood, I saw I had a further problem. I swore, the crack in my voice startling people nearby.

There were cops all over the corridor. They seemed to be there to limit access to the elevators — presumably to stop newspeople from getting up to the ICU. The cops looked harried and stretched. I assumed these were Sarasota cops, not directly tied to Barclay, but couldn't be sure. It could have been my imagination, but I thought I saw one of them scanning the crowds, looking for someone in particular. Maybe me. Maybe not.

I faded back into the mass of bodies. I was buffeted by the crowd meanwhile, pushed diagonally back into the hallway I'd just come along. More in hope than expectation I got out my phone and speed-dialed Steph's cell. I'd called her room before, but maybe . . .

No reply. I turned and started pushing back the other way, seized by an idea.

* * *

I found a stairwell back near the side entrance, with flights going up and down. Nobody was guarding it. I didn't imagine it would be long before the cops had the sense to plug this hole, so I ran up the stairs as fast as I could.

I burst out of the doors on the third floor and ran along the corridor. I blew straight into the reception area I'd visited that morning — dropping the pace down to fast walk, but still moving fast. There were a lot of doctors and nurses, people talking in hushed tones. Presumably most of the injured were up here in the ICU.

I heard someone else say — 'The shooter. Thirty seconds ago. Crash team's coming up.'

Through the white doors on the other side of the room it was quieter, a few people standing looking through windows in various degrees of unhappy. I ran to the end and yanked open the door to Steph's room.

The bed was empty.

It was empty and in disarray, however, and the room didn't look like it had been cleared in preparation for a new patient. Chanting the word *no* under my breath over and over, I darted across and checked the cabinet by the bed. Medicines, a spare gown. And Stephanie's purse.

So where was she?

Had someone got here before I did?

I couldn't find any sign of her clothes, which I hoped was a good thing. I ran back into the corridor, nearly colliding with a man in a white coat. Recognition cut in and we swung back to face each other. It was the doctor I'd talked to that morning.

'Where is she?' he demanded angrily.

'You're asking me?'

'You don't know?'

'Of course I don't know — or I wouldn't be looking for her, would I? I called the hospital half an hour ago. I got put through, so she was here then.'

'I came by your wife's room ten minutes ago but it was empty. I've been all over the floor looking for her.'

'Christ,' I said. 'Have you seen anybody up here? Anybody who shouldn't have been?'

'The entire hospital is full of people who shouldn't be here,' he said. 'Right now nobody has any idea who's supposed to be here and who's not.'

He seemed to suddenly clock my level of desperation, and took a mental step back. 'But . . . what kind of person would you be talking about, anyway?'

'Never mind. I'll find her,' I said, starting to back away up the corridor. Putting this guy on high alert wasn't going to make anything easier. 'Sure she's just gone for a walk. She's like that, hates being cooped up. If you find her, tell her to stay put, okay? Tell her I'm coming.'

'I will. Her condition's improving, but there's work to do. She needs more treatment, right away.'

'Gotcha.' I'd stopped listening by then — this guy had no idea of the real level of danger Steph was in, jeopardy that had nothing to do with the contents of a wine bottle — and hurried out into the reception area.

There was no point hurtling randomly around the hospital, however: run in the wrong direction and you're getting farther away from where you need to be. Much though I wanted to keep myself in constant movement, to be doing something, I had to stop and think first.

Assume no one had come for her.

I had to assume this. If I started to think otherwise, then I was too late and nothing I did could make any difference. I couldn't bear to go down that road.

So then, assume she moved herself.

This was a woman who'd been poisoned. I wasn't sure if she'd actually been told this, or if she'd properly absorbed the fact, but half an hour ago she'd received a semihysterical (or at least throttled and intense) phone call from her husband, telling her to get dressed. Thinking, 'Okay, that's weird, but he seems serious,' she does what he asks. He takes longer to arrive than she expects (I'd driven up from the house as fast as I could, but evening traffic stopped me from hammering it all the way). So she gets twitchy. She can't sit there in her room fully dressed, either, because a nurse could come in and read the riot act, ask what the hell she's doing, and insist she get back into bed like a good patient. So she takes herself for a walk around the ward or the floor, to wait for me, catch me as soon as I arrive.

I liked that version. I certainly preferred it to the scenario in which someone got there before me.

I wasn't sure what it meant I should do next, though. The doctor said he'd looked around the floor. How thoroughly? He'd presumably only been looking in the areas a patient might normally be expected to go (restrooms, the snack machines) and wouldn't have checked every nook and cranny. A hospital would have a *lot* of nooks and crannies. Did I have time to check them all — when Steph might not even be on this floor?

391

The area around the nurse's station was less crowded now. Someone was getting a grip on the situation, and one of the nurses gave me a hard stare as I passed, as if to check I was legitimate. I wasn't sure what the answer was. It seemed like everyone was looking at everyone suspiciously, and for a moment I was seized by the vertiginous conviction that *nobody* was here legitimately, that everybody was involved in something I didn't understand — the nurses, orderlies, supposed patients, and alleged relatives. That any single one of them could have stashed Steph's body in a cupboard and be enjoying the spectacle of me spinning around searching for her; that any of them could have a gun in their jacket or purse or white coat and be waiting for the most apposite or entertaining moment to drop me, to general applause. Maybe it was a competition. Maybe this was all just a set, and everyone in it actors and extras. Maybe it had always been that way, everywhere in the world, and I was the only person who hadn't known.

I did a fast tour around the floor and came up empty. Toward the end it occurred to me that she *might* have gone down to the exit on the ground floor and be waiting there. It occurred to me that this might even be the most likely explanation — Steph was sharp, good at cutting to what-happens-next — and that I was a total moron for not having thought of this in the first place.

I didn't want to take the elevator down into the middle of the cop zone, so I went back to the

392

far stairwell and clattered down that instead. I knew Steph hadn't been at the north doors — or at least that she hadn't been there ten minutes ago, because that's the way I'd come in. Within a few minutes I'd established she wasn't at the east doors, either.

Which left only the main entrance. I was going to have to go that way regardless.

I drifted quickly past the corridor that led to it. This area was less hectic now, though there remained a knot of people down at the end, including at least one person who looked like a reporter. I didn't know whether Steph would have thought being surrounded by people was a good or a bad thing. She'd been very foggy when I saw her that morning, and I doubted the intervening time would have been enough to clear her head. I should have given her a better idea of what I'd been afraid of. I should have laid it out for her. It would have been easier to predict what she might do if I knew she understood.

I tried calling her cell again. As it rang I realized I was close to hyperventilating and tried to calm myself down.

Suddenly I heard her voice in my ear, querulous, dislocated. 'Bill?'

'Steph? Where *are* you?'

'Cafeteria. Are . . . are you here yet?'

'Yes, I'm here at the hospital,' I said. 'I'm here. It's all good. Why . . . are you in the cafeteria?'

'I want everything to be right. And now is the time, yes? You always say that. Now is always the best time for action. Tomorrow starts now.'

393

'Steph — what are you talking about?' I was in movement again, searching the walls for signs, trying to find a map of the hospital. 'Wanted *what* to be right?'

'Everything.' She sounded confused but determined, as if trying to piece complex matters together in a mind that wasn't up to it. 'He called, five minutes after you. And I thought it didn't mean anything. It was just dumb. I was mad at you, that's all. So sort it out.'

'*Who* called, honey?' I finally found a map and located the cafeteria on it — it was at the other end of the hospital. I got my bearings and started to hurry in that direction. 'Who are you talking about?'

'You know,' she said reluctantly. 'He said we should meet, talk. And I thought, yes, get it done. Wasn't anything, anyway. I'm so sorry.'

And then I got it. '*Nick's* here?'

Nick — a man who'd started working at her office six weeks before, around about the time this whole thing had started to be put in motion. Who'd just happened to run into my wife last night downtown. Who'd now called her to arrange a meeting, just a few minutes after I'd run from my house, and from Barclay, who doubtless had a phone and could have made a call.

'Yes.'

'Is he there with you now?'

'Getting coffees. He wanted to go somewhere else, but I said no way, my husband's coming to see me. I'm staying right here in the hospital. I said that.'

'That's right. That was a good thing to say. Stay there, Steph. Don't move. Don't drink anything he gives you. Do *not* go anywhere with him.'

I started to run.

48

When I banged through the cafeteria doors I found myself in a long open space with low Musak and racks of things to eat, a place to pretend you or some friend or relative wasn't so sick after all and everything was fine and fixable through a latte and a skinny muffin. I hurried straight down the side of the room, scanning the tables. The room was scattered with a cross section of local humanity balanced on little designer chairs. It was hard to pick out anyone in particular.

Finally I saw her, slumped over a table right in the middle. She was in work clothes — the outfit she'd been wearing to go into the office yesterday, of course, before the meeting — but looked like she'd put them on in the dark. Her face was very pale. Her hair was lank. She looked like an old woman, far from home.

I scooted between the tables to her, leaned down, and put my hand gently on her shoulder.

'Honey, let's go.'

She swung her head up, took a second to recognize me. Close up she looked far too thin.

'Hey,' she said, and smiled. Her voice was weak, despite the warmth in it. 'I'm so glad you're here.'

'Me too.'

'I'm sorry about this. Just thought it was a good idea, you know?'

'Yeah, but it's not. We need to go.'

She blinked at me, then swung her head robotically to the side. I followed her gaze and saw Nick coming from the counter, a cup in each hand. He saw me, too.

'Don't know whether I can drink a coffee, in fact,' Steph said. 'Still feel sick.'

'That's right, honey. Your stomach's messed up. Coffee is a bad idea right now. Come on. Let's leave.'

Nick was quick getting over, but he stayed in character all the way. He looked cowed, as if he knew he was in the wrong but was determined to make things right. He was diffident. He looked exactly as he should.

He started talking from ten feet away. 'Hey,' he said. Muted, cautious. Concerned.

'So which is it?' I asked. 'Are you just an actor, or are you actually one of them?'

Nick looked at me warily. 'What?'

'Don't bother pretending. I know what's going on. So which is it? Player or filler? Emily never mentioned you. So I'm guessing you're one of them.'

'One of who?'

Steph looked more confused than ever. 'Bill, what are you talking about? Who's Emily?'

'Steph, seriously — we're going. We're leaving this hospital right now.'

'Leaving the hospital?' Nick said. 'You're not serious? Ste — Your wife is sick, sir.'

'I'm aware of that. And you and I both know how and why it happened, too.'

'I really don't, sir,' Nick said, with maddening

397

calm. 'I brought the wine bottle in, like you asked. I . . . I really think that the hospital is the place for her to be right now.'

'Is that so? I heard you tried to make my wife leave here just a few minutes ago.'

'Uh, no,' he said, looking confused. 'I just suggested we should go to the outside seating, so she could get some fresh air.'

'Bullshit.'

'Mr. Moore, I understand you're going to have a problem with me, in the, uh, light of things, and probably I should go, leave you guys to it now you're here, but her health is the priority, right?'

'We're leaving now,' I said, trying to ignore him, gripping Steph's arm in my hand, fairly gently.

A nearby table had started taking an interest — two middle-aged women and a man — and were making no bones about staring. I knew how it must look. A woman who really did look like the hospital was the only sensible place for her. A neat young man in pressed chinos and a spotless shirt, speaking calmly, talking sense. A wild-eyed older guy, in stained trousers and an old sweatshirt, last night's alcohol in a rank fog around him — and who was possibly also broadcasting on some psychic level the effects of having just seen two people shot to death near a swimming pool full of blood.

'Honey, please, let's just go.'

Steph wouldn't get up. Either she was too weak or confused, or she'd got it fixed in her head that the situation with Nick needed to be resolved, and was brooking no deviation until that was done. She'd always been like that, since college, since childhood, most likely. She wanted things sorted out. Squared away. That's a good quality in a partner, and I'd always loved it about her. I didn't right now.

'Bill, I . . . I don't know.'

The man from the nearby table was staring at me. He was bulky, wearing a cap, big gray mustache. He reminded me forcibly of the guys who'd got in my way when I'd seen the actor playing David Warner on the street opposite Kranks, and I wondered — had *they* been real? They'd certainly been very quick to intervene on behalf of a stranger. Did people do that kind of thing anymore? Had Emily told me everything? Had there been enough time to fill me in on all the levels, or were there lies out there I didn't even know about? Was the big guy in front of me running backup for Nick? Would there be other people in this room doing the same?

The guy stood. He was tall, paunchy. 'The kid's right,' he said. 'This lady doesn't look good. You shouldn't be taking her anywhere.'

He put his hand on my arm.

I shook it off. 'Get out of my face, asshole.'

Nick looked concerned. He looked insanely reasonable. He looked like the good guy, without a doubt. For a second I even questioned myself — wondered if I'd got this wrong, if I'd somehow got turned 180 degrees from reality and was doing nothing but swimming further and harder in the wrong direction.

'Mr. Moore,' Nick said, taking a step that,

probably not accidentally, put his body between me and the main doors. 'Why don't we just — '

'I don't know who the hell you really are,' I said. 'But get out of my way. Now.'

Nick glanced at the other man, making a mute appeal in the face of a tide of unreason. The guy saw his chance to be a hero, to aid this nice young fellow in front of the two women he'd been sitting with.

He put his meaty hand up, gave me a shove in the chest. 'Listen, buddy . . . '

I'd gripped the back of a chair before I even had a plan for it, then whipped my hand up and across like a vicious crosscourt half volley.

The chair caught the guy a glancing upward blow before making to where I'd intended — smack into the side of Nick's head. It was a light chair, but I'd swung it very hard and very fast, and Nick went straight down.

Suddenly there was a lot of noise — people gasping, standing, chairs being knocked back and over, somebody shouting for security, immediately, as if they'd been waiting all their life for the chance.

'Bill, for god's *sake*,' Stephanie said, aghast, staring at Nick on the floor. 'What are you *doing*?'

I was done with trying to talk anyone into anything, done trying to explain myself, done trying to deal with anyone at all except in the most basic terms. I slung my arm around Stephanie's back and started trying to get her out of her chair. The guy with the baseball cap threw a punch at me. It caught me on the side of

400

the head, but I turned away, head ringing.

'Come at me again and I'll kill you,' I said, in a voice I barely recognized.

The guy wasn't to know I was a Realtor, that I was just some asshole, the guy everyone over on Longboat had thought it would be fun to mess with. Bill Moore, everybody's punch, this season's recreational bitch. My voice said I meant serious harm, and he was closest to the firing line. He hesitated just long enough for me to get Steph's feet into stuttery movement.

I half dragged and half carried her toward the exit. People stared. People muttered. My heart was pounding, but I knew there were still cops in the building and we had to get out of here before they started taking an interest — or this whole thing was over.

When we made it to the door I glanced back and saw Nick pulling himself up off the floor, helped by the guy in the baseball cap, who was talking earnestly to him, doubtless telling him to call a lawyer or the army or to just get over there and kick my wacko terrorist ass. Nick was bleeding hard from a long cut across his cheek. He looked shaken, in pain, very disconcerted.

Acting? Could it be?

I pulled Steph out into the corridor and steered her toward the main cross hallway. She kept weakly protesting. 'Bill . . . '

'I'll explain in the car.'

'I don't feel good.'

'I know. But we have to go, Steph. Please just trust me on this, baby. We have to go.'

'Okay,' she said. 'Okay.'

* * *

I hustled her out the side door, moving as quickly as possible without looking like we were fleeing the scene. It was near dark outside now, the grounds and parking lot dotted by ornamental lamps. When we got to the car I held Steph upright against it while I fumbled for the keys. I levered her into the seat as gently as I could.

It was only when I'd got my door shut that I realized how sick Steph actually looked. In the harsh white of the courtesy light her skin was slick with a film of greasy-looking perspiration, and she seemed cramped over on herself, arms and legs spiderlike.

Her eyes were alert, however, and in them she looked like my wife. 'Where we going?'

'Don't know yet,' I said. 'Let's find out.'

I jammed the key in the ignition. Then in the mirror I saw Nick running across the parking lot toward us.

'Jesus Christ.'

Steph turned in her seat, saw him coming, too, his arm held out. 'What the hell's he doing?'

'What he was paid to do,' I said. 'Either he's behind on the game or Barclay's had a rethink — and decided he can do without me to carry the can after all.'

'Barclay? You mean *Sheriff* Barclay?'

'Yep,' I said, jamming the car into reverse.

'Bill — what are you talking about?'

I realized she didn't know anything that had happened to me today, or even who Hallam was/had been, never mind Emily or Cassandra. 'Later, honey.'

The car leaped backward, spraying gravel. I pulled it around too harshly and the back scraped someone else's car, grinding along it with a sound like an animal in pain. I yanked it up into drive and sent it straight toward the man now standing right in the middle of the lot. For all I knew he had a gun. I wasn't going to take the chance. I shouted at Steph to get down, reached over and shoved her when she didn't move.

He stood his ground. The car hit him full-on. He came crashing over the hood and into the windshield before tumbling off on the passenger side.

I stopped the car.

'He's getting up,' Steph said. She was right. He wasn't moving quickly, however. I was — and I had every intention of keeping it that way.

I ran around to where the guy was still trying to get to his feet. Gave him a kick in the chest to put him back down. In the last ten minutes I'd had more violent contact with other human beings than at any time since the playground, but now I couldn't seem to stop.

I stood on his wrist.

'Come after us again, and I'll kill you. Take the message back to whoever you're working for, too. Make sure they realize it includes them.'

He shook his head, as if he didn't have the faintest clue what I was talking about. I ran back to the car and drove away fast. At the junction with the main road I held it long enough to make sure I wasn't going to get broadsided, then took off into traffic, going right but then taking the quick left/right dogleg to head north.

Steph didn't say anything. She seemed mesmerized by the brake lights of the cars in front of us — either that or locked into an internal state of trying to process events. I didn't know how to start explaining. It wasn't clear in which order information had to be presented to make sense. Did I tell her that the guy she'd thought she'd been flirting with had been an actor — that she'd just had a walk-on part in some play in which people overturned my life for fun? Or did I lead with the news that when I'd left our house there'd been three dead bodies in it — corpses of people she'd never met, one of them the horrific remains of a young woman with whom I'd spent the night drinking?

'I don't understand,' she said suddenly. 'I don't understand anything that's happening.'

'We'll talk about it,' I said. 'For now, I just want to get us out of town for the night. Head up the coast a little way, maybe Tampa. Find a hotel, somewhere to stay. I need to work out what the hell we're going to do.' I remembered that my credit cards were dead, and my ATM cards could be by now, too. 'Do you have any money?'

'Don't know.' She looked vaguely around, then frowned. 'Don't have my purse. It's at the hospital.'

'Of course,' I said. 'Okay, well, never mind.'

This was bad, however. I couldn't recall how much I had left from the visit to the ATM that

404

morning, but it wouldn't be much. We had nothing with us, no clothes, no charge cards. We could wind up sleeping in the car, and Steph didn't look well enough for that. As we sat at the next set of traffic lights — me glancing in the mirror every two seconds, convinced someone would be creeping up behind, hiding in the run of traffic, waiting for the moment to strike — I realized my pocket was vibrating. I ignored it. I couldn't think of anyone alive who I should talk to, anyone who wasn't already in the same car as me. It stopped vibrating after a while. But then, thirty seconds later, came the sound of an SMS being delivered.

'Who's that?'

'I don't know,' I said, struggling the phone out of my jeans and passing it to her. 'Who's it say?'

She looked at it, and I felt the temperature in the car drop a couple of degrees. 'What?'

She shook her head. 'Sorry. I'm hardly in a position to be a bitch about it.'

'Steph, I'm driving. I can't see the phone. I don't know what you're talking about.'

She handed it back to me. The screen said:

I'm at home. There's weird stuff happening and I'm scared. Please call. Karren.

I did a U-turn that nearly got us killed.

49

'It's just about us now,' she says.

Hunter isn't sure that's ever going to be true, but he happily follows her out across the crabgrass. He's not sure life ever just lets people be alone. It's always on your case. Life is a dog that needs human attention at any cost and will worry at you until you give it some.

After a moment he notices that what they're walking on isn't grass after all, though, which surprises him — he's pretty sure he sat here in his car only yesterday and saw how much this place of theirs had been changed. Tonight this couple acres of the key seems to have reverted to scrub, however; tilting palm trees, straggly grass over sandy paths, a little swampy in parts.

A few minutes gets them down onto the beach. It's sunny there, so bright that it threatens to burn out into white. Sometimes evenings are like that, he supposes.

He holds her hand, and they walk along the waterline, watching their own bare feet. She asks him about where he has been and what he has done. He doesn't want to talk about it. That period was only ever a time of waiting, and it's finished now, and of no account.

He doesn't want to hurry, either, but he knows they have to keep moving. He knows there is someone on this beach with them.

When he eventually glances back, he sees her.

406

She is a long way behind, struggling a little in the sand. She is alone. She has had nowhere else to go in all these long years, and so she's waited for him.

There's nothing Hunter can do about her. She will always be there, some way back along his beach, forever following him. But she is fat, and old, and he and Katy are young. They can outwalk her, probably.

He thinks so, anyway.

They can try.

He thinks he hears a voice, then, though it could just be the rustle of the waves. The Breakers was always a dumb name for a place on this side of the peninsula. You don't get the big waves here. You just get these little guys, coming in and out like breaths.

He hears the voice again, louder, more urgent.

For a moment he wonders if the white surrounding them might not be the sun after all, and if the shadows over the beach are not merely from the wisps of insubstantial clouds up above but rather those of people leaning over a hospital bed.

It doesn't seem likely.

He rejects the thought, hooks his arm around Katy's shoulders, and kisses her neck.

'Let's see how far we can get,' he says.

She smiles, and nods.

And they walk.

★ ★ ★

'Yeah, he's dead,' the voice says. 'Mark the time and tell the cops.'

407

50

It took fifteen endless minutes to get back to the turn off the highway, during which Steph took some convincing that this was a good idea. I wasn't sure myself. My gut instinct was screaming loud, telling me to get the hell out of town, now now NOW, but I knew that if Karren was suddenly finding herself part of the cleanup, then I couldn't just drive away. We'd never been close, but if you get to the point where you'll let others be hurt through inaction, then darkness has fallen in your life.

I got Steph to try calling Karren back, but there was no answer. There was nothing I could do before I got there, so I just drove, fast, and on the way learned from Stephanie that Nick had started being attentive almost from the day he joined the magazine, that she'd politely resisted all this time, and it was only the pictures she thought I'd taken of Karren — and a lot of wine — that had broken her resolve yesterday afternoon. Nothing had actually happened, nothing would have happened, she said. I believed her, at least ninety-nine percent. I was certainly prepared to believe by now that all it took was a couple of tiny modifications, for someone to move the walls just a little, for a life previously solid to look like it had been made of cardboard all along.

Karren's apartment was in a development a

couple of streets back from the bay, half a mile north of downtown, an area favored by young professionals with money to spend and no kids to get to school. It was a three-story block, the building surrounded by small but well-tended gardens and angled so the upper stories got half-decent views of the bay. Karren had got into the development early. A smart buy. She was a smart woman. I knew the place a little, having once sold property in it.

As I parked in the lot, however, I realized I didn't know the number of Karren's apartment.

'Come into the driver's seat and lock the doors,' I said. I reached into the footwell on her side and picked up the gun. Steph stared at it.

'How have you got a gun, Bill?'

'Long story.' I got out. 'You see anybody approaching, anyone *at all*, just drive. Get away from here, okay? When you're safe, call me. Okay?'

Steph didn't move. I stuffed the gun down the back of my jeans, the way I'd seen Emily do it. Thus ended my entire knowledge of firearms. 'Honey, are you hearing me?'

She jerked back to life.

'Yes,' she said. She was lost in a combination of fear and dopiness that was hard to know how to deal with. 'But I'll move over slowly, okay? I really ache. All over.' She sounded about eight years old.

'Sure, honey. Of course. I'll be back soon. I'm going to shut this door now. Lock up after me, okay?'

She nodded. I shut the door. She locked it. We

gave each other a thumbs-up.

I trotted across the lot, glancing back when I got to the entrance to the building. Steph was laboriously hoisting herself into the other seat. I felt a twist of love for her that was so deep and sharp it hurt, and I wondered if I shouldn't leave Karren to sink or swim. She was just background, after all. Part of the filler God provides so you're not so aware of the joins and silences. But I thought back to the younger man I'd been — or hoped I'd been — and knew I couldn't leave without at least checking whether she was okay.

At the entrance to the building I realized there was another method of finding which was her apartment. I didn't know the number — but I could work it out. I changed course and went around the side of the block instead. When I got there I walked quickly backward into the grassy area, looking up at the windows.

I'd seen pictures of this structure recently, of course. The earliest photos in the sequence planted on my laptop had been designed to establish the environment, to make it look like the work of a voyeur homing in on his prey. The rear face sloped back, floor by floor. The window shown in the pictures had been on the extreme right middle floor. Now that it was in front of me, I recalled Karren extolling the virtues of a corner balcony, of having bought that apartment off-plan.

And there it was. There was a light on, but it was dim. I watched the windows as I tried calling her number again. She still wasn't picking up.

410

I ran back around to the front of the building. I didn't know what else to do but start pressing buttons on the entry phone. The first one with a 2 at the front was 201. A man's voice answered, and was quick to tell me he wasn't Karren. So then I tried the last number that started with a 2–204, which I hoped would be at the other end of the floor, thus at the other corner.

It rang, but nobody answered.

So maybe that was hers. But now what? I glanced back at my car and saw Steph in the driver's seat. Her head was bent forward, and I thought once more — *Christ, just leave it.* It's not like Karren was involved — why would they *need* to do anything to her? I could call her again and leave a message saying I'd gone out of town, that if she was concerned about anything she should call the cops (the ones in Sarasota, not Longboat, and certainly not Sheriff Barclay) and lock her doors and take care and blah blah blah. It wasn't as if I was going to be able to offer her more than that, anyhow.

Would that do?

Could I just leave it at that and live with myself?

I was on the verge of deciding I could when a pair of car headlamps swept into the lot from the main road. I took a couple of hurried steps into the shadow of a knot of palms by the entrance. When the car was parked I saw that the occupant was a large, harried-looking man in a suit, carrying a folder stuffed with papers. He saw me.

'Help you?'

'Hope so,' I said, reaching for the persona I'd used in countless meet-and-greets, good old Bill, the chap you'd trust to find you and your newly pregnant sweetheart somewhere perfect and yet affordable to start living your dream. 'Supposed to be picking Karren up for drinks. I know she's in, but she's not answering.'

'Karren? Karren White?'

'Right. I've tried calling up from the back but she's got music on loud. And we're running late.'

The guy looked at me. 'You her boyfriend?'

'Hell no.' I laughed. 'See the car over there? That's my wife. Karren and I work together. Far as I know she doesn't even have a boyfriend right now. Waiting for Mr. Right, you know how it goes.'

The man smiled, evidently cheered by the prospect of his neighbor being as single as he'd let himself hope, during long evenings alone in his apartment surrounded by paperwork and the remains of microwave meals.

We went to the door together. He let himself in, and let me follow. I thanked him without making a big deal about it, and as he went to the mailboxes I ran up the stairs, thinking: this is how people get killed, sometimes — someone is helpful to the wrong guy.

★ ★ ★

Up on the second floor I hurried to the far end. Two things about the door to 204 were immediately obvious. First, it was open, hanging slightly ajar. Second, there was a piece of Shore

412

Realty letterhead taped to the door. Someone had written a single word on it in big clear capitals. And underneath they'd put a smiley face.

I stared at it. The three dots and a little curved line. The word MODIFIED.

There was no doubt now, but I could still go forward, or back. I could push open the door, or I could back away and run.

I reached behind and pulled out the gun. I gently pushed the door. Beyond was a short wide hallway. It was dark. I stepped in, leaving the door open behind me. On the left, the hall dead-ended after a couple of feet in a wall with a couple of hooks on it. A smart blue jacket, a purse I semi-recognized. Both Karren's.

I looked the other way. There was a doorway on the left-hand side, four feet away. I crept along to it. A glance showed it was a half bathroom. Small, no windows. It smelled operating-room clean.

I backed over to the other side, keeping close to the exterior wall. I moved sideways along the corridor, heading toward the point where it hit the end wall and where there was a wide gap into the main apartment.

I flashed back in my head to the visit I'd made to a property in this block. It hadn't been a corner property — so the layout might not be the same. Given the length of this hallway, however, and how close I'd been to the extent of the building when I got to Karren's door, I thought the gap I could see likely opened onto the main living space, a large room with double aspect glass doors onto the wrap balcony I'd seen from the gardens below.

I took another slow, silent side step. I stood motionless for half a minute, listening. There was the sound of a car on some road, followed by a horn, even farther away. Both had a clarity, despite their evident distance, that made me wonder if the doors to the balcony were open. I hadn't noticed from outside. I put my other hand around the handle of the gun, the way I'd seen Hallam do it. I took the final step to the side, and looked through the gap in the wall.

The living room. A couple of dark red couches, three lamps, a coffee table partially obscured from my position by a big easy chair. Pale carpet. There was a bookcase against the wall on the right, with more books than I would have expected. Everything was very tidy.

There was nobody there.

Now what? Should I call out? Would that be sensible or dumb? How was I supposed to know? I opened my mouth, took in a couple of long, slow breaths. All I could hear was a ringing in my ears.

I took a step forward, to the threshold of the room. I noticed something on the near end of the coffee table, now revealed from behind the chair. A couple of small rectangles of cards, a few other pieces of paper, and Karren's cell phone.

I thought maybe I should call out. If Karren was in the apartment, in the kitchen or bedroom or bathroom, she'd be scared witless to see a man coming into her living room — especially if she'd already started to become nervous about

414

things happening in her life. But if she *was* here, why hadn't she responded to the last call? And even if she was shocked to see someone here, she'd realize soon enough that it was me.

But I couldn't get a call to come out of my throat. I took another couple of steps into the room instead. From there I could see that the things on the table looked like photographs: three stubby rectangles, like Polaroids. The other pieces of paper had the thin, curling shape of cash register receipts.

I moved diagonally toward the table, one step at a time, keeping my eyes — and the gun — trained on the door on the right, gateway to the rest of the apartment. I could see a kitchen, a couple of dim underlighters, a corridor that would lead to the bedrooms.

I got to the table, glanced down. Then looked again, properly. The receipts were for credit card transactions. I recognized the number, the last four digits. It was the number of my Amex card — the one I'd used in Jonny Bo's with Hazel — the card Sheriff Barclay already told me had been cloned to buy the gun that had killed his deputy. One of the receipts was for several hundred dollars, from a store called Hank's Sporting Goods. It seemed likely that was the one. There were a few more, for similar sums, but I didn't get as far as logging where they'd been spent, because I saw what was in the photos.

In the first, my swimming pool, taken from the living room of the house. In the second, the mangled body I'd seen floating there. In the third, that body, naked and facedown on a floor, before someone had undertaken the work of removing pieces of it.

Only someone who was part of the game would have access to these things.

I realized then that Karren White had been on the edges of everything that had happened in the last week. She worked in the same office. She knew my movements, was party to everything I did in working hours every day — and for months and months before.

She was the person who took the first alleged meeting with David Warner, and was then removed from the scenario to make way for me — dressed up such that I'd be only too pleased to step into her shoes.

She was the person who'd been conveniently in position at her window for someone to take the pictures.

I'd even phoned her a couple of times over the last forty-eight hours, handing her up-to-the-minute information about where I was and my state of mind.

I realized that it was possible I'd maybe been very dumb indeed, and that maybe Karren hadn't called me here because she was scared.

'Hey, Bill,' said a voice. 'Cool gun.'

I jerked my head up to see a woman in a robe leaning in the doorway to the kitchen. Her arms were folded. She looked relaxed and slightly amused.

It was Cass.

51

I stopped being aware of my hands, my feet, my body. I was merely eyes.

'Whoa,' she said with a delighted laugh. 'That is even better than I hoped. You totally look like you're going to fall down or something. Priceless.'

'Cass?'

'Glad to see the facial recognition software is still functioning. After such a hard day, too. You rule.'

I didn't know what else to say.

'That's okay, take a moment,' she said. 'You want a drink or something? There isn't much. Though it could be after last night you're avoiding alcohol, right?'

I tried to rethink everything since I got back to my house that afternoon. Since even before that — from the moment I'd woken in this woman's apartment to find a word daubed on her bathroom door, in what I'd thought had been her blood. I even took a faltering step to the side, to check I was seeing what I thought I was, not some ringer in makeup, that the effect worked from a different angle, that I couldn't see through her. That she was real.

'How are you not . . .'

'Look again at the photos.'

I looked at the pictures on the coffee table. I saw my pool. I saw the floating body. Then I saw the naked back in the third picture, and realized I perhaps should have wondered why someone might bother to strip a body before reclothing it in a black lacy blouse — a garment distinctive enough to make a man jump to the wrong conclusion when confronted with a corpse in his pool.

'That wasn't you.'

'Well, yeah, obviously.'

'So who . . . ?'

I put my hand over my mouth, suddenly convinced I was going to throw up.

'You can't guess?'

Who else was there? Whose apartment was I standing in? My voice was a croak between my fingers.

'Karren.'

'Yes. It is she. Target for your twisted affections, et cetera. I called her at your office this afternoon, saying I was a friend and that you were in trouble. She came running. Bitch was strong, though, when she realized none of the above was true. Scratched me quite badly.'

'But . . . why did you kill her?'

'Me? I haven't killed anyone.' Her voice sounded brittle, false. She stepped back from the door, gesturing for me to come through. 'Want to see who did?'

The door to the main bedroom was open. On the floor lay plastic sheeting covered in blood. Stained woodworking tools were scattered across it.

A man was tied naked to the bed. He seemed to realize that someone had entered the doorway.

He raised his head an inch groggily. His eyes found mine. I could not tell what I was seeing in them, if anything.

'David Warner,' Cass said. 'You meet at last. Though to be honest, he's not at his best.'

Sprays of blood were all over the walls of what had been Karren's bedroom. A place she'd gone to sleep, night after night. Read the books out there on her shelves. Given her e-mail a last check for the day.

And died.

I heard Cassandra walking away, back to the living room. I followed her. 'And Karren had nothing to do with any of this?'

'With what?'

'With the game the Thompsons were playing.'

'Nope.'

'What about the other one?'

'There is no other one. This whole sorry mess was a diversion played by oldsters with too much time and money on their hands. A jaded parlor mind game over brandies and margaritas that got derailed when an old victim came back to even the score.'

'Bullshit. I talked to the Thompsons just before Hunter got to them. They were scared to death. They knew something else was going on. Tony said he thought Warner had been putting parts into the scenario that they hadn't known about, trying to get back at them over some development deal they'd cut him out of.'

Cassandra shrugged. 'Okay, so you know more than I thought. There may have been something along those lines. But no, Ms. White wasn't involved on either count. In fact, I think she may even have been carrying a little torch for you. I found a few pictures in a drawer here. Nothing too stalky — just snaps of the handsome Realtor at parties, events, plus one of the two of you standing together at some tennis event. Sweet, huh.'

'But *why did you let him kill her*?'

'Containment. I didn't know what you'd told her, or if she could put you at the wrong place at the right time or just generally cause trouble and stop this thing being neatly put to bed. Though to be honest, using her as set dressing for your pool wasn't actually my idea.'

'So whose was it?'

She shrugged again, with an insolent little grin, a willful, gleeful child getting off on the power trip of screwing with an adult's mind. I decided I didn't have to understand what was going on. I started toward her.

'Don't,' she said. The emo chick disappeared, turned off like a light, and she aged ten years in front of my eyes. She now had a gun in her hand.

I remembered I had one in my own. I looked down at it.

'You won't,' she said.

'People keep telling me that,' I said thickly. 'Sooner or later one of you is going to be wrong.'

'Nah. From what I gather you've already had a chance to kill someone today, a guy who'd done you manifest harm. You didn't do it then. You won't do it now.'

'Don't be so sure,' I said impotently.

'I'm sure. You've been modified, but not that

420

much. The weird thing is that kind of means you win. In a way. Were it not for Hunter getting this thing so fucked up, you might be walking away from the game a richer man, friend of the Thompsons and lord of glorious new domains.'

'Where did all the blood come from? In the bed in your apartment?'

'Previous occupant.'

'Who was that?'

'Kevin.'

'That was *Kevin's* apartment? But, but you said . . . you said it was him who called you. While I was there.'

'I lied. The man I work for gave Warner my phone number and told him I'd help. He left a message.'

'Why would you kill Kevin?'

'He got a little too intrigued with what was happening to you. Ironically, he thought it would be a good excuse for trying to get to know me better. He called, I went around to his apartment, and . . . well, stuff happened. Though not in the way he'd hoped.'

'I thought . . . I thought all that blood was from you.'

'Sweet. No. I just used it to write you a message before I left to fetch Warner off the beach. You know, on the bathroom door. Funny, huh? Did you laugh?'

'Who *are* you? You're not part of the Thompsons' game, are you?'

'No. Nor Warner's, either. David had anger-management issues even by the standards I'm used to. His diminishing level of control had caused concern among acquaintances of his. They do not like any kind of attention being paid to their members. I was put in place here three weeks ago to keep an eye on him, and then — *bang* — the whole thing just darn explodes. Messy. Time to tidy up and put away.'

'Are you . . . Is this the group that Barclay told me about? The Straw Men, whatever?'

Any trace of levity left the woman's face very suddenly. 'Barclay said *what*?'

'Who are these people?'

'Nobody. They don't exist. Just an urban myth. A cracker sheriff getting things all mixed up, bragging on stuff he doesn't understand.'

'I don't believe you.'

'Believe what you like. But sometimes in life we pass by the side of things, Mr. Moore, like standing in the shadow of monsters in the night. Better to leave them be. Keep on going, don't look back. Lest you be turned to stone. Or dead meat.'

'What — now you're going to kill me, too?'

'Well, actually, there's the question.' She dangled her gun from one finger. 'My original plan was that you're found here, a suicide surrounded by evidence, appalled by the magnitude of the things you've done. Barclay will be dropping the gun by later, the one you 'bought' and 'used' back at your house. With everything that's been going on today down at the Circle, it will be a couple days before you're found — by which time Warner will have expired as a result of unnatural causes.'

'But why?'

'The trail has to end here.'

'*I'm* supposed to have done all this? Killed Karren, and Emily, and Hallam? Left Warner to die?'

'It does sound odd,' she said. 'But the acts of the deranged often do, at first, until we accept, yes, that's what they did. And it won't seem *too* out of line, in light of your recent Facebook activity.'

'What? I haven't been on there for days.'

'Right — you've been too busy. But, yeah, turns out you've been posting a load of subtle crazy shit up there in the last forty-eight hours. How Ms. White was making moves against you behind your back. How your secret friend Mr. Warner had started to give you ideas about how to teach chicks like that a lesson. And how finally you realized you don't need him anymore, and you can take vengeance on your tight-skirt-wearing colleague by yourself. Kind of dumb of you to have posted up those photographs of Karren this afternoon, but the flamboyantly deranged aren't always very smart.'

'No one is going to believe I did all this.'

'Actually, they will. People will believe anything that's lurid enough — we're all still looking for that sense of wonder. Plus, it sounds like you played the wacko very well in the hospital on the way. That'll help.'

'Is Nick . . . Which bit of this is he a part of?'

'Nick? I have no idea.'

'You know. You *must* know.'

'I really don't. This is intriguing.'

'He . . . he was the guy who was trying to have

an affair with my wife. Who was there when she drank the bottle of wine intended for the Thompsons.'

'I got nothing. That must just have been real life, I'm afraid. Sometimes it's hard to tell.'

'But . . . who *are* you? Where do you come from?'

'Out there. In the world.'

'And you're just going to do this to me, and go?'

'It's the way it is. I'm sorry. You're not actually a dumb guy, not totally anyway — you just got modified. I don't even mean by the old folks here — I mean by life. Everybody does. You start with an open road, but then the walls start to close in — day by day, year by year. There's no market for who you thought you were, so you become someone else. You get trammeled. You get crucified by the quotidian and you get smaller and smaller every minute until you die. Resisting that? It's tough. Staying true to who you are is the only real superpower. I have it. You don't.'

'But — '

'No, my friend, we're done talking. Are you going to leave the building, or what? I would if I were you, because what I'm offering isn't in anybody's game plan but mine. It's a cheat code, if you like. A secret side door. Who knows what you'll find on the other side?'

'You're going to . . . *let me go?*'

'It's why the balcony doors are open, dumb-ass.'

I looked across at the doors, but couldn't work out what she was getting at.

'Could be that you manage to get past me,' she said patiently. 'That you flip over the side before I can get a clean shot, and run off into the night.'

'But . . . why would you do that?'

'Why does anyone do anything?' She smiled, wide and innocent, looking for a moment exactly like the girl who'd served me mascarpone frozen yogurt on a hot afternoon not long ago. 'To see what happens next. My job was to tidy up the Warner situation and provide whatever collateral muddying seemed necessary or advisable. But as regards you personally . . . I have no instructions. I'm thinking it could be fun to watch. No one's going to believe a single word you say. About anything. And if they should ever start to . . . well, then I guess I'll just have to come and find you, right? So what's it gonna be? Do I shoot you now or later? It's your game. You choose.'

I walked out onto the balcony. I climbed onto the railing, all the while expecting to feel an impact, and then to die. I dropped down onto the grass, landing heavily, falling on my side. I got up.

Cass was on the balcony, looking down at me.

'I'll count to a hundred, Mr. Moore,' she said. 'Run and hide.'

★   ★   ★

The car was still there. I opened the driver's-side door. Steph looked up at me, eyes wide.

'Is Karren okay?'

425

'She's fine.'

My wife hauled herself across into the passenger seat. I got in and started the engine with hands that were not shaking and I drove away.

52

I drove for a long time without stopping, and as I took us up the coast and then north across the panhandle, I also talked. I tried to explain everything that had happened to me in the last days, to recount it, at least, but I kept getting tangled, caught up in trying to work out who had been running things at each point, and why. I couldn't think straight. I had not eaten for a long time. I was exhausted. I had seen people killed and I had seen what happened to them after that, without at any point understanding why. At first Steph asked questions, though not many, and in a voice that sounded increasingly tired. After a while she stopped asking and so I just kept talking, trying to put it all together and glad she was giving me the opportunity, glad that she was sitting next to me and letting me run. Sometimes that's what you need in your loved ones. Someone who just lets you run on, who provides a safe track for your thoughts and hopes to revolve around. It was a long time — in fact, only when I stopped for gas in South Carolina in the dead of night — before I realized that she'd fallen asleep.

When I'd gassed up I got back in the car, put a blanket over her, and went back to driving and talking to myself. I drove straight through the night, up into the woods of Kentucky, wondering how long it was since we'd done something like

427

this. Simply been in movement together, without an agenda, without a five-year plan. A world without walls. Eventually the sky started to soften and the forest on either side of the road turned from being an undifferentiated mass of black into individual trees. I tried to make something metaphoric of this, but I was so tired I was incapable of joined-up thought. I'd stopped talking by that point, had become content to keep driving with Steph sleeping in the seat beside me.

No matter how much I talked through the last five days, the final analysis remained the same. Everything we'd had was gone. There would be people who'd try to blame a lot of things on me, at least one cop who'd be ready to help, and as much evidence as they could need. It was all gone, then — everything, except for the two of us. After a decade of accruing baggage, of earning and seeking and building our lives layer by layer until we were held apart by our accretions of shell, it was back to just the two of us, naked in the world — and the weird thing was that it felt good. It felt like what I'd always wanted, back when I had an idea of who I really was and who I wanted to be. You put one foot after another, one word after another, and it makes sense at the time — until one day you look up and find you're lost in a future you don't understand, someplace you never wanted to go and do not recognize. That's what had happened to us: had happened, most of all, to me. You get up in the morning and look in the mirror and find a stranger looking back, and you brush your teeth and smile, and when you leave the room there's no reflection left in the mirror because you have climbed inside the fake.

What do you do if you realize this has happened? Go back to the beginning and start again? It isn't possible. Time flows but one way and all rivers make for the sea, and so we keep trudging on, writing our story-lives sentence by sentence, hoping that sooner or later we'll be able to steer them back onto a track that we recognize. It never happens. We just die, and in death it becomes contextualized. Everything makes sense at the instant we close the book on ourselves.

That's what happened, for better or worse.

I'm done now.

Good-bye.

In the end, a little after six in the morning, I got too hungry and tired to continue driving. I took it as a sign when, five minutes later, I glimpsed in the distance the blessed great yellow M of a fast-food outlet Stephanie and I had been going to for all of our lives together. So *much* of a sign, in fact, that it was only when I parked in the lot outside that I realized my face was wet. I sat looking up at the golden arches as if they were the gateway to the promised land.

'Hey,' I said gently. 'Look what we found.'

Steph was lying with her head propped against the window, wrapped up in the blanket I'd put around her. Her face was pale. She looked peaceful. It still took me a long time to realize that, at some point in the last few hours, Stephanie had died.

* ★ ★

She is buried in the woods near where I live. Her mother passed away a few years back, her father never reappeared. I'm the only person left to care. The world notices your passing, then turns back to the remaining group of revelers at the bar and orders another round.

I keep on the move. I have a cabin, but I spend long periods away from it. I walk, for days at a time, in broad circles along unpredictable routes. I stay a while near some hill town thirty miles away, then walk in the opposite direction to somewhere else. I spread the custom of my presence. I always come back, however. I'm not going to leave her alone for long.

I've grown a beard, and my hair is ragged. My nose got broken in a fight outside a bar, so I don't look quite the same as I did. It will do for now.

★ ★ ★

I used Internet cafés and libraries to track unfolding events down in Florida. It made the national media for a while, but it's instructive how short the news cycle is. There's always something else, another ring in the circus to stop us from looking too closely at any particular show. A war here, a celebrity death there, a recession, a crisis, something shiny going past. So much so that it might even make you suspicious.

Marie Thompson survived her wounds. The

deaths of her husband and Hazel Wilkins were accurately ascribed to the actions of John Hunter, disgruntled former local resident and convicted killer. Tony was much mourned, celebrated far and wide as one of the last big characters of the Florida boom years. Hazel didn't get the same coverage, on account of being just some old woman.

The deaths of Deputy Rob Hallam, Karren White, David Warner, and Emily Griffiths remain unsolved. As the bodies of all but Warner were found in the house of a couple who'd vanished, the media spent a day enthusiastically vacillating between claiming that Mr. and Mrs. William Moore were further victims, or else the murderers, egged on by circumstantial evidence relating to the purchase of a handgun used as a murder weapon. Once the stuff on my Facebook page became public, however, Steph rapidly joined the list of (assumed) victims, and I was shoved right into center stage — with David Warner emerging as a kind of shadowy accomplice/mentor figure who'd outlived his usefulness and met a grisly end in the apartment of one of my other victims, with whom I'd become obsessed.

The media were far too excited to look hard for inconsistencies in all this, being more interested in me being the first nutcase to unravel semipublicly via a social networking site. That was how Warner and I met, apparently, and then started to feed into each other's obsessions, creating a spiral of virtual insanity that eventually spilled out into the real world. Searching questions were asked about the online community's responsibility to keep an eye on its members, and hand-wringing editorials written about the need for the interactions of distant others to be monitored. It was a big deal. I had my own logo on the news.

Then it all faded away, and now the only ones who still care are a few conspiracy Web sites. According to these, I am either dead, or still alive, a stooge framed to divert attention from foreign policy shortfalls and/or rising CO_2 levels, a ranking member of a hidden elite, an actual psychopath but with supernatural superpowers, or I never actually existed in the first place. I prefer the last theory. To me, it has the ring of truth.

The cases remain open, as does speculation regarding the purpose of the structures discovered underneath David Warner's house. A small and powerless local pressure group, formed from relatives of missing women in the area, has called to have the building demolished so that its foundations can be examined. So far they have been totally unsuccessful. As the house has now been purchased by a holding company belonging to an unknown man based on the West Coast, it seems likely it will remain that way.

Peter Grant sold Shore Realty and left the state. The Breakers is still open for business. Marie Thompson lives by herself in that big apartment overlooking the ocean. Adrift in the present, queen of a diminished domain. Friendless, I hope.

Certainly alone.

A month after it had started to go quiet, I saw an article in the *Longboat Gazette,* and another lodged in the online version of the *Sarasota Times.* Local lawman Sheriff Frank Barclay had been found dead in his house, victim of a self-inflicted gunshot wound. A collection of child pornography was discovered on a hard drive in the basement. I doubt it was his. I doubt also that his final moments were quite as they were portrayed, or how he would have wished. I think he shouldn't have said as much to me as he did. I believe my telling Cassandra what he'd said was what got him where he was going.

I can live with that.

To the outside world, the two stories are unrelated, Barclay's death merely one of those nasty things that nasty men deserve. We're all pebbles on a beach. One lying here, one over there, another handful down by the tide line. They're all brought there by the same ocean, though, quietly moving us to and fro when everyone's asleep. Whichever way you're looking, there's a lot more going on behind your back than there is in front, where you can see. Count on that.

Only one other loose end remains, courtesy of a girl playing her own version of the game. That loose end is lying low. For now.

★ ★ ★

I have not been in contact with my mother. At first I kept away because I didn't want to put her in the position of knowing anything that might lead the police — or anyone else — to me. But the more time I spent alone, the more questions I started to ask. How well did I know her, in fact? There was no question she'd been there all the time I'd been a child. But it could be that while I was down in Florida she'd become different, that she could have been approached. It could even be that it had *always* been that way. Did I even have proof that I was actually her son? People tell you things, but that doesn't mean they're true. From there, further questions. Did my father really die of a heart attack? He'd always been very fit and healthy before. Did there come a time when, for some reason or other, it became better that he was no longer around?

Silly ideas. Probably. But are we ever more than details around underlying determinants over which we never have anything more than illusory control? The couple who go to church like clockwork but put on masks to record homemade S and M videos for sale on the Internet; the man whose alcoholic (and unfaithful and violent) wife presents so functionally to the rest of the world that he feels he's living in a dream; the mother whose angelic-looking child runs her ragged every morning to the point where she sits in the car for ten minutes — after she's finally uploaded her daughter to school, chatting with the other moms, who all seem to have everything *so* together — and sobs her heart out, fingernails cutting crescents into her palms.

434

We're all of us living Stepford lives, pretending in ways we don't even realize, having faked it for so long that we don't remember we're doing it, or why. But sometimes the edifice collapses, and we want nothing more than to burn down the entire world, just for some peace from the lies.

★   ★   ★

I have scoured the Internet for mention of the Straw Men. I don't even know whether there's anything there to be found. It could be that was just part of Cass's game, a red herring, an injection of apparent meaning into a meaningless narrative. The only thing I found was a paperback thriller. I read it. It was about a shadowed conspiracy of well-connected murderers, people killing others because that's what they do, and because they believe it's our natural way of life. It was a decent read, but it was fiction. Part of the game, too, perhaps, something planted to muddy the waters, to reassure us that these things only happen in stories and could not possibly exist in real life.

Once in a while I post something on a conspiracy forum, asking if anyone knows anything. The posts seem to be removed more quickly than I would expect. But . . . I suppose I would say that, right?

Whenever I find anything, or think I may be onto something, or come up with a new angle, I tell Stephanie about it. I tell her these things under my breath, all the time. Sometimes other people hear. They look at me strangely. That's okay. They have no idea what I'm learning. They have no idea who I'm talking to. They have no suspicion, either, that beneath the layers of thrift store clothes and what I'll admit is sometimes a significant layer of grime — my cabin does not have running water — my body is in the best shape it's ever been. I spend hours every night running through the woods. I have rocks and chunks of fallen tree that I use for working out. I eat what I can catch in streams and what I shoot in the woods. I have spent many hours practicing with the gun. I am very good now.

I feel ashamed I did not use it before, when I had the chance. And so whenever I am in a town I spend periods focusing on the backs of people's heads, imagining myself in the position of being behind them with the gun held out, readying myself: ensuring that when the opportunity comes I will be able to kill this time, to dispatch them as they deserve. If these strangers happen to glance around — which they sometimes do, as if they have felt a light touch on the back of their neck — I look away. They don't see me. And neither will my enemies, until it's too late.

They do not know how strong I am now, how developed I have become. I may be many things, but I am not crazy.

I am modified.